VENTHRALLI

by

TRAVIS STECHER

MULTICOSM PUBLISHING
LOS ANGELES, CA

Published in the United States by Multicosm Publishing
www.MulticosmPublishing.com

Printed by IngramSpark

Library of Congress Control Number: 2025905924

ISBN: 978-1-73-726664-8 (paperback)
ISBN: 978-1-73-726665-5 (hardcover)
ISBN: 978-1-73-726663-1 (ebook)

First paperback edition 2025

This book is dedicated to my oldest friend and sister, Keri Takano,
even though she gave me chicken pox.

CONTENTS

TS '22

DISTANCE

(Imperial units are scaled to equate to the size of the protagonists.
1 allo ≈ 6.58 feet / 2.01 meters)

		digit	≈	5 in
48 digits	=	**allo**	≈	20 ft
48 allos	=	**wheel**	≈	300 yd

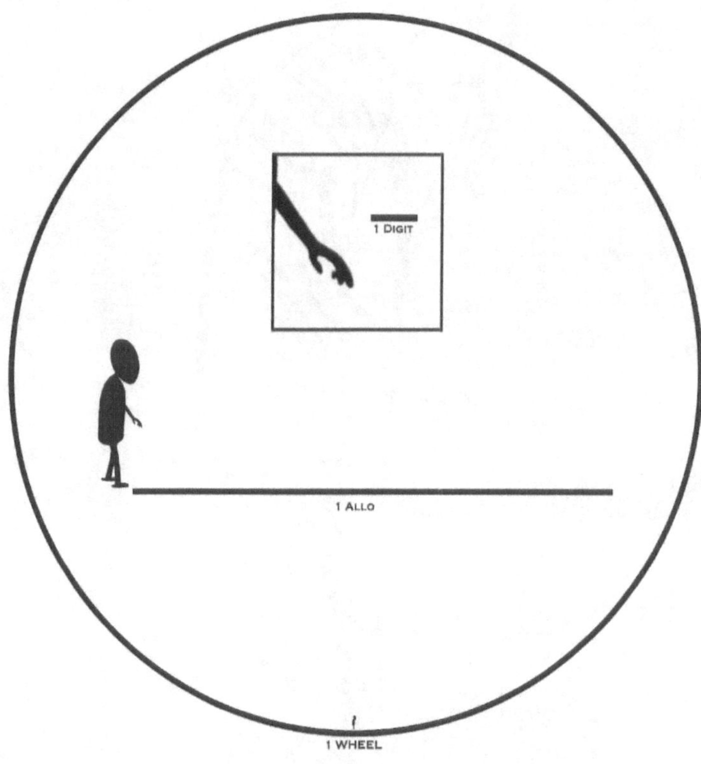

<u>TIME</u>

		beat	≈	1.2 seconds
8 beats	=	**roté**	≈	10 seconds
		10 rotés	≈	1.6 minutes
		100 rotés	≈	16 minutes
		1000 rotés	≈	2.6 hours
8000 rotés	=	**circayd**	≈	21 hours
42 circayds	=	**set**	≈	37 days
15 sets	=	**cycle**	≈	1.5 years

<u>TEMPERATURE</u>

(1 Syrolac ≈ 21 Kelvin)

°F	°C	**Syros**	
-459°	-273°	**0**	Absolute Zero
-423°	-253°	**1**	Hydrogen Boils
-126°	-88°	**9**	Earth's Lowest
32°	0°	**13**	Water Freezes
212°	100°	**18**	Water Boils
451°	233°	**24**	Paper Burns

The Myzer

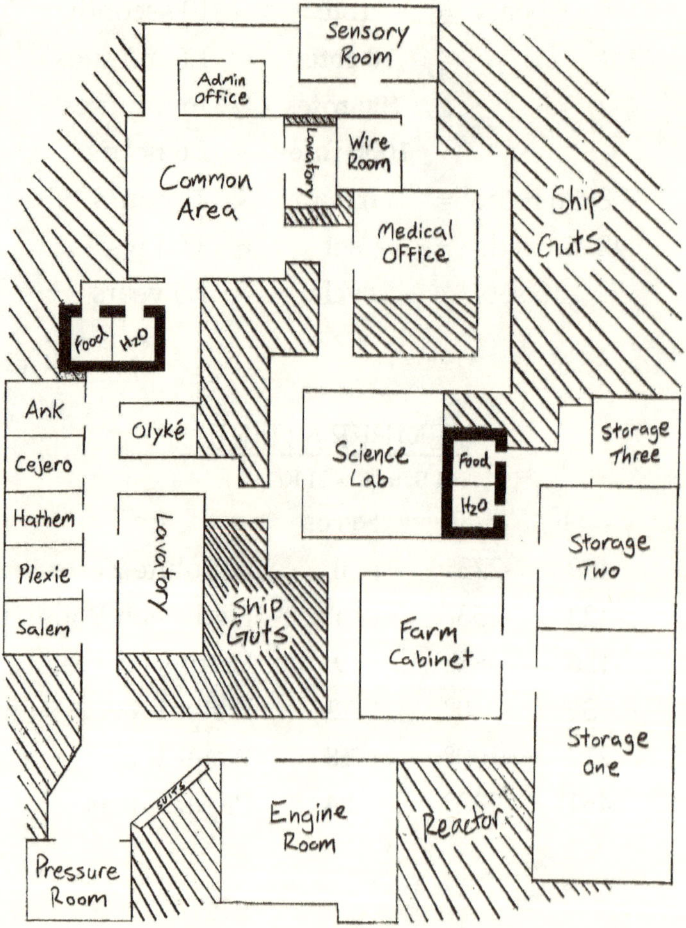
Sensory Room
Admin Office
Lavatory
Wire Room
Common Area
Medical Office
Ship Guts
Food
H2O
Ank
Olyké
Cejero
Science Lab
Food
H2O
Storage Three
Hathem
Lavatory
Storage Two
Plexie
Ship Guts
Farm Cabinet
Salem
Storage One
Suits
Engine Room
Reactor
Pressure Room

Introduction

First and foremost, the rant on these pages in no way reflects the tone of the story beyond.

Second-first and nextmost, thank you for opening this book! Time is our most valuable asset, and choosing to spend yours on my words fills my heart with a warm, gooey feeling. But not, like…in a concerning way. In a good way. Like when you see an old lady give a neo-nazi the middle finger.

Also, fuck nazis.

This book is, in a general sense, not like *Dilation*, and in many ways it's the opposite. It's slower, more linear, less grounded, and with fewer characters. *Dilation*, at its core, is a tale about humanity, whereas this story gives zero fucks about humanity.

And rightfully so. The Earth will be happy when we're gone; the universe won't even notice.

As an author, my intention has always been to write stories from different corners of the speculative fiction landscape. I chose to start with *Dilation* out of a lineup of about fourteen properties earmarked for novels—ghost stories and space operas and post-apocalyptic horrors and whatnot. It's the only book on the docket like it, just as *Venthralli* is the only one like itself.

My hope, ultimately, is that the aspects of my writing that persist between stories, such as the thriller style in which I tend to write (meaning "suspense," not "dancing with werewolves"), will be the aspects readers enjoy regardless of which speculative flavor it's seasoned with. Those similarities will certainly become more apparent as I release more varied works, but those works are also consistently delayed by the crippling anti-meritocracy of the capitalist hellhole in which I was born, so that reality is also many years away.

Tangentially—capitalism blows. I'm not going to get into it right now, because it's a whole can of rabbit wormholes, but the optimal outcome of capitalism is mediocrity. That's the best it can produce. These models are easily calculable; American businesspeople simply refuse to learn them because all of them are grifters, every single one of them, and they lack the talent and discipline required to understand the mathematics—

Sorry, sorry…I said I wouldn't.

Alright, where was I?

Oh, yeah. So, the point of this whole thing isn't to say, "this novel sucks so lower your expectations," but rather that *Venthralli* marks the beginning of a trend of writing dissimilar works of fiction. If you're expecting this to be *Dilation 2*, well…don't. As my therapist would say: manage your expectations.

If you've made it this far, thank you for indulging this dense chain of non-sequiturs. I'm relatively certain it qualifies as an introduction, though it may technically be a preface; I don't really know. I'm not an English-degree-haver, I'm a math-degree-haver, so I find these conventions to be arbitrary and pointless.

Like speling.

PROLOGUE
Attack of the Beast

Brackesh scoured through historical logs for any information that might help the *Domodo's* crew—some overlooked detail that could lead to their survival—but her efforts provided nothing.

Then, she transcribed the *Domodo's* final entry. Their previous one had indicated only that the ship was stranded, and their supplies were plentiful enough to await rescue.

Someone would be coming to get them.

The crew would not be there.

During their journey, the quartet of explorers had gained bounties of knowledge about the lightless frontier surrounding Venthralli's new home. Their efforts had outlined much of the space nearby. Its resources were plentiful, its navigation comparatively simple. And when a chunk of debris, sharpened by fate, had pierced the *Domodo's* fuel tank, sparing their living quarters, Brackesh had considered them fortunate; nobody had died. Had the main cabin been struck, though, the survivors could have sealed the breach and returned home. Even a lone crewmember.

Instead, they were stuck, safe and sound, waiting to be consumed by the only natural predator of their people.

The only predators in the universe.

There was a *clang* against the door. Brackesh jumped in her seat as two more followed—someone rapping against the bulkhead.

She opened the door, letting their ship lead, Prito, into the sensor array. Prito was sharp, experienced, and got his hands dirty whenever needed. And at this particular moment, he was preparing to fight with his bare hands what many considered to be a god.

"What have you found?" he asked, sealing the door behind him.

"Nothing, Skipp."

Prito peered over her shoulder at the transcription. "You've stopped?"

"I'm entering a log for the rescue team…" she explained, "so they can mark the zone as a hunting ground and not waste time looking for our bodies."

"We can't accept that," he said. "There has to be a way to kill it."

"But nothing to suggest how," Brackesh said. She looked back at Prito, her eyes dragging down to the alloy-cutter firmly gripped in his hand. "And *that's* not going to do it."

His fingers tightened around the instrument. Used to perform minor interior maintenance, the alloy-cutter wasn't even strong enough to cut through the notoriously thin exterior of the gascan tanker ships.

"It's better than nothing," he said, looking around as if there might be a discarded guide for killing predators. "Could we get something toxic inside it?" he asked. "Something poisonous?"

Brackesh shook her head. "We don't know what is or isn't hazardous to them. They eat fuel straight out of the reactor like it's fruit." Her shoulders dropped. She wanted to give up—she was ready to—but so long as Prito was fighting, she couldn't succumb to futility. "There surely *is* a way to kill it," she said, "but we have nothing new to go on."

A sound rattled through the cabin. One that no crews had heard, but all knew inherently. A siren of death for any who dared to leave the colony. A series of heavy *chunks* ran along the length of the ship.

The creature had grabbed them.

Beyond the bulkhead, the muffled *creaks* of bending hull plates pierced the air. A whine that made Brackesh's spine stiffen.

Prito's eyes bent inward, straining as he listened. "That's by the engines," he muttered.

"It probably wants to check for fuel residue."

"Or it just knows best how to pry open the can from that point." He turned to the door, slamming his empty fist against the button to break the seal. "As soon as you get that entered," he said, "find a weapon—anything. This omnivorous prat isn't taking us without a fight."

He stepped through and hit the button from the outside, pulling his arm through the closing door.

Brackesh didn't believe any of them could hurt the creature, but Prito's tenacity had gotten them through perils before. If anyone could fight off one of the predators, it was him.

Unfortunately, all of the confidence in the universe wouldn't change the fact that nobody had escaped the grasp of a zero beast. People had hidden on board and outside. They'd sealed themselves in their bunks with crates of food and piles of water, stowed themselves inside the floor panels. People had logged plans to kill themselves, hoping that their vacating body heat would prevent their consumption so they could be later found and brought home.

But nobody came home from an attack.

Ever.

VENTHRALLI

The Last Colony in the Universe

CHAPTER 1
THE MYZER

"Salem, guess what?!"

Ank's voice bounced along the hollow corridors of the *Myzer* and into Salem's room moments before she appeared in his doorway.

Salem glanced up. "What?"

"*Guess!*" she repeated.

"You found a faster route?" he answered with little thought.

"Better!"

"Um…we're having goopy peas for supper?"

"Ew, no. One more try!"

"What? No," he scoffed. "Not if you hate on my peas."

"Excuse me, but I *love* peas," Ank said, "More than *you*. I just don't like them being goop-ified. It's an abomination of texture!" She raised a water ball to her mouth, shaving a few layers off with her jagged teeth and crunching eagerly as she waited.

Ank, like Salem, was a venth—a citizen of Venthralli. Her body was encased in a hard carapace, her thin arms formed into hands with five fingers, each ending in flat, textured fingertips. A narrow neck supported her oval-shaped head, featuring large, black, protruding eyes designed to soak up every bit of light available. Typically, venth shells were dark grey, reflecting bright light with the faintest of purple hues, but due to a rare genetic mutation, Ank's shell had more purple than most, noticeable regardless of the lighting. Purple-shelled venth always seemed to have a sort of aura that drew others to them, and they were always viable gene donors.

Salem glanced down at half of a doodle he'd been making of a pea vine—he must have been craving them. He took some time to consider what might have gotten Ank so excited. It was her first excursion outside of Venthralli, so it was probably work-related.

The *Myzer* was an energy collector, performing the critical task of filling up its oversized fuel tank and returning home with the excess. The energy in question came in the form of starshards, frozen glops of discarded heat gel left over from the old stars after they died millions, even billions of hibernation cycles ago. Heat was the venth's most limited resource, and operating the colony consumed a lot of it.

Ank swallowed the melting water shavings. "Go on, guess!"

"Did we…" Salem mused, rhythmically tapping his feet on the metal floor, "find a floater?"

"We found a floater!" Ank cheered.

Salem pushed his doodle aside. "That's pretty neat, I guess." Floaters were small starshards that drifted idly through the outside. In practice, most of the shards they collected were floating outside, but when it wasn't the explicit target of their expedition, they called it a floater. They weren't very common anymore. Finding one mid-route was fortunate.

"Come on!" Ank squealed. "You gotta get it before it dies!" She threw the rest of the water into her mouth, practically swallowing it whole.

"It's not going to die this circayd, Ank. Even if we ignited it."

"Well, it's still losing heat," Ank said, her fingers clicked together in exhilaration, "so let's gooooo!"

Contrary to the stories told on Venthralli, starshards didn't exude heat on their own, and despite Ank's science-heavy training, the influence of those tales still appeared to affect her. Perhaps that was because, like most people, she'd never actually seen a starshard in person. As the ship's navigator, Ank had spent the first cycle and a half of her contribution period—which began at six cycles old and ended at around eighteen or twenty—learning how to locate shards and get a ship out to them, which was all studying.

Salem, on the other hand, had been on the *Myzer* for two and a half cycles. He was a shard handler—the one responsible for physically collecting the frozen mounds of fuel from the outside. It required far less training, most of which consisted of learning simple procedures and contingencies designed to keep him alive. Shard handling was exceptionally dangerous. Not from the shards themselves, which were a lot like water until they were refined and ignited, but because going outside was inherently risky. There was no air, no heat, no gravity, no light, and no sound. Often enough, a shard collection also involved walking around on a deadworld: rocks so large you could wander around one for a lifetime and never see the same place twice. Those posed different risks, such as falling to one's death or getting lost and suffocating.

Again, Ank clicked her fingers together rapidly, as if fighting to prevent them from jumping off her hand. Salem watched the digits move in sequence. It was oddly mesmerizing.

"Is there something else I'm supposed to know?" he asked.

Her eyes squinted in delight. "Mmhmm…"

Salem waited, watching her. She wanted him to ask, so he played the part. "What is it?"

"I *saw* it!"

Salem blinked—a visible refocusing of the optics beneath his hardened eye lenses. "You saw…what?" he asked. "The shard?"

"It's alight!"

Salem jumped up from the bedside. "How far?" he asked, bouncing slightly on his toes.

"It's in this zone. Come on, get dressed!" Ank skittered back down the hall, leaving Salem with his unfinished doodle.

Normally, starshards didn't produce their own light. They were all frozen, unrefined, and unignited. On rare occasions, something about the way the heat gel had originally flown from the exploding star made them harden chemically, rather than simply freezing. They were dense, crystal-like, and produced more fuel once refined, burning longer in the engines. With further rarity, those shards sometimes had a small, glowing ember inside, protected from the outside's heat void. Venth referred to them as light shards.

Salem looked down at his scribbled pea vine. He probably wouldn't have finished it, anyway—he'd already messed up several times—but the shard outside didn't require as much haste as Ank seemed to believe.

It had been burning for billions of cycles.

A few more beats wouldn't hurt it.

Salem's feet clanked against the metal floor as he leisurely made his way down the same hallway Ank had scrambled through. The excitement displayed by the *Myzer's* new navigator, and the absence of it from Salem, wasn't solely from her lack of shipboard experience. Salem had hatched at the end of a cycle, right before his first hibernation—what was called a "hibernation hatchling." As a result, he'd been awake for his entire first hibernation. It was why he didn't sleep well each circayd and had little energy. People always assumed he was a few cycles older than he really was. The *Myzer's* mechanic, Plexie, was ten, and often acted as if Salem were his elder.

For the first hundred circayds of his life or so, while the rest of the colony slept, Salem was raised by the hibernation crew. When the regular caregivers of the young, the brood rōshis, awoke at the dawn of the following cycle and resumed their duties, Ank hatched, making her a cycle younger than Salem by technicality. She was referred to as a "hibernation egg" or "perfect hatchling." Her regular sleep patterns were efficient, her energy appropriate for her age.

According to her, she'd timed it intentionally.

Salem passed through a doorway leading to the next section of corridor, minding his step over the slight protrusion as he left the bunk area. Like most venth ships, the *Myzer* was no more than an empty carapace, its walls and ceilings both comprised of the same alloy. The majority of its materials were contained in the outer lining to prevent heat loss, and ships went without the extra amenities of the colony.

Turning down the next hallway, he quickly crossed paths with Olyké, the colony administrator who ran the *Myzer*. Olyké worked for the Energy Department, as did Salem, reporting directly to the Power Panel: a small group who oversaw Venthralli's heat expenditures. It was the most important department other than water, though water required far less management.

Olyké had been a ship lead for almost six cycles. She was a big-picture sort of person who knew a little bit about a lot of things, so the diagnostic in her hand might contain anything from radiation signatures to nutrition information.

Salem knew almost none of those things.

"Time to get dressed," she said plainly, referring to Salem's space suit. The *Myzer* had six of them—one each for Salem, Ank, Olyké, and Plexie, as well as ones for Hathem, their doctor, and Cejero, their science officer.

"Ank just told me," said Salem. "How big is it?"

"Small, but Cejero thinks it's big enough to be a net gain," she said. Whenever someone opened the pressure door, the ship lost additional heat. For tiny shards the size of a toy, they lost more heat than they gained, and the longer they debated any of them, the larger the shard needed to be, because the *Myzer* was always losing heat. Excursions were only launched for confirmed shards, and sitting idly in a zone was almost as taboo as an excursion without a target.

"Do you want me to suit up and wait while they double-check?"

"No, just go out," said Olyké. She glanced quickly back down the hall. "I don't want to sit here longer than we need to."

Being a venth who typically held the expression of a rock, Olyké's jitteriness was unusual.

Salem fought back a smile. "Are you superstitious?"

"No. Don't be ridiculous," she spat. "I just don't want to sit around the zone figuring out *if* the shard is a gain, and ultimately make it a loss through our dallying."

Salem chortled. *"Dallying..."*

"Just get dressed," Olyké droned. She meandered back towards the sensory room, where the ship's instruments were kept.

Regardless of what she said, the light shard made Olyké uneasy. A few people on Venthralli told horror stories about them being unlucky or bad omens or whatnot. That breaking one could cause it to explode. They were just tales told out of boredom to scare hatchlings when the brood rōshis weren't around. Light shards were rare and mysterious, making them easy fodder for such fables, but few people actually believed them, and nobody who worked on an energy collector did. You had to be science-minded to operate a ship, and after traveling hundreds of zones without seeing one of the glowing gems, it was clear to Salem that people never returned with light shards because they never found any. By the time Salem had hatched, those stories had mostly run their course, but Olyké was fourteen or fifteen, so her clutch had probably heard them a lot.

And even if the supposed dangers of collecting a light shard were real, Venthralli couldn't afford to pass up on any form of heat. It needed constant energy to survive, which meant that running out of fuel was not an option. If that ever happened, all life on board—the venth, the plants, the agricultural bugs, even the bacteria—would die, marking the end of the universe's last civilization. The end of all life.

All but one…

If anything, light shards were lucky. This was a story he would be reciting in eleven cycles to venth just beginning their contribution periods. Salem didn't even know how long ago the last light shard was. There was a good chance he was about to become the only living venth to see one with his own eyes.

Salem approached the pressure room and opened the large cabinet containing their space suits beside it. He wrapped his dark, oval-tipped fingers around the rattiest one on the rack and unhooked it from its home. The light-grey material was tattered from countless collection trips. Functional, just coarse and frayed. A few of the other suits were lightly used, like Cejero's and Hathem's.

Plexie's to a lesser extent. The other two were as pristine as could be, only used in emergencies when everyone needed to go outside, or for entering and exiting through the dock. Ank's suit, which had to be made smaller, had been worn exactly once.

With his suit collapsed on the ground, Salem put his feet through the hole at the top of the suit and tried to pull the heavy, padded exterior up around him. The material didn't bend well, making it difficult to move in, but it protected him against the treacherous cold of the outside, which was all that really mattered.

While he struggled to get his shoulders through the hole, a pattering of footsteps grew from around the corner. Plexie appeared soon after, scuttling into view on all fours.

"Hey Salem!" the mechanic squeaked as he stood upright. "Want some help?"

"I think so," Salem replied. He should be able to effortlessly don his own suit by now, but they were nothing if not difficult to put on. "Does this mean the shard is a gain?"

"Oh yeah, at least thirty times the pressure door loss," Plexie said. He held the rim of the suit upright while Salem worked his body down into it. "Also, there's an issue with the external access port. It'll take too long to repair right now, so you'll need to bring the shard inside with you. I can fix the port while you and Cejero are on the deadworld."

Salem's shoulders popped through the opening of the suit, and it came to rest on his body. "Thanks," he hooted. He grabbed the worn helmet from the ground beneath the empty suit hanger and put it on, wiggling it back and forth until its latches met the suit's and clicked together.

Rotating his entire body, Salem turned back to Plexie. "Do you think it'll be as bright as people say it is?" he asked. "I don't want to hurt my eyes."

"No. One of my gene donors said they saw a light shard a long time ago, and it wasn't that bright. Do you want to use my dark lenses just in case?"

Salem considered the offer. Dark lenses were worn by people who worked with fire or something of a similar brightness, except for forge workers, who had to use blackout helmets instead. Plexie wore his lenses from time to time when welding. The torches all had their own protective screens, but the reflections could still be bright. At the same time, he often performed quick checks on the reactor without the lenses because it took so long to put them on.

"No, that's alright," Salem decided. "My helmet's already on."

"Where's your shard box?" Plexie asked, looking Salem up and down as if the large container was somehow hidden on his person.

"Will the shard fit in one?"

"Sure!" the mechanic chirped, reconsidering. "Well…maybe. Light shards don't soften when they warm up, do they?"

"They're not supposed to."

"Hmm," Plexie thought. "The box…might not close, then."

When bringing portions of starshards inside, a specially made rectangular case was utilized. Regular shards melted and evaporated quickly, so if you brought it on board a ship, it would loosen and get gel residue all over the place, which was hazardous. Because they were crystallized, light shards weren't supposed to melt at the same temperatures. It seemed moot, though, because if it started to melt, the box's lid would close, and if it didn't melt, the lid wouldn't need to.

Salem shrugged. "I might as well use one, I guess."

"I'll grab it!" Plexie said. "Hook yourself in." He scrambled farther down the hall towards the engine room.

Large spools of industrial line sat mounted on either side of the pressure room, the nearest of which Salem hooked up to his suit. Dull *clanks* echoed from the engine room, followed by a sharp screech as Plexie dragged the trunk out to Salem.

Shard boxes were made of a dense alloy, with molded patterns along the edges and a simple latch on the front. They weren't horribly heavy when emptied, but they were difficult for a single person to carry because of their size. The crate was as long as a venth was tall: just under a third of an "allo"—the width of a standard residential abode on Venthralli. For small measurements, venth often used "digits," roughly a finger's length, but the Energy Department preferred the use of portions of allos for consistency.

Salem was 0.296 allos tall.

"I can't wait to see it!" Plexie said. His eyes shined with delight. Salem suspected there might not be anything wrong with the external fuel hatch, and Plexie was just orchestrating the light shard to be brought inside. "Good luck!" he added.

Alone in the half-allo-wide pressure room, Salem shut the interior door. He gave the shard box a look over to make sure it wasn't damaged, then adjusted it so it would be easier to pick up once the gravity was gone. Then, he re-checked the cable attached to his suit and the clasp connecting them.

Finally, he took a deep breath and rolled his shoulders.

"Hey, Olyké?" he piped up. "Cejero?"

"Just me!" Ank's voice replied through the transmitter.

"I'm going to open the pressure door."

"Okay!" she said. "Why are you telling me?"

"I'm telling Olyké."

"But why are you telling her?"

"Because I'm supposed to," Salem said. "She monitors to make sure the interior door isn't leaking heat or anything."

"Oh yeah!" she squeaked. "I know how to do that, now."

"Nifty."

"Well, who *else* is going to do it if you, Cejero, Hathem, *and* Olyké all go outside?"

"Last time it was Plexie."

"Nope! Ank!"

"Okay, well, I'm opening the door."

"You are cleared to open the exterior pressure door," Ank recited, almost exactly the way Olyké did.

With his gloved hand, Salem grabbed the large metal handle beside him. As the lever's tension gave way and slammed downward, a gale of wind swept up, sucking the air from the room. Even through the thick layers of fabric, he could feel the air pushing against his arms. The upward pull of the air around his body.

Soon after, the pressure room became a vacuum. The *whooshing* around Salem died, the weight of his feet on the floor lightened, and the outer door opened.

Darkness.

A lot of people couldn't wrap their heads around what the outside was. Salem hadn't been able to at first. Not until he'd experienced it firsthand. It was nothing, but also everything. There was space. Boundless, infinite space. But it was entirely empty.

Mostly empty.

As if to prove that fact, a small dot of light gleamed against the oily canvas.

Salem smiled. He'd never seen light shining through the outside like that before. It was usually just black; the darkest black anyone could ever see. To find a shard, Salem had to go wherever it was supposed to be and then swing his flashlight around until the beam caught a piece of its icy exterior.

Not this one. It was shining *its* light at *him*.

Rocking his feet forward, Salem allowed the outside to pull him from the pressure room. There was no need to double-check the calculations or estimate his trajectory: the iridescent rock guided him all on its own.

Quietly, he sailed along for a while, watching the glassy object grow larger and move over his head. When he got as far as he needed, he poked a transmitter on the chest of his suit, locking the spool back in the pressure room. The line snapped taut, stopping his motion with a tender jolt. The shard box tugged at his hand as it tried to continue on.

Salem had timed his distance perfectly, coming to rest a couple of allos directly underneath the shard. From his hip, he unsheathed a tube-shaped canister full of pressurized air, giving a quick spurt towards his feet. The force pushed him softly upwards, dragging the weightless crate along with him to the light shard. He countered the force a moment later, coming to rest right in front of the gem.

"Magical" was the only word to describe it. The light shard didn't hurt his eyes at all. It was dimmer than an emergency lantern and had a slightly elliptical shape, more pointed towards its ends. The longest side was just a little shorter than Salem. The interior glow of the object accentuated its crystallized texture, like the clearest water tinted blue, although the hue might be from actual water frozen on its surface.

"I'm at the shard," he said.

"Good job," Olyké said from the sensory room. "Any give from the line?"

"No. Partial use of my puff canister. At most a twelfth."

"Got it." There was a pause as Olyké recorded the usage. They didn't want someone going outside with an empty canister, nor did they want to waste energy compressing a mostly full canister.

Salem tilted his head to change his perspective on the light shard. "It might be too long to fit into the box," he said. "I can probably cut it in two and fit both pieces inside, but that will probably snuff out the light."

Commotion stirred in the sensory room—Plexie opposing the notion of cutting the shard. Salem asked, "It's not actually going to blow up, right?"

"No..." Olyké said absently, listening to Cejero. "The light shard...won't explode. But it also won't melt. Just bring it inside so we can move along."

"Ooookie."

Salem reached his hand out to the light shard, hovering next to the surface to feel for excessive heat. He kept his hand as still as his heart would allow, and after eight beats without feeling any warmth, he placed the palm of his glove against the frozen surface. A slow, gentle motion, so as not to push the shard away.

Still no heat.

A good shard handler never tried to put a shard into a box. Not outside. Instead, they put the box around the shard. With deliberate motions, Salem opened the box and faced it towards the light shard. It took a while to move the box around the object without knocking it farther into space, though the visibility of the rare gem made the whole ordeal much easier to coordinate.

Once the two objects were resting together, Salem closed the lid as much as it could and angled the box so the shard was poking out towards the *Myzer*. He connected the box's handle to the back of his suit, which took some time, given how difficult it was to reach behind himself. Normally, Salem didn't have to worry about shards falling out of the box while being towed back to the ship, so he took his time on the return. He gave the tether a pull, hoping to approach at an angle he wouldn't later need to correct with the puff canister.

"You're at two hundred rotés," Olyké said.

"I'm coming back," Salem huffed with the shard in tow, "five rotés."

A roté was the length of time it took Venthralli to make one full rotation around itself, equal to eight beats. Salem's air tank lasted for around twelve hundred rotés depending on the type of use, so he was given benchmarks for time, the first being two hundred. His suit didn't lose air, exactly, but his body converted the air into different gasses, which, in turn, required energy to be converted back into breathable ones.

As the Department motto went: "Everything uses energy."

The pressure room was barely visible against the outside: a small, ethereal box hovering in the center of nothingness. A pilot lantern in the ceiling cascaded just enough light to see the mechanisms and spools from within, but it was too dim to function as a beacon. When Salem was off at an angle, which was usually the case, he couldn't see the edge of the opening until he was near the ship.

With precise motions, Salem positioned the box upright inside the pressure room. To prevent it from crashing down later, Salem maneuvered himself to the ceiling and pushed the container against the floor. Using the friction of his gloves, he slid himself along the ceiling until he was no longer above the shard box, then pushed himself back to the floor.

Rewinding the spool without gravity was a nightmare, so Salem pulled the excess cable freely into the pressure room, balling it up and pushing it towards the back corner. With his boots pressed into the floor, he grabbed the lever and forced it up into its original position.

A rush of wind fell over him. His knees buckled as the ground pulled at him once again. The jets pressed against his shell through the worn fabric of the space suit, and the pressure room equalized its atmosphere to the rest of the *Myzer's* cabin.

The interior door opened, and Salem was startled to see a full welcoming party. Everybody but Olyké had gathered in the corridor to greet the light shard.

The ship's doctor, Hathem, approached Salem in the airlock as he removed his helmet. She was an older venth of nineteen, on the last cycle of her contribution period. At over a third of an allo tall, she was larger than most venth, standing at least a head above everyone else on the *Myzer's* crew.

She unhooked Salem from the line, which had crumpled to the floor upon the gravity's return.

"I can re-spool this," she said. "Go ahead and take the shard in."

She gazed fondly for a moment at the edge of the crystal peeking from the side of the box, then turned to unlock the spool and recoil the flat tether's excess around it.

With considerable effort, Salem dragged the shard box towards its eager observers. Light shards were already so uncommon; finding one small enough to bring inside was practically unheard of. A shard of that size didn't contain enough energy to justify its own stop, and would only be grabbed if it happened to lie on the optimal jump path to a ship's objective. Add in the crystallization, the light...it was the greatest thing any of them would ever see.

Plexie and Ank could barely keep their carapaces together as Salem pulled the box inside. He flicked the lid open with his foot, causing even their science officer to recoil a bit, as if further exposure to air might cause the shard to blow up.

With his helmet off, Salem noticed that the light shard didn't look quite like a crystal. Certainly not the ultra-hard jewel he'd been led to expect. There was a viscous quality to it. Like the hardened sap from a bark plant.

"Wow…" Ank gasped, her eyes growing so large they nearly took up her entire head.

Plexie reached out to the shard, stopping his hand just shy of contact like Salem had. "Is it okay to touch?"

"Sure. It's not hot or anything."

Plexie pushed his hand softly against the resin-like surface, and Ank rushed to the box to do the same. Neither spoke as they felt the chill of the arcane object. They just smiled.

"Alright, let's see this thing," Olyké said as she rounded the corner to the pressure door. Reluctantly, Ank stepped away to make room for the colony admin, who looked at the crystal for no more than a beat. "That's pretty neat," she admitted. "How much energy will it give?"

"What would a regular shard of this size produce?" Cejero asked, leaning over the box to get a better look.

Sadly, Plexie examined the light shard up and down. "A little less than a jump's worth," he moaned.

"This will be about twenty percent more efficient by volume, so we might get a full jump out of it."

"Aw, do we have to burn it?" Ank asked.

"Yes we have to burn it," Olyké said. "We can't afford not to."

"But people back home will want to see it! I bet Brinka would put it in the museum."

"Next to the alien bones," Plexie mused. "You know, 'cause they both come from the outside—oh! Or with the first shard box!"

"Then we could go in and tell people, 'We found that!'"

Olyké shook her head. "The extra jump guarantees us a net gain so long as we get our full estimation from the deadworld. Plus, it exudes heat, so every roté it's not in the reactor, it loses energy."

"That's a very minor loss," said Cejero. "It's losing less in here than it was outside. As long as it's not melting, it's fine."

Hathem meandered out of the pressure room, the cable neatly coiled on the wall behind her. "It would be quite a sight for everyone at the colony," she said. "It might even be beneficial for the purpose of removing inaccurate stigmas. We always have the option of throwing it into the reactor later, should we find ourselves in need of fuel."

Plexie and Ank waited for Olyké's response with face-wide eyes, an obvious attempt to persuade her by appearing more hatchling-like. The ship lead ignored them, staring at the shard for a while. She turned to Salem, who, not wanting to destroy the shard either, made the same face.

She took a long, defeated breath. "Alright, fine," she said. "We can hold off on burning it unless we need to."

The three venth cheered, joined less enthusiastically by Cejero.

"I can come down a few times per circayd to make sure it's remaining solid," he said.

Plexie helped Salem move the glowing object to the hall outside of the engine room, as they didn't want to leave it near the warm machines inside. They were determined to do whatever it took to bring their new treasure home intact, a responsibility that would fall entirely on Salem in two circayds, when he would be tasked to find the *Myzer* enough fuel to return home with its required surplus.

CHAPTER 2
RUBBLE DUSTERS

The whir of the *Myzer's* engine softened as the ship landed from its jump. Each zone crossing took about half a circayd, with a reset time of forty to fifty rotés. Plexie had once explained to Salem why the ship required a pause before making another jump, but it hadn't made any sense to him, so he just thought of it as "cooling down" even though the engines remained hot during that time.

Salem lay in bed, getting whatever form of rest he could before his big mission on the deadworld. Ship crews were used to sleeping amidst the heavy rumble, but Salem was forever plagued by the timing of his birth. Venth were supposed to get between 1500-2000 rotés of sleep per circayd. Salem rarely broke 1000.

The procedure for touching down on a deadworld was lengthy. After arriving in their destination zone, the *Myzer* would creep slowly towards the deadworld, allowing the celestial body's gravity to pull on it. As that attraction grew stronger, they would then use the landing jets to slow their merging, and the ship would come to rest against the large sphere.

This time around, Salem may have actually dozed off for twenty or thirty rotés, but when he felt the lurch of the ship's impact against the deadworld, he knew it was time to get to work.

"Rubble Dusters, let's go!" Olyké shouted through the hallway. Salem was already at the pressure door, attempting to get dressed by himself, and had just about gotten his suit on by the time Cejero and Hathem joined him.

Historically, doctors never went outside because if something bad happened to them, it would create danger for the rest of the crew. Floating outside, anchored only to the pressure door, there was a notable risk, but on a deadworld, there was less. It was impossible to knock a venth free from one of the massive rocks' magnetic pulls, and dangers like falling into a ravine were primarily for whoever went first, which was Salem. Since Hathem had prior experience doing spacewalks—and was quite strong—she was useful to have on a deadworld, so at the beginning of the previous cycle, she was added to the ground team, marking the birth of the "Rubble Dusters," previously known as "Salem and Cejero."

As the ship's science officer, Cejero went onto every deadworld and asteroid. He collected dirt, and in the rare instances there was mist, he'd open up a jar and collect some of that, too. What Cejero was ultimately looking for within the dirt, Salem never knew, but whenever he finished before Salem, he would always help bring shard chunks back to the ship.

Ank flopped around the corner, her eyes slinky from sleep. She watched the three Rubble Dusters get their suits on by the door, waiting silently as she blinked herself awake. Around the time they finished, Plexie arrived with their homing radar—a device that told them how far and in what direction the ship was.

"This is where we landed," he said, showing the dim, infrared screen to Ank.

She stared at it for a moment, her expression foggy as she tried to do math early in the circayd. "Okay, so it's—umm…" she started.

One of the downsides to Ank's perfect sleep patterns was that, if she was woken early, she was sluggish and stupid.

Her left eye shrank. "Six point…two?"

"Why are you asking me?"

"I'm not…it's six-point-two…ish…wheels from the door."

A wheel was the circumference of the middle of deck one back on Venthralli—forty-eight allos. Salem would have to transport pieces of the shard a distance of several hundred homes.

"Why so far?" he whined.

"That was the closest we could get," said Plexie. "There's a lot of bumpy terrain around the shard signal. Mountains, we think."

Salem groaned and hopped backwards through the pressure door. To most venth, the mere concept of a mountain was appropriately otherworldly and fantastical. Salem had seen several, though, and they were inconvenient.

Cejero took possession of the homing radar so that Hathem could help Plexie into his space suit. Examining the device, he joined Salem in the pressure room. "Another external repair?" he asked.

"Yup!" Plexie said, worming his arm through the neck-hole of his pristine suit. "The insulation panels are sliding around near the farm cabinet, and it's wasting heat."

"I thought it was the fuel hatch," Salem said.

"Oh, that'll only take a hundred rotés. Two, max."

"This ship is always broken…" Cejero mumbled.

"How dare you speak of them like that," chided Plexie. "The *Myzer* runs great. Better than Venthralli ever does."

"That seems doubtful."

Plexie popped his other shoulder into his suit. "Cejero, if you had any idea how close Venthralli's reactor comes to breaking down every cycle, you'd never want to go home."

He followed Hathem into the pressure room while he fastened down his helmet. Cejero looked at him sideways, waiting for some whimsical clarification that he was only joking, but it never came.

"Okie," Ank said. "I'll be in the sensory room." She waved halfheartedly, lumbering off slowly to the other side of the ship.

With two-thirds of the crew ready to head outside, Salem cycled the pressure room. The exterior door opened, and they were met by a darkness dissimilar to that of a spacewalk. Their collective lights shined across the ragged, blue surface of the world just outside the pressure room, silhouetting a rocky outcrop two allos ahead.

Their flashlights weren't very bright.

A noticeable ache undulated through the arch of Salem's foot as it hit the ground outside. He walked an allo along the side of the ship to an unsealed cabinet beside the fuel port and grabbed a cart to transport the shard chunks—"chunk" being a non-technical term describing the largest amount of fuel one could reasonably fit into the external fuel port. During a typical collection, most of Salem's time was spent cutting the shard into chunks. Two people could carry a single chunk with relative ease, but they were still supposed to use the carts. On a deadworld this heavy, with their shard six wheels away, they weren't carrying anything by hand.

Salem returned with the cart, a loud tension in his legs, and the Rubble Dusters began their trek across the barren land.

The deadworld was a beautiful shade of dusty blue; Salem couldn't tell if it was a blue that was almost grey, or grey with a blue tint. Deadworlds often appeared blue, as many of them had layers of their old atmosphere frozen to their surface.

Before long, the exploration trio arrived at one of the larger outcrops, extending far up into the black. Finding a flat path between the jutting crags wasn't too difficult, but it became quickly disorienting. If not for the homing radar, they would've easily gotten turned around. When they reached the other side, the tall, canyon-like rocks separated and became sparse, though not so much that Salem couldn't catch at least one in his light.

They continued across the unnamed planet's surface for a couple of wheels, swinging their lamps across the rocks to gauge its geography. That reminded Salem of a task they had yet to complete. One of the utmost importance.

"Hey," he chirped, "whose turn is it?"

"Cejero's."

"Huh?" Cejero mumbled, lost in thought. "Oh, right, right..." He mulled over his responsibility for half a roté, then said, "I dub this deadworld...Hobblecob."

"Sorry to disturb you, Hobblecob," said Salem. "We'll only be here shortly."

Salem couldn't remember how the tradition had begun. They each took turns naming the deadworlds they visited, after which someone would apologize for disturbing the ancient being's eternal rest, lest they face its powerful wrath. The game was later was amended to include what job they thought the deadworld had in their fictional deadworld society, eons ago.

"Is Hobblecob a girl deadworld, or a boy deadworld?"

"Hobblecob is an *it*," Cejero said, grunting as he skipped his boot over a large piece of rubble. "In the old deadworld society, Hobblecob would be the equivalent of a work of art."

"I see it," Hathem agreed passively.

"Does that mean that *this* Hobblecob is a statue of an actual deadworld named Hobblecob?"

"No. It's a work of art all on its own called Hobblecob, and just happens to look like a deadworld."

"I love that!" Ank said through their transmitters. Salem jumped at the unexpected commentary. Olyké never said anything while the Dusters were on a deadworld; not unless it was mission critical.

Focused on the ground, Cejero abruptly stopped and leaned over. He touched a small pile of dirt by his feet, then rubbed his fingers together in front of his visor. "Hmm…" he mumbled. "Interesting."

Hathem turned back to him, rotating at the trunk to angle her helmet. "What did you find?"

"Powdery ground," he said. "Very fine."

"That is strange."

"It must be a compound of some sort." He retrieved a flexible container from his suit and scooped some of the powdery minerals from the surface into it. "Wouldn't be lucky enough to find a new element, but it could be exciting."

"Recorded," Ank said.

Cejero exhaled. "You don't need to record that, Ank. We're already logging the information with the deadworld."

"Well, the book says to record it. So I am."

"She's right," Salem said. "Nobody does it, but it's what the book says." Older people often forgot simple procedures that were commonly ignored for one reason or another. In this case, it was redundant, so the step was usually skipped.

"Olyké says I'm right, too."

Cejero grumbled, placing the container of dirt into a canvas bag he used for field samples.

The terrain between each of the large boulders became increasingly bumpy. The three venth huffed as their legs strained to move them through the heavy gravity. The cart behind Salem made a constant *shushing* sound as it slid along the frosty soil.

"Two hundred rotés," Ank's said. Her voice was fuzzy through the transmitter. "What's your angle?"

Cejero checked the homing radar. "Negative one-point-one."

"You'll land at around negative two-point-seven."

"Did you hear that, Salem?"

"Uh-huh," Salem exhaled, tugging at the cart with each step. Cejero thrust the tracking device into his hands.

"You're a little over a wheel away," he said. "I'm going to stop here and take some samples. There might be air materials in the surface dust, which would be worth verifying now."

"I'm simply old and tired," said Hathem. "I'll help Cejero. If you find the shard, give us a click."

With the small tracking device in hand, Salem continued along the dark tundra of Hobblecob. He couldn't actually "click" through the radio outside—his fingers were covered by the padded gloves of his suit, and the gloves were outside where no sound could carry. It was an old-timey phrase that only people Hathem's age used.

After a few rotés, the lights from the other Rubble Dusters faded into darkness, throwing Salem into isolation. The ground ahead crept silently out of the black, occasionally forcing him to stop and walk to the side before continuing.

When the radar showed him at five and a half wheels out from the ship, the surface of Hobblecob formed an upward slope.

"Urrrg," Salem growled at the large dirt pile.

"What's wrong?!" Ank queued in rapidly.

"Nothing…just a hill. It's really heavy out here."

"How far are you from the shard?" asked Cejero.

"About half a wheel."

"Well, at least it's early on for the trip back," he said. As the person who would be dragging the shard chunks back to the *Myzer*, Salem didn't feel like it mattered how early the hill was going to be. It was enough of a chore with an empty cart.

The apex of the hill fell away immediately into a downward slope, forming a shallow ridge. Salem stood at the top, catching his breath as he stared down the incline. His air tank hissed to keep up with his starving lungs.

With no one around to scold him, Salem pulled the cart to the lip of the ridge and sat on it. He pushed the surrounding dirt with his foot, allowing the immense gravity of Hobblecob to pull him towards the flattened landscape that surely existed below.

The cart's metal frame picked up speed and continued over the edge of the ridge. Soon after, Salem was rocketing down the powdery incline. Frozen dirt rushed towards him from beyond his flashlight; the uneven terrain bucked the cart side to side. He tightened his grip on the bars, struggling to keep from falling off.

Uh oh…

The bottom of the hill appeared at the edge of Salem's view and charged towards him. Before he could react, he hit the flat ground head-on and careened into the air, landing hard half an allo away from the base of the hill. Pain streaked through his carapace. The flashlight rolled across the ground by the cart. The homing radar struck the nearby dirt.

"Oof," Salem grunted, smacked in the stomach by Hobblecob. The impact was loud in his suit.

"Are you okay?" Hathem asked.

"Ugh," he groaned. "Hold on…"

Crazed, he rushed to his feet. How could he be so stupid? The cart might be broken, or one of his plates, or worse: part of his space suit. If he had a tear, he might be too far from Cejero and Hathem for them to save him. He might not even be able to find such a tear by himself.

Instead of fetching the flashlight, Salem paused and listened. There was no engine hum, no scampering footsteps, no rotational wind. There was no sound at all. It was the most silent place in the universe that any person stood in that moment.

He listened for half a roté. No rushing air.

"I'm fine," he finally answered. "I fell, but my suit's intact."

"Do you want us to come find you?"

"No, that's okay." He brushed flakes of frozen ground off of himself. "I'll let you know when I've found the shard."

Salem picked up the flashlight and walked back to the cart, retrieving the homing radar along the way. Its dim, infrared screen told him he was still a quarter of a wheel away, but the methods used to estimate the shard's location weren't as accurate as the homing radar itself, so Salem could be near the shard already.

Swinging the light around, he tried to get familiar with his new surroundings. The land flattened away from the base of the hill, and a large, sheer cliffside rose from the ground a few allos to his left. The vertical surface bounced his flashlight back brilliantly, Salem could just make out the jagged crest three allos up.

Salem walked towards the cliff, illuminating more of the smooth surface. It began to appear as if it were comprised of several rocks in series, or perhaps a single cliff that had been broken into multiple pieces. The ground nearby featured a few small rock mounds, each half an allo high and exceptionally flat. There was something off about the deadworld. Something that seemed almost—

Salem swung his flashlight back to the vertical face. His eyes bulged to absorb the beam's reflection, stretching the range of his sight to see as far as possible in a single eyeful.

He whispered, "No way…"

"What is it?" asked Hathem.

"I think you should come here," he said louder.

"Is everything alright?"

"Yeah," Salem said. He ran the beam up the pale rocks, craning his neck. "But I'm pretty sure these are buildings."

The lamps of Hathem and Cejero swept along the angled ground of the hillside as the two carefully descended. Few of their photons reached Salem from far away, making the beams dim through the darkness, as if seeing them through a black fog.

"Interesting," Hathem said.

Cejero stopped to look at her. "What?"

"I see tracks from the cart on the hill, but no footprints."

Her light shined up towards Salem, who shrugged sheepishly. "The cart must have covered them up behind me," he said.

"Uh huh…"

They walked past the cart Salem had abandoned at the bottom of the hill, joining him by the polished stone. With all three lanterns cast on it together, the entire cliffside appeared at once, confirming Salem's suspicions.

"This is…a city?" Hathem whispered, like the deadworld might awaken.

"Yeah—a city for giants."

"Wow!" Ank yelled; Salem winced.

"Aw, I wanna see!" Plexie whined.

"Are there any bodies?"

"Doubtful," Hathem said.

"Are there old lights?"

"We're not sure yet."

"Do you see any technology?"

"Ank—when we have information, we will let you know. I promise. Okay?"

"Okay…"

Excitement and terror swirled around Salem. Even with Hathem as Cejero beside him, walking towards the towering arches was frightening. He felt as if a two-allo-tall alien would emerge from one of the openings at any moment.

Buildings on Venthralli were generally wider than they were tall, but these were the opposite, with large, open doorways extending three decks into the sky. Each archway was surrounded by thick, square molding, all crafted from stone, and each roof protruded slightly from the wall, their peaks forming into a dull point at the top.

The three venth walked up to the nearest archway. Inside, their lights reflected faintly from the back wall, more than four allos deep. The building wasn't separated into multiple decks—it was a single, massive room, its ceiling nearly as high as all five of Venthralli's outer decks combined.

Hathem looked up at the monstrous doorway, running her light along its frame. "This is incredible."

Salem mused, "They look like they're only one deck high."

"I believe so," said Cejero. "There's nothing to indicate collapsed floors." He peered cautiously into the first building from the doorway. "That doesn't mean it's stable, though, so be careful."

"This is the best expedition ever," Salem gushed.

"I'll make a note!" Ank said. Hathem shook her head at Cejero.

Whatever lay farther along, it had to be at least as impressive as these buildings. Salem opened his eyes wide, taking in all of the room before branching off to explore on his own.

"I'm gonna go look for the shard," he finally said.

"Alright. Good find, Salem."

"Yes, good find," another voice came through the transmitter. "Hathem, it's Olyké. After you do your initial assessment, do a cursory biological search, then go into your full report."

"Understood."

Cejero went back to taking dirt samples. He would likely have to dig below the surface now, so Hathem could check for traces of life. Nobody ever found any, but scientists all insisted it was possible, so they had to check.

After all, zero beasts survived in the outside just fine.

A couple of buildings later, Salem realized that there was, in fact, a cliff behind them. The row of buildings sat up against it, their roofs carved just below the top of the jagged rock hanging over them. Passing each one, he shined his light into their stone archways, searching for the signature glint of frozen heat gel before sweeping it out across the nearby plain of dirt. He checked a few more, at which point the buildings stopped, as well as the cliff behind them.

"There's a cave here," he said.

"Where?"

"I think…eight more buildings? Nine total. There might be more of them on the other side; it's wider than my light."

"Aw, I really want to see this," Plexie said. "Can I go help with the shard after I'm done with the ship?"

"You'll get lost without the homing radar," Olyké said.

"But if we have to do lots of trips…?"

"Just take your time on that repair, and then we'll see where the collection is at."

Plexie always got antsy when they were on a deadworld. Salem didn't think the desolate landscapes were as exciting as he believed, though the presence of a giant stone city certainly made this trip more wondrous than the norm.

Struggling to focus on the shard hunt, Salem found himself repeatedly distracted by the different-looking buildings. In a general sense, they were similar, but each was different in some way. Unique.

"I have the cave noted," Ank said. "Don't disturb anything inside, or you may…" she paused as she read from the procedure manual, "collapse it on yourself."

"Thank you…" Salem droned, well aware of the dangers involved with spelunking. Unfortunately, caves were excellent places for starshards to survive, and this one was right where Ank thought the shard on Hobblecob would be—6.2 wheels away from the *Myzer*. And if that fact wasn't enough to draw Salem inside, the walls of this particular cavern were lined with more buildings, akin to those on the cliff, but smaller. Their ceilings stopped just below the top of the cave.

As boring as deadworlds tended to be, the fact that they existed at all was remarkable to Salem. The stars of long ago had been millions of times larger than a deadworld, trillions of times larger than the biggest starshards. Too big for any venth to truly comprehend. They were so massive that they had nuclear generators inside of them and were on fire all the time. Then, they all exploded. It just didn't seem possible for Hobblecob to have survived.

Yet, here it was.

Finding buildings was even more remarkable. These ones had likely been protected by the cave and cliffside. Most evidence of alien life had been found near a similar type of geological shielding. As for actual bones, there was just the one set in the museum, which Cejero thought was only about 4% of the whole alien they'd come from.

Salem searched quietly through the cavern's houses while listening to Hathem relay her findings to Ank. He was often envious of her job in the Rubble Dusters. This town had once been full of creatures—big ones, with shops and dance halls and tool makers. To be able to walk around and just think about what they were like—that was fascinating on its own, not merely as an afterthought while searching for fuel. Had Salem not been born at the end of the universe, he suspected he might have liked to be an explorer. He could draw pictures of the things he saw and display them for people who didn't get to see them.

Instead, he was passing by most of the oversized ruins, stepping lightly to avoid death during his search for the light shard.

The farther into the cave Salem went, the more dangerous it became. After the sixth building, he saw nothing but darkness ahead, so he decided to stop. The last building in the row was surrounded by rubble, which might indicate it was susceptible to collapse.

He shined his light across the structure. Its ceiling had fallen in, littering the floor inside with broken bits of crafted stone. The cave above had also collapsed in, exposing a hole directly to the outside.

Since the roof couldn't collapse in again, Salem walked into the building, stepping over the larger chunks of debris. He couldn't get very far. The building was shallow, nowhere near as deep as it was tall or wide. Salem thought maybe it had been a giant's utility closet or cabinet.

He walked up to the back wall, which was a different texture from the others: sheer, glistening in the atmospheric frost. Salem then considered that it could be made out of something other than rock, which could make it valuable to the colony. Or a special type of rock, like marble. His lantern reflected brightly from the perpendicular material, like polished metal, tempting him to feel the surface despite his better wisdom.

Making sure he stood below the hole above, he slid his hand along the wall. A bubbling feeling rose in his abdomen. He braced himself for the building to fall in, but it didn't.

The accent wall was smooth, almost slick. Sort of like—

Salem sprang back from the wall. Big, lunging steps that moved him completely out of the shallow building. He waved his flashlight up and down. A smile spread across his mouth.

"This is Salem," he said. "I've found the shard."

The back wall of the sixth building in the cave city on Hobblecob was neither rock nor alloy nor ice. It was a large, flat starshard. Three allos tall and one and a half across.

Once the realization hit Salem, the entire scene became obvious. The starshard had struck the deadworld above the building, breaking through the thin roof of the cave and the ceiling. The rim of the opening above had warped, melting as if near a forge, and the impact had collapsed the sides of the building.

"Ooh!" Ank howled upon hearing of the shard. "Recorded! How much is it? Is it at least three chunks' worth?"

"It's—" Salem tried to estimate how much fuel the boulder contained. It was one of the biggest shards he'd seen, and math wasn't his best skill. "It's more than the *Myzer's* tank could hold. Forty or fifty chunks, I think."

"Salem, it's Olyké. Did you say *fifty?* Five-zero?"

"Yeah, maybe more."

Salem peered around the sides of the shard to verify the depth without disturbing the site. It wasn't as deep as it was wide, but still over an allo.

"I'm bringing the cart over, now," Cejero said, wheezing with the metal appliance in tow. "Where in the cave are you?"

"Last building on the left," Salem said. He wrenched open a piece of twine that he used to measure his cuts, stiff from the cold. He measured out a cubic chunk, marking the shard with his heat saw by melting little dots in a 0.4-allo cube.

"Well, I'll be froze..." Cejero gasped. His mouth hung open, fingers tapping against the cart handle as he looked up at the starshard mountain.

"Not yet, you're not." Salem finished the first cut, and his eyes dragged up to the opening above. "There's a big hole in the ceiling where the shard came through. I think it'll be safe standing under it."

Cejero shined his light up. The ceiling dimmed as the beam swung over the opening, the photons escaping to the outside. "It's yours to collect," he said, "but I suggest we take a half-chunk back and grab the powered cart for the rest."

"Yup," Salem said. "Where's Hathem?"

"She took my samples back to the ship." He gestured up to the frozen heat gel. "This is a priority."

Salem halved one of his measurements, eyeballing the difference, then cut the half-chunk out of the combustible glacier. Traditionally, taking less than a full chunk was wasteful. It took roughly the same amount of time, the *Myzer* burned through the same amount of fuel, and their tanks lost the same amount of air. In the heavy gravity of Hobblecob, however, taking a half-chunk was wiser.

Salem tugged at the cart with all of his strength as Cejero threw his body into the back. One burst at a time, they dragged the first lode out of the cave and along the cliffside buildings.

Ever since Salem had first walked into the cave, surrounded by extinction, a question had formed in his mind. One Cejero might actually know the answer to.

"Hey Cejero, you're a science officer."

"That's very, ah…" Cejero took a deep breath and continued pushing. "Urg…observant."

"What do you think happens…" Salem pulled in time with Cejero. "Umph…at the end of the universe?"

"Technically, we are…at the end of the universe."

"Right, but not the *end* end. We're still…here…" Salem swapped his hand positioning and continued pulling. "Hobblecob is still here."

"Well, our dear Hobblecob…was likely very far away from any star when they went supernova. The deadworlds nearest the old stars—back when they weren't dead—they would have been destroyed; consumed by the expanding starfire."

They both ignored the hill approaching them, as if the obstacle might disappear before they arrived, but it didn't, so they took a break at the base of the incline.

"Give me a turn or two," Cejero said, breathing heavily as he leaned belly-first against the shard chunk.

"Turn" was a non-technical term used interchangeably with roté, though the two weren't entirely equal. About fifty cycles ago, in an effort to reduce Venthralli's energy expenditures, the colony's rotational speed was reduced. Since roté was a standardized measurement, it remained the same, and the time it took the colony to revolve once around its core—a turn—now took 1.05 rotés. Most often, turn was used colloquially to mean "a short while."

Salem fell onto his butt, lying back against the dune. "So how did the shard get here?" he asked. "If it was so far away?"

"Nobody tethered it to a pressure room," Cejero laughed. "There's a reason we tie you to the ship. Outside, nothing slows to rest."

"Isn't that what you said happened to the entire universe?"

Cejero nodded. "Entropy, but that's a little different. It happens over the course of hundreds of billions of cycles. *Trillions*, maybe. And, practically, it probably never truly ends." He took another deep breath. "I'm referring to classical mechanics: throwing an object or jumping up and down. Objects in motion outside just… keep flying until they hit something."

"What if they don't hit anything?"

"*That*, my young friend, is the universe's bane. Everything flies off forever and stops interacting with everything else."

"So then, when does it *really* end? Like, for everything?"

Cejero rolled over, leaning his back against the shard. "Who knows? For us—the venth, I mean—we'll eventually burn up all the starshards, extract all of the heat from the universe we can, and then freeze." He took a deep breath and rocked his body off the chunk. "Realistically, something else will happen that causes us to die sooner. Again, not you and I, specifically, but the venth of the future."

Salem sat against the hillside for another couple of rotés, catching his breath before standing up. "Okay, so here's the plan," he said. "We take this one back, grab the ladder and the powered cart, and return with Hathem. Then, I'll just cut chunks off while you two take them back with the powered cart and dump them by the engine."

"That's probably the fastest way to do this."

"Olyké?"

"I heard you," the ship lead responded.

"Can we come in to get the powered cart?"

"Are you sure you'll get more than three chunks out of this?"

"It's half the size of the *Myzer*," Cejero said.

"That doesn't mean we'll get it all into the ship," she said. "I don't want to cycle the pressure room an extra time just to hear that you'll need a circayd of excavation in order to get those chunks."

"We'll get way more than that," Salem said. "As it sits right now, we might be able to fill the tank."

"Alright. I'll leave it in the pressure room." She said. "You're almost at four hundred, by the way."

"Thanks," Salem exhaled. They'd be using a lot of air for this trip, but it wouldn't be an issue given the size of their haul. Their tanks wouldn't last for a full twelve hundred rotés with this much activity, but each trip should only take about one-fifty with the powered cart. Adding Hathem or Plexie's help, they might be able to fill the ship without anyone swapping a tank.

Grunting with exertion, Salem and Cejero pulled the cart up the incline. The shard bounced as they ascended, a happy sort of motion contrasting the true misery of their uphill journey. At one point, Cejero lost his grip, causing the cart to backslide. Salem dug the heels of his boots into the watery surface, leaning away from the cart until Cejero could help regain control. It only slid half an allo downhill, but it was easily a five-roté setback. Salem was thankful they only had to grit through this once.

Eyes weary, arms aching, and feet creaking, Salem eventually reached the thin ridge of the hilltop. He shined his light down the faded blue hillside, its slope disappearing beyond the light's edge.

Cejero joined him at the edge of the slope and groaned, staring down the hillside. "This somehow seems worse," he said, looking to Salem.

Without words, Salem walked behind the cart, grinned, and pushed. The cart's nose dipped down the hillside slowly, and once the back end cleared the ridge, it careened off towards the darkness.

Cejero tilted his head. "I suppose that works."

They followed the cart leisurely, watching it buck along the uneven ripples of iced soil. It reached the bottom just beyond their visibility, fading to a mere outline as it crashed into the ground and overturned, launching the fuel away.

"Damn," Cejero said. His body rocked stiffly back and forth in the space suit.

"That's alright," Salem said. "It was still easier than lowering it. Let's put it back on the cart."

"Negative!" Ank's voice cracked. She sounded on the edge of tears, listening to Olyké give orders elsewhere in the sensory room. "Abort the mission?"

"What?" Salem's voice pitched. "No, we're fine."

"Abort the mission!" she said forcefully. Salem turned to Cejero, arms raised in disbelief. Cejero shrugged.

"Why?" Salem asked.

"There's an un-venth!" Ank screamed. Salem's legs stiffened, nearly sending him tumbling down the hillside. He steadied himself on Cejero's shoulder.

The science officer scrunched the plates between his eyes. "What's an un-venth?" he asked.

"It's…what our clutch called the quarry beasts."

Cejero yanked Salem from his feet, dragging him down the hill in terror, and the two ran off towards the *Myzer*.

CHAPTER 3
THE UN-VENTH

Little was known about the quarry beasts. Venth knew more names than facts. The elderly used to call them "outside creatures." Grubs called them "un-venth." The words "hunter" and "predator" both referred explicitly to the universe's only other complex lifeform, and proper terminology included "quarry beasts," "zero beasts," and "venthhounds." In the past, many had believed the hunters were ships rather than creatures, but the truth was that no one knew for sure. Their carapaces were harder than the densest alloy, and the only time a dead—or deactivated—one had been found, Venthralli had wasted several reservoirs of energy failing to cut it open.

Unfortunately, most of the information known about zero beasts pertained to what would happen when caught by one. The hunters ate raw starshards, although none had been directly observed doing so. No ship had ever lingered in a zone with one and survived. The creatures preferred the refined heat gel found within a reactor and always prioritized attacking venth ships, sucking the liquid energy straight from their fuel tanks. The crews inside were a mere delicacy. Small, crunchy bags of nutrients that provided nowhere near the energy of heat gel, but were apparently worth the effort nonetheless.

Nobody knew how the space-faring creatures moved through the outside, if not because they were ships. Even more horrifying was the fact that they could follow venth ships through subspace, surpassing the physical limits of regular travel in pursuit of prey. Some of Cejero's colleagues suspected that the technology used by the venth to jump between zones, which predated colonial records, was actually based on an earlier species—or design—of quarry beast. Back before the venth were venth.

Regardless of how the hunters moved, escaping one was difficult. If you happened into a zone with one, you had to jump immediately. Chances were high that it would follow you to the next zone, so once you landed, you had to jump as soon as the drive cooled off to make sure you were gone before it arrived. Only then could you resume a route to your destination. Even with colonial support, plotting a jump in the time it took the engines to cool was difficult, especially when the prior jump was plotted in haste. Still, the two-jump evasion was the only proven way to escape.

And proven, it was. No ship had been lost to a quarry beast during Salem's lifetime, though one had been lost due to a bad jump during an evasion. Prior to Salem's hatching, several ships had been found after quarry beast attacks. Parts of the hulls were ripped off; the external engine ports were always gone, their fuel contents eaten by the creature—or salvaged by the inhabitants of a ship, depending on your beliefs. No bodies were ever found.

Most encounters occurred right after a ship entered a zone. They landed, spotted a previously unnoticed quarry beast, and immediately began the two-jump evasion process. That's how both of Salem's previous interactions had gone. They'd all waited as the engines cooled off, tense, wondering if the venthhound would catch them before they could jump, and eventually exited the zone. Then, half a circayd later, they did it all over again.

This time, they were on a deadworld. Far from their ship.

Salem's feet thumped inside his suit, his breath hissed loudly whenever his jaw wasn't clenched shut. He ran down the long slope half a step behind Cejero, attention focused on remaining upright.

"Hathem!" Cejero screamed. "Where are you?"

"Almost to the ship."

"Plexie, where are we with that repair?" Olyké asked. Her voice was steady: the way it sounded when she was struggling to keep it that way.

"I'm sorry," Plexie said. "It's not even half done."

"Get us flight-ready and close it up," she said. "Rubble Dusters, leave the cart and get back here, now!"

"We're coming," Cejero huffed. He and Salem ran down the slope, splitting apart to run around the capsized cart.

"Do we have enough fuel to get back?" Salem asked. "With the extra jumps?"

"We…should." Ank hesitated. " Yes."

Salem grabbed Cejero's arm past the fallen shard chunk. "How much time until it's here?" he asked, glancing back at the frozen block.

"Maybe a hundred rotés."

Salem pulled Cejero back to the fuel and ran around to the other side. He kicked the cart upright, crouching to pick up the frozen brick of heat gel. Cejero copied him silently.

"Go."

They lifted the shard chunk up onto the cart, grunting audibly through their helmet transmitters. Salem scrambled to the front and pulled at the handle with all his weight as Cejero pushed.

"Do *not* bring that chunk back!" Olyké shouted. "Run!"

"We're coming," Salem said.

Cejero paused and stood up. "Let's go, Salem," he urged, but Salem kept pulling the cart, slower without the added push. They wouldn't be able to run very fast in their space suits, so bringing the shard wouldn't add much time. They could easily get the shard into the tank before the beast arrived, and they needed the fuel.

Salem grunted, "Come on!"

Cejero watched him for a beat, likely coming to the same conclusion. He fell behind the cart and resumed pushing.

Running across the dark, rock-strewn surface with the shard in tow, Salem's legs began to burn. His plates ached; his tendons strained. He ignored the pain, focusing instead on following the cart tracks from their trip out, determined not to lose sight of them. They had meandered around a few times on their way out to the alien city, but it was a reliable path to the *Myzer*.

"No!" Cejero yelled as the tracks veered right. Salem looked back and saw Cejero checking the infrared display of the homing radar resting atop the shard fragment. "Go straight!"

Correcting to the left, Salem charged forward. He gasped at the air in his suit, lungs absorbing every molecule they could find. His heart raced, no longer comforted by the sight of their boot prints.

"Okay, it's closed up," Plexie said.

"Good, get in the pressure room," Olyké instructed. "Cejero, where are you?"

"One and a half wheels away," the science officer read off the display. He threw himself against the cart, toes digging into the frozen surface with each push. He screamed through his teeth, continuing through the pain.

Ank's voice came weakly through the radio. "I think…the un-venth just became affected by the gravity sphere of the deadworld."

"How much time?" Salem asked.

"Fifty rotés at most."

With every exhale, a growl emitted from Salem's throat. His vision became fuzzy from exhaustion, obfuscating the deadworld's surface even further. His grip loosened, sending him to the ground, and the cart halted.

The suit's thick material protected Salem from injury, but it also made getting up more difficult. Thankfully, he'd become quite adept at it, taking just over a roté to prop himself up on his elbow, then his hand, and pull one knee underneath himself to place the sole of his boot against the ground.

"Forty rotés."

Salem threw his weight forward, rebuilding the momentum of the cart. To the right, three sets of footprints crawled out of the blanket of darkness, casually moving in front of their cart as they raced towards the *Myzer*.

Again, Salem's grip weakened, and again his visor struck the icy dirt of Hobblecob.

He swore. He groaned. It took him longer to get to his feet this time. His arms ached, weak like melting plastic; his hands could barely close. He feared he might not be able to pull the shard anymore without resting.

They would have to abandon it.

"Come on, Salem," urged Cejero. "Half a wheel."

"Thirty rotés," Ank said.

Salem ran behind the cart, prompting Cejero to take the handle and pull. Leaning his body into the shard, Salem pushed with the front of his shoulder, arm lazily resting on top so he could angle the homing radar towards his face. Not long after, two faint beams appeared over the top of the shard, past the edge of Cejero's lantern, peeking dimly through the black haze.

"Plexie…" Salem wheezed. "Open it up."

The mechanic stood by the open pressure door, inside of which sat the powered cart. He looked back confusedly, then noticed the half-chunk of starshard between Salem and Cejero.

"It's in line of sight," Ank said. "Twenty rotés out."

Heat radiated up through Salem's lower abdomen—the anxiety of knowing that if they had impossibly strong flashlights, they'd be able to see the predator stalking them. That Salem might soon look over his shoulder and see its gargantuan form emerge from the blanket of darkness. Salem felt suddenly as if the quarry beast was so close he would have heard it grumble if not for the vacuum between them.

With long, waddling strides, Plexie sprinted to the fuel hatch and threw it open, joining Salem afterwards to help him push the cart the last allo to the ship.

"Alright, lift," he said. "Lift, lift, lift…"

"*Damnit, Salem!*" Olyké shrieked. "I ordered you to leave the shard! Get in the pressure room, *now!*"

"We were already halfway back," he lied. Hathem appeared beside him, adding the strength of her large, weathered frame. The semi-translucent crystal slid into the fuel hatch, hitting the back with a heavy *thunk* that vibrated through their gloves, and the door was slammed shut behind it.

Surrendering the cart to Hobblecob, they scrambled into the pressure room, squeezing around the powered cart Olyké had left inside. "We're in," said Hathem, slamming the lever to close the exterior door.

As the pressure room cycled, the *Myzer's* engines whirred. A wave of air spread across their space suits, and the ship rumbled, tilting as it detached from the pull of the deadworld. The four venth were thrown back and forth as the landing jets fought against Hobblecob's gravitational field—Plexie toppled sideways onto the powered cart; Cejero fell against one of the tether spools, hooking his tank on the end of the dangling cable.

The ship continued to gain distance from the deadworld. Once it had finally reached the edge of the celestial body's gravitational pull, the engine roared to its peak, and the *Myzer* jumped out of the zone.

Blood flowed down Salem's face, dripping onto his partially doffed suit. Instantly, it froze in the cold air.

"What the *hell* were you thinking?" spat Olyké, moments after hitting him in the eye. The lens had cracked, along with part of the surrounding carapace. Cejero ineffectively attempted to pull her away. "I *explicitly* told you to ignore the shard!"

"I'm sorry," Salem said, hand pressed to his eye. "But we had time."

"And enough energy to get home," she said.

"But if we ran into another one along the way—"

"We would evade it, as well, and then signal for a pickup. There was no reason for that risk."

"It wasn't just Salem," Cejero said.

"I'll talk with *you* later," she said over her shoulder. "But you would never make a decision so *unbelievably* stupid unless you were trying to get *him* back." She glared at Salem with an ire he had never seen in her, eyes steaming with rage. The crew watched tensely.

Olyké blew a lungful of air through her nose. "You're off my ship."

Salem blinked behind his fingers. "What…?"

"You disobeyed a direct order, and that insubordination endangered the lives of five other people. When we get home, I'm adding a restriction to the *Myzer* and getting a different handler."

"But we had time!" Salem protested.

"No, we didn't," she said flatly. "If that hunter had approached the ship from a perpendicular vector, we would all be dead right now. *You* didn't know that when you gambled our lives, and I won't allow anyone on this ship who puts the crew in jeopardy."

Salem stared at the ground, prying his hand away from his eye, gazing instead at the chartreuse blood on his palm. "I'm sorry…"

"Apologize to Ank. She's the one you dumped that responsibility on."

Jaw clenched, Olyké stormed off towards the sensory room, presumably to prepare for the rapid plotting of their second evasion jump. Cejero gave Salem a melancholy grimace and placed his helmet below his stowed attire. Plexie sulked off to the engine room. Neither spoke.

Salem finished removing his suit, the blood from his eye now freezing on the ground by the cabinet. Hathem hung her oversized gear on its hook, looking from Salem's eye to the floor, and sighed.

"Let's get you sealed up," she said.

Procedural devices and salves lined the shelves of the medical office, many of which Salem couldn't figure out the purpose of. Hathem grabbed a soft, malleable material used to absorb liquids and placed it on Salem's cracked eye lens.

"She just had to hit you in the eye," she said.

"Is it bad?"

"It'll require more than the cold, but you will live to scamper on."

Salem sat in silence while Hathem examined the wound, moving the itchy material up and down his eye to various places.

"Do you think she'll really kick me off the *Myzer?*" Salem asked while Hathem retrieved a bottle of thick liquid from the shelf behind her.

"It's hard to say," she mused, dabbing the liquid onto Salem's face. "She'll warm up a bit, but you did put the crew in danger by ignoring her, so I would not be surprised if she stuck with it."

Salem winced; the liquid stung the cracked portion of his eye lens. "What'll I do, then?" he asked. "The whole reason I'm a shard handler is because my genes aren't valuable. If I can't do that…"

"You can do something else."

"I can?"

"Sure. Not anything, of course. Some tasks don't need to be done; some require skills you would need time to master, but you can always start learning those now."

"Like what?" he asked.

Hathem walked over to a table covered with boxes and vials. "Like being a doctor," she said. She reached into one of the containers and produced a small, brown sphere between her fingers.

"I can't be a doctor. I'm a shard handler."

"And?" she said, handing the ball to Salem. "I used to be a shard handler."

Awestruck, Salem stared at the medicinal marble in his hand. "You were a shard handler?" he asked. "Really?"

"Really. Every turn I wasn't outside, I learned from our ship's doctor, Alizi. Cycles later, at the end of her contribution period, she recommended that I replace her."

"And you did?"

"I did. That's why I've always worked on energy collectors. I never learned any major procedures because they can't be done on a ship, and that's where I learned. And my time doing collections also gave me shipboard skills that most doctors don't have."

"Wow…" Salem said. He continued to stare at the small orb, taking in everything Hathem had just told him. "I don't want to be a doctor, though."

"First of all, you need to eat that."

Salem popped the medicine into his mouth and crunched down. The plates between his eyes scrunched; his cheek spasmed as he chewed. "That's gross."

"It's not candy," she hummed. "It's a coagulant." She pulled the bandage away from Salem's eye, checked the bloody side, then placed it back on the same spot. "If Venthralli had an infinite amount of energy, and everyone could do whatever they wanted, what would you do?"

Salem tried to imagine a world with infinite energy—how he would spend his time if he could do anything he wanted. Back on Hobblecob, he had thought that he would want to be an explorer, but that wasn't what most appealed to him. Exploring was really just a mechanism to see new sights.

After a roté of contemplation, he said, "I'd paint."

"What?"

"Like…using colors to—"

"I know what painting is, Salem." Hathem smiled. She never seemed bothered—like the entire universe tickled her. "What would you paint?"

"I don't know…things I've seen, only differently in some ways. Like deadworlds, but before they were dead. Liveworlds, I guess."

"Planets."

"Yeah. I'd think about what they looked like before they died, when the stars were heating them up, and paint them like that. Maybe they could have been orange. Or green. And maybe their canyons were filled with red liquid. Or something that looked like stew."

"I think that's wonderful," Hathem said dully, the way one would when pretending to listen to a grub. She wrapped a long, warm cloth around Salem's eye. "There's no reason you can't."

"But painting isn't a useful contribution."

"Why not? Venthralli needs art."

"It does?"

"It certainly does. Did you ever go to the care center up-ramp from the Civil Sector offices?"

"Rōshi Miri's."

"Do you remember the walls?"

"Yeah. They've got designs on them."

"Somebody painted them. That's why Miri's den is more fun and relaxing than, say, an energy collector. People need to recharge their own energy tanks, Salem. Sometimes that requires food. Sometimes it's water or hibernation. Sometimes it's art. Games, plays, paintings…" Hathem stepped back and looked at Salem's eye, much like an artist in her own right appreciating her work. "I think that'll do nicely, young grub."

"I'm nine."

"You're all grubs to me. Come find me at the end of the circayd, and I'll remove that bandage for you."

"Okay."

"In the meantime…" she grabbed a vial of liquid and a small, rigid bandage, thrusting both into Salem's hands. "Go clean up your blood so Olyké doesn't get more angry with you."

Salem cleaned his blood from the floor near the suit cabinet and as much as he could out of his space suit, then went to the sensory room at the other end of the ship. He crept slowly to the door, hoping not to bring attention to himself should Olyké still be there.

Thankfully, she wasn't. Ank sat alone in the sensory room, turning around as Salem stepped inside.

"Salem!" she yelled, falling out of her chair into a skitter. She stood up in front of him and hugged him tightly. "I'm so sorry!"

"I'm—" he started. "Wait, what? Why are *you* sorry?"

"Because I messed up! I should have seen it as soon as we landed in the zone!"

Salem blinked, confused. He had forgotten what it was like to leave the colony for the first time. The shock of learning what really went into fueling their home. He had once believed—like most colony-bound venth—that excursions always went according to plan. Sure, they were dangerous, but those dangers had been nullified by procedures perfected through generations. Every time the colony turned, it was proof of countless successful collections.

That belief must have been more profound for Ank. The last cycle of navigator training was practical, like an apprenticeship, with aid and oversight. She had located several shards from the colony and witnessed their faithful return, never seeing the gritty details.

The reality was that Venthralli rotated not from reliability, but from ingenuity. Ships rarely went from launch to land without going awry; that was just how ship travel worked. It was reliably chaotic. That was the reason for placing fresh navigators on ships at all—for them to understand the complications that occurred on the other side of the radio when they sent navigation information from Venthralli.

But Ank had never seen a full excursion, let alone a successful one. She still believed that the process, itself, was a science. To her, an error could only be explained by the newly added element: Ank.

Salem hugged her back. "It was behind a deadworld," he assured her. "You couldn't have seen it."

"But I should have!" she cried. She released him, scrunching her face. "What happened to your eye?"

"Olyké hit me."

She gasped, raising her hands to cover the bottom half of her eyes. "She *hit you?*"

"And she's removing me from the crew."

"What?!" Ank's eyes bulged. "No! She can't do that!"

"Yes she can. It's her ship."

"Okay, well, she *can*, but I mean…not reasonably."

"I ignored her. Twice. I put everyone in danger…I put you under pressure to save us."

"Oh, that was no biggie," Ank waved him off. "I just had to alter our escape velocity course to keep us away from the un-venth while the jump initiated. Difficult for many, but not for Ank!"

"Yeah, you're a smartie."

"You can't leave the *Myzer*!" she said. "We were supposed to be a team. Ank locks 'em, you box 'em! The diabolical duo!"

"Yeah…" Salem droned.

"I'll go talk to Olyké."

"No, I don't want to make things worse."

"That's why *I'm* gonna go make things worse!" She cackled. It was only partially sarcastic.

"Hathem thinks maybe she'll change her mind by the time we get back."

"And the doctor knows best! It'll be at least five circayds until we get home." Ank hopped back onto the chair she'd been working from, spinning around to face the computers. "That's plenty of time."

The prospect of having his sentence overturned gave Salem hope, but it would come at a cost. The good fortune they'd experienced during the trip out had finally turned, and would only continue to worsen.

CHAPTER 4
QUARRY

One of the many problems with the gascan-class tanker ships was that they had been designed under the assumption that there would always be some amount of fuel in their storage. Consequently, many of the ship's non-essential systems used those fuel stores as a back-up source of internal power. If the ship got stranded due to fuel loss, those systems died. It rarely happened—gascans carried fuel. It was their role.

In the unlikely event that one did run empty, the crew needed only to send a message with their coordinates, which, per protocol, Brackesh had done immediately after the *Domodo's* tank had been lanced. Little was impacted by the loss of secondary systems later on. The crew simply waited for rescue on a ship with air, heat, and purified water aplenty.

On this particular circayd, for the *Domodo*, losing their secondary systems was a big problem.

In previous cycles, Brackesh would have already given up by this point. The data on outside creature attacks was clear: the crew of the *Domodo* would not be returning home. In cycles past, Brackesh would have thrown herself naked out of the pressure trap. Quick and easy. Just exhale, wait a roté, and cycle the door without a suit on. She'd be unconscious in beats, and the outside could boil her blood without bothering her.

Over the last couple of cycles, though, Prito's "let's do something" attitude had infected Brackesh. There was no hope of escaping—she knew that—but she couldn't allow herself to do *nothing*.

A cursory glance around the sensor array showed nothing remotely weapon-like. A room full of computers and cables that fed outside to sensitive equipment. Nothing sharp or hot or acidic…

Acids!

Small amounts of chemical acids were kept on board the *Domodo* for use in experiments. Storing such compounds was dangerous on a ship, but any vessel with a science officer like Brackesh had at least one vial of the optimized solution, which maintained reactivity in the cold.

Leaving the door open, Brackesh sprinted out of the sensor array. The arched ceiling of the *Domodo* guided her along the singular hallway, along tapering walkways to the back of the ship. Another *creak* fired through the living quarters, threatening to burst the hull plates at any moment.

She found Prito standing in one of the ship's few junctions with their crewmate, Dwill.

"Where's Lyth?" Brackesh asked of their fourth.

"Checking on the engine room," said Prito. He looked down at Brackesh's empty hands with disappointment.

"I'm heading to storage," she said. "We have an acid solution that could be harmful to the creature if ingested. There's not much of it, but if it causes enough pain or discomfort, it might leave."

"I'll come see what else we can find in there," said Dwill. He'd been on the *Domodo's* inaugural crew, and knew it better than anybody—even Prito.

The living area of the *Domodo* formed a narrow hook, curving down by the engines at the aft of the ship and continuing partway up the other side. Brackesh continued through the corridor with Dwill, passing by the engine room without so much as glancing through the bulkhead. They tore around the bend towards the storage area, passing by a rough sawing sound—muffled, like a clawed hand dragging itself along the exterior hull.

Dwill split off with purpose to the far side of the storage area. Brackish threw her body against a few larger boxes, moving them off to the side. Behind them sat a medium-sized box of synthetic material and faded, blue color. The stamp atop denoted geological supplies: chemical materials.

Flipping the latch open revealed rows of plastic bulb vials. The acids were usually easy to spot by appearance. When mixed with melted water in particular amounts, the resulting solution remained fluid below the freezing point of either individual component, causing them to stand out in a box of solid chemicals that required heat to be of use. After multiple circayds at low power, though, the acid would be as crystallized as any water-based solution. The ethanol, too.

Brackesh plucked a vial out of the box, checking its content label.

Irrrk.

A conic dent pressed inward from the hull on the opposite side of the storage area. The exterior-facing wall.

Brackesh dropped the orb-like vial of alcohol beside the container, the frozen plastic cracking against the metal floor. She grabbed another vial, which contained pure, deionized water.

One by one, she tossed vials haphazardly next to the bin in search of the acid solution.

Trichloromethane, more ethanol, base powder…

Her hand gripped a sphere of partially-melted liquid. Moderately crystallized, like an icy slush. She double-checked the label, palms burning against the material.

"I've got it!" Brackesh said, springing upright. She stumbled over her own feet towards the door. "Let's go!"

"One roté…" Dwill called back. "I think we might have an explosive over here."

Brackesh stopped in her tracks, balancing as the friction from her heel stuck against the floor panel.

The ethanol!

With bounding strides, she returned to the crate and grabbed the uncracked vial of combustible liquid. Dwill sifted through a box in the corner, similarly tossing items that Brackesh couldn't make out in the darkness of the unpowered ship.

Thump, thump…

A second dent bent into the wall, larger than the first, the alloys whining under the strain. Brackesh retreated to the door, holding her hand by the once-yellow button, faded over time, that sealed the room off from the rest of the ship.

"Hurry!" she called. The second dent extended farther in, the metal wearing until it split open, sprouting a black, jagged tip.

The scythe-like carapace screeched against the hull, shredding through the thin alloy like worn canvas. Most of the opening was blocked by the creature's arm, expelling the *Domodo's* air slowly as it clenched tightly from underneath, filling the room with a deafening hiss and penetrating cold.

Dwill abandoned his pursuit, bolting for the door to escape the alien claw. Brackesh stood ready, hand by the seal to hit it as soon as he passed through the doorway.

Urrrrch.

The serrated limb squeezed harder, cutting further into the wall and leaving a sizable tear above.

With one foot past the door's frame, Dwill was pulled back into the storage area. Arms flailing, he tried to grab hold of the edge of the door. Brackesh dropped the ethanol, posting herself against the adjacent wall to reach for Dwill's arm.

Their hands connected at their forearms. The force of the breach pulled unbearably against Brackesh's shoulder as she clutched Dwill's arm. She dropped the acid in her free hand, using both arms to pull on him. She pressed her foot against the wall for leverage, screaming from exertion and pain.

The hull tore further, causing the weight of the depressurization to become too great. The force pulled Brackesh against the strip of wall beside the doorway—and the emergency seal button. With a dull *pth-unk*, the pistons above the door fired it shut, dragging both venth to the ground as they held each other.

The *crunch* of Dwill's arm rose above the roar of the gale, followed by the squishing of the meat inside his carapace, neither of which prevented the door from sealing shut, muffling Dwill's screams. His cries of pain faded a beat later as his body was pulled through the breach.

The venthhound couldn't catch the *Myzer* while it moved between zones, so for the half-circayd after their escape, the crew remained safe. The two-jump evasion typically used the shortest available jumps in each zone. They were the safest to calculate with little time, and the crux of their evasion technique was the rapid turn-around, rather than how far the jump was.

Jump paths were generally plotted in advance, with navigators on Venthralli making minor adjustments once a ship re-emerged from subspace, or "landed." Most of the work was done over circayds, even sets: a period of forty-two circayds. It couldn't actual-ly be done in the moment, so navigators had to prepare numerous jump paths ahead of time for the ship lead. It was quicker if another ship had previously taken the same route. The universe didn't change much over the course of cycles, so if another navigator had already plotted a successful path between two specific zones, a ship could use that same trajectory with minor alterations and little danger.

Salem didn't know everything that went into those calculations, of course, but he knew there were a lot of factors, like avoiding the sinkholes that sometimes hid at the edges of zones, strong enough to pull a ship clean out of visible space forever. Because of those factors—and the short time allotted—calculating viable evasion jumps for a ship under pursuit of a quarry beast was difficult. Salem imagined that several navigators were working frantically to pro-vide multiple jump options to Olyké upon the *Myzer's* landing, each of which would need to be altered based on the ship's actual loca-tion, all so she could select a single one.

The following circayd—after the *Myzer's* second evasion jump—Salem sat in the common area with Plexie, playing a game in which one of them picked a specific location of the colony and the other tried to guess it. It wasn't the funnest activity, but it used no power.

"Deck two," Salem said. The bandage on his eye had been removed the evening prior, just before the second evasion jump. The lens was still a bit callused and itchy.

"Wrong," Plexie said.

"Okay, well then it's probably three."

"Correct."

Salem thought to himself. He wasn't close to an answer, yet, and only had one question remaining, which wouldn't be enough to narrow it down.

He shrugged, "I give up."

"The storage closet in Valenio's house."

"That's waaay too specific!"

"Nuh-uh! You can specify any room."

"That's not a room."

"If cellars count, so do closets."

"You can walk around in a cellar. You can't walk around in a storage closet. Some flats even—

"Ank, Cejero, get to the sensory room immediately," Olyké's voice pulsed through the halls of the *Myzer*. "Hathem, Plexie, you probably should, too."

Salem shrank into his seat. Plexie sprang up and raced towards the front corridor. He stopped at the entrance to the hall, looking back at Salem.

"Come on!" he urged.

"She said everyone *but* me."

"Just come and wait by the door, you big larvae!" He turned and disappeared past the edge of the corridor. Other sets of footsteps pattered quickly around the adjacent halls. It did sound urgent.

Salem arrived at the sensory room to find Hathem standing in the doorway, arms folded. For the first time since he'd met her, she looked concerned.

"It must have been in the zone when we made the second jump," Cejero said from inside the helm.

"It wasn't, I swear!" Ank replied. "We did the second jump as soon as the engine was ready: 41.2 rotés after we landed. I remember it specifically."

Salem turned to Hathem, asking quietly, "Is the quarry beast here?" She nodded, never removing her eyes from the scene.

"It's coming right for us!" Ank panicked. "We need to jump *now*."

Olyké pointed to a screen near Ank covered in lines that held no significance to Salem. "This one should be quick to plot," she said, tracing her finger along. "Make the safest adjustments you can."

Ten rotés later, the engines spun up and the ship lurched. Salem lumbered off as the colony administrator explained to Ank the reasoning behind her selected path—keeping the quarry beast far from Venthralli without increasing the *Myzer's* return distance.

There was nothing for him to do but wait.

The ship landed during the crew's circaydly sleep. Ank was awake beforehand, plotting their next jump under the observation of Plexie and Olyké. Salem had heard their whispers and footsteps in the corridor when they'd woken. While trying to get back to sleep himself, he heard the engine whine down. Then, forty or fifty rotés later, it spun up again, and the ship jolted back into subspace.

There was no shouting, which was a good sign.

Tensions remained high that circayd as the crew waited anxiously for the ship to land in the next zone. Nobody had mentioned Salem's pending removal from the *Myzer* in the time since. Nobody knew if they would make it home.

That fear became realized before the middle of the circayd, when the crew found themselves crammed into the sensory room just after the end of their second evasion jump.

Their *second*-second evasion jump.

"It's here!" Ank shrieked. "How is it here?"

"I–I don't know," Olyké stammered. She watched lines appear on a nearby screen displaying feasible jump paths as they were confirmed by Venthralli and Ank, who combed through the ship's sensory data in a panic.

"Outside creatures only follow ships if they're in the same zone upon jumping," said Hathem. "It's the whole reasoning behind the two-jump evasion."

"That's a survivor's bias, though," Cejero said. "We don't know if it holds true for ships that were caught. We assume those crews would have documented such critical information in their vault boxes, but perhaps they didn't know."

Olyké stared at the crisscrossing vector map with her arms folded. "That means we've also assumed the rapid turnaround between jumps is the only part of the evasion that matters," she said, thinking aloud. Her eyes moved across the overlapping approximations. "Maybe our jumps need to be longer?" With a slight frown on her brow, body still, she studied the web of zone paths. A moment later, she let out an exhausted breath, tracing one of the lines with her finger. "Here," she said, moving to another path, "then here."

"That's almost directly away from Venthralli."

"We're not going to make it back to Venthralli," she said grimly. "We need to lose this thing."

"Okay," Ank's voice wavered. The crew watched as she dialed in the zone coordinates. The air in the helm was thick, warmed by their confined bodies.

"I can't," she finally cried out, "it's in the way!"

Cejero stared at the terminal with glossy eyes, helpless. Olyké gripped the back of Ank's chair so hard Salem thought she might crack a finger. "Angle back and around it," she ordered. Ank dragged a few switches and the ship lurched, burning through fuel like it was departing a deadworld. She rotated the vessel back, whipping the *Myzer* against its own momentum and throwing Salem into the doorjamb. Cejero fell into one of the chairs, glancing off the back and spinning to the ground on his rear. Plexie bounced against the nearby wall, ricocheting off his shoulder. He steadied himself, teeth glinting above his hanging jaw in the dim light of the sensory room's machines.

Salem's feet rocked slightly, knees bending to keep his balance. Once on stable ground, they waited for the comforting drone of the *Myzer's* engines pulling them into subspace; the soft jolt of their launch towards the next zone.

Then the ship lurched, but it wasn't along the typical plane of the engines: forwards, backwards, or side to side. It was as if the floor had been pulled away from their feet and slammed back into them. Their legs collapsed underneath them, and they fell to the chilly floor.

"No!" Ank screamed. She grabbed one of the lever controls and slammed it to its edge.

"What happened?" Plexie asked. The engines rumbled beneath their feet as they stood back up, but their footing didn't change.

"It's got us!"

The one thing Salem had been taught repeatedly was that if a ship was grabbed by a quarry beast, its crew was dead. Countless procedures were designed to stop that from happening, and the urgency of each was reiterated with the warning that any delay could result in being grabbed. "Grabbed" was synonymous with "killed," and they were to prevent it at any cost.

Looking around the sensory room, you would never know the ship was in the grasp of a venthhound. It looked like the helm of a ship currently evading one—frantic, panicked, but not without hope. Ank hit a pair of switches, leaned halfway out of her chair to flip a small lever, then pressed the large one back to its edge.

The cabin rocked, but the ship remained still.

A soft creak filtered into the sensory room from the hull above. Cejero's gaze darted up; his eyes bulged.

"It's going to break through the plating…"

Ank pulled at another control. "Plexie, turn jet four towards the bow," she said. The floor beneath them shook, but little else. "Hurry!"

Plexie bolted out of the sensory room, grabbing Salem by the arm as he ran by.

"Let's go!" he said.

The two venth sprinted along the *Myzer's* hallways, making their way to the opposite end of the ship. The quarry beast pulled at the vessel, sending them into the wall and knocking Plexie to the ground. He continued running on all fours, maintaining his momentum for half a roté before pushing himself back upright. They rounded the last turn at full speed, knocking into the opposite wall as they ran.

The engine room was second in size only to the common area. The ship's machines had to be stored inside, lest the outside siphon too much heat for them to travel. The air was wavy. The outer layer of Salem's carapace began to soften and peel moments after he entered.

Olyké's voice came through the ship transmitter near the door. "Hurry up, Plexie," she said. A grinding sound could be heard in the background—something being done near the helm.

Plexie ran to a large lever on the far wall and crouched beneath it, pushing up with his entire body.

"When I say, pull this back down," he grunted. The handle raised slowly, ending with a metallic *chunk* as jet four's positioning was released.

Tumbling over his hands and feet, the mechanic scampered across the room to a flat wheel fastened vertically along one of the machines. With each pull on the metal ring, Plexie's feet lifted off the ground, again using his weight to rotate the mechanism.

Ank's voice buzzed from the wall transmitter. "We need it now, Plexie! Before it moves below."

Urrrk. The hull moaned, bending underneath the creature's grip.

Many people believed the quarry beasts opened ships with their mouths, creating a seal before chewing through the ship's exterior panels. Salem wasn't looking to find out—

"Now!" Plexie yelled. Salem grabbed the pipe protruding from the wall beside him, lifting his feet off the ground as Plexie had. The mechanism started slowly, picking up speed as it rotated past the horizontal and locking into place at the bottom.

Salem slid off the handle, falling to the floor as Plexie ran past him to the transmitter panel.

"It's done!" he said.

The jet fired, sending Salem along the floor into the nearby wall with more force than the gravity beneath him. The zero beast pulled against the booster, flinging Salem back to the floor. Through the continual burn of the jet, a growl filled the room, unlike any Salem had heard in his life. It was an airy grumble—like broken gears—that physically vibrated the air surrounding him.

The ship spasmed again, and Plexie stumbled backwards into a machine whose purpose Salem didn't know. A high-pitched scream came from the mechanic's mouth, the sort made by someone being crushed or stabbed. His carapace hissed, fusing to the alloy as it melted through his back to the nerves within. He tried to push himself away, cooking his arm and palms.

Salem scampered over and grabbed Plexie's, tugging at him. His back sizzled, unwilling to separate from the machinery. He shrieked again, so close to Salem that it hurt his entire skull, distracting him from the gut-wrenching odor of his frying shell plates. The sticky, wet carapace peeled away from the machine, leaving a stripe of tar-like residue crisping on its metallic surface.

The engines spun up and the ship launched forward—a familiar, gentle disruption compared to those caused by the venthhound. Then, the cabin became still, and the *Myzer* was on its way. The engines rumbled around them, masking the sound of Plexie's cries.

* * *

The next jump took over a circayd, during which Plexie rested in Hathem's office. She said he would be fine, but Salem didn't know how fine "fine" meant. When he'd last seen Plexie, a large strip of the mechanic's back had been missing.

The crew met in the common area to discuss the problem at hand. Salem happened to be in the room at the time, drawing a deadworld covered in hot liquids he called "Soupworld."

"We got lucky with the damage," Olyké said. "There are a lot of dents, but only one puncture in storage three. The duct leading in was sealed off quickly enough to prevent significant air loss. The supplies were partially frozen out—non-essentials." She turned to Cejero. "How is this thing following us?"

"I don't know," Cejero groaned, staring blankly across the table. "Zero beasts evolved in the outside…we don't know much about their movement or senses. This one may simply be more acute than others; perhaps the recipient of a beneficial mutation."

"Any ideas we could try besides merely plotting longer jumps?"

He shrugged. "We can always heat-strip."

"That's the juncture I want to avoid," she moaned. Heat-stripping was the crew-instructed method of potentially hiding from a quarry beast. The practice involved separating all non-essential, heat-generating machines from the rest of the ship and launching them away, the hope being to trick the beast into following the shrapnel. It relied heavily on the unconfirmed belief that they sensed heat, and similarly on the hope that their other senses weren't keen enough to spot the cold ship's husk. If a ship was stranded in a zone with a quarry beast, it was preferred over sitting idly and waiting to be eaten, but not by much.

"I've sent a brief report to Venthralli," said Hathem. "In case the quarry beast follows us after the next jump."

"Did the colony give an estimation for a transfer or pickup?"

"A third of a set, depending on where we land and which crews have enough fuel to get us home," she said.

A third of a set—fourteen circayds—was a dangerously long time to be stranded.

Cejero put his head in his hands, the flats of his fingers spaced widely around his skull. Salem drew some splashes in Soupworld's liquid, like it was always moving around a bit.

"Well..." Cejero said, standing up from the table, "it has been wonderful working with you all. I imagine that, if we survive, we'll be anchored, what with a -140% return." He threw his head back. "Ugh...and that doesn't even include the transfer."

"It'll be closer to -300%," Hathem corrected, "but let's hold our assumptions. Our rate has been fine until this trip, and we have new information about the outside creatures."

"*Outside creatures*," Ank giggled. "With your *skipp* in your *gascan*."

"I'm glad you're amused."

"Nobody calls them that anymore, Hathem. 'Quarry beast' is the Energy Department's preferred terminology, and all of the cool grubs say 'un-venth.'"

Olyké grumbled, "Well, I'm calling this one 'Relentless Bastard.'"

"Sorry to disturb you, Relentless Bastard," Salem muttered idly, eyes nearly touching the viscous planet as he shaded it. "Now please leave us alone."

The circayd after being grabbed by the quarry beast Olyké had dubbed "Relentless Bastard," the *Myzer's* uninjured crew members gathered in the sensory room to observe the jump landing.

"At least the area is clear," Ank said once the engines had spun down. The possibility hadn't even occurred to Salem that a *different* quarry beast might have been hiding in this zone upon landing. "But, I'm not sure if..." Ank started, then hesitated. She punched buttons on the consoles that interfaced with the *Myzer's* many eyes. "If we have enough fuel for the next jump."

Her words sat for a while, as if the frosty air had slowed their reverberations. Salem looked to Cejero and Hathem. All three were silent.

"Take a shorter route," Olyké said after notable pause.

"I don't know if we have enough to *start* the jump, let alone get somewhere else."

"Perhaps that wouldn't be so bad..." Cejero said quietly.

"Running out of fuel in the middle of a jump?!" Ank said sharply. "We'd be stranded between zones—"

"And that might be preferable to heat-stripping. Look, I'm just kicking empty crates around, but there's still *no* evidence to suggest that heat-stripping actually works. There *is* evidence, however, though limited, suggesting we'd be safe in the arcane medium."

"But we'd be stuck there for *cycles*," Ank said. "And *die!*"

The area between zones—which were actually quite far apart in distance—was called the arcane medium. It wasn't traversable by regular means; part of why they had to jump through subspace to get around.

"I'm not saying it's a good plan, just that the odds might be better than heat-stripping. We could jump just outside of the zone, intentionally, even, and be pushed back in over the next few sets. It might keep us safe long enough for the quarry beast to get bored and leave."

"Assuming we're still alive once we get back..." Olyké added. She tapped her foot passively, eyes focused on the navigation screen. It only showed a few short line segments. If the crew was going to heat-strip the *Myzer*, they would have to start now.

Her head perked up.

"Wait a turn," she said. "We didn't burn the light shard."

Sitting down the hall from the engine room, in a shard box whose lid remained wedged slightly ajar, was a shard—small, but dense. Through all the stress of escaping the deadworld and running from the same quarry beast three times over, they'd forgotten about the light shard completely.

Nobody protested against its destruction this time around.

"My only concern," mulled Cejero, "is doing this without Plexie. To my knowledge, this reactor has never processed any hardened crystal shards, so we don't know how easily it will do that. There *is* a detonation risk if the gel is too, uh…chunky…when we jump. Whatever you'd call that."

"Under-levigated," Hathem said.

"Can Plexie be brought into the engine room?" Olyké asked.

"I can move him."

"Have him instruct Cejero through those checks, then." She turned to Ank. "How long until the engine is otherwise ready?"

"Thirty-five rotés…ish."

"The quarry beast will be here soon. Work fast."

Salem took a moment to appreciate the illuminated space rock before throwing it into the chamber, where it would be refined into a hot slush of volatile energy.

Burning the light shard was regrettable, but there was no other option. Hathem and Cejero carried Plexie over from the medical office, and for the following fifty rotés, he lay on a cushion by the door, guiding Salem and Cejero through the procedure of monitoring the light shard's addition to the fuel tank. The methods he used were surprisingly nonspecific. His instructions included actions such as smelling one machine to make sure it wasn't smoky and feeling another to make sure it was "just hot enough that you can't hold your hand against it, but not so hot it burns."

After confirming that the reactor had sufficiently melted and refined the light shard without overexertion or underprocessing, Cejero and Hathem took Plexie back to the medical office and Salem returned to the sensory room, where he found Ank peering at a monitor to angle their jump. Despite the added complications, it was only an extra dozen rotés after the engines had cooled before Ank was ready to initialize the transition to subspace.

She looked at Olyké. "Clear to—"

A bland siren emanated from one of the helm's panels. Ank's arms spasmed back to the launch controls. "It's here!"

"Jump!"

Before the word had fully escaped Olyké's mouth, the *Myzer's* engines began whirring up. The cabin swayed comfortably, and the ship took off.

"It saw us..." Ank said airily.

"Not necessarily."

"It was in the zone! Last time, it was in subspace when we jumped and it *still* followed us."

"So we'll prepare for heat-stripping as soon as we land," Olyké said, as plainly as if discussing a cleaning.

Jettisoning select components of the ship in a way that launched them across the outside and sealed off the openings created by the damage, all without blowing up part of the hull, was a difficult task. Each venth had a specific role to play in the rapid disassembly, and losing the hands of their mechanic would considerably complicate and slow the process. Frankly, Salem didn't think they could do it. Not without creating a vacuum breach or blowing themselves up.

Several cups of synthetic carapace later, however, Plexie was up walking around. A thick, black streak of the artificial compound ran down the length of his back. He clenched his teeth any time he sat, stood, or moved his right arm, but seemed otherwise to be recovering well. It gave them a realistic chance of heat-stripping the ship without catastrophic error.

The ship's engines faded and were reduced to silence, running through the remainder of their fuel to land in the zone. There was no idle hum. It was the sort of silence only experienced outside.

Olyké sent the *Myzer's* jump path back to Venthralli. If the colony didn't hear from them the following circayd, they would cancel the fuel transfer and instead organize a salvage team.

The *Myzer's* crew stood at the ready for its heat-strip, with Salem and Plexie switching their jobs due to Plexie's injuries. Salem had practiced his new task throughout the jump, miming the ritual destruction of a significant portion of the engine room, then running back into the rest of the ship before its hottest parts were flung away. Plexie, in turn, would seal a bulkhead leading to the back half of the ship in case the damage exceeded the confines of the engine room.

Ideally, Salem will have passed through it first.

Fifty rotés after landing, he stood in the engine room beside the thrust systems. The dormant machines no longer generated the heat that typically plagued the area. He tapped his toes nervously against the cold floor. Waiting. Ready to perform the eight-step process and sprint back to the safety of the bunks.

Sixty rotés.

Seventy.

After eighty, Ank's voice emitted from the wall-mounted receiver.

"How…uh…long might it take for the un-venth to follow?"

"Generally up to four hundred rotés," answered Hathem.

For obvious reasons, the engine room wasn't heated like other rooms in the ship. After a hundred rotés with the reactor off, the air inside had become problematically cold. Salem's plates began to stiffen; his motions would be sluggish.

At the two hundred mark, he began to breathe easier, even though his lungs ached with every intake of frozen air, heated only by what transferred through the open doorway, and every exhale reemerged opaque. As their official name would suggest, quarry beasts weren't known for delaying when pursuing a meal, and two hundred rotés was a pretty long window for any quarry.

Five hundred rotés after landing, the crew left their standby positions. Salem ran to his room and stood under the life support vent, allowing the warm airstream to emanate across his body until his plates loosened again. The outcome they had dreaded would not be occurring on this circayd.

Instead, they drifted through the black pitch of the outside, stranded on their immobile ship.

CHAPTER 5
VENTHRALLI

The crew of the *Myzer* lived aboard the stagnant ship for thirteen circayds after Relentless Bastard gave up chase. Not knowing when the rescue would arrive—or if the ship that came would run into any problems themselves—Olyké lowered the temperature inside the *Myzer* by one syro and froze out the areas they didn't need, restricting as much of their power usage as possible.

Venth measured the amount of heat in a location using Syrolac units, named after somebody thousands of cycles ago and usually called "syros." Zero used to be the temperature at which everything froze, because people had assumed that, if everything was frozen, no more heat existed. Then, scientists discovered that the outside was even colder, and starshards actually started to evaporate at negative two syros, so the entire scale was shifted down by three.

The outside was always zero. Even when heat escaped from the pressure room and dissipated through the universe—which one would assume would heat the outside up slightly—it was still zero. Venthralli was set for comfort at eleven syros, whereas the *Myzer* usually ran at nine to conserve energy. The melting point of water was thirteen syros, and the inside of a healthy venth's carapace was just over that, leaving little room for body temperatures to drop. The lowest temperature someone could reasonably handle before dying was about five, but only electricians ever experienced such low heat levels without a space suit.

Wire rooms were cold.

On its return to Venthralli, an energy collector called the *Chaziro Cubar* stopped to unload a portion of its heavy tank into the *Myzer*. Their colony admin, an old venth named Rello, asked Olyké about their escape while the *Cubar's* mechanic oversaw the transfer. Olyké omitted Salem's defiance in her retelling, which he was thankful for. He would soon be awaiting assignment, and that could become problematic if the other ship leads thought he was a problem.

"It probably arrived in the zones right as you jumped," Rello said upon hearing the tale. "A fast venthhound."

"It didn't," Ank insisted. "The only times it arrived before we jumped were the time it grabbed us—when we had assumed it couldn't have followed us—and the last jump, which is the only time it *didn't* follow us."

The *Cubar's* administrator tilted his head back and forth, debating internally. "That's contrary to every encounter to date."

"It wasn't a typical quarry beast," said Olyké.

"They can't see heat between zones."

"Thermal senses are speculative at best," Cejero said. "We're not even completely sure they're animals."

"They're animals, Cejero."

"That's the leading theory, yes."

"And for good reason. One of my clutch had a gene donor who was on the team that salvaged the *Domodo* way back...Eragio, I think his name was. Died many cycles ago. Anyway, she said that *he* said that the inside of the ship was covered in a strange salve their science officer later identified as genetic material."

Cejero's neck jerked back. "He...*what?*"

Rello nodded. "Digestive fluid or saliva or something. Mucus, maybe."

"That...can't be true." Cejero shook his head. "It would be part of the standard S.O. materials."

"Well, this was long before my first cycle as a science officer, so it's all hearsay, but my understanding is that, at the time, the Panel forced the Bio Board to keep that information tucked away because they didn't want to deter people from working in the old gascans any more than their reputations already had. As for the substance on the *Domodo*, unless the crew was jumping around with a shipful of some *other* alien's fluids, never logged the interaction, and then happened to be attacked by an outside creature during that same trip...the salve came from the thing that ate them, which was an animal."

"Plus, ours screamed," Salem added from the side of the room. He'd been trying to stay out of sight so Olyké wouldn't mention his removal and prompt more questions from Rello about it, but it seemed to him that everyone aboard the *Myzer* would know after their attack that quarry beasts were, in fact, beasts.

The entire room turned their heads in unison.

"What?" Rello said.

"When?" asked Cejero.

Salem blinked at the sets of staring eyes. "When we burned it with the jet."

"Why didn't you say anything?" Olyké chided.

"I thought everyone heard it..." he said.

"Sound doesn't travel outside," Rello said, tapping his chin, "and no ship has ever survived physical contact with an outside creature, so there's never been a documented vocalization. It would make sense for this to be the first report of hearing one. Are you sure it wasn't something from the ship, Salem?"

"No."

"But it happened while the jet was burning it?"

"Uh-huh," said Salem. He did his best to describe the low, windy growl, but nothing on Venthralli compared. Truthfully, it was best described as the sound of an animal that ate other animals.

"That could be mechanical," Cejero said, arms folded.

Plexie appeared from the corridor behind Salem. "It wasn't mechanical," he said. The *Chaziro Cubar's* mechanic, Pisque, joined him by the doorway. "I've heard every type of machine there is. Every broken one, too."

"Well *that's* an exaggeration," Cejero said, but Pisque nodded along with Plexie, as if it were a well-known fact among engineers that Plexie possessed a cataloged memory of broken machine sounds.

"We've started the transfer," Pisque said. "It should only take about forty rotés or so." He looked at Ank, who was bored beyond sanity, and shrugged his perfectly reflective shell up towards his head. "We're gonna bring some food over while we wait. Wanna help?"

Ank sprang up from the table, eyes twinkling like the light shard Salem had destroyed.

"Yes, please!"

She scurried off quickly with Pisque, animatedly describing their run-in with the quarry beast. Everybody in Salem and Ank's clutch loved Pisque. He was the older grub they'd all looked up to when they were little, and it didn't wane until he began his contribution period and stopped hanging around the brood areas. Even then, whenever they saw him, they'd all beam. He was funny and upbeat and charming…

Salem hated him.

Rello shot an intense look at Olyké and Cejero. "You need to tell the Bio Board," he said. "This is a big deal."

"Big enough to stop the Panel from decom-ing us?"

"You're not going to get decommissioned," he said. "What's your return going to be? -200?"

"-324."

"Okay…that's not great." Rello's teeth chattered a bit. "But it's not an extinction event or anything. Ships have done much worse without being disbanded. You were in the 4000s last cycle, right?"

"4486."

"See? That's outstanding." He guided her to Ank's vacated seat, the flats of his fingers directing the top of her shell. "The Panel *needs* you, 'Lyk. You're just going crazy from being stranded for so long, that's all. Sit down, relax. Let the grubs bring over some fresh rations."

Olyké closed her eyes, the beads within her lenses unfocusing entirely, then took a deep breath.

Rello looked to Salem and Cejero. "Now, ah, where might I find that doctor of yours?"

"Is something wrong?" Cejero asked.

"It will be if I don't stop in while we're here."

Cejero showed Rello the way to the medical office, leaving Salem alone with Olyké—a situation he didn't want to be in. He took his drawing of Soupworld back to his bunk, where he remained miserable through the rest of the circayd.

Hathem and Salem waited by the pressure door as the *Myzer* moved across the Talesk-Venthralli zone, where the colony had been since Salem was born.

Every other generation or so, when the energy collectors began nearing their communication limits to retrieve fuel, the colony migrated to a new zone in a shard-rich area. The next migration would likely happen during Salem's lifetime. The conversation had come up twice already. When that happened, the abandoned zone would again be referred to simply as "Talesk." The compound name was designed to provide context in logs and other dated documents. A quarry beast in Talesk was concerning. A quarry beast in Talesk-Venthralli was apocalyptic.

Venthralli was a torus-like sphere: a ball with a wide, cylindrical hole through its center, around which the colony rotated once per turn to create gravity. The circular cavern extended two-thirds of the way through the core, lined with a short helix of rooms that stored ships like the *Myzer*. It ended at a stationary wall, which insulated the colony's heat-generating systems on the other side—namely, a large thruster with surrounding engines and reactors. It also housed the metal forges, which further benefitted from the core's lack of rotation and proximity to the reactors.

The docks took up the majority of the inner decks that lined the core. They weren't really decks in the traditional sense, but rather large areas of specific purpose with no interconnecting structure. The rest of that space was taken up by systems that benefitted from low heat and gravity, such as energy reservoirs and electrical rooms. Heating the inner decks required too much energy, so the docks instead absorbed some of the heat being pushed past them, from the reactors to the outer decks. When closed, the docks reached two or three syros this way. It was warm enough to prevent ships from freezing over and breaking, which is what happened to dormant vessels outside, but still lethally cold for the venth, requiring ship crews to disembark in their space suits.

The *Myzer* coasted into the docking spiral, stopping near the mouth of their dock and idling. Maintaining the needed ranges of gravity in Venthralli's outer decks—the furthest areas from the core—required the colony to rotate too fast for a ship to dock without collision. The inner decks stopped and started all circayd long as people moved up from the outer decks or down from the core. Ships leaving or returning had to ensure that their designated cross-section would remain locked from rotation throughout the process.

For the last time, Salem exited the *Myzer*. It wasn't unusual for people in his line of work to change ships. In fact, with the unfortunate exception of those who died early in their careers—a rare occurrence for shard handlers these circayds, though certainly more common than in other roles—every shard handler worked with multiple crews throughout their contribution periods. Old venth retired, vacancies needed filling. It was guaranteed.

Still, the *Myzer* was the only ship Salem had known—a change made even scarier by its suddenness. He hadn't been able to prepare himself. And since he was being removed, he worried further that he might never get to work on a ship again.

All he wanted to do was go home and cry, but he couldn't. Not for a while, anyway.

Instead, he spent the rest of the circayd crammed in a small room with the crewmates he no longer worked with. Every returning crew was held in quarantine for a minimum of half a circayd while they were examined for alien viruses. As slim as the chances were for life to survive outside, it wasn't impossible, and far more likely on a deadworld. Pathogens could remain dormant in the ice or frozen in the soil, and it only took one to eradicate their species.

Extinction was at the forefront of Venthralli's collective focus. A domestically evolved virus had once almost wiped out enough venth to prevent sustained propagation, and the potential of an alien virus was even worse. Cejero and Hathem routinely mentioned the ongoing discourse about whether digging up ice and dirt for analysis was more or less dangerous than leaving it, with the consensus being that, since someone might bring back a pathogen either way, identifying them was safest.

The same concern existed for overpopulation, which had also nearly eliminated them once. The brood rōshis taught Salem's clutch about a time when, for about four cycles, Venthralli euthanized the elderly to prevent food from running out until the population reduced. Luckily for their species, that period of population excess never overlapped with the Swelter Famine: when the garden was exposed to too much heat, and the venth forever lost two species of vegetables, and, with them, a crucial vitamin. For generations, hatchlings died from diseases surrounding that nutrient deficiency, and the venth teetered on extinction, not knowing if those whose bodies weren't hungry for the vitamin would be sufficient in number to keep their species alive.

After each instance of near-eradication, laws were created to prevent the future demise of the venth.

In this case, a medical quarantine.

Hathem spent a few thousand rotés running exams while the *Myzer's* crew, plus Salem, were confined to the dock's attached suit room. The room was small, making it quick to heat up and lamentable to be confined in, especially after just having been stranded for thirteen circayds.

A few times during their confinement, the section of the inner decks in which they resided was started or stopped, preempted by a bland tone emitting through the dock twenty rotés before.

Syringe in hand, Hathem paused as the sound blared across the *Myzer's* home.

"Well, that's inconvenient timing," she said, in the upbeat way a brood rōshi would speak to a hatchling. And for all Salem knew, she had once been a caregiver. He hadn't known about her shard handling career until half a set ago.

"Maybe we should wait?" Plexie said nervously, watching Hathem prepare to take his blood.

"We have plenty of time," she hummed, sticking the thick syringe between the plates on Plexie's side, spurring a sharp whine.

Nineteen rotés later, the force of Salem's feet against the ground began to lighten. After three more, the faint pressure caused by his toes against the floor became enough to push his body away from it. He always tried to see if he could keep himself still enough that he would remain touching the ground once the deck stopped moving, but he never could. The more he tried, the harder it was. Pushing his butt toward the bench only served to move him away faster.

Some time later, the deck started up again. The legs of their suits swung to the side of the cabinet, slowly angling down until they hung as they would on the *Myzer*. During the spin-up, venth were supposed to float to a bench and pull themselves against it, allowing the rotational gravity to be imparted on their body steadily while their section sped up to match the colony. If one were hovering in the air, they would float towards the edge of the room and slightly downward due to air friction. They would speed up until they hit the wall, at which point they would then slide down the vertical surface to the ground. It was the more fun way, so in the absence of mental stimulation, that's what many people did, including Salem and Plexie.

With nothing but happy bacteria in their bodies, the *Myzer's* crew climbed down the ladder to civilization—the outer decks. Venthralli was split into three hubs, each with its own set of long, circumferential decks curving around the core. As a person descended, each concentric thoroughfare became longer, its gravity heavier, all the way down to the exterior hull. Each deck was wide enough for buildings on both sides, though few had a singular road all the way around.

The *Myzer* was docked over Bendil, the frontmost hub, furthest from the thruster. Salem hopped off the ladder to the top deck of the hub, which they referred to as Bendil 1. Both Bendil and Kairv—the rear hub below the reactors—had three decks, whereas the central hub, Venthia, had five. All three rotated in unison, their misaligned decks connected by wide ramps.

Bendil 1 was taken up primarily by the Burrow: the large barracks in which the venth hibernated between each cycle. The first round of hibernations for the Darkwatchers—the people who ran Venthralli while everyone else hibernated—had just ended. Most of them slept in their homes, but some found the noise of their fellow venth too difficult to sleep through, so part of the Burrow was kept available to them during their hibernation times. For now, it was closed and cooled, and would remain that way until the second round of Darkwatcher hibernations began in a couple of sets. Until then, the top deck of Bendil was desolate.

At least, it was supposed to be.

"Look out!"

A small grub, no more than 2 or 3, flew through the air towards them. The six adult venth separated, watching the grub soar in a large arc up towards the ceiling.

"Careful," Olyké cautioned, gazing up at the youth. Farther up the thoroughfare, by the door to the Burrow, two others each held the end of a long, springy rope.

It wasn't that long ago that Salem would come up to the top decks and shoot his friends down the wheel. In theory, if you had the right force and angle, you could fly around the wheel forever. In practice, you always wound up running into something or touching the wall, and as soon as you made contact with the ship, the centrifugal force sent you plummeting to the floor. If you launched too slowly, you'd sink to the ground. Too fast, and you'd curve downward and crash into it.

These grubs had likely been going too fast, and rather than correcting by slowing their velocity, they'd angled the slingshot up more, resulting in the high arc of the small venth. It wasn't so dangerous that Salem was worried about her, but she certainly could hurt herself.

"Don't touch the ceiling!" Cejero said loudly.

"I know!"

After the grub passed the apex of her flight, slowing from air friction to form a lopsided arc, the *Myzer's* returning crew continued diagonally across the deck to a pair of wide, shallow ramps, one of which led up to Venthia 1, the other down to Venthia 2. The floors of the central hub were half a deck above their adjacent equivalents, and in most places, you could zigzag all of the way down or up the ramps between the hubs.

The warmth of Venthralli hit Salem as soon as he stepped onto the incline. Not just the delightful eleven-syro temperature that enveloped him from down the ramp, but the sounds and smells that emanated up from there, as well.

The crew split apart at the bottom, heading off to their various homes or errands. Venthia 2 was one of the decks that consisted of a single thoroughfare all of the way around the wheel, lined on either side by buildings for services, tradespeople, food, and recreation. The ceiling hung more than an allo above Salem's head, considerably higher than the corridors of the *Myzer*. The upward-curving thoroughfare could be seen an eighth of a wheel in either direction, disappearing up behind the ceiling.

Directly across the road was another pair of ramps. One went down to the science and research facilities on Kairv 2, the other up to the Darkwatcher homes on Kairv 1. The top decks of each wheel, being the easiest to power, were designated for areas that required heat during hibernation: the Burrow, the Darkwatcher homes, and the garden, which spanned the entirety of Venthia 1.

Venthia 2 was always bustling. Music played a few buildings down the road; orange light spilled out of a nearby kitchen as meals were being prepared. Salem walked along the fairway, soaking in the homely feelings he'd been hungering for. He had no particular place to visit, but he lived on the other side of Venthralli and wanted to be amidst the colony during his half-wheel walk home. A slight breeze touched his face—a common occurrence on Venthia 2.

"Salem, you're back!" called a voice from amidst the clamor. Salem's head swiveled on its narrow post in search of the source. A few buildings up-wheel, a chef from his clutch named Teemeru stood in the doorway of one of the kitchens, one arm wrapped around a thin, metal bucket. She primarily made unheated foods, insisting that it was the cuisine of Venthralli's future.

Salem hooked back to greet her.

"We're back."

"What a relief!" she exhaled. "People were saying that the *Myzer* was stranded?"

"Yeah. For thirteen circayds."

Her eyes bulged. "That's so long."

"We were pretty far away."

Teemeru looked around hesitantly, almost fearfully. She leaned in close to Salem, her voice hushed. "I heard..." she whispered. "You were grabbed by an un-venth?"

"Yeah, we were," he said. The contents of Teemeru's bucket nearly spilled out of her arm. She fumbled with it for a couple of beats to regain control. Salem wasn't surprised to find out that news of their attack had already spread throughout the colony. People talked, and if the topic was a quarry beast encounter, it spread like an unchecked illness.

"That's—terrifying!" she squealed. "And everyone's okay?"

"Uh-huh," he said. "Well, no. Plexie was hurt, but he's okay now. It wasn't the quarry beast."

"That's good," she said. "Well, not *good*..." She slowly shook her head, unsure of what words could be said about such an event. She looked back into the kitchen. "I imagine you're eager to get home after all of that."

Teemeru reached into the bucket and removed a small ball of water, extending it out to Salem. Its surface glinted burgundy in the light of the promenade. "Here, take this," she said.

Salem inspected the colorful orb. "What is it?"

"Just water with crushed-up berries. The yield was high from the harvest, so I get to try out new recipes with the excess."

Salem took a full bite of the berry-flavored treat, slightly sweet, but not as pronounced as a handful of the fruit would be. "That's good!"

"And hydrating!" she said brightly. "I've been calling it berry water…" She made a face. "I need to think of something better."

Salem crunched on the berry water, staring at the large crater his teeth had made in the ball. His eyes dropped. "How hard is it to cook?"

"Well, I don't cook them, so they're technically 'juiced,' I suppose, but they're simple to make. I wanted something that would be quick to make."

"No, I mean in general. Like…to be a chef? Is it difficult?"

"Hmm…" Teemeru thought to herself, surprised, like she'd never considered the difficulty of her craft. She scratched her chin. "It's not hard, I s'pose. It just takes practice—trial and error. I had to learn a little bit about crops, but not as much as an actual gardener. Same with nutrition, anatomy, and heat science, although I don't use much of that anymore because I don't use heat."

"That sounds hard."

"I guess, but you kind of learn it as you're doing it, so it's fun!" She tilted her head. "Why? Do you want to be a chef?"

"Not really," Salem shrugged.

Teemeru stared at him quizzically for a few beats. The top of one of her eyes raised up. "What's wrong?"

"Nothing. I'm just…I'm not sure if I'll be on an energy collector much longer. That's all."

"I don't think anyone could blame you after what happened," she said. "Maybe you could talk to the Civil Sector? They certainly have tasks that need doing right here at home. You know, where it's *safe.*"

"I might just do that."

"You should," she smiled, glancing back through the door. "I've got to check on tomorrow's veggie slush, but if you ever *do* want to learn about cooking, I'll show you!"

"Okay. Thanks, Teemeru."

"Mmhmm," she hummed musically and carried the bucket back inside. Through the doorway, Salem saw a dull, teal design on the wall: a zigzagging stripe with a large, jagged arc underneath.

He took a starving bite of the berry water, chomping off half of the remainder at once, and continued along, making his way to the ramp that led down to his flat on Kairv 3.

Many people on Venthralli fulfilled two roles when their primary duty didn't occupy much time. This was rare for ship crews since they couldn't be relied upon to return on a schedule, so when Salem was home, he spent time doing simple labor tasks through the Energy Department Domestic Loan Program, which provided overworked venth with the aid of crews while they were grounded —what people called an "added two," in reference to hands, eyes, or earholes. Most commonly, it involved moving things in and out of storage or the docks.

Visually, the storage area on Venthia 5 was Salem's favorite place in the colony. It was twice as wide as every other deck, extending partway below Bendil 3 and Kairv 3, so rather than looking like the inside of a wheel, as the other decks did, it looked like a long basin. It was cool.

It was also cold. The storage area was both spacious and far from the engines, making it too energy consumptive to heat to eleven. Salem should be used to it after spending so much time on the *Myzer*, but for some reason, he wasn't. He didn't like being cold when he was home.

Using Venthralli's highest-gravity area for storage seemed cruel at first, but it would be more harmful overall to have regular foot traffic on it. Salem didn't mind the extra weight as much as others did. Energy collectors augmented ideal venth gravity, so even though he spent more time on Venthia 5 than most, his body endured less overall gravitational wear than people who lived in the colony cycle-round.

There was also a half-circayd maximum for work involving the lowest deck, which was a limit that venth rarely reached. Often enough, there was nobody on the deck at all.

That was not the case upon the *Myzer's* return. Having arrived a set before the mid-cycle festival, Salem found himself working on deck five during the busiest time of the cycle. It took forty circayds to set up the event, which spanned the entirety of Venthia 4. It was the only time in the cycle that every venth would be in the same place at once, ship crews and Darkwatchers included.

With no excursion in his near future, Salem went to work setting up the festival. The crises surrounding the event's preparation were enjoyably domestic compared to those Salem had returned from. Someone needed to access a storage lot that was blocked by another; an item required three people to move safely, but no one else was available. It was almost relaxing.

Up until the fifth circayd, that is, when Salem was called in by the Power Panel. His stomach bubbled as he made his way up the zigzagging ramps to the government district on Bendil 2. With every step, the weight of anxiety pressed further into his gut, and the weight of his body lightened.

Most of the Panel's members were present when Salem arrived. He had only been in front of them twice before, both times when he was first being assigned to a ship. He knew one of them was named Gairrd, but not which. They spoke concisely and directly: too busy for pleasantries during this set. They were in the midst of their semi-cyclic analysis, assessing the colony's energy needs, expenditures, and crew performances to schedule excursions for the second half of the cycle.

As soon as Salem stood before them, one of the Panel members spoke without preface.

"Please give us your account of Recovery 67-223-MZ."

Salem swallowed hard, then tried to describe the events of the *Myzer's* most recent excursion as best he could. He told them about the light shard, the city, their brush with the quarry beast, and their eventual rescue. They asked him pointed questions about the quarry beast—the sound he'd heard, when it was made, at what point he destroyed the light shard, how long he believed it took for the light shard to be destroyed once in the refiner...

Then, they reached the part he'd been dreading.

"Why has Administrator Olyké placed an immediate restriction against you for the *Myzer*?"

Salem shifted uncomfortably. "I...disobeyed an order that put the crew in danger."

"To leave the shard chunk behind?"

Salem nodded silently.

"We see no record of a prior formal reprimand. Is that accurate?"

"Yes," he said pointedly.

One of the Panel members who had been silent thus far cleared her throat, as if to comment, but continued to stare curiously at a chart in her hand. For a full roté, she said nothing; no one else on the Panel spoke, all seeming to wait for her.

Finally, she spoke.

"Without that partial chunk of fuel," she croaked with old, worn vocal cords, "your ship would have been unable to make the jump after you escaped the quarry beast's grasp, is that correct?"

Salem paused.

Was that true?

Salem tried to quickly replay the series of jumps in his head. How many had they made after escaping?

Two. And then the one they did after burning the light shard. The shard from Hobblecob had probably fueled the first of those jumps in some part.

Salem couldn't tell if there was something more to the question he was supposed to explain, so he kept his answer simple. Simpler was better.

"Probably," he said.

"Is it possible that your actions saved the crew?"

"Well..." he started. The Panel member looked up from the chart when Salem trailed off, spurring him to anxiously finish the thought. "I think the un-venth...I mean, the quarry beast...might have stopped because we destroyed the light shard. So, if we'd had to burn it sooner, the quarry beast would have stopped following us sooner."

Her head nodded softly. "There's no way to truly know what the outcome would have been, of course." Her eyes returned to the sheet. "But by other recounts, you played a key role in the *Myzer's* survival after being caught by the quarry beast," she said flatly. "That is an unprecedented achievement."

"I see," he said, though he didn't really.

"Regardless—ship leads cannot perform their duties if they can't trust a member of their crew. With the new restriction in place, you are hereby removed from the *Myzer*, effective immediately, and are pending assignment to a vessel should the need arise."

"In that event," another venth from the Panel continued, "your actions in their entirety will be provided to the ship administrator so that they may make an informed decision on accepting or rejecting your placement." The venth sat back in his seat and folded his arms. "Candidly, it is unlikely for this lone offense to outweigh your successes, especially within the context of Recovery 67, but there are no guarantees. If you are unable to be assigned by the end of the cycle, your contribution capabilities will need to be reassessed by the Labor Department at the beginning of the following cycle. We recommend using this time to consider what other roles you are able to fulfill for Venthralli in the event that occurs."

"I understand," Salem choked. Part of him had thought Olyké would change her mind, perhaps because of the insistence of others that she would. Hearing the intimidating, nameless figures declare his removal from the *Myzer* made it feel like it was happening all over again.

"That concludes the Panel's involvement in the matter of your service with the *Myzer*," said the Panel member who'd first addressed Salem. They looked to the venth sitting on either side of them. "And we would also like to thank you for your efforts in the *Myzer's* extraordinary escape. Informally."

"You will be notified as soon as there are any changes in your assignment status," another said abruptly. "The earliest that would happen is after the mid-cycle festival."

"So, try not to fret in the meantime," added the one on the far end, who gave Salem a slight smile.

CHAPTER 6
FESTIVITIES

Salem didn't cross paths with the crew of the *Myzer* during the set leading up to the mid-cycle festival. For as compact as Venthralli was, the inner decks had a combined area of almost 3400 square allos, so it was common to go entire cycles without seeing some people. Everyone had areas they tended to stay in—their role, their home, the kitchen room they preferred. Salem lived near a ramp leading down to Venthia 4, so most circayds he only saw people who either lived near him on Kairv 3 or were also helping with the festival set up.

Salem got a few breaks from working on decks four and five. He spent a few circayds assisting Teemeru in her heatless kitchen, which helped him realize that he *really* didn't like cooking. Should he be forced to spend the rest of his life stuck in the colony, he'd rather work in the storage area. He also spent a couple of circayds helping one of the scientists on Kairv 2 while her research assistant recovered from a mild burn. The research had something to do with heat efficiency—trying to make the colony's thermal systems last longer with the same amount of fuel. For Salem, it meant standing across the room and reading numbers when asked.

It might have been the single most boring task he'd ever done.

The last energy collector, *Aborenth*, returned home a few circayds before the festival. Salem helped connect the fuel transfer, which was sort of fun. He'd merely functioned as the hands for a colonial engineer, sort of like when Plexie walked him through refining the light shard, but it was an opportunity to go outside, even if it was just in the cylindrical cavern of Venthralli's core.

Then, after forty circayds of preparation, the fete arrived.

Having been more involved in the setup process this time around, the experience was different for Salem than in cycles past. He'd watched Venthia 4 go from husk to park over a set, imagining along the way what it would eventually become once filled with people. The anticipation was exciting; so much so that Salem barely slept at all the night before.

Not wanting to fall back asleep so close to morning, Salem got out of bed early, careful not to wake his sleeping housekin as he exited their home. He meandered towards the nearest ramp; his pattering footsteps echoed softly along the barren alley. In the absence of conversations and pedestrian traffic, Venthralli actually made quite a bit of noise. *Whirs* and *thumps* and *hums*.

When he arrived on the deck below, Venthia 4 was nearly empty. A few event workers had already started their tasks for the circayd. Some night workers came by to get an early glimpse before heading to bed. A few other hibernation hatchlings, like Salem, had come by, unable to sleep. Salem made his way 'round the wheel to check in, writing his name on a piece of parchment coated with warm gum on the opposite side so it would stick to his carapace.

One of the rōshis on that side of the wheel had already brought over a small group of hatchlings, who were running out of their shells in anticipation of the games opening up. A couple of new games had been added this cycle that looked interesting to Salem, but the young venth all swarmed around the ones they already knew and had yet to tire of.

Water Fight was forever the favorite, and was as simple as the name suggested: you threw balls of water at moving targets. It had been around for hundreds of cycles; the sign had been remade and repainted countless times due to wear. Salem had grown out of the game, but there was still something enjoyably primal about it. He didn't know what or why. There couldn't be much of a benefit to their ancestors throwing water.

In recent cycles, the game for bragging rights had become Flip Toss, one that required quick, precise juggling of objects. Because of the rotation, throwing an item up and catching it without moving was no easy task on Venthralli, and people who worked on ships were usually bad at it. They'd throw objects over their heads, then watch with momentary confusion as the item arced up-wheel and away, rather than falling straight down as it would on a ship.

Much of the appeal of the classic games came from the forge workers' tradition of molding little toys out of soft alloys for grubs to win. This cycle, they'd made Winged Chrills: mythical creatures that stole people's shells and flew away. Last cycle, it was a character from a grub's story called Sawtooth: a venth with a giant mouth and huge teeth, whose bite was so strong that she ate venthhounds from the inside out. Cejero had a toy gascan in his bunk on the *Myzer* he'd won as a grub.

By late morning, a thousand venth were scattered throughout the communal deck, enjoying music, dancing, snacks, and events. A handful of engineers made piles of sticks that shot electric fire from the end, which the grubs all waved in the air as they ran around. The light almost hurt to look at, but it was hard not to.

They were so…sparkly.

The circayd was split by a large supper with enough food to sate every venth for two circayds—the biggest feast any of them would have until the following cycle's festival. Traditional dishes were accompanied by ones made from overstocked crops. Multiple foods used the berries Teemeru had been given some of the excesses of, although there was no sign of berry water by any name. Salem particularly liked the Bendil bread covered in vine noodle cream, a combination he'd never had before, so he got seconds.

After the meal, Salem found himself sitting with Cejero, eating hot cakes made of alingroot and grains. Neither spoke about their previous excursion, opting instead to discuss the events they'd missed on Venthralli during that time.

"Have the second-half schedules been sent out?" Salem eventually asked. It was painful to bring up future excursions the *Myzer* would be doing without him, but the information could give him some insight as to when other ships might be trying to add a shard handler. It would be more useful to know if the *Myzer* had found his replacement, which would likely spread to openings elsewhere, but Salem didn't want to ask about that. Not during the festival.

"Not yet," Cejero said. "Some of the other science officers and I were actually talking about that earlier in the set. We think that shards have become so hard to find that the folks on Bendil 2 are reconsidering migration. That probably clogs up the works a bit, especially in the Energy Department." He took a small bite of his dessert. "What about you? Any word on a new assignment?"

"The Panel said it wouldn't be until after the festival, if not later. I've just been doing the stuff I normally do when we're home, only more of it. I set up a lot of the decorations here." Salem leaned back, eyeing the table at which they ate. "I moved this table up here."

"Oh yeah?" Cejero chuckled. He similarly inspected the table, as if there might be a telltale sign Salem had moved it.

"I reckon I'll probably move it back."

"Doing a service to your people."

From behind Salem, a voice arose. One he knew all too well.

"There you are," it said, and from around the side of the table, Olyké walked into view. "Hi Salem," she said casually, as one would to someone they knew through friends.

A fresh bite of steaming cake found its way early down Salem's throat, singeing the sides. He took a generous bite of water to cool the inside of his neck, waving meekly in response.

"Ank was looking for you by the games," she told Cejero. "She said it's important."

"Do you know why?"

"No. Just that she wants you to look at something scientific."

"Must be urgent for her to be dealing with it during the festival."

"So I presume."

With a sigh, Cejero pushed himself lazily up from the table. "Alright," he said. "I'll go look for her—wait here in case she comes by. And don't eat my cake." He wormed his way through the grid of park tables, soon disappearing into the crowd.

Olyké remained by the table as Salem ate. She looked at him intensely, like she was analyzing his chewing skills.

"Salem, I'm sorry I hit you."

"Oh…" he furrowed his brow and swallowed the masticated grains. "It's alright."

"No, it's not. It was emotionally charged and unprofessional. That being said, I'm responsible for every person on that ship, and I can't allow their lives to be put in jeopardy against clear instructions. I don't hate you, Salem; I just need the ship to operate smoothly so that, if there's a complication, we have the room to accommodate for it without putting us in danger."

"I understand," he said. He waited for a couple of beats, then slowly took another bite of his cooling dessert. Cejero reappeared from beyond the mob, alone, searching across the tables.

"But, regardless of everything else that happened…" Olyké started. "You, Ank, and Plexie are the reason we escaped the zero beast. So…thank you."

Her words took a while to make their way into Salem's head. The situation was difficult to read; Olyké was difficult to read. Salem gulped down the bite of cake. It scratched mildly against his burned throat. "You're…welcome?" he said.

Cejero returned to the table, taking Olyké's attention. "Did you find Ank?" she asked.

"No," he grumbled. "You'd think she would be easier to find." He stood up on his toes and gazed over the crowd. "I know she's small, but she's also in a field of slate. We must've circled—"

"Cejero!" Ank yelled above the music. Her vibrant frame popped up amidst the tables, hopping over the heads of nearby venth before winding her way towards the science officer. Her body bobbed up and down as she ran to the table, a piece of parchment clenched in her fist. "Oh good, both of you," she said to Olyké. Her gaze moved past them. "*And Salem!* Aww—it's like a little reunion. Are you back on the *Myzer?*"

"He is not."

"Well, maybe now," Ank chirped. She pushed the paper into Cejero's hands. "Look at *this!*"

Cejero stared at the page for two full rotés. His protruding eyes danced up and down the sheet, paused to narrow on something in the corner, then scanned back to the other side. "Is this...?"

"A shard!"

"Oh, okay..." he shrugged, nonplussed. He looked at Olyké. "We can still submit this for our first excursion after the mid-cycle, right?"

"No, look at *this*," Ank pointed to something on the page. "Remember how I told you about those searching methods?"

"Uh, yeah. Selective-something?"

"Selective rescanning. It uses deep-wave signal aggregation to identify shards, instead of trial-based frequency isolation."

"That means very little to me, Ank."

"All of the zones around Talesk-Venthralli are empty, so it's only a matter of time before we have to relocate the colony—"

"Heh, Salem and I were just talking about that."

"But what if we had *really* good long-distance data? The number of jumps per excursion would decrease, the radius of empty zones could increase without tribulation, and the colony would migrate less often."

"That would certainly save us energy," agreed Cejero. His eyes lingered on the page.

"Almost as much as hibernation itself!" she said. That was no small benchmark. Hibernation had been a key turning point in the venth's survival tens of thousands of cycles ago. By bringing everyone together, lowering their biological functions, and turning the heat off in most areas of the colony, their overall energy and nutritional requirements were heavily reduced. It was so critical that, if someone were to die during hibernation, their lineage would be removed from the gene donor list, much like Salem's had been. Unfortunately, it often happened to elderly venth who were simply old, but with so many unknowns looming towards their potential demise, it was a risk Venthralli couldn't take.

Nor did they need to. Only a quarter of the population needed to lend their genes for the venth to propagate safely, and in a crisis, they could get by with a tenth.

Ank clicked her fingers together in sequence against her thumbs. "Anyways, that's how I found *this!*" She poked the page in Cejero's fingers emphatically.

He blinked, refocusing on the printout. Olyké leaned over to look at the sheet, scrunching her face. Neither venth seemed to give the reaction Ank had expected. She looked between them for a beat, then poked the page again. "That's the shard!" she said.

Olyké tilted her head, as if looking at the information from a different angle would make it clearer.

Cejero shook his head. "That's an error."

"Nope!" Ank beamed. "Shard!"

"This wouldn't even be considered a shard, Ank. It would be the size of a deadworld."

"I know!" she squeaked. The young navigator practically exploded out of her violet carapace, head pressed back into her shell like it was coiled to launch away.

"Then you know it's an error," said Cejero. "A shard of that size would have been found back when the colony first arrived in Talesk. We would be able to see it through regular means."

"We *can* see it! It's just *really* far away! I angled a basic receiver at the location and left it to absorb while we were out at Hobblecob. It didn't show up for a whole set, but it finally did! It's there!"

Olyké plucked the page from Cejero's hand and pulled it close to her face. Salem scurried around the table to look at the data sheet, though once he did, he wasn't sure why he'd bothered. Nothing on it made sense to him.

"If it's not an error," Olyké mumbled, "this would fuel the colony for hundreds of cycles." She scrunched the plates over her mouth. "How far is it, exactly?"

"Around forty-one mean jumps away."

Olyké dropped the sheet back on the table. "Let the Panel know. I'm sure they'll take it into consideration when planning the direction of Venthralli's migration."

Ank's face dropped, her head rose back out of her shell. "But… we should be migrating *there*," she said. "We just need someone to scout it first. That someone could be us!"

"Ank…" Olyké sighed. "That's twenty jumps past the excursion limit. They wouldn't approve a trip *one* jump past it."

"What if we shard-hopped?"

"Absolutely not," Olyké said quickly, but as the words left her mouth, she seemed to give it a second thought.

Shard-hopping was the process of jumping past a ship's fuel reserves by locating starshards along its path and using the power from each to get to the next. It was a practice reserved for emergencies, when no better alternatives were available. Had Relentless Bastard left the *Myzer* alone with enough fuel for a single jump, they could have attempted to shard-hop home.

In theory.

In practice, shard-hopping never worked, and it wasted a lot of fuel. Continuing the chain of jumps required winding, convoluted paths that ate up a lot of extra shards, and in order to get back through the evaporated zones surrounding Venthralli, a ship would have to build up a reservoir of at least five jumps of fuel in that manner. Had Relentless Bastard *actually* left the *Myzer* alone with enough fuel for a single jump, the Power Panel would have ordered them to stay put and wait for the *Chaziro Cubar*.

However, as ludicrous as a forty-one jump shard-hop sounded at first utterance, it wasn't so unrealistic. Most of that trip would take place outside of the excursion limit, where the zones were shard-rich. And since the destination was a giant shard that would fill the energy collector to the brim, it wouldn't be surprising for a ship on such a mission to re-enter the excursion limit with a full tank, as well.

If the ship re-entered. Every danger that came from traveling outside was amplified past the excursion limit, plus a slew of unique perils experienced only by the dead.

Salem was not surprised by Olyké's response.

"Why not?" Ank whined.

"Because it's suicide," Olyké said. "Which is why the Panel will hear it only as losing an energy collector and its crew. There's not a ship in the fleet that can carry enough fuel to rescue us at forty-one jumps."

"We won't need a rescue," Ank said confidently. "Our rate is over 100%" She gestured to Salem, whose head perked up at his inclusion.

"That's an average, most of which took place while you were here at Venthralli with all of its resources and aid. If there's a 300% slump outside of the excursion limit, there's nothing we can do."

"This is *huge*, Olyké." Ank pointed to the readout again. "If we can confirm these data and explore the way, Venthralli could migrate there permanently."

Olyké stared at the paper, deliberating the hypothetical trip more than Salem would've assumed. She collapsed into a seat at the table and propped her head up with her hand, poring over the information with focus. Salem watched like a phantom in the corner while she mulled the data over.

"If anyone was wondering," Ank said cheerfully, "the longest possible rescue would be sixteen mean jumps by the *Venth Queen*, which can hold fifty jumps' worth of refined gel."

"It can barely do six without needing repairs," said Cejero.

"I said *possible*."

Olyké stood back up. "Before I take this to the Panel—in *any* capacity—we need to be absolutely sure it is what it appears to be."

She handed the paper to Cejero, who flicked the corner as he looked up and down the information. "Let's triple-check everything on here," he said. "If there are no inconsistencies tomorrow, we should be able to get it to the Panel before they start sending out the next round of excursions."

"Be thorough," Olyké said, leaving the picnic area.

Cejero pursed his mouth while he looked around the festival. "I'm...going to grab another piece of cake before I head up to Kairv. See you there in about thirty?"

"Okie!" chirped Ank. Cejero worked his way through the tables towards the food carts.

A short grub ran past Ank with a sparkling decoration held high in the air, screaming while another chased after them.

Ank smiled at Salem. "You're welcome!"

She skittered off, calling to Hathem through the crowd.

After the circayd-long celebration was complete, the seasonal supplies began their collective voyage back to the storage deck. At least twice as many people as had worked on the set up assisted with the strike down, making the process considerably faster. Even with the half-circayd work restrictions for Venthia 5, the entire task took barely more than three circayds.

A heavy gust hit Salem in the face, pushing him back a step. He gripped the handle of his nearby cart, steadying himself against the pressure. The lower decks moved faster and had more space for pressures to form, so wind tended to be more intense on them. They were also colder, which apparently mattered because people created larger variations in temperature. Gusts weren't too common on Venthia 5 because of all of the stuff, but when they showed up, they were sudden, powerful, and could knock you right over if you weren't paying attention. They also sometimes came at an angle because of the deck's width.

The gale subsided quickly, allowing Salem to resume his task. He unfastened the last box from the cart and shoved it off the lip onto the cold ground. He wiggled the box in place so it sat nicely against the crates on either side, then grabbed the rolling platform and returned up the ramp.

The procedure closely resembled that of moving shard chunks on a deadworld. Every trip down the ramp reminded Salem of the hill on Hobblecob he'd slid down. The whole excursion now seemed like a dream: the fantastical buildings, the light shard, the unending pursuit. What else would they have found on that rock had their trip not been interrupted by Relentless Bastard?

After returning to the communal deck for the fifth or sixth time that circayd, Salem was met with an early removal from cleanup.

"Salem!" one of the organizers called over to him—a Darkwatcher named Leiff who worked in the electrical rooms. "Your presence is requested at the Power Panel."

The cart handle hit the floor with a *ting* as Salem released it.

"Did they say what for?" he asked.

"No. But they asked about twenty rotés ago—said to have you come as soon as you were available," Leiff said. Whether the summons was reason for excitement or dread, Salem didn't know. Venthralli was a few circayds into the second half of the cycle, so maybe the Energy Department had found him a ship assignment. That didn't warrant a meeting with the Panel, though.

"Alright. Thanks, Leiff," Salem said flatly. He moved the cart off to the side, then left Venthia 4 and the ghostly remains of the mid-cycle festival.

His limbs drank up the pressure relief as he ascended the ramps to the pleasant, airy weight of Bendil 2. While most public buildings had open entryways, government structures featured metal doors that slid to cover the opening, similar to residential homes or bulkheads. Salem trotted a quarter of the way along the wheel until he came to the door leading into the Panel's chambers. It was closed, blocked by four venth waiting idly in the walkway: Ank, Plexie, Hathem, and Cejero. The rut in Plexie's shell had healed, leaving a thin divot that ran vertically down his back.

"Salem!" Ank called past Cejero. The others greeted him warmly, albeit surprised by his arrival.

Salem looked between them. "Why are you all standing around?" he asked.

"We're waiting for Olyké," said Cejero. "She's in with the Panel right now."

"How have you been, Salem?" Hathem asked, as if he might be dying. "Have you been assigned to a ship yet?"

"I think that's why I'm here."

"Huh?" Ank grunted, rotating her head sideways.

"Leiff said the Panel wanted to see me, but they didn't say why."

"*At* the Power Panel," she said giddily. "*By* me!" She gestured to Salem. "And here you are!"

Hathem frowned at the young navigator and began scolding her for misleading Leiff. Partway through, she was interrupted by the light grinding of the door's bearings.

Olyké emerged, downtrodden. She gazed across the group, eyes passing right by Salem before doing a double take.

"Salem."

"Hi."

"So?" Ank bounced on her toes, hands clasped together. "What did they say?"

"They denied it, again."

Plexie groaned. Cejero hit his fist against his shell.

"The formal proposal?" Ank asked. "For a *full* excursion?"

"Yes."

"Buuuut…" She raised herself up to the tips of her toes. "What about the plan—?"

"Yes," Olyké said. "They will allow us to shard-hop."

Ank and Plexie bounced up and down, cheering.

"You're joking?" Cejero said. Olyké put her hands up to settle down the younger venth.

"The Panel recognizes the value of a multi-generational energy source, as well as the need to confirm its location prior to migration.

They also need to consider the security of the colony's energy reserves. They won't let us leave with a full tank."

"How much will they give us?"

"Enough for six jumps."

Plexie's feet stuck flat to the ground. "*Six…?*"

"That's barely enough to get through the evaporated zones," said Cejero. The zones within five jumps or so of Venthralli had all been scavenged clean of even the smallest floaters—a sphere of about seven hundred zones centered around the colony. An allotment for six jumps wouldn't afford the *Myzer* much possibility of getting to the excursion limit.

Perhaps that was the point. Or perhaps the Panel wanted to test Ank's methodology, to see if it was really so accurate that she could shard-hop a ship all the way to the excursion limit.

"That's the deal," Olyké said flatly. "In any other case, they'd probably plan an exploratory team for next cycle, but because of the accuracy of the data in the proposal, they seem to believe there's enough of a chance of success to do this now."

"Or need to migrate Venthralli has become more severe than we believe," said Cejero, "and finding this now is worth a heavy risk."

Olyké raised her palms up. "If I knew either way—"

"I know, I know…" he said. "Don't want you to lose your role or anything. What's our next step?"

"This is a volunteer mission," she said. "The likelihood of failure is high, and the Panel won't send a rescue or transfer past the excursion limit. We'll *have* to find shards as we go…"

"Probably along the way back, too," added Cejero. "We shouldn't assume that a deadworld-sized shard will be usable."

"If anyone isn't willing to go on this, now's the time to say it. No judgements."

Again, Olyké looked between the crew. Her eyes met Salem's and lingered briefly, but gave no addendum of exclusion or offhanded comment about finding a shard handler. Salem imagined it would be difficult to fill volunteer spots for an excursion like this, and time consuming—something Olyké would need to begin immediately if someone objected. Salem thought Plexie might have abstained. Even the laziest possible engineering work was a significant contribution to the colony, and Plexie had a lot of cycles ahead of him. He also had a lust for adventure, though, and that usually tipped the scales.

After five beats of silence, Ank cheered. "Yay!"

Plexie was retaken immediately by his excitement. "Let's go be heroes!"

"Heroes…" Cejero laughed, "fools who get lucky."

"Let's go get lucky!"

Hathem turned to Ank, whimsically, as if the whole conversation were hypothetical. "Are you sure you can find a consistent path of shards?"

"Yup!"

"Well, then," she shrugged. "What more do I have to look forward to, other than five cycles of boredom?"

"That's the spirit!"

Despite Hathem's customary indifference, Salem could tell she was eager to find a deadworld made of pure fuel. How could she not be? It was the biggest find of the century; all of them were excited.

All except for Olyké, who seemed to begrudge the entire mission. Almost as if it wasn't voluntary for her. Salem wondered if the Power Panel would actually force her to lead such a dangerous excursion.

"Alright, Ank," she said. "You're being given full access to the colony sensors to collate, and have ten circayds to find us a path to the excursion limit. I want a 300% tank plotted to that point."

"Aye aye!"

"There is no room for mistakes. One failed recovery and we're dead." She turned to Salem. Her eyes narrowed in a shattering combination of disappointment and ire. "*No* going rogue."

Salem nodded, afraid to hear his own voice.

"Ten circayds?" Cejero confirmed.

"Ten circayds."

"I'll go do a full diagnostic!" Plexie said, jittering with wide eyes as he took off down the wheel.

Ank skittered towards the nearest ramp. "Come on, Cejero!" she called back. "We've got shards to find!" She disappeared around the corner of the incline, the pattering of her limbs fading behind the ambient hum of the rotating hubs. Cejero and Hathem made their way more leisurely in the same direction.

Salem had momentarily forgotten that Ank was the one who had summoned him to Bendil 2, and he didn't actually have an audience with the Panel, so he started his trek back down to Venthia 4.

"Salem," Olyké said, stopping him in place. She gave no smile or warmth; her face was entirely business-like. "This is not a reinstatement," she clarified. "It's a volunteer mission."

"I understand," he said.

She stared at him for half a roté, like she'd had more to say, but then decided against it. Standing alone with her in the middle of the road of the government sector…it might as well have been a whole cycle.

"Welcome back," she said finally, returning to the administrative building and sliding the door shut along its alloyed bearings.

CHAPTER 7
MOUNTAINS

Despite the danger of the trip ahead, Salem was excited to get back outside. His time in the colony always felt like limbo: passing time until the next shard grab. The feeling had been elevated this time around, not knowing whether he'd set foot on a ship again.

Then, Ank found the mega shard.

As life sometimes happened, however, something new was brought into Salem's life on Venthralli during the ten circayds leading up to the *Myzer's* departure. Something good. He wanted to help Ank with her historic discovery, but for the first time in his life, Salem found himself also wishing he could stay home instead.

What he really wanted was to be in both places at once.

A couple of circayds after the Power Panel approved the *Myzer's* under-fueled excursion to locate the mega shard, Salem strolled along Venthia 2 after his mid-circayd meal. The idle tasks that usually occupied his time between excursions had yet to pick up after the festival—a major contrast to the scramble leading up to it—so he had little reason to be anywhere besides his flat. In those situations, he sometimes found himself walking along the thoroughfare of the trade district. Just to see what had changed since his last period of limbo.

Venthia 2 was as flurried as always. Salem peered into storefronts as he passed, realizing he wasn't sure of the purpose of many of them. He stopped to watch a trio of venth play a strategy game he wasn't familiar with, themed around fictional, combative ships, and then he hopped his way through a crowd of hatchlings being taught a silly dance by two of the rōshis.

At some point, he found himself standing in Teemeru's kitchen, staring at the wall of blue-green lines. He hadn't intended to enter the kitchen; he was barely aware that he had. He just stared at the wall, hypnotized.

"Are you hungry?" asked Teemeru, cooking knife in hand with small slices of tuber stuck to the side of the blade.

"Huh?" Salem blinked slowly. He looked around the kitchen. A pair of venth sat eating whatever the supper leftovers were.

Teemeru glanced between Salem and the wall. "Are you hungry?" she repeated. "That's usually why people show up."

"Oh, no…sorry," he said. "I already ate. I just wanted to look at the wall again."

"It's nice, isn't it?"

"Yeah," he said softly, turning back to the design. It was just a pattern, neither picture nor portrait, but there was something hidden within the errant lines that called to him. An image beneath.

"It looks like a mountain," he added finally.

"Why do you say that?"

"Because…it does," he said. "Don't you see it?" As he asked the question, though, it occurred to him how unusual it was to see such a shape on Venthralli. There weren't many things in the colony structured like the jagged design, and with only perhaps twenty living venth who'd ever seen a mountain with their own eyes, most people wouldn't see what Salem did when he looked at the wall: ground that jutted upward forever.

He poked his finger at the top of the tallest lines, which formed a point. "That's the peak," he explained. "These are the sides. That might be a little offshoot or spiky bit."

"They have peaks?"

"Yeah," he said, befuddled. "Haven't you seen one?"

"Most people don't leave the colony, Salem."

"But you've seen a picture somewhere."

Teemeru shrugged. "I don't think there are any."

"Really?" he asked. The space between his eyes scrunched. It seemed impossible for no one at home to know what a mountain looked like. They were a signature feature of the deadworlds, and venth often used the term to describe something large or insurmountable, though only the first of those was true. Salem had climbed two of the rocky slopes thus far, which were a pain. "I'll draw you one," he said. "They're kind of neat."

"Salem!" she yelled out. He jumped back from the wall, checking the ground to see if he'd stepped in something. "You should draw it on the wall!"

He looked back at the zigzags. "Here?"

"Yes!"

"What about the design?"

"That's been there forever," she said. "This could be like...an upgrade."

"You'd let me do that?"

"I think it would be wonderful! *And* informative."

Salem bounced on his toes a couple of times. "Yeah..."

"Are there other things like mountains?" she asked.

"On deadworlds?"

"Yeah."

"It's really just rocks and water, but they're shaped differently, like cliffs or valleys."

"I think people would love to see things like that," she said. "Without having to leave Venthralli and travel across the outside. You were looking for things to do here at home."

Salem had never thought to catalog the different sights he saw on deadworlds. Most of their surfaces were boring, and the geological structures that sparsely covered them had no relevance to people on Venthralli. For a shard handler, though, understanding those features was critical to their survival. If one didn't know that the ground might suddenly disappear, they could walk right off a cliff, which Salem had almost done once. He and Cejero then threw a crisis lamp off the edge to see how tall it was, and the light was almost invisible on the ground below—hundreds of decks down.

Features on deadworlds were impossible to absorb in a single eyeful, as they were far too large to illuminate in any significant amount, so the only way to truly understand them was to traverse them. Then again, Venthralli had also never been seen in its entirety. There were images of what the colony looked like. Its shape was well known, but then again, so were winged chrills, and those didn't exist. The only truly accurate images of the colony were, ironically, ones that provided no sense of its shape: the schematics from which it was repaired.

Rather than try to draw mountains and caverns as they appeared outside, Salem could draw them more in the spirit of the images of Venthralli, giving them the same sort of majesty as their civilization.

In fact, that was something he already did regularly.

"I could make them different colors," he said. "They're usually all the same, you know. Or, similar. But I've been drawing dead-worlds the way they looked when they were alive—planets, I guess —and they might have been a whole prism of colors."

Seeing the joy in Teemeru's face at the mere prospect of having a deadworld mural in the kitchen and thinking about all of the scenes he could paint—large, vivid renditions of his liveworld drawings, like a big, maroon crater or a lavender valley—made Salem feel for the first time like it might not matter if the Energy Department couldn't find him to another ship when the *Myzer* returned. He liked being on a ship and would miss it, but the more he thought about the murals he could design, the more eager he became to create. He could paint ancient civilizations, too. Like the one on Hobblecob. An icy, aqua-green cliffside with muckflower-yellow buildings.

Salem nearly fell down the ramp to Bendil in his haste to get to the Civil Sector.

Unlike the Power Panel, civilian administrators were known for operating quickly. Energy was handled on large scales: half-set excursions and multi-cycle consumptions. Civil workers were more plentiful, and they primarily dealt with circaydly problems. If a heating system broke on Venthralli, it was not the Energy Department that dealt with it, but a civil engineer.

In the same fashion, the civil administrators gave Salem an answer right on the spot.

"That sounds novel!" exclaimed the Head of Communal Building Design—a venth named Keige.

"So…it's alright if I paint the mural?"

"If the Panel doesn't have anything for you to do through the Domestic Loan Program," said Keige. "You do still work with them, yes? I see a recent assignment here."

"We're leaving in eight circayds, but I think I could finish this before we leave." Salem hesitated, tapping his toes. "And, do you think maybe when we get back…if people really like it and want something similar…that I could paint more? Instead of the 'added two' things I usually do when I'm docked?"

"Hmm…" Keige drummed the flats of his fingers on the table. He looked to the venth on his right, who didn't give any sort of gesture to help his mulling. "I suppose that would still be up to the Panel, based on their scheduling and whatnot, but if people want them and we have the material supplies available, I can't see why not. It's been some time since any of the interiors have been colored." He gave a final tap on the desk. "We may not be able to get you a definitive answer before you return from your collection —you know how the Panel is. How long is this excursion?"

"We're not sure, exactly. Probably around two sets."

"Two *sets?*" Keige repeated, nearly falling out of his chair. He held the edge of the table to steady himself. "As in eighty-four circayds?"

"If everything goes well."

"That's, ah…*ahem.* Well, yes. I imagine that would be plenty of time to get a response from the Panel."

It was Salem's dream. If only for the last hundred rotés or so.

He thanked the civil administrators and turned to leave, but was immediately stopped by one of the others.

"Hold on a turn, Salem," they said. Beside them, Keige was eyes-down in a collection of papers, teeth grinding as he flipped through them. The other administrators watched quietly, like they couldn't continue their own work until he'd found whatever he was looking for.

Finally, he stopped at one of the sheets, scanned it thoroughly, and smacked his finger down at his goal.

Loudly, as if dictating through a fuzzy radio transmission, he read, "5-5-B-2!"

"55B2?" Salem echoed. It was a storage grid location, but he'd been done working there for a couple of circayds.

"It is a lot in the storage area on Venthia 5," Keige explained.

"Yeah…"

"That's where the paints are stored," he said, smiling. "If I recall, they'll need to be warmed up a few syros before they can be used."

Since Salem wanted to paint more murals around the colony, he decided not to make them all look as they did outside; otherwise, they'd appear too similar. He did have an idea for a sort of info-mural, showing the different ways deadworld rocks could be organized, like ravines and oceans, along with explanations for each.

Not that anybody on Venthralli would find themselves in a ravine, but they could still know about them.

He could paint that one the way most deadworlds looked, then the rest could be the way he imagined liveworlds to have been: colorful, vivid, and active. A landscape that was truly alive.

After moving the paints up from Venthia 5, Salem spent the rest of the circayd thawing and mixing small amounts of different pigments together in Teemeru's kitchen. It appeared that whoever painted the original design on the wall had used the same paints. Salem's concoction was a bit more blue, but close enough that it would only be noticeable when painted beside the existing design.

Realistically, Salem could have finished the mural in a couple of circayds, but it would have been little more than a spiky triangle, barely discernible from the zigzagging lines underneath. He had six whole circayds to work on it, and he wanted to make the long-dead landscape revive the way a liveworld should.

The mountain he painted was based on one he'd seen during his first contribution period, while disturbing a deadworld named Gellig. The large starshard had been lodged halfway up the summit, and Gellig's excessive gravity had pulled at him the entire way. Once the shard was dislodged, though, getting it down the mountainside had been wonderfully simple. Gellig had even been kind enough to break it into chunks on impact.

As Salem painted the underlying peaks, dozens of people stuck their heads into the kitchen to see what he was doing.

"How do you know?" they'd often ask of the mountain.

"I've seen them," Salem would reply.

"Really?" Aghast. "Where?"

"On the deadworlds."

Salem spent so much time outside of the colony that most people didn't know him, let alone what he did, and upon finding out, they would generally ask more questions about deadworld collections. People who spent their lives on Venthralli didn't realize how often shard handlers went onto the monstrous rocks. It was a low percentage of their overall collections, but considering how many shards were plucked out of the lightless, empty expanse each cycle, there were always a few on deadworlds.

After Salem completed the general shape of the mountain, he began to struggle with his vision. Having been fortunate enough to see a mountain illuminated by the *Myzer's* engines, he actually had a good idea of what they looked like in a general sense. In painting the entire vista, though, he'd somehow lost its monstrous essence. The feeling it gave when seen up close. The way mountains were experienced by every person who saw one. Perhaps that was just a consequence of painting one differently from how they looked in reality.

Salem stepped forward and pushed his eyes close to the wall, so he could only see part of the shape. It still looked more like the wall's previous design than it did a geological feature. He stepped back, nearly bumping into a table that had once sat against the wall but now resided in the middle of the kitchen. He tilted his head sideways at the mural.

It looked flat. That was the problem. It didn't appear rocky or round.

Shades.

When Salem drew deadworlds—or anything, really—he made parts of them darker to give an appearance of width. He didn't even think about it much anymore, but he did it by coloring more in those areas. Adding more paint didn't seem to darken the area in any noticeable amount, so he mixed several new colors of slightly varying hues, and with every stroke of darker shades, the jutting object began to appear more like the liveworld he imagined.

Throughout the entire mural project, the only box Salem had to move was the one on which he stood to paint the peak. He'd never actually seen the peak of the mountain on Gellig—he would have died from soreness trying to get there—but he had seen a smaller peak partway up, as well as the mountain outlined in its entirety by the *Myzer's* engine glow, and that was more than enough for his mind's eye.

Partway through the fifth circayd, Salem stood in the middle of the kitchen, looked at the wall, and saw a mountain. Not just in shape, but in character. He moved his eyes close, taking in a narrow view of the base as it would appear to those who'd surmounted such objects.

It was done.

The mural filled Salem with a sense of pride unlike any shard collection, which was a surprise in itself. Grabbing shards kept their species alive; it was important. At times, it was extremely difficult, and Salem succeeded despite those challenges, victorious through his own skill. Some even called shard handlers "heroes."

This was just…paint.

Salem couldn't stop smiling at it.

I made that!

He didn't think the mural was as good as many of his drawings, but that didn't stop the feeling of accomplishment from coursing through his arteries. Drawing on a large scale was harder, and he didn't have the option of crumpling up the wall and starting over.

A number of people came by to see the alien landscape while Salem cleaned the paint splashes on the floor. One venth spent about thirty rotés staring at the mountain, allowing her eyes to soak up the color in wonder, as if the wall were an opening to a teal landscape on which Venthralli was derelict.

"Are any of the deadworlds purple?" she finally asked.

"Maybe," he said. "Once upon a time, anyway." Salem had never seen one that was purple, specifically, but the hue was similar to a deep blue, so it seemed a more likely color for a liveworld to have been. "None of them look like this anymore," he explained, "they're all dead and frozen, but back when there was heat, who knows?" he shrugged. "We have purple paint."

"That would be nice in the metalworks," the venth said. "Purple always kind of feels cool, doesn't it? Reminds me of sorbet."

"I'd like to do more of them; it was fun. I have to leave in two circayds for a shard, but hopefully the Panel will let me work with civil on more of them when we get back."

"Oh, your role is on an energy collector?"

"A shard handler, yeah."

"*That* makes sense," she said, nodding at the mural knowingly. "So you've actually seen this?"

"Uh-huh."

"How big was it?"

"I'm not sure, exactly. The shard was eighty allos up, so the whole mountain was at least a few wheels tall."

Her eyes bulged. "Oh, wow…I thought maybe a couple of allos or something." Her gaze trailed up to the peak jutting into the metallic fold between the wall and ceiling. "I don't think people will know how big it's supposed to be," she said. "What if you painted Venthralli near it? For reference?"

Salem mulled that idea for a couple of rotés. Something about the mural would be lost if everyone thought the mountain was only a few decks tall, but he didn't want an image of the colony to take away from the landscape's features. He also didn't think he would be able to paint Venthralli very well in such a short amount of time.

The next circayd, Salem stacked the paint containers back onto pallet 2 of row B in section 55 on Venthia 5. An idea sprang into his head, so he kept out the remaining light grey paint, along with the brush he'd made from an old cleaning block, and made his way back to the kitchen.

For twenty rotés, he stared at the mural and tried to imagine how small a venth would appear next to the mountainous outcrop. Once he felt confident in his estimation of "as small as he could paint," Salem got to work on a little grey shard handler climbing up the cliffside. The brush wound up being too large for what he needed, so he used the curved tip of his finger where the flat met the knuckle.

Despite taking up a minuscule amount of space on the wall, the little figure took nearly half a circayd to paint.

Just as Salem finished the mural, Ank came to the kitchen and immediately pointed to the little venth on the mountainside.

"It's Salem!" she chirped.

"Not necessarily me," he said. "Just a shard handler. Or any venth, I guess. Just to show how big the mountain is."

"But you did that!"

"Well, yeah…"

"So, it's Salem!"

The impact of the tiny rock climber on the landscape was immense. People looked at the mountain for a roté, noticed the venth climbing up the side, then took a second look at the mountain with added wonder. Salem liked seeing their faces when they realized the majesty of what they were looking at. It reminded him how he'd felt when he first encountered one, back before they were simply a nuisance.

After returning the paint and brush to 55B2, Salem ran up the nearest ramp to the government district to see if someone from the Civil Sector would come see the finished project. One of the structural engineers, a venth named Bao, had some time to come look near the end of the circayd.

"My, my…" he said, hands on his carapace. He leaned back to absorb the visual, then pointed to the rock climber. "Is that you?"

Salem gave his now-rehearsed answer. "It's anyone," he explained. "Any venth-like creature."

"Ahh…but that's something you do, isn't it?"

"A couple of cycles ago, yeah."

Bao smiled, looking at the mural in its entirety before returning his focus to the little climber on the side. "That sure would be something to see."

The entire experience had given Salem a craving. He was almost disappointed to be leaving on what was easily the most incredible expedition in Venthrallian history.

And now that he had the attention of the Civil Sector, he was more optimistic about his future than ever before. His worst fear from the last set had become his dream: if the Panel was unable to assign him to another ship and he was stuck on Venthralli, that might allow him to paint murals permanently.

He'd simply be…a painter. As a role.

And if things went *really* well on their excursion—if they actually found a shard the size of a deadworld—they would put an end to shard collecting entirely.

CHAPTER 8
THE LONGEST JOURNEY

The wind stopped; the sound of the outside creature became nothing more than gentle vibrations in the floor. The bulkhead slammed down in front of the cracked lens of Brackesh's eye. Chartreuse blood flowed from the openings in her foot and hand, far too rapidly to clot in the cold before she died.

Her only goal prior to that fate was to update their final log, to outline the information the *Domodo's* crew had died for: why the venth couldn't hide, why bodies were never found. It would create more questions than answers, but the answers provided could save lives. At the very least, it would give the venth a tangible understanding of the dangers posed by an outside creature. Knowledge about what they'd face. Knowledge that was now known only to Brackesh. The serrated limbs; the pale tendril; the spiky, blood-colored—

Scratching came from the other side of the bulkhead. Rapping. Brackesh had barely closed it in time. The metal appeared thick enough to hold. For a while, at least. Longer than she needed.

She filled her lungs with diluted air, taking in three full breaths for every one she required. The ship jostled back and forth with a dull, repeated pounding.

The sound grew louder, melding into more of a scraping.

The creature was moving. It was trying to cut off her retreat.

Brackesh took off towards the sensor array, her steps uneven. She forced her legs to propel her along the corridor, a spotty trail of blood in her wake.

The rhythmic *thuds* of the moving creature quickly reached her position. The walls caved inward, illuminated by sparks cascading down from the ceiling. With a pitchy whine, the *Domodo's* carapace bent further in, closing the hallway around Brackesh as she limped along.

She was almost at the sensor array.

Two allos left.

One…

Brackesh ran between the jagged walls as they pinched together. The ceiling bent in front of her. The floor panels popped up to form a metallic hill blocking her path. She fell against it, righting herself to climb over, gasping for air. She took one step up the mound and was knocked back prone.

The creature's vise squeezed the cabin harder, jutting the floor up into Brackesh. The ship's panels flayed, the torn metal slicing into her shin. Sparks arced up from the broken flooring as she screamed, brightening the crushed corridor for one final beat before the *Domodo* was engulfed in darkness.

The pressure against Brackesh's aching body lightened. She tried to push herself upright, but the floor had pulled away from her. There was nothing to prop herself against.

She had pulled away from the floor.

With nothing to run or stand on, Brackesh hovered weightlessly between the uneven panels. As her eyes adjusted to the darkness, she could see the jagged walls around her, reflecting dim light in a sort of prism.

There was still power in the sensor array.

Droplets of yellow-green blood misted the dark hallway around her. She probed her uninjured leg downward in search of the busted floorboard, her toes tapping at air until they finally touched metal. She kicked off, sending herself soaring towards the helm. It wasn't a difficult target to hit from an allo away, nor was it difficult to grab hold of the hatch's frame as she passed through and swing herself against the wall beside the protruding yellow door button.

Brackesh might only have a few beats left; whatever she wrote would have to be simple. There was a lot to log—information that could answer long-held questions about the hunters; information that might save a future crew from the onslaught of an outside creature.

To ensure the log returned home, Brackesh swapped the input storage to the *Domodo's* vault box: a fast, powerful, zero-syro computer that was fastened to the ship's exterior in a protective casing. No matter what state the *Domodo* was found in, the salvage crew would take the vault box home, and that would—

Two blade-like arms punched into the sensor array from above, stabbing repeatedly into the ground until one of them finally caught Brackesh through the back of her shell, impaling her into the floor. The limb pulled her out of the ship, boiling her blood and icing her skin as her body was placed into the gaping maw of the creature's mouth, where her carapace would then be broken apart by smaller claws, making the toughest parts of her body easier on the beast's digestive system.

"Your port's unfrosted, *Myzer*. Opening up."

The voice of the inner deck dispatcher buzzed into the helm of the energy collector, followed soon after by the gentle rocking of the ship leaving its bed. Even with residual heat emanating from the outer decks, the doors of the docking spiral were perpetually frozen over. Every departure and arrival required heat to open the door without damaging the machinery—yet another cost of exploration.

"How's the repair holding up?" asked Olyké.

"Let's see. Storage three's pressure is..." Plexie punched a button at the side of the sensory room and looked over the readout produced. "Normal."

"Good," she exhaled.

The crew remained oddly blasé as the *Myzer* made its first jump towards the unknown, as if it were any other excursion. The profundity of their mission hit Salem within rotés, however, removing whatever apprehension he'd held about leaving his artistry. For the first time in his life, he was on a ship *without* the sole purpose of obtaining a heat gel surplus, like the explorers of the past—a dynamic both strange and exciting. The *Myzer* could burn through a full tank of fuel, post a negative return, and still succeed in their mission. All they had to do was return with confirmation of a near-eternal energy supply.

Simple.

The first jumps away from the colony went as smoothly and poorly as expected: no dangers, no shards. A straight shot through the sphere of evaporated zones surrounding the colony. With so little fuel, though, the crew's concerns thickened after each landing without a shard.

Once they made it through the evaporated zones, it didn't take long for them to run into the first complication of their journey.

In the helm, Ank explained, "With the way these zones have been excavated, the most direct route will take us through a couple of surely-empty zones. There's always a chance of finding a tiny remnant once we're there, but I don't even see a shimmer from here."

Olyké peered at one of the navigation panels, arms folded. "What's the up-wheel route like?"

"Less known, so we might find a small floater once we land, but I don't have eyes on one from here."

Olyké fingered the radio. "Plexie, I need a fuel estimation," she said. As they waited for their mechanic to figure out precisely how much refined energy rested in the *Myzer's* reservoir, Olyké discussed their possible paths with Ank.

Where most navigators would have planned a single route from Venthralli to the excursion limit, Ank had plotted dozens, each contingent on ranges of fuel recovered from different groupings of zones. The routes she had estimated to be the most fruitful were of the kind Olyké had characterized as "up-wheel": a long way to travel a short distance. As if one had run around an entire deck just to get a couple of allos away. In this case, the up-wheel route was an indirect path that weaved the *Myzer* through the outside in ways that would otherwise be wasteful, but still required them to find floaters in zones presumed to be empty.

Fifty rotés later, Plexie walked his results up to the helm. The three discussed each potential course as the ship idly burned through heat in the desolate zone. The fuel estimation showed just enough fuel to get them through the straight path, guaranteed to provide no additional fuel. The up-wheel route was poorly traveled, making it a more promising gamble. The *Myzer* was still within the excursion limit, so if they came up with nothing, they would get rescued. The excursion would be over, their contribution records would be tarnished, Olyké might even find herself no longer working for the Energy Department, but they would get home alive.

They took the long route.

The goal of their mission was not speed, but distance and efficiency, and for that task, Olyké might be the best ship lead in the colony. Even when looking at gritty details, her sight remained on the whole. It took a sort of imagination Salem didn't have. He fantasized, imagining places that didn't exist or couldn't exist; things he'd seen in his past. Olyké imagined possibilities both good and bad. Every problem that could happen, but likely never would.

In times like these, Salem wondered if perhaps those issues never happened *because* she thought about them.

They landed in the first zone of their up-wheel route, and within rotés, Ank cried out, "Found one!"

The crew had come to expect these sorts of results from Ank, but it was still refreshing to see firsthand that shard-hopping could be a feasible method of travel for the *Myzer*. It was tangible proof that Ank could locate hidden shards after entering a zone, dissolving much of the crew's concern about the upcoming journey. In theory, the farther they got from Venthralli, the larger and more plentiful the shards would become.

"How big is it?" asked Plexie.

"*Tiny*—not even half of a chunk. Buuuut I'm pretty sure if we find another one like it during the next three jumps, the detour will be an improvement over the direct route."

Plexie pointed at a readout in front of Ank. "I don't think one more will be enough. Not unless it's bigger."

"Nuh-uh! See how short these jumps are gonna be?" She traced her finger along the lines.

Plexie blinked at the screens. "Why are we doing those?"

"To find shards!"

"Half a chunk is good enough," Olyké said dryly. "Suit up, Salem. I want gel in the tank within two hundred rotés."

"Easy!" Ank said on Salem's behalf. "We're almost touching it."

Ank wasn't exaggerating. When Salem rocked out of the pressure door, he immediately expelled part of a puff canister to stop himself from floating past the shard. It was practically resting against the hull, no more than two allos away from the fuel port. The collection had primarily consisted of him getting in and out of his suit and cycling the pressure door twice.

The next zone was empty, sandwiched between two half-circayd jumps, but the one after yielded a sizable shard, larger than any of them would have believed could be in a zone so close to the colony.

"How is this here?" Hathem asked. "We're not that far out."

"This zone was only traveled three times," Ank said cheerfully. "The first was a full-circayd collection that filled the ship, and the other two were lengthy stops during a return."

"So you suspected smaller ones were passed up…"

"And they were!"

"Very clever, grub."

"That's the Ank guarantee!" she smiled, more than a little proud of herself.

Once the *Myzer* finished its unorthodox detour, Ank and Salem fell into the groove she'd envisioned. Ank lined up starshards like residential abodes, Salem grabbed them, and the *Myzer* jumped on towards the next. The path they took to the edge of the excursion limit was long and winding, routing them through zones less traveled, but more likely to contain small, overlooked shards. It was a common point of question whether the elongated path was more optimal than going straight through to the edge, but with every chunk of frozen gel Salem deposited into the *Myzer's* tank, the convoluted route appeared more and more beneficial.

Until it wasn't.

Salem stood by the pressure room, checking over his suit to make sure its seams were holding strong through frequent usage, when Plexie came scampering past him on all fours.

"Sensory room," he huffed, "come on!"

The flats of Salem's fingers paused as they ran along the interior seam between the suit's forearm and elbow. He looked up.

"What's going on?" he asked.

"A quarry beast!"

The suit fell into a pile on the closet floor. "Is it here?" Salem asked as he ran after Plexie.

"I don't know."

"Well, is it coming after us?"

"I don't know, Salem!"

Plexie's arm and leg rose up along the wall as he skittered around the corner in a full sprint. Salem's blood warmed, struggling to keep up with Plexie all the way to the sensory room, where the mechanic pushed himself upright and jogged the last half allo to the doorway.

"Is it here?" Salem called through the entryway as Plexie clomped into the room.

Olyké responded quietly, eyes locked on one of the monitors. "No."

"The colony confirmed its last location as being the zone directly between us and the first anchor shard," Cejero explained. "That was a circayd ago, so it should be gone when we land. However, if it's not, we might not have enough fuel for a two-jump evasion."

"And we can't rely on the two-jump evasion anymore," Olyké drone. "We know it doesn't always work." She clicked her tongue against her teeth, mulling the situation. "Fuel is going to be scarce if we try to go around," she said. "I don't want to risk getting stranded in its path. How many methods do we have on board for checking the zone without alerting the creature?"

Ank's mouth turned sideways; she looked around the instruments at her sides. "Two, I guess. There's a lot of uncertainty right now about radiation pings. After what happened last time, we should probably assume that *some* un-venth can sense them."

"Take the circayd to do those checks—not the rad-ping. Pre-plot the shortest two-jump evasion from the next zone, just in case." She turned away from the screens. "Plexie, fuel diagnostic. Cejero, double-check with the colony about those sightings, see if they can give us a prediction of its path."

"What if we can't two-jump to the anchor shard?" Ank squeaked. "We'll be outside of the excursion limit…"

"You have one circayd to find us an emergency landing zone with a starshard in it," Olyké said. Ank's face drained, the burden of their survival now resting on her back. "It's all unexplored," she added. "There will be shards."

"Yeah…"

"One circayd," announced the colony admin. "Turn the reactor off, reduce life support to six syros."

"*Six?*" Plexie wailed. "That'll be miserable!"

"Not as miserable as being eaten."

Plexie sulked off to check the fuel levels and idle the reactor, mumbling something Salem couldn't hear.

"How far is the first anchor shard?" asked Hathem.

"One long jump past the excursion limit," Ank answered, "about twice the median. In a zone I'm naming 'Plessionat.' It should fuel us all the way to the second anchor."

The notion of an anchor shard was new. No expedition had been planned with a reliance on floaters before, nor had detailed information been available past the excursion limit. The Power Panel had asked Ank for a thorough report on how she'd determined those anchors, which were essentially "the easiest shards to find through aggregate scanning." Ank took the request to mean that the practice might become standard in the future, lowering the required energy allowance for all excursions.

So, in a way, their trip had already become historic, reimagining the industry that kept the venth alive.

Salem's hand arced slowly across the parchment: a hill formed over billions of cycles to curved perfection. It was perhaps the finest line he had ever drawn.

There were few benefits to living in six syros. Covered in thermal sheets, trapping what little heat their bodies radiated, it was still painful, and if they lived in it for too long, it would be lethal. Venth bodies slowed down in extreme temperatures to preserve energy, which had made all of Salem's lines smoother, steadying his hand to beautiful results.

Not results worth dying over, of course.

It also seemed that time had been unable to escape the slowing force of six syros. Two thousand rotés of reduced life support felt like a circayd all on its own. Salem had shambled into the engine room at one point in search of residual heat from the reactor, but it had been off for too long. Ank ignited a leftover festival sparkler that she'd brought along, hoping maybe it could heat a small room up a little, but all it did was strain their eyes.

The crew splurged on a hot meal for supper—a comparatively minimal expenditure. The hot rations were disgusting, but easily the best part of the circayd. Salem savored every steaming spoonful; the warmth cascaded down his body's tubing and into his stomach. It made him seriously question Teemeru's notion that the future of cuisine was uncooked.

Cejero sat stiffly beside Salem with his own bowl, steaming in the icy air. "Plex, there's clicking in the ceiling past the engine room," he said casually, downing a spoonful of hot, syrupy nutrients.

"Yup," Plexie said. "Probably the ducts. Thinner metals warp when the temperature drops, and the ship is quieter."

"Shouldn't you check it out?"

"Temperatures drop *way* lower in the docks, 'Jero. The *Myzer's* engineered for this…" His fingers slapped the edge of the table. "Oh! That's near the depressurization site, too. The duct probably dented inward, which also causes creaking."

Cejero set his spoon down. "It's our life support, Plexie."

"Plexie is hardly going to ignore potential issues with our life support," Hathem said with a smile. "If it persists, he can check."

"Okay…but our life support is perfect," Plexie said indignantly. "The airflow to storage three is slightly reduced because that's what happens when there's a depressurization, but the spiral engineers didn't think it was worth fixing. I sure can't do it out here."

"Vacuums also create build-ups of residue in the corners," Hathem noted. "In the gascans, we had to remove the ceiling panels entirely and pull down each section of the ducts just to—"

Ank screamed from the sensory room, startling Salem. His spoon flipped end over end along the table, splattering a line of his bowl's contents along the smooth surface.

"I found it!" she yelled. The patter of her hands and feet against the frosty metal grew as she skittered through the twisting halls—a vigor no venth should have in such temperatures. "I found it!" she repeated eagerly in the common area. "I got a hit from the subspace sonar."

"Where is it?" Cejero asked.

"In subspace, duh," she joked; Cejero narrowed his eyes at her. "It left the next zone, Leire, at some point during the last circayd."

"Just as well," he said, pushing his bowl away. "We got nothing else from the colony."

"So, we go?"

"Do we have escape jumps prepared?" asked Olyké.

"Yup!"

"With a starshard in the final landing zone?"

"Yeah…" Ank hesitated. "I think so."

"What does that mean?"

"Well, it wasn't conclusive. *But*—there *is* a sizable shard in Leire, which we can grab now that the zone is unoccupied."

Olyké tilted her head back, deliberating. The crew watched her gaze at the low ceiling. Olyké rarely, if ever, made idle movements as most venth tended to do when emotional or focused. She was always still. Her entire body concentrated in sync.

"Screw it," she said to the roof panels. "Let's go now."

With reserved excitement, Ank nodded and scampered back to the sensory room to prepare their jump.

Olyké lowered her head; her eyes fell onto Salem.

"I want this one done as quickly as possible," she said. "Make sure you're suited up a hundred rotés before we land."

Helmet clutched under his arm, Salem waited by the pressure door for a dozen rotés before meandering back to his room. He lay on his bed, waiting for the ship to land, eyes gazing unfocused at the grey panels above.

He wondered what the mega shard would it look like. Would it be a sphere, like a deadworld, that he could walk around on? Would it be a different color? Something about it must surely be different to have allowed it to survive with so much mass.

In all of Salem's fantasizing about future paintings, he'd never even thought about starshards. He always drew landscapes. Imaginary ones, usually, sometimes an individual plant or ship or a monster from an old bedtime story, though Salem wasn't very good at drawing things like hands or faces. He could certainly paint a starshard, though. There were already drawings of them to give people an idea of what they were, but those were more like the schematics of Venthralli.

"Salem!" Plexie shouted, waking him. "Olyké says we're almost there."

"Oh…" Salem groaned, shifting over on his bed.

Plexie scrunched his face. "That's really gross, by the way."

"Huh?"

"Sleeping in your space suit."

Salem gazed around his room like he'd awakened in a new land. Lying in bed rarely resulted in sleep for Salem. Certainly not after a few rotés. It was a constant problem.

He rolled off the mattress and trotted back to the pressure door. The *Myzer* had returned to its typical, uncomfortable cold, made uncomfortably hot for Salem by lounging in his suit. He stumbled a step as the floor dipped beneath his feet.

They had arrived.

Once again, Salem waited with his helmet under his arm. It took a little time for Ank to relocate the shard and orient the *Myzer* accordingly. Plexie scampered off to the engine room to examine the post-jump diagnostics, returning to Salem a few rotés later.

"Alright, Ank says it's a few wheels away," he reported. "Negative fifteen and…" His face contorted. "Negative forty?"

"Got it," Salem said. The coordinates described the shard's relation to the pressure door: fifteen and forty were angles, with negatives being to the left and bottom, and a few wheels would use most or all of the cable that tethered Salem to the ship. The measurements were all approximate; the shards were moving, the ship was moving, though Ank was quite good at locking the ship's velocity with a shard's.

Salem grabbed a puff canister, lifting it a couple of times to be sure it was mostly full. He hopped into the pressure room and sealed his helmet down. The air tank's hiss began in sync with the cycling of the pressure room, and in complete silence, the exterior hatch slid open.

Nothingness.

It's all Salem ever saw when the door opened, but it always felt strange. Disorienting. As if reality itself had suddenly ended.

Moving himself towards the ground, he pressed his feet against the right side of the door frame and swung his body down below the floor, pushing off in the direction of the shard.

The cable's friction against the edge of the opening buzzed softly into his suit as he soared through the outside. The farther he got, the fainter the vibrations became. He angled his flashlight ahead, shining along his path on the off chance that he'd angled himself directly into the shard—a one in a million chance, but not worth gambling.

There was no visible beam from the flashlight, no lightening of dust in front of him, no landmarks to give him a sense of speed or angle. There was just darkness. His only guides for direction were the technique in which he'd launched himself from the ship and the tether pulling against him. He waved the beam of the lantern in a tight circle in front of him, his arm dimly outlined by the lights in his helmet. When the gentle circles hit their apex on the side closest to his face, he could sometimes see a weak glow from the material encasing the beam, a faint semicircle against the black, but nothing beyond that.

Salem had become excellent at estimating his travel speed, having kicked off the ship so many times while using the homing radar. Once he felt like he'd traveled a couple of wheels—twelve rotés later at eight or nine allos per roté—he slowed his separation from the ship with the puff canister.

Salem swung the light beam across the outside, searching for the small glint of the distant shard, but there was nothing. At this angle and distance from the *Myzer*, he couldn't even see a glow from the pressure room's pilot light when he looked back. Were he to stare long enough, he might be able to make out the thin line at the top edge of the doorway, but he would hit the end of the tether long before that happened.

Just as he was about to heat up the homing radar and ask Ank for a precise location, the frosted, translucent rock bounced some photons back at him. It was twenty allos away—close enough to the end of the line that Salem allowed it to snap taut naturally, sparing the wear on the gears that locked the spool in place when the tether was still coiled around it. He was careful not to lose his grip on the canister as the line tugged back at him.

Salem puffed himself towards the reflective surface. It grew slowly in his viewport, eventually filling up more space than his visor could capture. Its mass wasn't noteworthy, perhaps two trips' worth, but it was long. He'd have to cut at least twenty-four digits off the tip—half an allo—to fit the remainder into the fuel port.

This presented Salem with a dilemma common to the shard handling process: would he cut the shard here, or back at the ship? Transporting small pieces was usually more manageable—they fought less against changes in momentum—but they required more attention and time to get back. Losing control of a larger shard, however, often required more energy than was available with the gas on hand.

No risks, he reminded himself.

Vibrations ran through his hand when he activated the heat saw, its light blinding after thirty rotés of near-total darkness, the sound deafening after thirty rotés of near-total silence when he touched the readied blade to the side of the shard. Specs of frozen residue sprayed from its surface, vanishing against the outside. The loss of shard material from cutting always bothered him a little, even when he didn't consciously think about it. He repositioned the blade a few times, cutting from alternate angles to eventually meet in the middle.

Soon, he would be forced to decide how he wanted to haul the first half back. He'd gotten pretty good at moving two semi-chunks at once, pushing one towards the ship lightly and correcting it along the way as he hand-carried the other, but there was no reason to get fancy here. He had enough air to make sure each piece was—

"Salem," Olyké's voice came through fuzzy over the radio, obscured by reverberations in his suit.

There were a number of procedural updates that Salem generally didn't provide because they were boring and no one wanted to hear them, but he was supposed to be doing this by the book. And since the shape of this shard was going to double his collection time, Olyké was about to become very grumpy.

Whoops.

"Salem, do you receive?" she said.

Salem scrunched the plates between his eyes. "Yeah, sorry," he said, turning off the heat saw. "I'm at the shard, but I'm going to have to cut this in two, and I think—"

"Return to the ship, now."

Salem blinked at the glistening peak. "Huh?" he grunted. "But I'm actually ahead of—"

"Get back to the ship!" she shouted. The volume nearly caused Salem to drop the heat saw.

"It's back!" Ank yelled in the background. Salem's carapace stiffened: a physiological reaction venth had to fear.

Somehow, it had known.

The quarry beast had returned.

CHAPTER 9
BREACH

Every plate on Salem's body screamed for him to pull himself back to the ship. To scramble up the line attached to his suit as quickly as his arms would take him. It was the safest way to get back, but it wasn't the quickest, and at this distance, a faster start would compound itself nominally.

Fighting those instincts, he carefully pulled himself half an allo along the cable, stopping himself with the puff canister. He rotated perpendicular to the shard, the soles of his boots facing the icy jewel beneath him. His toes grazed its surface when he swung his feet.

"Salem?" Ank's voice quivered. "Salem? Are you there?"

"Yeah, hold on," he coughed.

Outside, the most reliable way to navigate back to the ship was to follow the cable. It was simple; intuitive. The homing radar was great for navigating deadworlds and useful for showing distances, but in the dark, three-dimensional landscape, it required a lot of trial and error to find the necessary angle of trajectory. Salem often forgot to bring the radar altogether.

With the briefest possible tap of the puff canister, he pushed himself down towards the shard. He allowed his legs to coil up, as if squatting on solid ground, and the combined mass of the two objects continued along, drifting ever so slowly away from the ship. He pointed the flashlight up along the cable, which extended off into darkness, disappearing four allos away.

Salem took a few beats to aim, already ten or fifteen allos behind where he would have been had he pulled himself along at the cable.

"Salem!?"

With a grunt, Salem pushed the shard away with all of his strength, rocketing his body toward the *Myzer*.

"I just sprang off the shard," he said. As he sailed along, the line immediately began drifting away: he was off target. He slammed his finger into the canister button, exhausting a long burst of gas to remain parallel to the tether. Once he felt that his trajectory was aligned with the metal cord, he stowed the flashlight, loosely gripping the pliant cable as it dragged along his fingers.

Soaring through the black with nothing in sight but the dim outline of his arm and the first eight digits of tether, Salem listened to the thin cable's instructions, adjusting his angle whenever it pressed against his hand. Multiple times, he changed his trajectory only to reverse it later, tricked by the curve of slack that had formed from the kinetic friction of his glove. He prayed that the puff canister would last until he returned. He couldn't properly gauge its weight without gravity; waving it around really only told him if it was low. At some point, it would simply stop working.

"We have to leave in ten," Ank said dejectedly, meaning that in ten rotés she would have to maneuver the ship to evade the quarry beast, at which point Salem would be pulled in tow and killed instantly.

If he was lucky.

Just after the ten-roté timer began, a faint, vertical line materialized before Salem. The side frame of the pressure door, dimly lit by the indicator light inside, was well above his trajectory. The cable began dragging upward against his fingers; a sound like ripping canvas swelled up into his suit. He gave the canister a couple of quick jets, correcting his path leisurely towards the doorway.

Another roté of soaring towards the *Myzer* and the outline of the pressure room became sharper—a phantom square whose walls Salem had yet to make out. He was still too low, but far enough to be able to correct it with a small spurt, allowing him the rest of the can to slow at his destination.

He held the button down for a beat. The force of the canister pressed against his hand for an instant, like a small creature jumping off his palm.

His direction didn't change.

He tried again, bracing his arm against the pressure of the can, but there was none to brace against—no resulting thrust, no muffled *pfft* crawling up his sleeve.

The can was out.

Careening towards the underside of the *Myzer*, Salem pressed the button as far in as it could go, ready to break the mechanism entirely. He tried again. He shook the can vigorously, which sometimes helped, but the effect went unchanged. He chucked the can at the ship, starved for any negative momentum he could get, but the resulting sway was insignificant.

The doorway moved high above his peripheral, signaling his imminent collision with the ship. He braced himself for the impact, his only sense of speed being the cable rubbing against his gloved fingers. He had to remain conscious to pull himself to the pressure room.

Flicking the lantern on, he raised the beam ahead, towards the *Myzer*. He waited for its alloy to capture small flecks of light and throw them back to him, so he could time his impact.

It wasn't there.

Another beat, moments from impact. It still wasn't there.

The outline of the pressure room disappeared above him. The cable pulled roughly towards it.

Salem wasn't about to collide with the *Myzer's* floor…

He was going to pass underneath it entirely.

With no time to think, Salem tightened his grip. The pliable cable pressed down against his index finger, collecting slack in front of him, but only for a moment. The line tightened, whipping Salem up towards the ship's underbelly.

He sped along the arc, jaw clenched as he fought to keep his hand around the cable. His body pulled against his arm, threatening to rip itself from the joint. Agony jutted along his elbow plates to his shoulder socket. All he could think about was holding on.

The flashlight slipped from his other hand, spinning away like an alarm meant for nobody but him and the quarry beast. Maybe it would chase after the light? Maybe this was the moment they learned that quarry beasts loved spinning lanterns? Nobody had probably—

Salem crashed into the underside of the *Myzer* faster than he'd ever traveled in his life. The breath in his lungs was knocked free, his insides battered, and the last thing he saw through his cracked visor was the strobing light of the lantern, floating off to join the dying cosmos.

Then his fingers released the cable.

Ank's plates were stiff. Her body wanted to tremble. It certainly would have if not for the rigidity of her outer shell. For that, she was grateful. She didn't want to appear nervous in front of Olyké. For Olyké to think her ill-fit to pilot their nigh evasion.

Not that Salem was being afforded any extra time by having Ank at the controls. Were it up to Ank, she would wait another two rotés, but that's because Ank knew she could surely pilot around the un-venth at that distance. But it wasn't up to Ank, it was up to Olyké, and Olyké didn't know how good Ank was at inner-zone navigation, yet. Not really.

In training, Ank and the other would-be navigators often played a strategy game designed to exercise and condition their brains. The game was played in three dimensions, along various two-dimensional grids and up and down between them. Ank knew how to control one board from another, how to lure people into a column when she desired.

Ank beat everyone, always.

She beat the algorithms, always.

Ank was queen.

Without noticing, Ank tapped her finger against her thumb. They hadn't heard a word from Salem since he'd kicked off the shard. Twelve rotés of deafening silence.

Salem was more clever than he believed. Most venth would have scrambled up the line, which was only natural, but it contained a problematic velocity limit when weightless. One could only climb arm-over-arm so fast. Once they were traveling around six allos per roté, seven at the most, they couldn't pull on the cable any faster, and attempting to do so would likely slow them down from the friction of the grab. That would, in turn, add extra slack, making later pulls less effective. It also wobbled the return course back and forth, adding further—

Thump.

A deep, obscured sound pulsed through the radio. Salem had done something, or something had changed. Ank assumed he'd bumped into the ship, and since she hadn't heard a similar *thump* near the sensory room, he was probably somewhere closer to the pressure door. That was good, because in a little over five rotés, Olyké would tell Ank to evade the un-venth, and then Ank would kill Salem.

"Salem, what's going on?" she said, trying to keep her voice steady. The way Olyké would.

No response came.

Ank waited a couple of beats, anxiously tapping her four parallel fingers to their opponent before she tried again.

"Salem?"

No response.

He might just be focused. Doing whatever it was he needed to do to get inside the pressure room and close the door. Usually, if Ank called multiple times, he would respond. Even just a word to tell her that he was fine or busy.

"Salem!" she yelled. "Can you hear me?"

No cough, no groan.

Ank stifled a whimper. Something had gone wrong, and as the timer neared zero, part of her hoped she didn't hear from Salem again. At least then she could wonder, even convince herself, that Salem had been dead before she'd moved the ship. She wouldn't be able to handle hearing him respond right before she moved the ship, hearing the snap in the background as his radio went silent, spending her entire life knowing what she'd done, hearing the sound of his broken carapace every beat she was alone.

"Salem!" Ank cried. She looked at Olyké. The ship lead's face was a husk, blank and stoic, a carapacial mask she used to make life-and-death decisions. It was something Ank could never do.

Ank checked the un-venth's distance.

Four rotés left.

Tick, tick.

Someone tapped on Salem's visor, drawing him awake. Only Ank or Plexie would do such a thing. Hathem would gently rock his shoulder. Cejero would say his name quietly until he finally woke. Olyké would yell it for a quicker response. As a matter of fact, so would Plexie, so it must be Ank tapping on his face, amused that he'd fallen asleep in his suit. He could hear her crying with laughter, saying his name.

His helmet strobed. The dim indicator light within was amplified rhythmically whenever the departing lantern pointed towards him.

Crack.

The break in Salem's visor was larger than when he'd collided with the *Myzer's* hull. The periodic ticking of the spreading fracture had become a timer for the weakening material, slowly breaking under the pressures of the outside.

Rather, its lack of pressures.

But the ship was still here, though, yet to snap Salem in half. It hadn't moved away from the approaching quarry beast.

"My helmet's broken," he said, not completely sure why he decided to tell the others. They couldn't do anything about it. There was something Salem wanted to know, but he couldn't think…

"Oh, no," Ank said unsteadily. "Salem, we need to leave in four rotés. You have to hurry!"

The lantern had flown too far to illuminate the ship's hull, so all Salem knew was that the metal was not a few digits in front of him. He waved his arms around in the darkness, searching for the underside of the ship, but his limbs swung freely.

He'd bounced away.

Panicked, he lashed his arms more, fruitlessly trying to rotate his body without a puff canister. Something grabbed him, squeezing the pit of his elbow. A fat, metal worm.

With both hands, Salem grabbed the cable and pulled himself along.

He didn't move.

He sped up the motion, but served only to spool more of the cable nearby.

Salem checked to make sure he wasn't pulling at the end connected to his suit—the length of cable that ran down towards the shard, away from the *Myzer*—but he wasn't. It was definitely the portion that he'd grabbed earlier, which ran directly to the spool.

With fervor, he pulled at it again, waiting for the slack to tighten and allow him to move along, but it didn't.

Somehow, the cable had been severed from the ship.

There was no way for Salem to get himself—

Wrong way!

Fumbling with the tangled mess he'd accumulated, Salem pulled himself along the same portion of the cable, but in the opposite direction—towards the pressure door. He soared along the cable, holding his hand loosely around the line to prevent building up more slack. When he started to float away, he pulled himself back along, bouncing his suit against the hull towards the cable's fulcrum.

Tick, tick…tick, tick…

Reaching the lip below the pressure door, Salem's body continued past the corner. He squeezed down on the cable, allowing the remaining length to swing him up over the door in a large arc. He didn't dare try to choke up on the rope.

Just as he'd hit the bottom of the ship, Salem slammed face-first into the hull twenty digits above the pressure door.

Csshh—tssss.

Splintering lines spread across his visor, clear in the reflected light of the pressure room. A small piece was abducted by the vacuum, glinting farewell as it flew off into the darkness. Behind it, filtering through the hole in Salem's tattered helmet, went his air.

The roar of the gale cushioned the high-pitched whistle created by the narrow opening, like someone had put a steam machine inside his helmet. And much like the sting of steam, the cold stabbed at Salem's face through the wind—so cold it felt hot. Every moment, the air vacated faster. The *crunch* of his weakening helmet became more frequent.

"I'm almost at the door!" Salem shouted over the forsaking gasses. He dragged himself down to the opening, exhausting his nutrient-starved lungs. Hands out, he coasted into the floor of the pressure room, cushioning his impact to prevent further damage to his visor. He righted himself, lunging at the lever for the exterior hatch. His fingers vised around the metal handle…

He paused.

Something told him not to pull the lever. Something in the back of his mind. At any moment, the rest of his visor could be pulled into the outside, freezing his eyes and boiling his insides. The *Myzer* might roll away from the quarry beast, splattering him into the wall, or worse, throwing him out of the pressure room to be snapped in half by the cable.

The cable!

Salem hadn't triggered the remote re-spool because it would have taken too long to pull him back. Now, three wheels' worth of the thin, metal line hung out of the pressure room door. It wouldn't close, and the pressure room wouldn't cycle.

Salem cursed himself. He would have had substantially less cable to collect right now if he'd started the re-spool. Hand over hand, he pulled the cable into the pressure room and threw it helter-skelter into the corner. The *hiss* of his vacating air began to dim; he could feel the lenses of his eyes pulling away.

It was going to take too long. Even if he could gather the entire cable before Ank moved the *Myzer*, which he certainly couldn't, his suit wouldn't hold for that long.

Salem yanked the heat saw off of his belt with so much vigor that it nearly flew away from him. His carapace stiffened for an instant, and he flailed to regain control of the device. Salem didn't know if the heat saw would work on the tether. Starshards required very little heat to melt through, but the saws were also capable of cutting through rock, although slowly.

White-blue light flared up from the line, brighter than anything Salem had seen before: brighter than cutting through rock, brighter than looking into the reactor. He screamed and turned his head towards the dark corner of the pressure room, but the image of melting metal was burned into his eyes, pain like being stabbed in the lens with a pick. Reflexively, he tried to hold his hand to his eyes for comfort, slapping his palm against the visor of his suit and sending another splinter of glass off into the pressure room.

Every breath Salem took was a fight against the pressure loss to pull air inside his body. He pressed the saw down blindly, only mildly aware that he was whining audibly through the agony. The silver-grey walls of the pressure room were vivid, their surfaces tinted blue from the light of the melting cable. For a full roté, Salem pressed the saw into the cable. Ank said something, but over the dying whoosh of his air supply and the searing of the cable, he couldn't hear her.

Then, finally, the sound stopped. His hand pressed through and struck the floor beneath.

He dropped the saw, allowing it to float wherever it pleased, and kicked the broken end of the cable out of the pressure room. Frantically, he unhooked the clasp on his suit, grabbed the tangled ball of cabling behind him, and chucked it out the door in a similar manner to how he'd coiled it.

Throwing himself at the wall, he planted his feet and shoved the handle upward.

"I'm in!" he cried over the *thunk* of the closing door. The room became black, the white image of burning cable branded in the center of his vision, and the ground pulled down on him. The gentle whistling of his suit air became consumed by the rush of the pumps, normalizing the pressure room to the rest of the ship.

The floor underneath his boots lurched, sending him stumbling into the opposite wall. He slid down to the floor, clawing to remove his helmet and toss it aside. He pressed his palm desperately against his eye, crying alone in the darkened pressure room.

CHAPTER 10
STRANGE MATTER

Deja vu struck Salem repeatedly as Hathem bandaged his eyes. Both of his ocular casings had been damaged from the flash burn, one considerably more than the other.

"This eye has seen better circayds," Hathem said with a grimace. She wrapped a flexible bandage around Salem's head to hold a restorative salve in place on his eye. "But, it's seen worse, too."

"It can't see anything, now."

"That's just the bandage. It will heal fine."

One of Salem's eyes was only half covered, giving him some visibility. Venth eyes were larger in proportion to their heads than any bug in the garden or extinct species on record, and their heads were large, themselves, so wrapping even part of an eye required a lot of bandaging.

Hathem unwrapped part of the soft material around his head, then rewrapped it. "Next time you plan on cutting through alloy with a heat instrument, you should perhaps use a blackout helmet."

"I wasn't planning on doing that."

"I know, Salem. I was just trying to lighten the mood." She took a heavy breath, carefully layering the cloth on itself. "That was very clever thinking out there."

"Thanks."

She looked to the door. "Do you need something, Plexie?"

"No," the mechanic said, obscured to Salem in the peripherals of his fully bandaged eye. "I just...don't really know what to do now."

"I don't think there's much any of us can do at the moment," Hathem replied calmly. She tucked the bandage firmly into itself behind Salem's head. "Alright, you know the routine," she told him. "Keep that on until I tell you to remove it."

"I will, thank you." Salem spun on the examination bench toward the door. The top half of Plexie slid into view. "Are we going to have enough fuel for two jumps?" he asked.

"Barely. Ank tried to find a shard before we left, but we had to go so quickly, she couldn't." Plexie sighed. "Hopefully, she can find one between jumps. We're going to pass the anchor shard."

"It's Ank; she'll find one," Salem said matter-of-factly. "We can probably jump back to the anchor shard, too."

"Maybe…" Plexie looked down at his feet. Or the floor. Salem couldn't tell.

"Something else going on?"

"Well…" he droned. "I guess some of the tests she uses to find stuff outside will change depending on weird factors, and…she's pretty sure this is the same quarry beast as last time. Whatever Olyké called it."

"Relentless Bastard? But why would it even be over here?" asked Salem. Hobblecob was in a different direction than the *Myzer* had traveled this excursion. Salem didn't know the exact angles and distances, but it had to be at least twenty jumps away. Maybe twice that.

Plexie shrugged. "I dunno, but…two jumps might not work, you know? And turning back for the anchor shard won't be safe, either."

"Right…" Salem said. He, too, looked at the ground, obscured by the dark bandage.

"I'm sure we'll prepare a heat-strip if necessary," Hathem said with her back turned. She placed the remaining medical supplies from Salem's treatment back into their homes. "Until then, there's nothing to gain by dwelling."

"It's hard not to think about."

"Even if this outside creature hounds us as it did before, I believe in Ank's ability to land us beside a shard, just as I believe in Salem's ability to get the ship fueled before the engine is ready and Plexie's ability to keep that engine strong." She smiled, as if they were merely experiencing a social hiccup that all young venth encountered. "Go do something recreational. Play a game."

"We're not hatchies," Plexie grumbled.

"You don't have to be a hatchling to play a game," Hathem said. She shooed them out of the medical office. "Go do something you enjoy, and believe in Olyké to let you know when there's something you are needed for."

Plexie laughed. If there was one thing they could believe in, it was that the colony administrator wouldn't let them sit around when there was work to be done.

Amidst the cosmic silence, while the *Myzer's* engines cooled into their second evasion jump, Ank scraped up the location of a low-mass shard within range of their estimated fuel reserves. As meticulously as possible, she calculated the jump during the time available, aiming to land within spool distance of the shard.

Due to the lack of velocity data from afar, navigators usually didn't consider landing within that sort of proximity, but Ank seemed to believe she could approximate that information. If she was successful, and the small shard didn't require any cutting to fit it into the reactor, Salem could actually get it refined before the engine cooled off. They weren't entirely certain that the beast in their wake was Relentless Bastard, but if it was, expediting a third jump could be the deciding factor in the creature's pursuit or forfeiture. For all they knew, escaping it could be as simple as a three-jump evasion.

Despite Hathem's suggestion, Salem and Plexie did not play a game during their flight. Salem didn't draw anything. Cejero didn't tell them about anything he'd read. They all rested quietly, not unlike a circayd of meditation. The second jump took them past the excursion limit. It should have been a momentous occasion, but they were all too tired and scared to celebrate. They had been on the *Myzer* for twenty-seven circayds, and because of the convoluted path along which they'd traversed, they weren't even a quarter of the way done. It was the longest Salem had ever been on a ship, including the time they were stranded.

Unable to sleep that evening, Salem wandered around the halls of the *Myzer*. Strolling through the areas he rarely visited helped him feel less confined; it gave him the sense of being elsewhere. The effect was pronounced by the bandages over his eyes, which made everything darker and more difficult to discern.

After a hundred rotés, he found himself in one of the storage rooms looking at scattered containers of varying shapes and sizes. A surprising number of them were labeled poorly. Or in a way that was difficult to see.

Reminded of their last excursion, Salem walked leisurely to storage three, where the creature had punctured the hull, and checked out the repairs. There wasn't much exterior hull in the *Myzer's* smallest storage room, just a single section opposite the door. It was barely wider than the pressure room, curving slightly inward on its way up to the ceiling.

It took Salem three rotés to find the six-digit-long gash near the floor of the far corner. The damage was barely visible; the engineers in the docking spiral had done a fantastic job.

They always did. Repairing the exterior of an energy collector was a top priority task.

Quarry beast arms were always described as long scythes that reaped the inhabitants of a ship, but Salem didn't know how wide they were supposed to be. It seemed like the tear had been big, and he wondered if the limb had punctured through into the next room.

Careful to avoid waking anyone, Salem shifted a few boxes in the chilly air of storage three. With the side wall no longer obscured, he lowered his head close, his half-covered eye digits from the wall as he looked up and down the smooth surface.

It seemed normal.

Salem stood up, bored, and gazed across the various containers in the cramped room, feet planted as he rotated his torso around.

There were even fewer crates labeled in here. He doubted whether anybody on board actually knew what each box contained. Perhaps it would be beneficial for him to open each crate and see what was inside. There could be something useful for their travels that none of them knew about.

No, Olyké would certainly get upset. And some of the crates were marked for scientific supplies, so Cejero would get annoyed, too. Plexie would be disappointed if Salem couldn't find anything exciting or interesting. He also might be the person who knew exactly what every container held. In fact, as Salem thought about it, it seemed likely that many of these boxes contained engineering parts. Obscure components for fixing the *Myzer* that were unlikely to be used.

Sidling between the wall and the stack of boxes he had moved, Salem made his way out of the corner, leaving the boxes where they were. There had been no clear organization, and they were in more or less the same locations as when he'd entered.

Salem stopped.

His foot hovered digits from the ground.

He'd nearly stepped on something. An item that had fallen out of one of the containers he had moved. With Salem's luck, it would have been something fragile. Or valuable.

It was both.

Feet together, forehead scrunched, Salem stared at the item, head tilted to see it above the bandage line. Perhaps it was sleeplessness, or prolonged confinement on the ship, but he found himself struggling to rationalize what it was.

He blinked, the refocusing less impactful with three-quarters of his ocular shells covered in bandages.

Is that…?

He didn't quite know what it was, but at the same time, in a general sense, he knew exactly what it was…and it was important. It might even be useful to them.

Salem closed his eyes for a couple of beats, cutting the light from his lenses entirely before reopening them.

It was still there—peaceful, dangerous.

And exposed.

Salem ran back around the crates, along the far corner, and out of the storage area.

He needed a real adult.

Eyes pressed together, Cejero tilted his head to the side, then back the other way, observing the item from a different angle.

His shoulders clenched.

"Holy shit…"

"You can say that again," mumbled Olyké, standing by the far wall with her arms folded. She watched the science officer examine the small spike on the floor of storage three.

"Holy shit!" he said again. He fanned his arms out, stepping back from the alien material. "Hathem, we need a—"

"I'm on it," the doctor replied. She jogged slowly past Salem, back through the corridors of the *Myzer*.

Olyké scrunched her nostrils. "Maybe we should leave the room?"

"Definitely," Cejero agreed. He exited the storage room with the ship admin, waiting near Salem in the hallway. "It had to have broken off during the attack," he said, "which means we've already been exposed to it for nearly a set, so we should be alright. And airborne pathogens aren't likely to spread in these temperatures, so the risk of contactless contamination is low. Were I to heat the specimen up—"

"It's part of a *quarry beast*, Cejero. They *live* in the outside."

"It is presumably part of a quarry beast," he corrected. "The point of the apparent break is dark magenta, almost brown, much like a synthetic oil. It could be a part from a tool that the spiral engineers use, or a mutated plant ration that was left here. We

won't know until I can examine it, which I can't do until we have
—"

"We're all here," Hathem called from down the corridor. She returned with safety equipment for handling biological materials; the last two members of their crew followed in tow.

"I can't believe you weren't going to tell us!" Ank wailed.

Olyké wrangled the three young venth in the corridor, forcing them to stand far back while Cejero and Hathem dealt with the potential contaminant. "You are all waiting back here," she said. "Understood?"

They nodded, disappointed, and watched from afar.

Salem had always believed the hunters to be indestructible. That's what everyone always said about them. Finding a broken piece of venthhound—if that's what this really was…

Salem might get a medal.

"What do you suppose it might be?" Cejero asked through his mask. He wrapped the spike carefully in a synthetic film. "It seems likely that it's part of their arms. A tine or quill. Like the leg hairs on bugs."

"Perhaps a tip," she said. "Something that could break off."

"Yeah…" Cejero grunted. He rotated the pick curiously in front of his eyes as he folded the film around it again. "That's what's strange, though. Nothing like this was described on the dead one they autopsied—or, tried to autopsy—and absolutely nothing on that specimen could be broken or cut through."

"With shipboard tools," Hathem said.

"That is true…"

"And we know that jet bursts cause it pain."

"That is also true…"

With the remnant wrapped, Cejero placed it into a sealable container and set it off to the side. It was a small spike, a digit long and yellow-green in color, quite similar to venth blood, only a little greener. It was also pale, or its color had faded in death.

"Perhaps this is a different type of quarry beast," Hathem said casually, as if it were a fun logic exercise. "It displayed heightened capabilities when it hunted us last excursion. Perhaps it's a different breed: less durable and more aware."

"Entirely possible," Cejero said. "We've only visibly examined the one." He began scraping the floor where the blood-colored stick had been, pulling all of its particles into a sterile bag. "I keep thinking about what Rello told us—about the *Domodo* wreckage."

"That crossed my mind as well."

"I checked that report to see if there was any indication of genetic material found on the ship, and there was none. In fact, there was surprisingly little information in that regard."

"Is that uncommon?"

"Those reports actually tend to be quite overindulgent. It's a common joke among S.O.'s that salvage reports include unrelated details like missing rations because the reporting science officer wants to appear thorough or clever. Still, it would be easy to overlook a bare entry as laziness or pragmatism, and given what Rello said, it does make me wonder."

The two venth spread multiple chemicals along the floor to kill any remaining cells or viruses not already collected into various specimen containers.

"Specifically," Cejero continued, "I wonder if this remnant came from inside the quarry beast. We know nothing about their interior anatomy. Rather than a different breed, it could simply be a common aspect of their interior morphology that's vastly different from our own."

"Something that could be broken."

"Yes."

They picked up the specimen cases and walked back through the corridor with Olyké, the younger venth following eagerly behind. Ank skittered in bursts up to Cejero's heels, pausing for a beat to give him more space before catching up quickly again.

"However, the third-hand information about the salve in the *Domodo* has me thinking of something more familiar to us," Cejero said. "Like a tongue or tooth."

"A tongue that reaches into ships?" Ank asked. "And licks up venth? Getting spit all over the place?"

"Perhaps." Cejero removed his mask. "With tines like these to prevent shards or prey from slipping away."

Ank scrunched her face. "Ewww," she groaned. She stood up, matching their pace on her back legs.

"Should we head back to the anchor shard?" Cejero asked Olyké.

"I'm considering it."

"I think it would be safer to go forward," Ank said. "We know the anchor shard is in the natural range of this ultra-observant unventh, and finding shards past the excursion limit will be much easier, so—"

"We may not be continuing the excursion, Ank."

"What?!"

"At the very least, we should go back within the excursion limit," Cejero said. "To see what the colony wants us to do."

Olyké stopped at the bend by the crew bunks. "And for that," she said, "the anchor shard is a good grab." She looked at the container in Cejero's hands. "I *am* hesitant to send that information to the colony without knowing if this is actually from a zero beast or not. Can you verify that on board?"

Cejero considered the question for a beat. "Not specifically if it's from a quarry beast. We don't know their genetic make-up."

"And this could be from the *other* creature that punched a hole in our ship," joked Plexie.

Olyké spun on her heel, glaring straight through him.

"I did *not* request engineering input," she scolded. Plexie's plates seized with a jolt. Olyké looked between the three younger venth. "Not another word from any of you or you'll be confined to your bunks for the circayd. Am I clear?"

They all nodded quietly. Plexie looked at his feet.

"It should be easy enough to determine if it's biological," Cejero continued. "Unless its genetic makeup differs so significantly from Venthrallian life that it appears mineral-like."

"Any chance of finding out more?" Olyké asked.

Cejero shrugged. "No clue—probably. Simply cutting through part of this would tell us something, but I presume you're asking about biohazards? Or what might harm it?"

"Yes."

"No clue."

"Figure out what you can before we land. I don't want to double back on the hunter and end up without enough time to chunk off part of that anchor shard all because of a warped tuber."

Plexie squeaked and covered his mouth. Eyes bulging, he looked at Olyké, then raised his hand meekly.

"Go ahead, Plexie."

"Well, it's just that…we never figured out why this quarry beast's senses are better than others. Maybe it can…I don't know… smell the spike or something?"

"It can't," said Cejero.

"Do we *know* that? I'm just saying that, with how narrowly we're escaping everything, maybe it's safer to just…get rid of it?" He looked at Olyké, who, to his credit, seemed to consider his proposal.

"Absolutely not," Cejero scoffed. He shook his head in disbelief. "This could tell us how to repel the quarry beasts. Even *kill* them! We're not going to 'get rid of it.'"

"Well, it's not your decision, is it?"

"Actually, it is," Cejero said. "Bio takes jurisdiction when alien material is involved. In this situation, I supersede Olyké."

Plexie looked to their colony admin, who simply nodded in confirmation. Salem had never heard of this dynamic before, but he'd also never found an alien body part. It sort of made sense.

"For now," Olyké said, "we need to focus on the immediate issues: figuring out what this fragment is, lining up jump options in both directions, and getting this next shard collection done as quickly as possible. If we get stranded outside the excursion limit in a zero beast's range, it won't matter what's on board."

Cejero and Hathem took the specimen containers to the science office, and the rest of the crew returned to their bunks to try to get some sleep before they landed.

Salem didn't sleep, of course. He lay awake in bed, remembering every detail he could of the tongue tine he'd found, practicing for the circayd in which he would try to paint it from memory.

CHAPTER 11
Unbeaten Paths

A trail of foamy, chartreuse blood dripped out of Dwill's severed arm, which remained clinging to Brackesh's own. She swatted futilely at it, her groans the only remaining sound after the storage room's depressurization on the other side of the closed bulkhead. Eventually, she broke the grip of Dwill's necrotic fingers, and his forearm landed on the ground beside her.

With the round vial of acid in hand, Brackesh rushed through the corridor, sprinting around the sharp curve near the engine room. Around the blind turn, she nearly ran into Prito, standing by the open bulkhead with their mechanic, Lyth.

"Part of it's by the reactor door," Lyth explained. "There's some kind of wiping sound inside, and creaking in the floor panels." Her head swiveled down each corridor. "Where's Dwill?"

Still catching her breath, Brackesh shook her head. She couldn't bring herself to explain what had happened. To describe the reaper's scythe that had torn their can apart, or the *Domodo* crushing clean through a venth's carapace.

Lyth's eyes fell to Brackesh's leg, wet with the sputtering blood of Dwill's arm.

"Did you find it?" Prito asked.

Brackesh held up the plastic orb, its contents already softening at the edges where her hand gripped. "We need something to melt it quickly," she huffed.

Lyth gestured with her welding flame. "Will this melt the vial, also?"

"Yes, but it'll have to do." Brackesh held the vial up to her eyes, gripping the protruding cap with her thumb and forefinger. She rotated it to examine its state. "When we're ready, I think we can just hold it—"

With a *crash*, the hatch to the reactor flew up into the ceiling, bouncing roughly onto the engine room's floor. Instead of the usual orange glow, there was darkness, and from that darkness emerged a long, pink tendril, slimy and hot, like a narrow cone that bent every which way.

It was the actual flesh of a zero beast, the thing of nightmares, here inside the *Domodo*.

Brackesh recoiled back from the engine room, stunned by the sight. Lyth stepped through the bulkhead quickly, striking the torch igniter a couple of times until a narrow, blue flame appeared. The creature's tongue slithered along the wall of the reactor, leaving a disgusting, translucent-white film along the floor.

The tendril touched the opposite edge of the room an allo away, then swept blindly across, smacking into Lyth and pinning her against the wall just inside the doorway. Brackesh could feel the heat exuding from the beast's appendage, smell its stench. She wanted to run inside and pull Lyth away, but her legs were locked in place. She could see Dwill's arm clutched between her hands as it was crushed underneath the door.

Then the beast let Lyth go. The slimy tongue inexplicably pulled away, leaving the mechanic free to run.

Without hesitation, she took the opportunity. The creature's tongue retracted back towards the hatch from which it came, just far enough to pass behind Lyth. She made a single stride toward the door before the tongue darted forward, skewering through her stomach.

Prito called out to the mechanic, who looked down languidly at the bloody, wet cone emerging from her torso. The tip of the prehensile tongue hooked around her, whipping her up into the ceiling. The welding torch jumped out of her hand, bouncing off the metal paneling above. The shadow of her body, suspended on the tendril, danced along the wall in blue light.

Before the torch hit the ground, the tongue disappeared, pulling Lyth back through the broken hatch. The welding tool landed in a nauseating trail of blood and saliva, which bubbled underneath its flame.

If the *Myzer* landed where Ank believed it would, the shard would be right beside the hull. All Salem would have to do is go out and nudge it, and the ship would be on its way as soon as the engines cooled down.

Suit on, Salem lingered by the pressure door. Ank's mismatched helmet hung by his side, less worn than his own had been even before its visor was shattered across the outside. She wasn't likely to need it until they got back. And if she did, it meant they had bigger problems.

Salem shuffled lazily towards the spool that held their last cable, guided to its faint outline by his uncovered eye. His hand extended out to grab the end of the line dangling down from the coil.

His fingers never found the cable. The *Myzer* launched upward, throwing Salem headfirst into the ceiling and back to the floor. Ank's helmet rolled across the ground, white lights flashed across Salem's eyes—both of them—and although he had never been ejected in such a way, his initial thought wasn't to wonder what had happened, nor to acknowledge the sharp pain searing through the top of his scalp during each heartbeat.

At least I wasn't wearing the visor, he thought. They couldn't afford to lose a second one.

Salem groped blindly around the pressure room for the dropped headwear. Olyké and Plexie wailed in pain nearby as they recovered from the event, then Olyké's footsteps thumped away towards the sensory room.

"What just happened?" Salem called out. He got to his feet and ran after her, stumbling a step in dizziness before taking off towards the sensory room. His head throbbed with every step, and by the time he reached the helm, his carapace was clammy from the insulated material.

Ank sat in front of one of the information readouts, shell plates shaking as Olyké stood hunched over her shoulder.

"I'm sorry!" she cried.

"Did we hit something?" asked Salem. He shifted his suit to rest evenly on his shoulders.

"No," Olyké said flatly. "We ran out of fuel—"

"I thought we had enough!" Ank whimpered.

"—and that's what happens when you get bucked out of subspace. The reactor softens the transition, but if you have no fuel…" She skittered around Ank to check another panel, eyes darting across its information. "Then it can't do that."

"But that all happens at the very end of the trip, right?" Salem asked. His voice cracked. "So we're not in between—"

More footsteps approached from behind. Cejero's voice bounced through the corridor ahead of him. "Did we reach the zone?"

Olyké lingered a beat before answering. "Maybe…"

Cejero's body stiffened. "What does 'maybe' mean? Are we in the medium or not?"

"Just hold on!" Ank said, punching at the controls.

Most of the universe, including all of the space between zones, was filled with a chaotic energy called the arcane medium. Really, it was more accurate to say that zones were areas of its absence. Ships were tossed around in unpredictable ways by the medium. *Incalculable* ways. And since their instruments and sensors didn't work properly, either, it wasn't just difficult to move through; it was impossible to jump out of. Ships like the *Myzer* spent as much time and effort as they did calculating trajectories because messing up a jump could cause a ship to vanish forever.

Physical matter that wound up inside the arcane medium would eventually be pushed into a nearby zone, but it happened over the course of eons. That was why starshards and deadworlds had all ended up in the zones, and why sinkholes, which were far stronger than the medium's forces, were more likely to be in the medium, which occupied most of the space in the universe.

A ship arriving just outside of a zone would take cycles to be pushed into navigable space. In the rare event that a ship's momentum was still on the right course, there was a chance it could drift into the zone over the course of several circayds or sets. However, transitioning from subspace to real space usually altered a ship's momentum vector—the speed and direction in which it traveled—and the arcane medium altered it constantly, which made that outcome unlikely. Technically, it was also possible for a ship to limp into the zone on its engines, but with no means of navigation from within, that also required the ship to emerge on its original vector—which the crew would have no way to confirm—and then be piloted forward into the zone before its heading was altered too much by the harassment of the medium.

Both of those scenarios were flukes. Most likely, the vessel would reappear generations later as a ghost ship.

Thankfully, ships used additional fuel at the beginning and end of each jump, so a small error in their estimation typically caused a ship to drop inside the zone at the wrong location or on the wrong trajectory. Ending up in the arcane medium required a huge mistake, or several large ones compounded.

"Is that really possible?" Salem asked Cejero quietly so as not to disturb Ank while she worked. "That they missed the zone?"

"Unfortunately, yes," he said, his face hollow. "There's no way to prepare coordinate information for jumps out here like we do in the colony, so the variance is extremely high."

"Variance?"

Cejero watched Ank for half a roté as she shut down an entire suite of sensors. "Jump calculations are approximations," he explained. "We have outlines for most of the zones within the excursion limit, now, so we know exactly where they begin and end. The accuracy of each depends on the age of their most recent scans, so before every excursion, we generate more accurate parameters for the zones we might end up in. If Plexie makes a really bad fuel estimation and Ank makes a really bad consumption estimation, we'll still land near our target because the coordinate data is so accurate."

Ank flicked one of the same switches off, waited, then turned it back on.

"Out here," Cejero said, "it's based entirely on what Ank gathers en route, as we're traveling. That provides less leniency."

"Do you think she can pilot us in?" Salem asked. "If we're not in the zone, that is." He hoped to learn that there was a special piloting technique that few venth could master, but would allow a ship to be piloted through the medium, because if there was, Ank could probably do it.

"Well, we're out of fuel," Cejero said. "So, no."

Salem frowned. He'd already forgotten that part of their situation. There were too many problems to keep track of.

"But nobody can pilot through the medium," Cejero noted. "It's not a matter of skill. The medium is a nonlinear field of probabilities, and Venthralli doesn't possess the means to collect the data needed to approximate them."

"We can see!" Ank cheered. "We're in!"

Cejero's entire body softened. "Well, that's a relief," he said. "How fast are we moving?"

"Very."

"Too fast to grab that shard?"

"Definitely."

"Okay…" He slinked past Salem into the sensory room. "Plexie thinks we can use the rotation jets for that."

"But we're out of fuel…" Ank moaned. Salem began to feel the desperation in full force. Every possible solution was hindered by one of the other problems. Salem couldn't do anything about them, not unless they could get close to the shard.

"The jets don't have to use the reactor's power matrix," said Cejero. Salem blinked.

That was true.

"He's right," Olyké nodded. She turned quickly to Ank. "Turn off all non-essential systems, now. Lower the heat and life support..."

"Okay."

"Lights. Gravity. Everything."

It was an obscure fact about their ship that Salem had long ago learned and forgotten. The reactor generated all of the *Myzer's* energy, and because it *could* power the jets directly, it did. That was just common sense. If you used the capacitors to power the landing jets, you'd just recharge them with the reactor, anyway, which created unnecessary energy loss.

That functionality meant they could power the jets with the same pool of energy as their life support systems.

The flats of Ank's fingers slammed into the controls, depleting the *Myzer's* energy expenditures. The sensory room plummeted into darkness, dimly lit by faint, multicolored indicators from its various instruments. A series of small, yellow-green pilot lights lined the corridor behind Salem. With one eye covered, it might as well have been pitch black. Then, the pressure on his feet softened.

"Get us belly-forward," Olyké said, "then run the jet until we're at critical power."

Ank angled the *Myzer* up, as if cushioning the ship's landing against a deadworld that wasn't there, and slowed. Simon's legs buckled, the pressure worse than on Venthia 5. After a couple of rotés of continuous strain, he lowered himself to all fours to relieve the pressure on his legs: a position made all the more uncomfortable by his suit.

"Go ahead and kill the gravity," Olyké said, pressing her arms into the top of the chair beside her. It took Ank a while to deactivate the ship's gravity altogether. There were safety measures in place to prevent that, just as if someone were to completely shut off the heat or air. You also couldn't close off gravity to one area like you could with a vent, so any change was shipwide.

The change in force was barely noticeable to Salem—he'd had ten grubs piled on top of him and one had been pulled off. The *Myzer* braked harder than any landing or docking in Salem's career, and for a lot longer, too. By fifty rotés, he was lying flat, his carapace slick from the heat.

Another hundred rotés later, the crew's exhale clouds became entirely opaque, making Salem thankful for the cumbersome, venth-shaped incubator around him. His face was chilly in the air. His chest stung with every frigid breath.

"It's so cold!" Ank wailed from her seat.

Cejero's teeth chattered. "You can s-s-say that again."

"It's so coooold!"

"It does appear that the quarry beast didn't f-follow us," he said. "Which could indicate a number of v-very exciting things."

"Like what?" Salem asked.

"Later," said Olyké. "We need to get this shard before we all frost over." Her silhouette turned to Salem in the darkness. "You did a mobile handle once, didn't you?"

"Yeah," Salem wheezed from the ground. During his first contribution cycle, he had collected a shard that was moving at a much different speed than the ship. Mobile handles required a shard handler to go outside early and push themselves ahead of the ship, affording them enough time to match their speed to the passing shard's. They'd bring a second cable to wrap snugly around the shard, then speed themselves up as fast as they could to reduce the impact of the ship pulling the tethers on the backswing. At that point, the shard would be dragged along with the ship in near-lockstep and could be cut normally. The velocity differential had to be small; otherwise, the handler wouldn't have enough time to match the shard's speed and fasten it before it was gone.

Not if they wanted to live through the tether snap, at least.

Olyké leaned close to one of the displays, her face basked in dim orange. "We're almost at critical power. These jets are burning through the electron backup. What's our relative speed?"

Ank read off one of the displays, "Sixty-four point five allos per roté."

"Is that slow enough?" Olyké asked Salem.

"I think so…"

"Cut the jets now. Get the work lighting on. Keep the heat off."

The pressure on Salem's body stopped. Wearily, he stood up, and his feet drifted away from the floor. He had forgotten that the gravity was completely off.

More lights came on, enough to illuminate the rooms for work purposes. Salem reached out and grabbed the top of the newly visible doorway to steady himself.

Olyké rechecked some of the panels. "We're coasting at fifty-six, Salem. Get to the pressure door."

"Okay…"

Salem pulled himself through the door and sailed down the halls to the pressure room, pushing himself faster whenever he drifted close enough to a wall. He was sad he wouldn't get to hear what Cejero thought he'd learned about the quarry beasts. He probably didn't need to get ready this quickly. He would likely spend the next hundred rotés hovering by the pressure door, just waiting for the shard to get nearer.

Still, the shift from doom to bloom was delightfully unexpected. They weren't in the medium, they could collect the shard they'd come for, and their evasion had worked.

And why shouldn't it have worked? Ank thought this quarry beast *might* have been Relentless Bastard because it looked similar in whatever sensors she had used. Maybe they were just related—a common gene donor or something. They could call this one "Apathetic Jackass."

Arby and AJ, Salem giggled to himself.

As he'd expected, he spent sixty rotés floating near the lever in the pressure room while the *Myzer* got close enough for him to go outside and begin the mobile handle.

He launched himself ahead of the *Myzer*, which was directly downward, below the floor. A dozen rotés later, when he reached the cable's end, he allowed it to pull taut, slowing him to match the *Myzer's* speed. There was a slight bounce, so he gave himself a short puff to stay as far ahead as possible.

Every time Ank's voice came over the radio, Salem's heart sped up, certain it was the call where she told him that Arby—Relentless Bastard—was back, but it never was. She just kept reminding him that she was cold and wanted him to hurry so that they could turn the heat back up.

The 56-allo-per-roté difference between the two objects made the mobile handle somewhat rushed, further complicated by Salem having destroyed the other tether.

Using two puff canisters, he accelerated himself away from the shard for a roté, reducing the difference in their velocities by fifteen or twenty allos per roté. Then, he allowed the shard to hit him, matching their trajectories, as well as slowing the shard in relation to the ship a little—maybe one or two apr. It didn't feel great, but it gave him over five rotés to tie his cable slack around the shard before the ship towed it.

Normally, Salem would leave the shard to be pulled by the second cable, accelerating himself as fast as possible so that, when the ship finally pulled him along, there wouldn't be much force. This time around, he was connected to the shard, which was far too heavy for him to speed up in the time available.

Salem placed himself in front of the shard, his belief being that, rather than being pulled at full speed, he would first be thrown forward by the shard, speeding him up before the cable yanked him along—the portion that connected him to the shard. That way, rather than one impact at fifty-five apr, he would have two impacts at around thirty.

Unfortunately, those impacts ended up being more like twenty and fifty. When the tether pulled the shard along, Salem glanced off to the side, thrown diagonally compared to the *Myzer's* path. That didn't soften the second blow much, and when the cable pulled on him directly, it hurt.

A lot.

However, those were oddities that Salem had expected before he'd left the *Myzer*. Much to his surprise, his first collection past the excursion limit went exactly as planned: smooth, without unforeseen problems.

After spending some time checking for signs of the quarry beast back in the excursion limit, and for shards farther away, Ank, Cejero, and Olyké decided that getting farther from the creature's domain was their safest bet, rather than trying to double back.

So, with a couple of jumps' worth of gel in the tank—and a few more waiting in the next zone—the *Myzer* carved its way forward through the unexplored outside. No contact with Venthralli. No rescues.

They were on their own.

Shards were more plentiful past the excursion limit, which was indicative of how thoroughly the zones within Talesk-Venthralli's sensor range had been scoured.

The colony had limited information about the zones the *Myzer* now traveled. They'd ruled out the possibility of other colonies like Venthralli, as well as full, proper stars, but nothing could be gleaned about shards or deadworlds. That might change in the near future, with the methods Ank had used to locate the mega shard, but it wasn't available to them now. The only data they had was what Ank gathered herself. Similarly, the only information she had available to plot jumps with was collected in real time. As the *Myzer* pressed into the unknown, Ank periodically idled the ship for a circayd or two while identifying their best leads. After their near-miss with the arcane medium, they had no intention of rushing their coordinate calculations without good cause.

Ank's diligent work didn't come without its perks. When the Rubble Dusters bestowed names onto the anthropomorphized celestial bodies they disturbed, it was strictly for their own amusement, to pass the time. It wasn't recognized or recorded by any colonial agency. The names Ank assigned to the zones in which they traveled, however, were very much permanent. A fact she enjoyed quite a bit.

After idling for two circayds in the zone officially recognized as "Clickbug Frenzy," Salem had become unbearably bored. He sat at the table in the common area, staring passively at a half-eaten brick of rations, lost in thought about the murals he might one circayd paint. Hathem sat beside him, cataloging something with a marker and pad. Olyké and Plexie ate their rations leisurely, whereas Cejero scarfed his down like they might be his last.

He gazed at the empty table, as if another serving might appear before him, then turned his head up to the rest of them. "I have developed my leading theory," he said. "If anyone is interested."

"On what?" Olyké droned between bites.

"On this persistent quarry beast we've found ourselves entangled with, and, in turn, the un-venth as a whole."

"Wait! I want to hear!" Ank shouted from down the hall. Her footsteps pattered along the cold floor like a wonky gear. The sound swelled until she arrived beside the table. "Did you say 'un-venth?'"

"Yes."

Her face ignited. "Yay!" she cheered, looking eagerly for a space to sit before finally squeezing between Salem and Hathem. "Okay…" she said. "Continue."

"Given that we're fairly certain this was the same quarry beast that we encountered at Hobblecob, the question arises—why were two jumps suitable this time?"

"We didn't have a light shard," answered Salem.

"We considered that possibility last time, yes, but we haven't had a light shard at any point during this trip, including when the beast turned around to hunt us down. There's no plausible reason for a quarry beast to suddenly zag back between zones with no quarry in sight. They're roamers."

"But Relentless Bastard has super senses, right?" asked Ank. "It can see through subspace or something."

"Until it can't, and that's the quandary. It followed us through five jumps last time, so why only one this time?" He lifted his hands in question to everyone, obviously in possession of what he believed to be the answer.

"I think they're not the same," Salem said, giving the half-hearted guess he'd made circayds before. "They're related, and that's why they look the same, but this one's not as keen."

"Think back to when we burned the light shard. What else happened?"

"We jumped," Ank said.

"And then?"

"Hmm..." she pressed her lips together in thought, then gasped, eyes wide. "Oh! We got stranded!"

"We got stranded."

"And we were stranded this time!"

"Yes."

"What would that imply?" asked Olyké.

"That it senses the active reactor."

"Interesting..."

"*Specifically* the reactor," he clarified, "because we didn't actually run out of fuel last time, right? We just didn't have enough to jump anywhere. The capacitors, the sub-reserves, the distribution systems...everything in the reactor's power matrix was running..."

"But we ran the reactor dry exiting subspace," Olyké said. "The engines were dead." She folded up the wrapper of her finished ration brick. "You said this hypothesis might pertain to zero beasts as a whole?"

"It is significantly less likely for an organism to mutate an entirely new sensation than it is to acutely improve an existing one. Like Salem said...this beast certainly has keener senses, but there's no reason to believe it somehow hunts *differently* than others of its kind. It's simply better at it."

Hathem quietly set the marker down in front of her. "That fact might be of use for us out here," she said. "If we find ourselves in a situation where this quarry beast—"

"Relentless Bastard," Salem said.

"Whatever its name is—"

"*Relentless Bastard!*" Plexie insisted.

"Settle down, boys—if this *or any* outside creature pursues us out here as Relentless Bastard has, heat-stripping is not a viable option because we won't be rescued." She pressed her hand against the carapace near her shoulder, popping the space between the plates. Cejero scrunched his face. "But, we could preemptively siphon heat gel into shard boxes, then run through the remainder by jumping. The engine won't be scattered across the zone, and we can put the gel back into the reactor once we're safe."

"Putting refined gel into a shard box is not recommended," Plexie said. "You'd have to open the box and let the contents liquify before pouring, which will corrode the inside. Especially if you're pouring carefully."

"Then we should make sure it doesn't come to that," Olyké said, "by making each jump count."

She turned to look at Ank. The young navigator stared back blankly for a moment.

"Alright..." she groaned, slinking off the bench and lumbering back to the sensory room.

The *Myzer* further distanced itself from the excursion limit, retrieving Ank's second anchor shard without abnormal crises.

Even after the ship was filled to the brim, it spent a third of its journey idling, synthetic eyes open to the universe. Their fuel supply was comfortable, but that didn't negate their need to find the most lucrative zones as they traveled.

Cejero stood by a specimen table, temporarily ignoring the blood-colored spike resting on its side. With little else to do as the ship traveled, he had spent a considerable portion of the last thirty-four circayds in the science office. The alien material was certainly the most pressing task for him, though he didn't think there was much for them to learn that would aid them in the short term.

After confirming that the specimen was, in fact, alien biomaterial, he had considered turning the ship back to the excursion limit. Legally, he could have invoked Article 25, taken control of the *Myzer*, and done whatever he believed necessary in light of the situation. He still could, if he really wanted to. The Bio Board didn't trust the Panel's ship administrators to accurately assess the large-scale ramifications of cellular threats, let alone dictate the necessary steps to contain them. If there was a disagreement over biohazards, a ship's S.O. had the final word.

In other words, Cejero was the person responsible for placing the survival of their species over the survival of his crewmates.

Thankfully, Olyké was more likely to make that call than many science officers, and there was no doubt in his mind that she would heed any warning or suggestion he made pertaining to his expertise. Cejero didn't want control of the *Myzer*. He didn't want to make those sorts of decisions.

He also didn't think going back to the excursion limit would have been the right call. On an intellectual level, the alien material was probably the most notable discovery in hundreds of cycles, but on a practical level, the near-infinite source of fuel was more beneficial to the colony.

With the flat side of a knife's edge, Cejero scraped some particles of blood from the torn end of the spike. His heart raced. It was easily the most dangerous action he'd ever taken in his life: inviting particulates of alien biomaterial into the air.

Multiple dishes of fluids sat on the adjacent counter, filled with particles from the last scrape he had made. One had turned blue a couple of circayds ago, the significance of which he was still consulting chemical texts for. Some of the residue from the outside of the spike, which had not yet appeared anywhere inside of it, sat on the microscope lens. The substance was consistent with dried or frozen saliva, adding a little evidence to the "tongue tine" theory, though it would also imply that the creature's saliva was secreted from elsewhere.

It could also be a tooth, which inspired frightening imagery.

The only results Cejero had found so far were simple, but significant nonetheless. The alien material could be damaged by lab equipment—which, if it was indeed part of a quarry beast, was incredible. There were also notable similarities and variances to venth anatomy, such as the overall structure of the spike's carapace and lack of an internal skeletal structure. Nothing so far that would change their future, like a volatile reaction to sodium or anything.

Cejero set the knife down and collected the particulates into a tube, sealing it closed. From behind him, the door opened, followed by Hathem's voice.

"What did you need, Cejero?"

"Mask," he said. "And close the door, please." He recognized that closing the door didn't provide much safety on a ship, since everything was connected by their life support systems. It was still a good practice. "I've come to realize," he explained, "that, over the cycles, I've lost some of my edge with this sort of work, so I'd like a second opinion."

"That only gets worse as time goes on," she said with a smile. She connected the mask ties behind her head, one up between her eyes and over the top, the others around her cheeks.

Cejero led Hathem to a dish of xenomaterial on the side counter. She looked over the parchment beside it, which was covered in notes documenting the timing of various reactions.

Once upon a time, Cejero had done quite a bit of biological research. He preferred it to geology, but what he preferred most of all was adventuring through the outside, and to do that, he'd had to switch to geology. A good science officer was versatile, though, and

Cejero enjoyed studying a variety of topics, but what he needed to know about most were minerals: the elements that would be on a deadworld. His primary task was to survey and identify rare materials that Venthralli required to continue functioning.

It was…monotonous.

And now that Cejero was faced with an epic, story-like scientific investigation—the studying of a never-before-seen alien fragment, recently living, while completely isolated from the colony—he had come to realize that it had been nearly five cycles since he'd done any real research.

Fortunately, Hathem was also versed in biology.

"Lab work isn't my forte," she hummed pleasantly. "But this might suggest that the cellular metabolism is slow. Very slow."

"That was my take."

She leaned back from the sheet. "Fascinating."

"Yes," he agreed. "Especially if this is indeed from a quarry beast. We think of them as constant roamers, but maybe they're not. Maybe they hibernate for long periods of time and only mobilize when certain criteria are met."

"Or maybe the act of traversing outside isn't energy-intensive for them."

"Yeah, maybe…" Cejero droned. He stared at the small, chartreuse fragment.

Hathem stared at him for a moment. "Was that all?" she asked lightly.

"Huh?" he grunted, looking up from the spike. "Oh, yes. Thank you. It hasn't been easy figuring out the meaning of a lot of these results."

"I can imagine," she said, depositing her mask in the sterilization receptacle by the door. "Probably more interesting than a bag of dirt."

"Quite a bit."

Hathem left the science office, leaving Cejero to sterilize the metal surface of blood shavings. He put the remainder of the cleaning block away, then checked around the office to see if there was anything to tidy up before he left.

His eyes fell again on the unusual biomaterial.

Something about the spike had started to feel off, recently, but he couldn't figure out what. Nothing from the examinations or tests, specifically. Just when he looked at it. He could see every little bump on the carapace, the frayed, frosted blood on the end—like the spike had become so clear and vivid that it appeared fake. The way words sometimes sounded after you heard them too much.

And that's probably all it was. His mind wanted desperately to identify a bizarre, xenological phenomenon, where he'd simply spent too much time looking at a strange object.

Anything else would be ridiculous.

CHAPTER 12
NEGATIVE INFLUENCES

Sixty-five circayds had passed, and they were still far from their destination. And whenever they did finally reach it, they would only be halfway done, though their return should be quicker if the mega shard fills the *Myzer's* belly to the brim.

Salem stared at a piece of paper in front of him, crispy from another bout of decreased heat in the ship: the new norm while they loitered.

Why is there a hand here? he asked himself.

On the page was a hand, but not one drawn by Salem. He never drew people; he was no good at it. The hand was simple and sloppy, like a grub had carelessly traced the hand of an adult venth.

Salem peered at the edge of the hand. It did look like his line work, but he was sure he hadn't drawn it.

He *had* been sketching, but he'd been drawing...a bug?

A plant?

Something from Venthralli. To help remind everyone of home. As he thought about it, though, he couldn't actually remember drawing anything like that at all...

Not much was known about the illness that had killed Salem's gene donor. They didn't even know if it could be carried to Salem, but the possibility was enough to remove him from the donor list. All Salem knew was that it was deadly, and it had made his gene donor act strangely before he'd succumbed to it.

What "strange" meant, Salem had never truly known.

His breathing deepened. His blood surged. Pressure swelled in his head, blurring his thoughts. Somehow, he just knew...

This is it, he thought. *It's happening to me, too.*

Salem looked at the paper. The crudely drawn fingers almost seemed to wiggle at him. In fact, they very much did appear to wiggle. If Salem hadn't known it to be impossible, he would have believed it to be happening.

How old had his gene donor been when his illness finally took him? Ten? Eleven?

Roughly Salem's age…

Salem spilled out of his bunk and into the icy halls of the *Myzer*, falling to the ground. He pressed himself up, straining to breathe or think. His head felt like a puff canister without a button.

A deep, rumbling voice pressed outward to his skull.

"You aren't sick…" it said. *"Not yet."*

It wasn't his voice. It wasn't even sound. Salem heard it as clearly as if someone were standing beside him, but with none of the physical vibrations. Just pressure.

"What's going on…?" he said quietly. He looked around the hallway, down to the pressure room, as if something would stand out. Nothing seemed off about the *Myzer*. Nothing to explain the hidden voice.

"You and I…" the voice growled, *"are connected…now."*

Salem wheeled backwards into his room, tripping over the edge of the door frame. He clawed his way onto the bed and turned to sit up against the wall. His carapace was hot and clammy, melting the bed underneath him. He scooched to the side to check. To figure out how it was melting.

It wasn't. It was just wet from the heat.

Everything was normal.

"Not normal," croaked the voice. *"Not for you…not for I."*

Struggling to force his own voice out, Salem choked on his words.

"Who—" he squeaked to himself. To nobody. "Who are you?"

"You…know."

He gasped. The pressure in his head swelled without relief, leaking out the bottoms of his eyes as melted water would.

"R–Relentless…Bastard?"

"Relentless…yes."

"Salem?" Plexie's voice preceded his entrance to Salem's room. He found Salem on his bed, sitting with his feet curled up to his stomach. "Hey, what have you been up to?"

Salem struggled to comprehend Plexie's words. They sounded strange, somehow. "I've…" he said. "I've been drawing." He pointed to the hand lying on the floor.

Plexie picked up the parchment, squinting one eye at the drawing. "Salem, you've been in here all circayd."

"All circayd?"

"What is…circayd?" Relentless Bastard asked. Salem did his best to ignore it. To understand the words of the venth in front of him.

"Yeah," Plexie said. "I thought you were sleeping or something."

"Maybe…" rasped Salem. "I don't remember much of the circayd."

"Circayd—your time."

Plexie stared at Salem. "Maybe you should go see Hathem," he said, gently placing the drawing at the edge of Salem's bed.

The pressure waxed and waned in Salem's scalp, rhythmically, like a song of endless brutality. He stood from the bed, legs shaking slightly. "Yeah…" he mumbled. "Can always…see the doctor."

"Yes," the soundless voice croaked. *"Show me your medicines."*

"No!" Salem shouted, holding his hand up. Plexie jolted at the sudden yelp, his entire face taken up by his eyes. Salem tried to even his voice, to ward off Plexie's suspicion. "I'm…I'm fine," he said. "I'm just…sick."

Plexie leaped backwards through the door, yelling, "That's not fine, Salem! You need to go see Hathem right now! What if you infect everybody?"

"Hathem…" the voice graveled.

"Shut up!" Salem snapped. He didn't want Arby to learn about the venth. Not because of his thoughts. He wouldn't let himself be the reason.

"Don't be mean," Plexie said, wheels away. "I'm just trying to help."

Salem waved Plexie off. "Not you," he said.

The mechanic's face drained, like he had just watched Salem set fire to the garden.

"Then…who, Salem?"

"Nobody," Salem mumbled. He spun around, hoping to somehow turn away from Relentless Bastard's mind games. "It's no body."

"Salem, calm down."

"No, buddy…nibodnnin…"

The pressure in Salem's head burst. A blistering pain fired down his forehead, between his eyes, and the room disappeared.

Streaks of grey crossed Salem's field of vision. Dark, but grey. The lines were jagged, stretching as far to the side as he could see. Beneath them was more grey, but lighter in color. And smooth. Like metal plating.

It *was* metal plating.

He was in Hathem's office.

Again…

Probing the bandage around his head, Salem sat up. A groan escaped his mouth; his forehead pulsed beneath the wrap. Moments later, Hathem returned, ducking her head beneath the doorway to pass her towering figure through.

"Hey, grubbo," she greeted. "How do you feel?"

"Bad."

"You hit your head pretty hard. What happened?"

"I…don't remember," Salem strained. It was all so fuzzy. Had he been sick? He seemed to remember something about—

Relentless Bastard.

Salem shot off the table; his legs buckled underneath him. The creature had wanted to see the medical offices, and now he was here.

"Whoa, hold on there," Hathem cooed, steadying him upright. "You need to rest."

"I can't be in here."

"Why not?"

"It'll see."

"What will see?" Hathem asked casually. She cuffed her hand around his arm and guided him back to the examination table. Salem took in a deep breath, ready to answer, but silenced himself.

Hathem lowered her chin, staring at the uncovered part of his eye. "Salem," she said sternly, "tell me."

She wouldn't believe him. She didn't know what the quarry beasts were capable of. None of them knew.

"I need to talk to Cejero," he finally said.

"You can't."

"I have to!"

He started to rise again and Hathem placed her hand on his stomach, pushing him down onto the table.

"Don't make me restrain you, Salem."

"Then let me talk to Cejero!" he yelled.

"He's resting," she said. "He had an accident."

Salem stopped struggling and looked up at Hathem. "What do you mean?" he asked. "What kind of accident?"

"He's suffering from outside sickness," she said, removing her hand from his carapace. She lowered herself into a chair across from the exam table and leaned back. "He cut off one of his fingers."

"What?" Salem said. His voice squeaked. "Why?"

"Because that's what outside sickness does," she said. She leaned forward. "Delirium, disorientation, hallucinations, memory lapses, paranoia, mania, panic..." Her eyes narrowed on Salem. "Is any of this sounding familiar to you?"

He looked at his knee plates. "Some of it..."

"Do you remember talking with me about quarry beasts earlier in the circayd?"

"No."

"I don't imagine you would, but you spoke of them a lot. What do you need to talk with Cejero about so badly?"

Salem tried to recall his conversation with Relentless Bastard. He didn't intentionally omit anything, but it was difficult to remember it all. As Hathem probed further, he recalled the drawing. It all sounded like the symptoms she had listed.

"But that doesn't mean it's not Arby," Salem insisted. "We don't know how it communicates."

Hathem frowned. "You named it?"

"Olyké did. Relentless Bastard: R.B."

"Gotcha—well, I can tell you that people have spent their entire lives attempting to communicate with zero beasts, using every conceivable method, including forms of mind linking. It's not possible. We send them hails every time we do an evasion jump, just in case they *might* be ships of creatures who haven't decrypted them until now." She looked at him intently. "Do you know what *is* possible? And well documented?"

"Hm?"

"Auditory hallucinations from outside sickness," she said. "Did the zero beast tell you anything that you didn't know prior?"

"It wants to learn about our medicine."

"That's paranoia."

Salem nodded. He looked at the ground sadly. "So it's my fault, then? I'm the reason Cejero was hurt?"

"What in the—" Hathem shook her head vigorously. "How did you arrive at *that* notion?"

"Well, we aren't going on deadworlds, really," he said. "I'm the only one going outside, so it had to have come back with me, right?"

"No, Salem..." Her shoulders dropped. "Outside sickness isn't a virus or pathogen. It's a psychological ailment that causes physiological symptoms."

"What do you mean?"

"It's from being isolated for so long. Stress hormones are flooding your body for extended periods of time, usually resulting in sleeplessness, which then creates more stress hormones. It's something your brain creates naturally; you're just producing more than your body can handle. Historically, it only affected frontier explorers who became stranded for extreme amounts of time, hence the name. We've been separated from the colony longer than any ships in modern cycles, and under very extreme circumstances. Did you sleep at all last circayd?"

"I don't think so."

"I'm not surprised," Hathem smiled. "You just slept for six *thousand* rotés in my office."

"Really?"

"Really." She tilted her head to the side, her smile fading away. "Do you hear it now?" she asked. "Relentless Bastard?"

Salem shook his head.

"You seem engaged in our conversation. Are you having trouble focusing?"

"Not really."

"That's good."

Hathem turned to the shelf behind her and opened a thick, armored box. She removed a needle and closed the lid, switching its heavy lock over. "It's just about time for bed," she said, "and I reckon you won't be able to sleep now that you've just woken." She held the needle up. "This is something that will make you sleep without fail."

"That exists?"

"It does, but we rarely use it. The resources are scarce, and more importantly, it's dangerous. You're going to have to sleep here so I can monitor your vital signs. I know it's not the most comfortable setup, but you won't notice while you're out." She took a deep breath, smiling again as she leaned over Salem. "Any other questions?"

"Yeah—why was there pressure in my head?"

"Well, the hormones are in your brain, and they use blood to move around, so that's one possibility. It could also have been a hallucination of its own. They're typically auditory or visual, but not necessarily." She pointed the syringe at the bandage around his forehead. "That's from hitting your head after falling unconscious."

"Right..."

Hathem waited for a moment to see if Salem had anything else to ask before she drugged him. He'd never been given a needle before, except perhaps when he was too young to remember, and he didn't like it one bit. Hathem heated the tip of the syringe first, allowing it to more easily puncture the lining underneath Salem's carapace when pressed between his plates. He could only rue the pain in his side for an instant, and then he was asleep again.

Wild dreams skipped through Salem's mind as he slept under the influence of the medication: Ank locking herself in her room because Salem was sick—because everyone was sick; Relentless Bastard floating inside Salem's head and living there; Olyké praising him for being the best shard handler in the colony. Every degree of good, bad, and strange, all without prior context. When Salem awoke, he'd nearly forgotten them all, reduced to obscure feelings in the back of his mind. He tried to grab them as they fled, realizing that he never dreamed when he slept. Not in any way he could remember.

The bandage on his forehead had been removed during his sleep. A wire had been stuck to his stomach carapace that led to a box with a purple light on it. He removed the connector from himself, jiggling it a bit to unstick it.

Salem felt...

Amazing.

Rested, energetic...

Is this what everyone feels like after they sleep?

With a bounce in his step, Salem left the medical office. He found Hathem and Ank in the common area. It seemed early in the circayd.

"Good waking," said Hathem. "How are you feeling?"

"Better still, thank you."

"I got it, too," Ank said. Salem scrunched his forehead; there was a tinge where he'd bumped it. "Outside sickness," she clarified.

"You did?"

"Yeah. Not as bad as you or Cejero. I heard you both were sick, and I thought everyone was going to get infected and die, so I locked myself in my quarters."

"I thought I dreamed that."

"Nope! That was real Ank!"

"Everyone needs to start reducing the amount of time they spend alone," Hathem said matter-of-factly. "It is not in our nature to be isolated from the colony for so long, and adding individual solitude for extended periods of time will only make matters worse. I know it's not ideal with how much time we already spend confined together, but we don't have a colony of people. We only have each other."

"How's Cejero?" Salem asked.

"He'll be alright. He's up and about somewhere."

"He was examining that alien spike," Ank said excitedly, like she was telling Salem the plot of a new play, "and thought it was coming back to life to attack him. Then he tried to kill it, but thought his hand was a part of it."

"Wow."

"Right?! And the pain didn't stop him because he assumed it was from the spike attacking him."

"He wins the medal for 'most extreme case.'"

Ca-chunk.

The floor bounced. The lights dimmed. The comforting hum of the engines disappeared.

"What, now?" Hathem gazed over her shoulder, calling down the hall. "Plexie?!"

"Are we out of fuel again?" Salem asked.

"We can't be," Ank said. "We had at *least* five jumps' worth after we landed here. We've barely moved since."

Olyké burst into the common area, continuing through to the opposite corridor, down towards the engine room.

"Damnit, Plexie!" she yelled. "What's going on?" Cejero followed shortly after, hand wrapped in a frosty, chartreuse-soaked bandage.

Salem and Ank looked at each other, then sprang up and scurried down to the engine room. Plexie's voice reached them before they rounded the last corner, alleviating Salem's fear that something terrible had happened to him.

It had happened to all of them.

"We can't!" the engineer yelled. Tears fell down to his mouth.

"Tell us *exactly* what you did, Plex."

"You don't understand. You don't!" he cried. "We can't bring it back with us!"

The engine room was almost as dark as the rest of the ship, lit by the concentration of lights coming from the machines. They were all the wrong colors; bad colors. A bloody, yellow-green.

Olyké screeched, *"What did you do to my ship, Plexie!?"*

"I didn't do anything to the ship!"

"Then what the hell is going on?"

"Oh, shit..." uttered Cejero. His eyes gazed across the same blood-chartreuse lights. *"Shit!"* he shouted, turning to Plexie. "Why?!"

The mechanic fell to the floor, crying. "Because...it'll get back to Venthralli."

Somehow, Salem knew exactly what Plexie feared: that an unventh had somehow gotten into the ship, and planned to smuggle itself back to the colony.

He helped Plexie up, patting his carapace as Hathem arrived to check on him.

Olyké watched Cejero examine the machines, hesitating before asking, "What is it?"

The words dripped out of the science officer's mouth. "He jettisoned the fuel…" he said despondently, "and…disassembled the reactor's power matrix. That's why we're on auxiliary power."

Fury rose in Olyké's eyes in a way that Salem had seen exactly once before. She spun on her heels and charged at Plexie. Hathem released the sobbing mechanic, leaving Salem to support his weight, and used her massive shell to block the ship lead.

"Olyké, leave him," Hathem said.

"I want him confined to his room."

"No. That's why he's ill in the first place."

"He can recover back in Venthralli."

"We won't get back to Venthralli without him. And you won't be able to lock him anywhere, Olyké. He's a mechanic."

"Then tie him up," Olyké said. "We can't have a saboteur jeopardizing the crew."

"I'm not a saboteur!" cried Plexie. "I did it to save the colony!"

"We know, grub," Hathem consoled him; her eyes remained on Olyké.

Olyké's face rested into its usual state of determination, abandoning her attack on Plexie. "Keep an eye on him then. We need to get that fuel back into the ship."

"That might not be possible," droned Cejero. "It didn't leak out; it was jettisoned. Refined gel is too hot to freeze immediately upon exposure to zero-Syrolac temperatures, so it'll separate first, causing it to be spread across the zone as a powder. Collecting even half a chunk's worth would take more than our collective air tanks."

"Then we'll recycle the tanks."

He grimaced. "The tanks recycle through the suits…it's not part of the infrastructure. It *has* to be powered by the reactor matrix."

Olyké clicked her teeth together, mentally listing their solutions.

"We should definitely check," Cejero added. "We might have gotten lucky with the splash. Just…maintain expectations."

"Alright," Olyké nodded. "In the meantime, Ank, get to the helm—find us *anything* in the zone we can feed the tank."

"No!" Hathem snapped. "Nobody but you or I should be alone. And even then, only when *absolutely* necessary."

Salem had never heard Hathem speak to the ship lead like that. For her to bark orders at Olyké in that manner, it had to be something serious: essential for the crew's survival.

Olyké must have come to the same realization, or she was afraid of Hathem.

She inhaled deeply, shoulders bobbing. "Why only you and I?"

"Males produce more of the hormones that cause outside sickness, making them more susceptible, and all venth produce less as they age. If you need Ank to find us a shard—"

"*Of course* she needs to find us a shard!"

"—then two people need to go with her. We should stay in a full group as often as possible, and in groups of three on all other occasions."

"Even when we pee?" asked Salem.

"A few rotés is fine, we just need to minimize our total amount of isolation. Going forward, we should all sleep in the common area, as well."

"Fine," Olyké grunted. "Salem, go with Ank. I'll be there after we take Plexie to the medical offices. Cejero, can you figure out how to reverse what was done in here?"

Cejero looked around the engine room, tapping a finger from his uninjured hand to his chin. "I don't know," he bit his lower lip. "Plexie's the only one who really knows these systems."

"We'll have to stick to pairs for now. We need to find a shard, reconnect the engine, and get Plexie to medical, and none of that can be deprioritized."

Blessing the three-pairs plan, Hathem took Plexie to the medical office and gave him the same drug that Salem had taken the circayd before. Salem left with Ank so she could find more fuel, leaving Olyké in the engine room to watch over Cejero.

For over two thousand rotés, Salem sat quietly in the sensory room while Ank used the instruments at her disposal. The room was dim and cold once again, their power limited.

The eerie silence was eventually broken by Olyké, arriving beaten and exhausted, fingers stained with stale oil. She fell into the chair opposite Salem and closed her eyes.

"What have you found?" she exhaled, rolling her head backwards.

Ank tapped her fingers on one of the readouts, like it might suddenly provide more information, but it didn't. She dropped her head into her hands, body shaking, and pressed the flat sides of her fingers into her scalp.

"Nothing," she squeaked. Her voice fought to escape her throat. "There's nothing here."

CHAPTER 13
STRANDED

For circayds on end, Ank scoured the zone for starshards, examining each pixel of their surroundings with the fastidiousness of an energy expense auditor. Anything larger than a chair would give the *Myzer* a short jump that could, in turn, take them to a more bountiful zone.

Salem tried to collect as much of the powdered fuel as he could, opening a shard box and pushing it through the densest cloud of material underneath the *Myzer*. Spotting a shard outside was difficult enough on its own. In a powdered form, it was impossible. Most of the gel cloud had already spread past the cable's range. And with how meticulous the process was of angling the opened shard box and moving it without spilling any of the powder already inside, Salem didn't recollect much by the end of his air tank. Enough to cover the loss of the pressure room usage, but only by the raw numbers. They wouldn't be able to get all of the residue out of the box and into the reactor, let alone start the power matrix.

If Salem and Hathem both went outside—one tethered, one relying solely on puff canisters—and used all of their remaining air tanks, they might be able to collect enough fuel to pour into the reactor. The reactor would process the already-refined gel quickly, and they could then start the ship. It wouldn't be enough to jump to another zone, but it might be enough to jump partway. Then, if they were lucky, they would get kicked out of subspace into the arcane medium on a trajectory that would cause the *Myzer* to be pushed into another zone before their life support failed, at which point they might be near enough to a shard to get moving again.

It wasn't their preferred option.

Salem had suggested using that same fuel to turn on the reactor and replenish the air tanks while he scooped up more fuel, but Ank had said the attrition would be too high.

For the first few circayds, they traveled in pairs. Salem was always the person to be switched elsewhere in order to balance their groups, because Salem didn't really have anywhere to be. He sat in the engine room while Cejero tried to undo whatever Plexie had done. He helped Cejero as an "added two" from time to time, but Cejero mostly just stared at the different machines, then made a change, shook his head, and changed it back.

After Cejero and Olyké both failed repeatedly to fix the *Myzer's* engine, Olyké finally agreed to let Plexie back into the engine room. Hathem was there to make sure he remained healthy and spot the early signs of outside sickness. At least, that's what she claimed. Salem reckoned the real reason was that she didn't trust Olyké around Plexie, but he kept that thought to himself.

The implementation of their safety groups didn't affect Salem much. Rather than passing time by drawing in his bunk or the common area, he drew in the sensory room with Ank and Cejero. The common area was littered with bedding, like a bunch of grubs had been given a deck to themselves without supervision. The oils that secreted onto their shells had iced over, their photon-hungry eyes strained to see through the scarce lighting.

For a crew already suffering from outside sickness, it was a dangerous situation to live in.

Seven circayds in, Salem sat against the wall of the sensory room, hunched over while he practiced drawing the light shard. He had decided it was his highest priority for painting when they returned home, but, unfortunately, the most remarkable thing about a light shard was its glow, the beauty of which Salem couldn't seem to capture justly with a pen.

He crumpled up the page and tossed it aside. The sphere of paper bounced up into the corner, slowly descending through the *Myzer's* reduced gravity to the ground beside an identical ball of discarded parchment. He leaned back against the wall of the quiet sensory room, deciding to take a break from his doodling. There wasn't much parchment left in the helm, and Salem didn't know how long it would be until he could go get more.

"Hey, Cejero?" he said.

"Hmm?" the Science Officer grunted. His focus remained on the tome in his hand.

"Do you know how quarry beasts talk to each other?"

"Is this about the voice you heard?"

Salem shifted. "Hathem told you about that?"

"Yes," Cejero said. He set down the bound document, noticing Salem's discomfort. "Salem, I understand." He held up his half-finger, the end of which now consisted of a flat carapace that appeared melted. "She also asked me that very same question. Had me check the colonial logs for evidence of extrasensory communication and everything."

"What did you find?"

"Well, Salem, nobody knows one way or the other. Quarry beasts might have some form of unrecordable communication, but they also might have no ability whatsoever to communicate at a distance. To my knowledge, you and Plexie are the only people on record to hear the voice of one at all."

"Wasn't that the outside sickness?"

"I mean when it grabbed us. That rumbling you heard."

"Oh, right..." Salem droned. He'd forgotten about the rumbling voice. Plexie had heard it then, too.

"Think of it like this," Cejero said. "If you were to eat a cleaning block, you'd probably get sick, right?"

"Yeah."

"And if you got sick after eating a cleaning block, would you assume to have spontaneously developed Corrosive Lining Syndrome?"

"What's that?"

"A disease believed to have been eradicated from the gene pool generations ago, which caused the lining of a person's stomach to be eaten away by digestive acids, eventually killing them."

"Ewwww," Ank said.

"Yes, it was very bad, I'm sure, but the point is that, even though we don't *definitively* know that CLS is gone forever, if you felt a sharp pain in your stomach after eating a cleaning block, you wouldn't assume CLS, you would assume the cleaning block. Similarly, auditory hallucinations are a *very* common symptom of outside sickness. Right up there with paranoia."

"I guess..." Salem said. He flicked the edge of the top sheet of paper with his index finger. "But...isn't it a strange coincidence?" he asked. "That Plexie and I both heard the voice in the engine room, and are the only ones who heard it speak to us? Maybe the extrasensory thing is happening *because* we heard Arby's voice?"

"Hah," Ank chortled, face glued to the displays as she calculated inputs for the *Myzer's* sensors. "Arby..."

"Because he's 'Relentless Bastard.'"

"Oh, I'm aware."

"That's quite an imaginative stretch, Salem." Cejero tapped at his stomach plates. "But no, I don't think it's strange at all. What's more likely is that, having heard the *actual* voice of a quarry beast—something most people consider terrifying merely in concept, mind you—your minds both borrowed from that experience when undergoing paranoid hallucinations."

"Yeah, I guess..."

"And as Hathem would say, there's no use in worrying about it, anyway, so your health will be better off—"

"Eeee!" Ank jumped out from her seat, her vocal cords clicking together rapidly. "It's here!"

Salem's heart stopped, his frosted shell plates seized.

His voice came out in a whisper, as if his fears might materialize if asked aloud. "W-what's here?"

"A shard!" she squealed. Salem's plates began to relax; a cloud of white gas appeared in front of his mouth.

Ank thrust a scribble-covered page into Cejero's hand. He gazed over her math for a roté, then scrunched his forehead. "Is this enough for a jump?"

"I think so!"

"Outstanding," he said. "I'll go get the others."

"Wait!" Salem cautioned; his body still coursed with the chemicals of panic. "We're not supposed to go alone…"

"Oh, I'll be fine," Cejero said, rising on shaky legs. "We're not supposed to spend our circayds alone in a general sense—it's hardly dangerous for me to walk to the common area, is it?"

Salem shrugged. "How would I know?"

"Precisely," he said, leaving the sensory room to walk through the *Myzer's* darkened corridors.

After Lyth was taken by the outside creature, a gargling, rumbling sound vibrated through the floor of the *Domodo*. Not a cry of pain or satisfaction, nor damage to the ship. It was a voice unlike anything heard on Venthralli. The demonic growl of a creature from the abyss.

Prito took the vial of acid from Brackesh's hand, thrusting the alloy-cutter in its place. "Wait here," he grunted, taking a step towards the hatch. He paused, glancing back over his shoulder. "Whatever you learn from this…"

Brackesh nodded. At this point, they both knew that no amount of persistence would save them. But what she *could* do was warn Venthralli about what they'd witnessed: the tendril, the growl. There was nothing like it in the colonial records. And on top of that, Brackesh would learn if temperature-diluted sulfuric acid could harm the organs of a venthhound.

On soft feet, the ship lead walked into the engine room, denying the creature of his thumping stride. He approached the blue welding flame that burned idly across the room, slowly and silently leaning over to retrieve it. The wavering light rose in his hand, flickering his silhouette against the wall behind him.

As Prito neared the reactor hatch, more sounds emitted from the shrouded opening. Nothing like the growl they'd just heard. It was higher. A collection of short hisses that popped up and faded in an instant: possibly the sound of the tendril raking along the inside of the fuel tank?

Prito stopped. His chest heaved, lungs guzzling the air. It took him four beats to summon the strength to move forward another step, towards the opening. He kept the flame low, not yet ready to melt the container.

Prepared to sprint to the sensor array, Brackesh watched Prito hold the acid near the hatch, far from his body, waiting for the tendril to reappear.

His thumb flicked the back of the torch, tripling the flame's length. The room flooded in shimmering azure, so bright the walls became painful to look at.

Prito waited, body still, shadow dancing along the wall. The only sound was the burning torch.

Then, the hissing sound returned, growing louder. As it did, it changed. It wasn't a series of hisses, but a rapid clicking, masked by puffs of air. Almost like a chitter.

The source of the sound emerged from the broken door, and it wasn't the foul, pink tongue that could perforate the carapace of a healthy venth, nor the jagged talon that had ripped through the outer hull of a functional gascan.

It was a swarm.

Tiny creatures, barely larger than a hand, spewed forth from the opening, running on six slim, pointed legs, each as long as their bodies, scraping against the floor with every step. From the front of their soft, blood-colored carapace sprouted two claws, large and curved. Each critter moved independently, attached to neither the beast beyond nor to each other.

They had come from inside the zero beast.

They *lived* inside of it.

Age-old debates raced through Brackesh's mind. Were these yellow-green critters the real enemy of the venth, and the so-called quarry beasts merely their ships? Were they a symbiotic lifeform, like the strains of bacteria that resided inside every venth? Her deliberation was brief, vacating her mind in exchange for a simpler, more appropriate thought...

"What the *fuck*?" she exhaled.

Again, Brackesh found herself frozen in the presence of a sight too overstimulating to process, but Prito didn't share her hesitation. He lunged back from the bacterium creatures, angling the torch's heavy flame at the plastic casing. The thick jet of fire completely engulfed the acid vial, blazing the tips of Prito's fingers.

One of the small critters lunged through the air, digging its scythe-like claws smoothly into Prito's abdominal carapace. Neither the acid nor its spherical container had melted enough to be of use, and within moments, the rest of the swarm had engulfed Prito's legs. The small aliens lacerated their way up his body with jagged claws, not too dissimilar from the large, black one that had dug into the storage room.

Are these its...offspring?

Prito screamed. A dozen serrated daggers punched into his carapace, snapping through the plates like bark and dousing the creatures in blood of matching color.

The vial finally melted, splattering its corrosive liquid across Prito's chest. Shrieks erupted from the creatures caught in the splash, and the rest clawed their way up Prito's neck, anchoring their bladed hands through his spine and cheek.

He fell backwards, still.

The creatures' claws dug into his carapace, tugging him by the legs back towards the opening.

A lone bug skittered past the herd. Its pointed, green-yellow feet clicked along the floor, claws striking together like a dangling chain.

Brackesh tightened her grip on the alloy-cutter, recognizing that it would be too clumsy a weapon to hit the small, agile gut-critter. The lone alien leapt across the ground, landing at Brackesh's feet, and with all of the weight she could muster, she stomped on it.

Pain seared through the arch of her foot. She cried out through her teeth, slowly lifting her leg up.

The vermin remained attached to the bottom of her foot, body spasming as she tried to shake it free. She pinched the base of its claw, slick with her blood, between the flats of her fingers and slid it out of her foot. The minuscule serrations on the blade pulled shards of carapace from her, followed by a fresh surge of thick, chartreuse liquid.

The other claw swung upward, slicing into the side of her hand. She howled in pain, flinging the dying creature back into the engine room. It landed awkwardly, injured, flipping backwards on itself past two others that charged the door.

Brackesh sprinted down the hall with uneven steps, making sure not to slip on the blood of her open wound. The creatures gained on her with terrifying speed, hopping lightly over the bottom of the bulkhead to the engine room.

She just had to get to the next section of the hall. Then, she could close off the back third of the ship.

As Brackesh stepped through the doorway, a deep, grating *creak* came from behind her. The outside creature shifted, unsealing the hole it had thus far been covering. Brackesh was forced backwards by the wind. Her hand lashed out to grab the door frame; her fingers gripped the metal, but the gale continued to slide her legs towards the opening.

The floor rushed up to Brackesh's face. She avoided impaling herself on the alloy-cutter, instead cracking the lens of her left eye against the metal. The repair tool shot out of her hand, through the air towards the breach, bouncing along the ground. The winds dragged her a dozen digits back. The alien bugs clawed at the ground to avoid the same fate.

Then, the gale stopped. A soothing breeze swept over Brackesh's shell as she lay face down on the floor; a light *hiss* came from the engine room. The tiny footsteps resumed, haunting her without pause.

Brackesh punched her palms into the floor, pain pulsing through the cut on her hand, and launched herself to her feet. She hobbled through the bulkhead, jaw clenched with each step on her wounded foot, and hammer-fisted the button that sealed off the rear third of the fuselage.

One of the quarry beast's long, serrated limbs stabbed into the engine room in search of Brackesh, slicing open one of its minions in the fray. The soft breeze intensified, pulling Brackesh towards the engine room for the briefest of moments, and the bulkhead slammed shut in front of her cracked lens.

Prolonged exposure to the extreme cold had slowed Cejero's movements. His joints, his plates...his whole body was stiff. It was an evolutionary advantage in the universe wherein the venth lived. As far as they knew, they were better suited to survive cold temperatures than any other species in natural history...sans the quarry beasts.

Cejero walked through the corridors of the *Myzer*, feet gliding along the floor with every step, delivering messages in person like they were on a damn gascan.

He flicked the ridge of his thumb against his severed knuckle, more sensitive to the cold now that it was coated with scar casing.

Cejero couldn't blame Plexie for what he'd done, even though the crew would likely die as a result. None of them could have anticipated that the trip would be prolonged this much, nor that they would all be susceptible to outside sickness.

Objectively, it was fascinating that all three male venth had fallen ill within a circayd of each other. And that Ank had developed any symptoms at all. Chromatic venth should be the least likely to develop outside sickness, but as Hathem had pointed out to Cejero, they were also known to mirror the stress hormones of people nearby, which seemed to offset the genetic stability.

Either way, there were specialists on Kairv 2 for whom the case study would be a dream. Hormonal psychologists could spend the rest of their contribution periods using it to study the strength of the sub-psychological connections their species had mostly evolved past. The *Myzer* hadn't been derelict prior to their symptoms' onset, either, which might indicate a hard limit for the amount of time any small group could—

Click, click, click...

Cejero looked up at the ceiling panels, the outline barely visible in the glow of the pilot lights.

He hated hearing the creaks of the ship: the warping of the metal that stood between him and near-instant demise. It was louder, again. Agitated by the cold. Amplified by the silence.

He turned down another corridor: long, dark, and empty.

There was no risk of Cejero relapsing, not this quickly. Still, whenever he stared down the lightless narrows, he could feel the sickness knocking. It was a sight that made him inexplicably uneasy.

With an even gait, he started down the hallway.

Reclining against the wall, Salem looked over the sheet Ank had shown Cejero. He recognized most of the symbols, though he didn't understand what any of the scribblings meant.

He hadn't wanted to start a new version of the light shard drawing because he wouldn't have had time to finish it, though, at this point, he probably could have. Cejero had been gone for fifty or sixty rotés. Of course, if Salem now decided to start another draft, the rest of the crew would probably arrive.

There was no way for him and Ank to communicate with the others. External transmissions were a critical system, but internal comms were a convenience. If he wanted to check on them, he would have to either walk down to the common area, or—

"Cejero!" Ank yelled with so much volume that the air rattled. "Where are you all?"

They listened to the responding silence for a few beats. A shuffling of footsteps rose from down the corridor, followed by mumbling.

"Coming!" Cejero called back. A roté later, their footsteps became pronounced, their voices clear.

"Once the power matrix is back on," said Plexie down the hall, "we can force hot air through to soften the material and blow it out of the way, but it's a lot of heat for no real benefit."

"We're not wasting power on that," Olyké muttered, entering the helm. She walked directly to Ank and examined the nearby display panels.

Salem brought Olyké the sheet of handwritten numbers. Her eyes dragged slowly from the readouts to the parchment, then back to the data.

"Show me the yield, again," she said. Ank flicked a pair of switches below one of the panels, showing mass estimations of the shard. Olyké considered them for a moment. "And what about our approach vectors?"

Ank punched at the unlabeled switches, writing down information she needed to hold onto. For over thirty rotés, the crew waited quietly as she worked. No engine hummed beneath their toes, no air pulsed overhead. There was only the pressing of stiff keys and the occasional marker scribble.

Finally, Ank spun around, face glued to the last piece of parchment on which she wrote.

"There's a *very* small window for movement that will give us a shot at a mobile collection," she explained, "outlined between the infimum and supremum of these sets." She pointed to one of the figures on the page. "If we exceed this speed, we won't be able to stop, outlined by this set of velocities. Too slow, and we'll run out of life support before we get there—this range here; the backup power burn."

"Let's keep it safe," Olyké said. "Get us just below the middle of that window—Salem can do a mobile pickup at fifty."

Ank nodded and began setting the ship's path. Olyké loomed over her, grinding her teeth as she watched Ank prepare the jets. The sound sent needles down Salem's shell.

The landing jets weren't designed for this type of travel. They were blunt instruments with no mechanisms in place for precise trajectories. Ank had to calculate the required angle of thrust for each jet, which changed depending on the direction the ship was facing, and how long each jet needed to fire to achieve their desired trajectory. Then, she had to input those combinations for the jets to fire in sync, with specific delays between each movement.

It took a while, but eventually, a feeble whir vibrated up Salem's legs from the floorboards, and the *Myzer* was pushed along Ank's vector chain by the landing jets. The movement was subtle. Even in minimal gravity, it was barely more than a wobble.

It wasn't even a wobble.

"Are we not moving?" Salem asked.

Ank furrowed her brow at the screen. "Something's wrong," she said. She reversed two of the main controls, then repeated the command for the landing jets to run the desired sequence.

The result was the same.

"Stop!" Plexie shouted. Ank's hands retracted from the controls. "It's sending power to the jets, but they're not activating," he said. "There's a mechanical problem somewhere."

"Oh no…" Ank whispered.

The jets hadn't fired, but the ship had still used energy trying to activate them.

Twice.

Five sets of eyes turned to Olyké, who shot a sideways glance at Plexie. "I thought we fixed everything you broke?"

"We did," he said. "I didn't do anything to the landing jets or electron backup."

"Then why can't we activate the jets with the backup anymore?"

"They've been iced over," Cejero mumbled, eyes closed. "Something broke in the cold."

Olyké stared at the floor, arms folded. She tapped her chin with the flat side of her finger. They watched her, waiting for her to come up with a solution. To realize something they'd all missed.

She finally spoke, her voice wavering a tinge. "How long would it take to fix the mechanical problem?"

Plexie answered reticently. "Maybe a circayd..." he whimpered, teetering on the edge of his breaking point. That only added to Cejero's despondency and, in turn, Ank's. They'd come so close to salvation, and it was now fleeting.

"You can't speed that up?" Olyké asked.

"Well, I...I need to get underneath the jet," Plexie said. "To diagnose it." The bottoms of his eyes squeezed upward. "That has to be done outside. And...a lot of damage can be done. It's difficult to do quickly in a suit."

"Okay," Olyké said, her voice even once again. "Ank, will a one-circayd setback crunch down on our safety window?"

"Yes. But I think we might still have one. Hang on."

Ank's hands flew across the panels surrounding her, shaking as she punched at the various inputs. Olyké's breath rumbled, eyes locked on the readout.

"No..." Hathem growled. Her sudden vocalization startled Salem. She sounded angry, which was reason enough for both Ank and Olyké to stop and turn back.

"What?"

"We have three full tanks of air and two partials," Hathem said. "Even if Salem uses a minimal amount getting the first chunk into the reactor, Plexie only has half a circayd of air to do the repair."

"Then we'll have to..." Olyké started. Her eyes lost focus, dropping to a spot near the bottom of the machine. The repair couldn't be done without refilling the tanks, which couldn't be refilled until they refined the shard, which they couldn't collect without doing the repair.

For a long while, Olyké grilled Plexie for detailed explanations of each possible repair the jets might require: how long they would take to repair, how long they would take to rule out, whether any part of their diagnosis could be done from inside…Ank charted those fixes by speed and accuracy, hoping to identify the best way for Plexie to use his half-circayd of air.

Salem didn't pay much attention; it was all very technical and confusing. Far more detailed than any of his training had been. He'd learned things like how to measure the air in a tank, how to fix a space suit outside, how to replace a—

He got an idea. One that could solve all three of their problems. And it had nothing to do with draining the electronically pressurized gas lines that ran parallel to the jet's distribution sub-reserve or breaking open the air tanks to manually replace trace amounts of breathable gasses.

Salem stared at the one and only piece of information on the readouts he recognized…

The distance to the shard.

"I can get it," he said morosely.

Olyké paused in the middle of her conversation about removing the *Myzer's* interior plating up to the hull. She turned to Salem, sighing. "I know, Salem," she said. Her voice was strangely soft, almost nurturing. "But we still have to get you close enough."

"No, you don't," he said. "Not if I take all of the tanks and puff canisters with me…"

The room fell still. Hathem looked away, refusing to condone his plan without a reasonable objection.

Ank spun in her chair. "No! You'll get lost!"

"I'll bring the homing radar."

"You wouldn't be able to find the shard in the first place," Cejero said. "At this distance, even the smallest fraction of a degree off on your approach would have you passing dozens of wheels away from the shard."

Hathem turned back around. "Could we repurpose the homing radar?" she asked. "Use the information we have about the shard's direction and distance?"

Cejero blinked. "Actually…yes, we can. Pretty quickly, in fact." He considered the process for a few beats, then threw up his hands. "He wouldn't be able to find his way back. We would need two homing radars for that to work."

They sat quietly for another roté, thinking of ways for Salem to get the shard back without a cable.

"Crisis lamps," Hathem blurted. "We have a few, and they should be bright enough to see from a distance."

"Not from that shard."

"But from quite far away. Much farther than the shard's reflection would appear from during the descent. Especially if we place one on the hull, like the mirror of a flashlight, and one at the end of the tether, as a sort of beacon."

"That is the better use of the homing radar…"

Olyké bent her head to the side. "I'm not sure about this," she said. "Will the puff canisters even get him to the shard before his air runs out?"

They both looked to Ank.

Ank wasn't eager to do those calculations, but she did them anyway, leaving the crew in another unsettling silence accented only by the punching of metal inputs and clouds of frozen breath.

According to Ank's math, Salem would be able to get to the shard with minimal use of the puff canisters and still be alive to get the shard in motion with the remaining pressure. Salem noticed that the return trip, with the shard, was slower than the trip out.

Everybody else seemed to notice, too, because they got into a really long conversation about optimizing their stock of puff canisters for Salem's mass, the shard's mass, and their combined mass. They discussed a complex strategy in which Salem would essentially set the shard on a slow heading towards the *Myzer*, fly ahead and get on the ship, then go back out to retrieve the shard later. It seemed a bit far-fetched to him, nor did he think it wise to abandon the shard during its journey. Not if a small alteration could have it missing the ship by dozens of wheels.

Since nobody could think of a surefire plan to get Salem back, he spent the rest of the conversation thinking about what he would do when he ran out of air, deciding that he would just take his helmet off. People said the outside was so cold it would kill you instantly, and that seemed preferable to suffocation. He'd also heard the opposite, though, that it took time. It had something to do with holding your breath. Was it that holding your breath was bad, which, in this case, would be good?

Hathem would know. Salem didn't want to ask her.

In the end, Olyké agreed to gamble their lives on Salem, which he took to be complimentary. There was no consensus on whether there would be enough force in the canisters to get the shard back before the *Myzer* ran out of power, let alone Salem before he ran out of air. Olyké didn't seem to think he would make it, insisting on keeping one of the partial tanks in Hathem's suit to collect the shard if Salem died along the way.

Still, she believed he could save the rest of them, and half a tank less wasn't going to prevent him from getting the shard in motion.

CHAPTER 14
UNTETHERED

A large, high-density fiber sack sat on the ground. Air tanks, puff canisters, and crisis lamps were piled near to the brim, making the satchel almost as heavy as an empty shard box, though significantly easier to carry.

"I think this will be easier than a box," Hathem said, handing the sack to Salem. "Just keep one of the crisis lamps on inside. That will warm it enough to open."

Plexie bounded over from the engine room with a small tube in his hand. "This is a zero-syro adhesive," he said. "Put some on the back of a lamp and press it wherever. It'll be stuck good a few beats later." He dropped the dense tube into the bag. "The casing should absorb enough warmth from the lamp to allow you to squeeze the glue out, but you can also hold it in your hands for a couple of rotés. Just don't get any on your gloves."

Salem smiled at the tube and cinched the bag shut. "Thanks. Both of you."

"Yeah…" Plexie mumbled, clicking his toes on the floor. "We can worry about prying them off the ship when we get home, right?"

"Right."

The mechanic stood idly for a beat, then threw his arms around Salem and pulled him close. Salem couldn't recall Plexie ever hugging him before, and almost wished he hadn't then. The rest of the crew followed suit: Ank, then Hathem and Cejero. Even Olyké.

"We're going to lose you about halfway there," she said. "So don't panic when that happens. The suits aren't made for this kind of range. You'll hear us on the way back."

"Got it," Salem nodded. The unspoken goodbyes made him uneasy. He tried to avoid thinking about his chances of returning, but between Olyké's worrying and Plexie's quiet crying by the wall, it was difficult not to. It was like he had already died.

Cejero handed Salem the homing radar. The dark-ultraviolet line on the screen shook back and forth above a number so large it made Salem's stomach turn over on itself.

"I think you're going to be alright," Cejero assured him. "I didn't set the radar to the shard's coordinates like we'd planned; it's still programmed to the ship's sensor. The values have just been shifted based on the interception point we've aimed you towards. That's why it's confused right now: because you're still on the ship. Once you get going, the guide will lock on."

"Okay," Salem said. He watched the line jiggle around.

"This way, after it's turned off and back on, it'll reset back to the ship without needing to be reprogrammed."

"Okay..." he mumbled again, brow furrowed. He wasn't sure why Cejero was so concerned with reprogramming the radar back to the ship. That is, until he realized that *he* could turn the device off and on at the shard, setting it back to the ship. "Oh, wow," he said. "Thanks, Cejero."

"Like I said, you'll be alright. Coordinates are etched on the back here, just in case: 45.3, 22.8, 3573.1. Start in that direction and it'll pick you up a couple of allos out. Make sure to leave it on until you get to the shard."

With no time to spare, Salem put his helmet on and lumbered into the pressure room, enduring the weight of the overloaded satchel until he could leave the *Myzer's* gravity. The entire spool of cable was already unwound, ready to be dragged to its length with minimal friction.

Before Salem could close himself in, Ank scurried around the bend into the pressure room. She whispered some final instructions to Salem, barely audible through the outside-tempered material surrounding his head. They were detailed, explicit; best for only the two of them to hear.

She smiled, stuffed one of the leftover festival decorations into the satchel, and raced back through the interior pressure door.

Offensively bright in the darkened pressure room, a single crisis lamp glowed atop the spare tanks and canisters with the oversized bag. The luminescence of the homing radar barely discolored the satchel's walls, flooded by the volume of light produced by the lantern.

Through his glove, Salem could feel no heat emanating from the bulb, but it was there, ensuring he could later open the bag. He removed two of the deactivated crisis lamps and cinched the satchel shut.

The unspooled cabling lay neatly on the floor so that it would neither tangle nor create resistance as Salem traveled. He wrapped the cable loosely around the bag twice, hoping that the static friction would keep it trailing with him until it reached its end, at which point it could slide off the bag without stopping him.

Using the care one would reserve for handling explosives, Salem applied a dollop of the engineering adhesive to one of the crisis lamps, then pressed it against the cable just past the bag.

"One, two, three..." He whispered off the beats, lingering for a couple more just to be sure. When he released his grip, the lantern remained attached to the cable, and his glove did not. Its radiance seemed less powerful than it had inside the satchel.

"I'm going to open the pressure door," he said aloud, resting his hand on the metal switch across from the emptied spool. He waited for Olyké's confirmation, though the protocol seemed silly in the present circumstance. If there was a temperature leak or mechanical failure, what could any of them do about it?

With a heavy breath, he threw the lever.

The pump that equalized the pressure room to the vacuum outside wasn't part of the life support systems, so the whoosh of air that normally accompanied the door didn't occur. Salem's legs were snared from behind by the air of the pressure room, vacating through the opening at the base of the door. He clenched the lever, grunting at the unexpected force. His feet swept out from beneath him easily in the absence of gravity. The door opened further, the gale extended upward, and by the time it reached his body, it had stopped, the air now dispersed indefinitely across the outside.

Activating the second crisis lamp, Salem placed some industrial glue on its dim side, reaching around the bottom of the doorway to hold the light against the *Myzer's* hull.

He retrieved the half-used puff canister and the homing radar, double-checking the coordinates carved into the back. With his air now in use, he couldn't afford much delay, but it was worth taking an extra roté to gauge his angle of approach. Any adjustment he made afterward would come at a cost.

Once he felt confident with his estimation, he pressed both feet against the wall and sprang off into nothingness.

Only, it wasn't nothingness.

Below his trajectory—what would have been through the floor of the *Myzer*—was a tiny, white speck.

Salem refocused his eyes, just to be sure. Then, a second time.

"It's a light shard!" he said.

"Are you sure?" asked Olyké.

"I can see it."

"Outstanding!" cheered Ank. She and Olyké had opposing feelings about the rare phenomena, although they didn't seem to be quite so rare. The once-in-a-lifetime occurrence had become a twice-in-a-cycle find for the *Myzer*.

That experience had torn Salem between the opposing views. Seeing the shard's light from thousands of wheels away was invigorating and electrifying; a distance that only one or two venth had ever witnessed with their own eyes. But after the events surrounding the last light shard, he was starting to wonder if there was a factual basis to the superstitions; if those tales existed because quarry beasts were drawn to the incandescence.

Salem wanted to ask Cejero if he thought that they might encounter another super hunter like Relentless Bastard, just so Cejero could tell him that he was being ridiculous, but Salem couldn't bring himself to ask. He had that now-familiar feeling that mentioning it aloud would bring the reality to fruition. Or worse, that Cejero would give some indication that he *did* think an outside creature was en route. And what good would that do anybody? If Salem panicked, they were dead. If a quarry beast showed up, they were dead.

Best to cover his eyes with his bedding, as they say.

Puff canister in hand, Salem referred to the homing radar for guidance. The shard's light would help guide him, but he still wanted to use the coordinates to avoid wasting puffs later on. Ank helped align his direction and speed using the *Myzer's* limited sensor capabilities, but in doing so, revealed another problem.

"Hey…I don't think these coordinates are correct," he rasped. There was some commotion in the sensory room as the crew moved around. Salem squinted his forehead at the homing radar's display, refocusing his eyes again on the dim light.

"Salem, did you turn the radar off?" asked Cejero.

"No."

"Then it's correct," he said. "Ank and I both triple-checked those calculations."

"But I can see the shard, and it's way below my vector."

"Did you say 'below?'" Cejero asked. He sounded disappointed for some reason. "How far?"

"A lot. Like twenty degrees."

The crew conferred indecipherably for a roté before Cejero returned to the communicator. "Salem? Ank is going to check again," he said gently, "but for now, you need to follow the device and make the adjustments she tells you. And try to slow your breathing, too."

The last instruction took Salem by surprise. "Huh?"

"We don't want you using additional air," he said. "We're going to continue talking to you until you leave radio range, but don't respond. Just give mumbles if applicable—mmhmm and mm-mm."

"What's going on?"

"You might already be hallucinating."

"Oh…" Salem exhaled, wasting air. His body wanted him to breathe more, tried to make him panic. And with everything that still lay ahead of him, it all seemed impossible to stave off.

"Don't worry," Hathem said. "Just relax your lungs. If you start to hear voices again, remember that it's only the outside sickness. It will go away once you get back. Does that all make sense?"

"Mmhmm."

"Very good."

The tether hit its end and tugged back on Salem, slithering around the bag before parting ways and hanging free against the universe. After a quick correction for the rotation imparted on him by the cable, Salem held down the partial canister and sped up his descent into darkness. By the time he reached ninety allos per roté, the canister's pressure had weakened noticeably, but hadn't completely run out.

For seven hundred rotés, the crew talked to Salem in shifts. Normally, it would have been insufferable—non-stop talking about nothing. Hathem told him an entertaining hatchling's story he'd never heard before, about a garden bug that didn't want to eat plants. She engaged him periodically, asking him questions like, "You'd think she would have given up, right?" And Salem would reply, "Mmhmm." The constant reminder that others existed nearby was helpful, but after a while, Salem began to wonder if they, too, were hallucinations. If he was already out of range and had replaced his crewmates' voices with psychosis.

When he neared the edge of his suit's radio range, Ank had him make a few final adjustments to his approach, burning through the remainder of his first canister before putting it in the bag.

Then, partway through Plexie's explanation about why electricity moves faster outside, his voice began to scramble.

"But the —rons will fl— aro—"

"Plexie, I'm going out of range."

"—an't —ou. Talk —n."

The static died, suspending Salem in lightless silence.

The bag resting against his shell was a poor substitute for the comfort of a tether, leaving Salem with only the speck of light below his bearing to anchor him to reality. And it wasn't even real.

Ironically, it was that act of rationalization that had grounded him. The light hadn't moved, as it would have if it had been a shard, nor had it grown larger or glinted. He didn't need anyone to tell him the speck of light was a hallucination. It served only to remind Salem that his will was stronger than his outside sickness. He almost dared the auditory hallucinations back, just so he could reject them.

Almost.

With nothing to do and no one to talk to, Salem spent the next portion of the trip compulsively checking the radar every few rotés. Eighteen hundred wheels. Seventeen ninety-five. At some point, he realized he had been humming idly, wasting air, and stopped himself.

At around thirteen hundred wheels away, something changed about the universe around Salem in a way he couldn't describe. It had become even more silent to his ears, quieter than nothing, and in a single beat, all of the effort he'd spent controlling the outside sickness fell apart. Phantom pains spread through his organs, up his thin neck to the bottom of his face.

The more he tried to slow his lungs, the more they sped up. His breathing deepened fruitlessly, like he couldn't breathe.

He *couldn't* breathe.

His first air tank had run out.

Salem was breathing in the byproduct of his exhales; he was suffocating.

Pulling the satchel around to his front, Salem cranked open the top, blasting his eyes with violent, white light after twelve hundred rotés of blackness. He cried aloud, wasting precious air, shielding his face from the concentrated reflection of the crisis lantern. The low oxygen percentage had already blurred his vision quite a bit; he was dangerously close to fainting.

Scrambling to fetch one of the full tanks, Salem tried to remain calm. He swiped at the valve behind his back: a frustrating task to accomplish in the cumbersome space suit.

Why didn't I practice this before?

Lungs heaving, he disconnected the empty tank and moved it to the side, allowing it to hover. The sting of cold stabbed at his back through the thin fabric underneath the tank. The containers beside him appeared as barely more than deformed blobs of plastic, the bag muddled within the light of the crisis lamp.

Familiar with the motion, now, attaching the new tank was a quicker process. Salem groaned through each heavy, useless breath, pained by the frostburns developing on his shell, until finally the tank was connected in place with the valve open.

Salem's lungs sucked down the gasses as quickly as they entered his helmet. For the first time, his nostrils noticed the air's delightful scent, his ears the comforting *hiss* of the valve. The bag returned to focus, distinguishable again from the light inside. The spare tank formed into its proper shape beside him.

Every time Salem shifted, the fibers of his suit grated against the frostburn on his back.

It was going to be unbearable by tank four.

Long after Salem had lost his sense of time, the homing radar dropped into double digits. He swept his flashlight around, eventually spotting a glint amongst the black. The radar showed him as only five wheels from the location they had expected.

Salem was impressed.

He shut off the device, which had to be nearing the end of its charge. With a fresh puff canister, he slowed himself and corrected his path, finally meeting with the small boulder of fuel. It was larger than he'd anticipated: easily a chunk and a half.

"I'm here!" he whooped. He ran the beam of the flashlight along the shard's reflective surface, his face adorned with a smile. "And it's a good size, too. We're gonna be okay."

His smile faded. Nobody could hear him. The crew didn't know he'd arrived, nor that they were getting more than a chunk of fuel out of this shard. Not yet, anyway.

"Nor will they."

A squeak ran up Salem's throat and out between his teeth. He couldn't stop it. The deep, crackling voice boomed through his helmet as if something had struck it. He tried to ignore the sound, but the volume of the rumbling was so great he couldn't hear himself think.

"So much food," it said. *"So...isolated."*

Salem cranked his neck in every direction, waving his flashlight in search of a large, approaching shape. Most of his surroundings were blocked by his helmet, and as he gripped the puff canister to rotate himself more easily, he realized he couldn't afford to waste any of its pressure entertaining fiction.

He stared carefully at the iridescent point off in the distance, allowing his beady eyes to absorb every wave it produced.

"The light calls," it said.

"Ignore it!" Salem barked to himself.

"Ignorance...saves none."

"You're not even real!" he shouted. The difference he heard in his own voice, the aerial vibrations it created, helped bind him to reality, just as his prolonged focus on the dot of light hadn't made it any clearer, either. Salem couldn't let Arby waste any more of his time.

He had work to do.

He pried open the icy satchel, re-exposing the blaze within to the cosmos. One by one, he removed his tools: the deactivated homing radar, the heat saw, the measuring twine, and the festival decoration. Each item hovered where he placed it, like a floating workbench beside the puff canister.

Flicking the radar on, Salem sighed with relief to see the compass pointing him back towards the *Myzer*, though it reminded him that he was 3578 wheels away. He moved the device around to get a general sense of which way he needed to go, then shut it back off. He inspected the shard to determine which orientation would be best for moving it, deciding on facing the flattest side away from the ship.

Voiding the rest of the puff canister, he slowly rotated the crystal, using the last dying spurts to get himself back to the satchel for a fresh canister and an armful of unused crisis lamps.

Salem became quite skilled at using the outside adhesive without getting any on his gloves. He placed a dollop on each lamp, placing one on every side of the starshard except the flat one. The surface became a beautiful cobalt, blending into ruby closer to the center whenever a lamp was angled just behind the edge. It was a feature Salem had been completely unaware of until then. He wanted to study the ephemeral color shift, the way it changed as one of the lamps moved further behind the shard.

Instead, he warmed up the saw and moved on to the next phase.

Having already identified the part he wanted to cut, Salem spurted himself to the tip of the longest side and, using his fist as a guide, melted through a knob protruding from the end of the shard.

Salem metered his movements carefully, juggling his tools by gently placing them where he needed. The process was long and tedious. He placed the measuring twine by the dark side of the shard and measured twelve digits away from it, requiring both of his hands to prevent the already uncoiled wire from moving. That's where he placed the freshly-cut ball of heat gel—repeatedly, as the icy exterior kept sticking to his glove when he tried to let go. Then, he had to go fetch the homing radar, which had drifted a bit too far for his comfort, and return it to the workbench area. He took the festival decoration over to the gel ball and placed it opposite the starshard, leaving the three objects to float together in lock. He retrieved the satchel, stowing all of the items he no longer needed.

Then, it was time.

Salem floated back to the constellation of items, the added mass from the satchel nearly causing him to run into the shard. He placed his feet against the center of the shard's flat surface, curling his legs so he could fit his head underneath the gel ball.

Holding the knob in place, Salem expelled puffs from the canister at it. As Ank had predicted, the gas was just warm enough to melt the gel, but not enough to vaporize it as the heat saw would. The makeshift floor beneath Salem was heavy enough to prevent him from moving away much, at most a quarter of an allo per roté.

"*Don't…*" Arby said. "*You will become…inedible.*"

"Piss off," Salem said aloud.

The surface of the ball began to shine, and the next few puffs sent mist onto the decoration, coating it with unrefined gel residue. The soggy exterior of the knob didn't stick to Salem's hand this time. He carefully puffed himself out from between the two objects, retrieving the festival decoration that had begun floating away.

He touched the sparkling end against the fistful of fuel, and with the heat saw on full blast, pressed its blade against the bottom of the decoration's shaft.

He winced in anticipation of the reaction.

Nothing happened.

He blinked at the sparkler, then repeated the motion with aplomb, waiting for the gel-covered wrapper to ignite. Only a cloud of smoke appeared, collecting itself around the contact point.

"Did it already freeze?" he asked the universe, frustrated by the mystery science not working as explained. He didn't know if re-freezing would prevent the gel from—

Pff-tsss.

Salem's visor flared as the base of the decoration ignited. He dug his finger into the puff canister, backing away from the reaction as quickly as the jet would take him. The ignition raced up the side of the cylinder, faster than Salem had anticipated, and he was only half an allo away when it reached the sparkling end and detonated.

The concussive force hammered into Salem's plates, bludgeoning his stomach and pulling the wind from his lungs. He flipped end over end backwards, his body careening away from the starshard.

Pfft, pfft...pfffft.

Salem fired the puff canister liberally to slow his spinning. His chest burned, but miraculously, the suit fabric hadn't been torn in the explosion. Pressure grew in his head; blood pooled in his skull. He labored his breaths to avoid vomiting in his helmet.

Pfft-pfft.

Muted, the pressurized gas vibrated through Salem's gloves. The spinning slowed to manageable speeds, and Salem oriented himself back towards the shard.

But the shard was gone.

Salem stared at the vacant zone, jaw agape. Ank had assured him the explosion wouldn't destroy the rest of the shard. He had placed the siphoned piece far away, melted the outside, angled the spray—

"*Good,*" the voice gargled. "*You still...are. We will arrive.*"

Fake Arby was right: Salem still was. If the shard had exploded, he would be a chartreuse mist right now. It was just traveling fast.

Too fast. The shard was already far enough away that Salem couldn't see the lantern cluster. He'd have to make his way back towards the *Myzer* and hope he spotted the lamps.

Fumbling with the homing radar, Salem flicked on the infrared display, discovering that he had a completely different problem to deal with first.

Where the display had shown *3578* after the reset, it now showed *3596*.

3597…3598.

The shard wasn't moving too fast; Salem was. The explosion had flung him away from the *Myzer* at twice the speed of his descent, covering the entire circumference of Venthralli every few beats.

Bracing his arm against the exhaust, Salem pushed his finger into the puff canister. Using the explosion to propel the shard had afforded him a couple of extra canisters for his return trip, but he'd also need a lot of force to slow the boulder of fuel once it reached the *Myzer*.

Salem kept the flat side of his finger pressed until the canister was completely expelled, but his distance continued to rise.

3610.

He chucked the empty canister into the void behind him, pawing through the contents of the bag to do the same with the expended air tank. They provided a negligible push, but their absence also lightened him. He retrieved the next canister and slammed his finger down.

Half of a puff—the canister he'd expended on the way out.

"Shit," he whispered, tossing the puff-less can behind him. He dug around for a roté, wiggling his fingers down past the tools and air tanks until he found another canister. Relieved to feel the mass of a fully compressed container, Salem laid on the button.

The radar slowed, came still at 3626, then began counting back downward.

3625.

Counting the beats between each tick of the radar, Salem got himself moving towards the *Myzer* at around a hundred allos per roté. He didn't know how accurate his angle was, other than that it wasn't bad enough to create a noticeable lack of acceleration towards the ship despite his canister usage. He looked around for the clutch of lamps, stretching his neck to peer out the edges of his visor. The longer it took him to find the shard, the less likely he would be to find it at all. It would be a miracle for the explosion to have launched it directly at the ship, but it weighed a lot more than Salem, so it wouldn't be moving too fast to correct.

Before long, a white, wobbling pinpoint appeared above Salem's trajectory.

He angled himself up, requiring a longer puff than he expected based on the angle. The wobbling light separated into distinct lamps, intertwining as the shard spun. The spinning motion quickly became pronounced. The shard's size grew rapidly.

"Uh oh..." Salem said. He fired another puff of gas to slow himself down, but couldn't waste more. He didn't know how much would be needed to correct the shard's path, and he'd have to impart as much speed as possible onto it.

Tilting his helmet away, Salem plummeted towards the large rock of unrefined heat gel.

Phthump.

He collided with the translucent crystal, battering the upper right half of his torso, pinching his arm beneath his body. The impact spun him slowly, imparted from the shard's wheeling rotation. It was an easy fix compared to last time, requiring a few quick puffs to stabilize himself.

Correcting the shard's course required a healthy amount of compressed gas. Every adjustment Salem made to the shard caused him to absorb some of its spin, twirling him in response and requiring quick canister bursts to negate.

By the time the whole process was done, the shard was moving faster than it would have been had Salem moved it with puff canisters alone. It had taken more force than he'd intended, which would make stopping the shard problematic later on, but he was on track to return home before his air ran out, and that was a victory.

Dreading the inevitable frostburn, Salem staved off the changing of his air tank for as long as possible. He placed the new tank in position, ran through the entire process in his head, and then performed the swap. To his credit, he managed to change the tanks much faster the second time around, but it hurt a lot more. Removing the old tank felt like being dragged across a bed of pins, and placing the new one on was exactly like being dragged back over it.

With little else to do, Salem spent hundreds of rotés thinking of ways to perform the tank change without exposing the under-insulated part of his suit. All he came up with was facing his back towards the crisis lamps, which weren't even warm enough to soften the starshard's exterior, let alone protect his carapace from the outside.

Fatigued, tortured, and lightheaded, Salem did the third swap. It took longer than the second; just reaching back to disconnect the old tank was agonizing.

"Ahh, ahh, ahhhh!" he yelped throughout. By the time he finally switched on the airflow, the shard was nothing more than an azure blur beside him. He felt about to faint, his voice raw from screaming through the poor air concentration.

As he wheezed in the air from his last tank, he heard a voice.

"Salem, what's happening!?"

Salem blinked.

"Huh?"

"What's happening?" Olyké repeated. "Why are you screaming?"

"Uh…" he wheezed. His head felt thick from suffocation. "Frost-burn," he said. He took a deep breath of the fresh air, rasping as the shard came back into focus.

"Do you have a tear?"

"No, I just switched the last tank in," Salem explained. He filled his lungs up again. "Somebody should really insulate the part underneath them."

Laughter arose in the background—Salem didn't think it was very funny. He couldn't move any part of his body without feeling a knife ice sawing into his carapace.

"That's great!" Cejero's tiny voice said from elsewhere in the sensory room.

"It's not great," Salem grumbled. "I'm burned really bad."

"I mean that it's great you're only now using the last tank," Cejero said. His volume swelled as he neared the transmitter. "Sorry about the burns; I forgot that's how the suits are built. You're the only person I've known to remove their tank outside. How far away are you?"

Salem turned on the homing radar. He would now be able to get an accurate speed by giving them two measurements. Even without the *Myzer's* main systems on, they'll be able to tell him exactly how long it would be until—

Salem stared dumbly at the blank screen for half a roté, waiting for the infrared display to light up. He turned the power on again.

Still blank.

"Oh, no..." he moaned.

"What's wrong?"

Salem tried again to no avail. "The homing radar is out of power."

"What was the last distance you saw?"

"Thirteen eighty-something. I think 1388?"

"How long ago was that?"

"I don't know," Salem said. "A while before I changed the tank."

"Do you know how fast you're moving?"

"Around seventy or so."

"Wow, great pace," Cejero said. He paused for a roté while Ank spoke indecipherably to him. "Okay, so...Ank says she saw the shard's...redshift. You should be here in around nine hundred rotés. Plenty of time to spare."

"This is the partial tank, though."

"Well...still time to spare," he said. "Just breathe easy. And stop screaming."

Having spent fifteen hundred rotés fine-tuning the shard's trajectory using changes in the homing radar's distance, Salem only had to make a few alterations before the crew resumed yapping at him about nothing.

Some time later, Salem moved himself to the side of the shard and allowed his eyes to absorb every photon that may lie ahead. He must have stared for fifty rotés before a pair of small, white dots appeared: the crisis lamps stuck to the cable and ship. As he neared, he eventually saw part of the tether, accented against the outside by bouncing light from the lamp.

With a pair of lengthy puffs, Salem guided the icy rock's path towards the cable. The end of the cable became visible even after turning his lenses away, then the lamp underneath the pressure door. The lights grew closer, and Salem's gawking eyes could make out the hull of the ship around the lamp, then the edges of the pressure door.

The beacon light whizzed towards him at seventy allos per roté.

He wouldn't be able to slow the shard enough.

"Um…hello?"

"Go ahead, Salem."

"How much can I slow this with one canister?"

"Hold on…"

The full outline of the *Myzer* appeared against the space beyond, illuminated by the residual light of the lanterns. The beacon soared past him, the cable brightened in the shard's lamp cluster.

"I need to know soon," he urged.

"It depends on the mass of the shard and angle of the canister," Olyké responded. "Not seventy."

Why didn't Salem think to cut the shard en route? There had been so much time to do it. He could have probably slowed half of it. Certainly enough to divert it harmlessly into the—

Salem held down the jet of his last puff canister. The stream came out as a thin haze in the brightness of the lamp array, like spittle dissipating out into the darkness. The edge of the *Myzer* moved in front of the shard's path, only a wheel away.

"Hey, uh…" Salem curled his legs up, rotating his body so his feet would rest against the flat back of the shard. "Everyone should get away from the engine room."

There was rustling in the sensory room. Olyké said, "Why?" but Salem didn't have time to explain. As the *Myzer* rushed towards him, he kicked off the side of the shard, leaving it to careen into the floor of the engine room.

"Impact!" he yelled.

He didn't think the force of the puff canister would slow him enough to survive an impact with the ship, so he fired the remaining gas to the side to get out from under it, angled slightly forward in the hope of slowing himself enough to clear the edge of the hull.

The crisis lamp beneath the pressure door sped towards him, moving up over his eyeline as the ship grew in size. The shard moved ahead of Salem, its lamps reflecting off the *Myzer's* grey surface.

The ship was rushing at Salem too quickly, its edge too far. His entire field of vision was taken up by the hull, now only twenty or thirty allos away. In a panic, he angled the puff canister directly ahead, just hoping to survive the impact. The mist collected in front of him, obscuring the metal beyond.

His trajectory curved as he slowed; his sideways movement compounded. Arcing back into his view, not five allos away, came the edge of the ship.

The edge he was about to strike at sixty apr.

Salem strained the elastic tendons of his legs, pulling his limbs in as tightly as he could, fighting against the rigidity of the space suit. He heard the hollow *bong* of the shard's impact reverberate through the ship and into his radio, barely more than a whisper in his ear while he cleared the edge of the ship by a toe.

"Seal it!" Olyké shouted as Salem soared past the pressure door.

"Sorry—I couldn't stop it," he grunted, hastily correcting his course and returning to the impact site. The shard had bounced off at a slight angle, but remained near. The crisis lamps were still attached, highlighting a crack in the shard and an indentation in the hull. He shined his flashlight along the *Myzer's* new dimple. "I don't think it broke through."

After a few precision puffs from the dying canister, Salem met up with the rebounding starshard and stabilized it against the ship, allowing the masses of each to hold the other close. He wouldn't be able to cut the shard up with the air he had left, so he maneuvered back to the pressure door and went inside.

Evidently, that was the right choice, as Salem spent damn near the remainder of his last air tank manually winding the cable back so he could close the outer door.

CHAPTER 15
SECOND WIND

Met by a small chorus of helmet-muffled cheers, Salem cycled in from the pressure room. The interior door opened instantly, guzzling another cube of air from the remainder of the ship. As soon as the gale hit Salem's legs, he pried his helmet off and dumped it in the corridor, swelling the mild sounds of celebration. He gasped at his first breath of fresh air in over half a circayd.

He never guessed he would one circayd describe shipboard air as "fresh."

"Very impressive, Salem," Olyké said, resting her hand on his shoulder. "Not many could've done that."

Before he could respond, she made her way back to the bridge. Salem smiled to himself; she'd walked the entire length of the ship just to say those words.

Suit on, Hathem walked into the pressure room, patting Salem on the back as she walked by.

"I can get it," he told her.

She gave him a flat smile. "No. That's enough outside for you."

Not one to argue in favor of going back outside after a half-circayd spacewalk, Salem began the process of removing his suit, made arduous by his burning shell plates.

Ank hopped in front of him, eyes bulging around her head.

"Guess what?!"

Salem stared at her. He wasn't in a place to be processing mysteries right now. "Um…I don't know?"

"I saw the light shard!" she said.

It took Salem a few beats to realize what she was referring to. He had forgotten all about the tiny speck of light from his descent, long ago dismissed as a hallucination.

His head juddered. The singular idea that had that kept him sane for the last forty-five hundred rotés was the knowledge—the *fact*—that the light shard wasn't real. That Arby's voice wasn't real.

His stomach folded over. "It can't be," he gasped. "I traveled thousands of wheels towards it, and it never moved. It never got bigger."

"That's because it's very far away," explained Cejero. "Moving a few thousand wheels doesn't change the angle of observation enough for our eyes to recognize."

"And it's big!" added Ank. "For you to have seen it at all."

Salem stared at the floor.

"You look upset," Cejero noted.

Salem didn't want to sound crazy, for people to think he was suffering from outside sickness again, so he chose his words carefully. "I just..." he hesitated, "Arby said it was going to stop here to eat us, and then move on to the light shard."

"Arby isn't real, Salem."

"He is too!" Plexie called from the engine room. "He grabbed us!"

"No, I mean..." Cejero paused, frustratedly formulating his words. "The voice you heard, *Salem,* is not real. Whatever it said isn't true."

"But it said the light shard was real, even when you thought I was hallucinating. And it's true."

"*You* thought it was a light shard, first. Remember? You were right, not Arby."

"Silly Salem," Ank patronized, "you can't use the antecedent of a conditional as its consequent." She clicked her fingers against their opposing digit. "And with how big this shard has to be, it'll probably get us all the way to the mega shard!"

Salem nodded, staring down at the floor. He knew it was good news—the location of a shard big enough to prevent them from getting stranded again—but he couldn't shake his concern. If light shards did attract quarry beasts, even just ones as keen as Arby, an anchor-shard-sized one would be even more dangerous.

"How does Olyké feel about this?" he asked.

"Ummmm," Ank stalled. Her face scrunched. "She thinks it's the right course for us to take."

Perhaps Olyké and Salem were more alike than he'd thought. In almost three cycles of working on an energy collector, he had never once believed that any cosmic superstition could be true until then. And while it was obvious they couldn't pass up a shard of that size, his dread of the mysterious crystals only escalated.

Running the *Myzer* on low power for extended periods of time posed damage risks to some of the machines and electronics running throughout. After Hathem fed the first half of their cracked shard into the reactor, the crew went to work running diagnostics on the newly abuzz instruments. Salem's suit lay in an empty pile on the ground, converting waste gasses into breathable ones, and that was the extent of his equipment responsibilities. While he waited for each tank to refill, he pressed buttons and shined flashlights on command, or held machines in place while someone torqued on them in some manner.

Once the ship was finally deemed safe by Plexie and Olyké, the comforting hum of the drive kicked up, and they jumped out of the zone of dereliction.

Category-five frostburns covered the back of Salem's neck. In order to prevent carapacial decay, Hathem made him hold hot mesh against his nape for the rest of the circayd, swapping between two different pads as one cooled and the other reheated. He didn't get a beat of sleep that evening. He tried lying in every possible position, and was met each time with sharp, grating pain along his shell. Relaxing enough to doze into a micro-slumber was outside of his reach, so he lay awake and listened to the increasing number of odd mechanical sounds emitting from the *Myzer*.

As it turned out, the explosion Salem used to propel himself through the outside had nearly burned through the thermal lining of his space suit. Ank's suit was too small for him to use, so for subsequent shard collections, he donned Cejero's. It was in much better condition than his had been even before the explosion, sans the helmet, of course, which had been Ank's. The new suit felt warmer, too; the insulation thicker.

When he left to grab the next shard, his nerves were on fire unlike ever before. He was ready for something to go wrong, for him to be placed under strain or stress in unforeseen ways. He expected it. The shard was a quarter of a wheel from the *Myzer's* external fuel port. Salem cut it into four chunks and pushed each one effortlessly into the reactor.

The whole thing took two hundred forty rotés.

He had actually forgotten how easy a normal collection was.

With every pause, Salem gazed off towards the small dot in the distance, just to make sure it was still there. Even after a couple of jumps, it hadn't grown in size at all. It made Salem question whether the pinpoint of light should be of comfort at all, but everybody insisted that it was to be expected.

All of the data Ank had compiled over the course of the previous set of jumps had finally started to pay off. As she'd looked around nearby zones, she'd gathered fragments of information about the zones farther away. As a result, she now spent less time trying to quantify their options between jumps. It still wasn't as easy as traveling within the excursion limit, but it was noticeably smoother than when they'd first left it fifty circayds ago.

Plexie had grown concerned by the amount of wear being placed on the *Myzer's* systems without proper maintenance, informed in some way by the slew of mechanical checks the crew had completed to get the ship jump-bound. The wavy path along which they'd traveled, often requiring unideal zone transitions to conserve or obtain fuel, had prolonged an excursion already destined for mechanical strain. More jumps had been placed on the *Myzer's* engine without a refit than perhaps any ship in the colony, and it had been repeatedly powered down in zero syros.

Taking advantage of their complication-free jump spree, Plexie did a series of involved diagnostics, examining components from the outside while Ank plotted their next course. After a couple of examinations, he discovered that the fuel injectors were crystallizing inside, so during one of Salem's shard collections, he took on the lengthy process of cleaning the injectors. It involved a complex disassembly of the injector casings, so Olyké and Hathem went with him to expedite the process.

Salem quietly cut the shard into three pieces while he listened to Plexie give the other two venth instructions. After the last chunk was placed into the fuel port, Hathem insisted Salem return to the ship rather than wait for them to finish up. The *Myzer* had comfortable levels of energy, and Salem wasn't supposed to be outside any more than needed.

In the common area, Salem sat with his heavy skull propped on the palm of his hand. He chewed reticently on a vegetable, watching Ank and Cejero wander slowly around the room.

The crew's energy levels, unlike the ship on which they served, had dwindled. Every ship produced some of its own food through renewable rations—nutrient-dense plants that grew quickly and tasted terrible, like they were spoiled even when fresh. It didn't grow fast enough to feed a crew, so the majority of each ship's circaydly intake was prepared on Venthralli and stored on board in areas that were insulated against the rest of the ship, allowing their stores to be preserved for cycles by the outside. An energy collector like the *Myzer* could stock several excursions' worth of rations and, if needed, could complete an entire trip to the excursion limit and back without consuming any renewable rations whatsoever.

This trip, however, had surpassed its expected timeframe, which was already five times longer than the average excursion. Even with the *Myzer's* additional nutrient allotment, the entire crew was on reduced rations, which was taking its toll. They were one jump away from the light shard, which should have been exciting or frightening, but they were all just tired.

Once the ship's fuel injectors had been serviced, the other half of the crew joined them in the common area, shambling in from the back of the ship.

Plexie sat down next to Salem, similarly balancing his head in his hand. "Alright, the injectors are good," he said. His voice sounded loud to Salem after sitting in silence for hundreds of rotés. Plexie rolled his head to Cejero. "And I fixed that stupid clicking sound for you."

Cejero stopped pacing. "Oh…thanks," he said.

Plexie nodded, dipping his face down into the palm on which his head rested. "Just so you know, it was a pain in the ass. I had to move the thing using a series of pressure loops and T-junctions until it fell into a pocket in the wall that drops down a little."

"What was it?"

Plexie shrugged. "I dunno. I can't get into the vents." He gave a heavy sigh, sinking into his hand. "I swear, though, if one of the spiral engineers left a tool in there…" he shook his head. "It could have been sucked back into the condenser."

"Let's get out of here," Olyké said. "Ank, how many alternate routes do we have?"

"Huh?" Ank blinked. "None. This is the jump to the light shard. The long one. Did you want to do an up-wheel route instead? Two jumps?"

"No, I mean after we land. What have you pre-plotted in case we run into a problem?"

"Ummm, just the general outlines, I guess."

"Pre-plot approximates before we leave—the quickest ones as well as multiple three-jump evasion paths—but get us going within the next two hundred rotés."

"Okie…" Ank mumbled. She rolled off the bench awkwardly, landing somewhere between all-fours and upright.

With a similar lack of exuberance, Salem got up to follow her.

Cejero patted his hands on his shell, looking between the remaining venth. "I'd like to start a round of chemical tests on cells from that fragment," he said. "Plex, can you go to the sensory room, as well?"

Plexie looked to Hathem, like he was going to ask why she couldn't go with Ank, instead, and then realized that she needed to be involved with the alien contaminant. His gaze shifted to Olyké, arriving at the same conclusion.

"Fine..." he groaned, sliding off the bench. His feet clanked unevenly against the floor as he shuffled off with Ank and Salem.

On the floor of the sensory room, Plexie lay on his stomach, face turned to the side. Salem sat in one of the chairs near Ank, fighting the urge to play with the controls while she worked.

Being confined to the sensory room didn't bother Salem as much as it did Plexie. Right now, they had it better than the other half of the crew, who were stuck in the science office. Salem and Ank had spent sixteen hundred rotés there earlier in the circayd, watching Cejero update his tests. It had been too cramped for the three of them. There was too much equipment, leaving nowhere to sit that didn't require moving elsewhere soon after.

It had also been *exceptionally* boring. All of the information was on a scale too small to see: cells and their parts and whatnot. The spike hadn't even been out to look at.

A pair of footsteps came up the corridor towards the sensory room. Salem shallowed his breathing and tilted his head, listening to the rhythmic pattering.

One of Salem's strangest and most adept skills was identifying his crewmates by the sound of their footsteps. He heard them often, lying awake in his room, and each had their own combination of pace and intensity. The easiest to decipher was Ank running on all fours. Plexie ran that way often enough, but he sounded more machine-like; his limbs struck the ground with equal force at even intervals. Ank ran haphazardly, like her limbs were fighting to stop her from falling into the floor.

The nearing footsteps were quick and strong, approaching with purpose. They were footsteps with an objective.

Definitely Olyké.

The colony administrator took one step into the sensory room before dropping her gaze to the flattened engineer. He turned his head towards the door, stomach still pressed to the floor.

"Come on, Plexie. We have to hunt down some chemicals in storage for Cejero and Hathem."

Plexie stared at her, unmoving. "Why...?"

"Because both of them are contaminated right now, and it will take some time to collect it all."

Plexie considered her rationale for a moment, his shell rising and falling as he breathed. "And you can't be there by yourself for long?"

"Correct."

"Not because you need an engineer?"

"That's right."

"But I'm tiiired," he whined. "I was outside all circayd working in my suit. Can't Salem go?"

"Fine. Come on, Salem," she said.

Salem hopped off the chair and lumbered to the door, walking past Plexie's head and into his eyeline.

"Thaaanks, Salem," he mumbled, face pressed against the floor.

Trotting to keep up with Olyké's determined strides, Salem wound around the corner leading to the common area. She thrust a sheet of parchment into his hand featuring a dozen compounds written in Cejero's scrawl.

"What're these all for?" he asked.

"Cellular tests," she said blandly. She stepped over a pile of bedding that hadn't been fully pushed to the edge of the room, exiting through the side hall. "Cejero needs those items to complete the remainder. Some of them aren't safe to keep in the offices, the rest he's run out of."

They arrived in the medium storage room—storage two—as the *Myzer* bounced into subspace, rocking them back and forth on their toes for a couple of beats. They began systematically checking each crate, pulling aside any that featured chemical warnings or medical markings. Had Salem inventoried every box like he had considered, it probably would have only taken them a dozen rotés to collect everything on the list, but he hadn't. He'd found the spike, then proceeded to forget all about his plan for storage organization.

Plumes of thick haze blew from their mouths as they worked. Without sufficient nutrients to keep their bodies warm, the frigidity of the storage room quickly became a burden.

Arms shivering, Olyké removed a small metal tank from within a larger metal box. "Nitrogen here," she said, hissing, "Oh god, that's cold…"

She ran to the door and set the tank down roughly, practically dropping it beside the box of chemicals they'd already found. The echo from its dense *clang* lingered in the storage room as Salem marked nitrogen off of the list, which he'd stuck to the wall with frozen spit.

"Six more," he said.

Olyké left storage two and walked to the main storage area, which featured an intercom. Her footsteps faded into gentle taps, her voice filtered through the corridor.

"Plexie, my blood is about to freeze," she said. "Divert some heat down to storage two, will you?"

Salem couldn't make out the words of Plexie's response. Olyké returned, sliding the container that had once held the nitrogen tank to the edge of the room, pushing with all of her weight until the crate slammed into the far wall.

Olyké stood upright, hands resting on her hips, and looked among the remaining crates. The room warmed, reaching a temperature that was still uncomfortable.

After a couple of rotés, she moved one of the unchecked crates away from the others and opened it. Two of the items on their list weren't dangerous enough to require special storage or markings, and they could reasonably be stored with a handful of different supply types. At some point, they would have to dig through half of the containers that weren't purpose-built. The items were all supposed to be in storage two, but that didn't necessarily mean they would be, so there was also a slim chance they would have to check in storage one, which would take all circayd.

As Salem rotated an assortment of finger-sized vials with long names, occasionally checking one against the list because they sounded similar, a *click* came from out in the hall, up by the ceiling panels.

Then another.

Olyké paused, listening as the sound rattled along the corridor. "I thought Plexie just fixed that?"

"He said it was stuck in the wall."

Olyké grumbled at the objects in the large crate, "Well, it's not." She extended her arm down towards the bottom to push some of the items around. The clicking moved farther down the life support trenches, ending in a hollow *thunk*.

"It is, now," Salem said, and to his delight, the corner of Olyké's mouth turned upward as she looked through the crate.

"So long as it's not in the condenser…" she mused.

Listening to the gentle *whoosh* of warm air being added into the storage area, Salem and Olyké each searched through one of the basic storage containers, removing items to look underneath, careful to remember how they were packed so they could fit back in their homes.

The clicking came again; sharper, but farther away. It didn't sound like the *Myzer's* regular creaks, which Salem heard often while lying awake, but rather like someone in the next room hitting sticks against the floor.

The sound grew louder, moving into the hall. Salem looked up to see who it was, and more importantly, what they were doing.

The tops of his eyes curved outward, confused and fear-stricken.

A small creature, neither quarry beast nor venth, appeared in the doorway. It stood low, barely higher than Salem's ankle. Its carapace was blood-green with faint, purple blotches. Each of its five legs was the exact shape of the spike in Cejero's office, a stub where the sixth leg should be. It had no noticeable eyes on its body. Two scythe-like arms extended outward.

Salem opened his mouth, but his throat closed up as if about to cough. He didn't know what to say. What to call the animal that had conjured itself into the *Myzer's* hallway mid-jump.

"Th—the door!" he spat out. A chitter rose from somewhere inside the creature's mouthless body. Deceptively endearing, like laughter.

As if she'd been spat out by the storage container, Olyké pulled her upper torso out of the crate, spinning on her heel towards the alien sound. Her gaze fell on the strange being, and she backed into the crate, eyes bulging out of her face.

"What the fuck is that!?" she yelled, lunging sideways around the corner of the opened container.

Frozen in fear, Salem watched as the creature screeched and rushed towards Olyké, bladed arms forward. It leapt up high, and in her haste to back away, Olyké's foot caught on the crate lid, and she toppled onto her back. The alien critter landed on her abdomen, digging one of its scythes into the center of her stomach.

Olyké cried out, meekly, her lungs unable to scream. Salem looked around for something to hit or trap the tiny monster with. All he saw were closed boxes and an assortment of chemicals never to be thrown on a ship.

Another blade dug into Olyké's side, and again the ship lead howled airily.

Salem picked up the lid from the container beside him, gripping it with both hands to swat the creature. He ran to Olyké, but she had already grabbed it between her hands and pried it away from her chest, talons shredding her carapace as it tried to hold on. She tossed the pentapede over her head and across the room, where it smacked into the wall, its crackling vocalizations showing no sign of agony.

Dropping the lid, Salem lifted Olyké up, one arm around his neck and the other pressed to the largest of her wounds, and the two shuffled to the door.

The critter's feet tapped gently as it scurried around the line of boxes they'd placed by the wall. At the edge of Salem's vision, a pale green blur lunged into view, growing larger as it soared through the air towards his face.

Swatting his free hand in front of him, Salem struck the creature with his palm somewhere along its three-legged side. It wasn't terribly heavy, maybe as much as a thick, empty can of the same size. A bladed limb dragged across the back of Salem's hand, slicing his carapace open with frightening ease.

The violent alien flipped backwards into the open container, and the two venth moved through the corridor. Salem held the ship lead as best as he could, moving away from the storage rooms as quickly as her injuries would allow. After a couple of beats, the tapping of pointed feet resumed, growing in volume behind them.

They couldn't move fast enough like this.

"This way," Salem said, pulling Olyké down a short hall on their left, which led to the T-intersection by the engine room. Sneaking a peek over his shoulder, he saw the creature hobbling towards them in its five-legged gait, just one allo away.

As the wall ahead grew nearer, so did the chittering animal behind them. The rapid drilling of its feet grew louder, maybe only a quarter of an allo behind them, now.

They turned the corner; the clicking stopped.

The alien shrieked as it lunged, its drumming voice mere digits from Salem's ears. Salem's plates seized, ready for the sharp blade to slice the back of his neck or dig into his temple.

It never came. No stabbing pain; just soreness in his legs and the cut on his hand.

Clang—the claws hit the wall behind them. Not daring to look, Salem rushed them to the door ahead, not even half an allo away.

The animal's footsteps clicked along the ground, again growing near and again stopping as the creature shrieked and lunged through the air. Salem curved around the lip of the door, fell against the wall inside, and hit the close switch.

The metal pane slid down agonizingly slow to seal off the engine room. The creature landed on the floor past the bulkhead, just out of Salem's view. It turned back with a shrill cry, reappearing in the opening below the closing door.

We're going to be trapped with it, he thought. Mere steps away from the door, the creature lunged through the narrowing opening, arms raised, coiled to dig into the soft shell of Salem's legs. He didn't know why the door wasn't instantly closing like it normally did, why time had slowed in such an unfortunate way that the bulkhead could seal gingerly while their pursuer moved with haste, but the creature had won its race against the closing door.

The blades extending over the creature's head *clanged* against the thick metal dropping in front of it, pausing its eyeless face for an instant before disappearing behind the hatch.

Olyké collapsed against the wall beside the intercom, allowing the room to prop her up while she pressed her bloody finger into the button. "Contamination!" she called out. Her chest heaved; blood flowed between her fingers, pressed against the large wound. "Something's on the ship!"

"Where are you?" Cejero replied, his voice flat.

"Engine room," she said. She tilted her hand away from the gash in her chest to examine it. "I need Hathem…" A labored breath filtered in and out of her lungs. "But it's not safe here."

"How do you mean?" Hathem asked. Her voice rose as she neared the science office's radio. "What sort of contaminant?"

The engine room had a thin stack of parchment for working out mechanical problems, which Salem sometimes borrowed at night when he didn't want to go all the way to the storage area. He handed the entire clump to Olyké, who placed half of the stack over each opening in her carapace, wincing at the roughness of the parchment pressing against her exposed flesh.

She nodded at the intercom, indicating for Salem to hold the button.

"The spike is a leg," she said. Her voice was breathy. "From an organism on the ship." She slid to the ground. "You need to seal off this half of the *Myzer*."

"What about you?" Plexie asked.

Olyké turned her head, listening for the creature, waiting for it to bang at the bulkhead again, but it didn't.

It was gone.

Salem couldn't remember how long ago its last strike had been. Judging by Olyké's face, as reserved as it was, neither could she.

"Wait, don't!" she yelled. "It's not down here anymore." She thought to herself for a moment, head resting against the metal behind her. "Lock yourselves in."

There was silence as the sensory room and science office doors were sealed. All six venth were locked in their respective areas, and nobody knew where the angry parasite roamed.

What Salem did know was that Olyké was bleeding steadily, and in the closed engine room, it was too warm for her wounds to clot.

Due to the water-based nature of venth blood, most open wounds closed themselves off within a few rotés. The 13.2-syro fluid left their bodies, became exposed to the sub-thirteen-syro air of the colony or ship, and crystallized, quickly freezing over. This process, called "frost-clotting," was a critical survival mechanism for the venth. Their blood was thin, allowing it to flow easily through their cold arteries.

For more extreme injuries, those that occurred between shell plates could be treated easily. The soft tissue was flexible, allowing it to be warped closed and fastened with sutures. Injuries within a plate were much harder to mend. The plates weren't pliable at all, preventing wounds from being pushed or sewn closed. Doctors had to break the plate in two and allow its halves to be squeezed together. Synthetic carapace was dangerous to slather haphazardly onto open wounds, since it could potentially flow back into the body and kill the person. The old technique of placing a bandage over the wound as a barrier for the synthetic carapace could prevent the shell from fully healing due to the foreign material.

Twenty-three out of every twenty-four punctured shells were healed with nothing more than frost-clotting.

"Fold those pages to roughly the width of the wound," Hathem said. "You're going to push the folded end into it."

Salem folded the top few sheets from the stack—the ones yet to soak with blood—and then folded them again. The stack became a little wider than the wound, but they would compress down a bit. Olyké looked at the fibrous wedge, groaning at what was to come.

Salem frowned at it. "Maybe we can just go outside, now?" he suggested. "And let the cold do its job? I think the alien's gone."

Olyké shook her head slowly, rolling it back and forth along the wall. "Way too risky," she huffed. "It could be right in the hall."

Salem pressed the intercom. "Okay, it's folded."

"Now, press the rounded side into the wound," Hathem said, her voice tiny and buzzy. "If there's any excess sticking out past the edge of the laceration, fold it in and away so the pages can get farther into the cut."

Moving the wad of parchment to Olyké's stomach, Salem waited as she peeled back the blood-slicked pages. His hand hovered by the digit-long opening. Fresh, yellow-green blood oozed out from the frayed carapace, the edge of which Salem touched lightly with the fold of paper.

"Don't be mad at me," he said, and then forced the pages into the jagged opening in Olyké's shell plate.

She screamed, her pointed teeth clamped shut. Salem folded back the excess material as instructed, pressing the improvised bandage deeper into the wound. She screamed again, her mouth only a digit from his earhole, searing his skull.

Once the pages had been wedged to the depth of the shell plate, Olyké took hold of it, her hand coated with drying blood.

"Done," Salem said into the intercom.

"Good job. Now, does anyone hear it?"

There was a pause. They listened carefully for sounds of the creature wandering their corridors.

"No," Salem finally said.

"Not up here."

"Neither do we," Hathem said. There was another pause. "We can't wait," she continued. "I'm coming down to the engine room."

"Press the button," Olyké told Salem, adding loudly, "What if we shut down the reactor? How long would it take for the engine room to cool?"

"Frost-clotting isn't my only concern. The wound needs to be cleaned and treated with bacteriostatics—"

Salem blinked at the intercom.

He knew that word…

"—so, either we're meeting in the medical office, or I'm grabbing everything and bringing it to you."

"I can get them," Salem said into the transmitter.

"It'll take you twice as long to get over here, Salem, and then—"

"Not from medical," he clarified. "From storage two."

He waited for Hathem's response, but there was none.

After a roté of silence, he started to get nervous. Maybe the alien had shown up. Most likely, she was just talking to Cejero. "I know where that stuff is," he added. "We just went through the medical supplies in storage two." A few more beats, still no response. Salem looked to Olyké, pressing the button. "Hathem?"

"I'm here," she finally answered. Salem's shell relaxed. "We think we can probably lure the creature up here. You would be able to go to storage and back without crossing paths."

Hathem then gave him a short list of items to retrieve, occasionally asking him to repeat something back.

"Lastly, the disinfectant," she said, rounding out the list. "I think the only ship-safe acid in storage is the aqueous hydrochloric acid solution. Did you get that?"

"Hydrochloric acid."

"List it all back."

"Adaptive cell syringe," Salem repeated, "antibiotics, PGH wrap, hydrochloric acid."

"Give us six rotés to make some noise, then go."

"Got it." Salem released the button. "Will you be able to close the door from there?"

"No," Olyké said. She stood up weakly, one hand pressed to her side, and the other holding the parchment wedge, and leaned her shoulder against the wall beside the intercom.

Six rotés later, Salem stepped into the cool air of the corridor. He listened for signs of the creature—no clicks, no chitters, no shrieks.

The bulkhead closed behind him, shutting him out of the engine room. He set off towards the storage area, jogging on his toes through the maze of halls in which the alien roamed.

CHAPTER 16
THE KIKOGEN

By the far wall of the medium storage room, Salem dug into the first of two chemical crates adorned with the medical symbol. He shuffled through the supplies, careful not to break any of the items as he searched for the words repeating in his head.

He quickly found a syringe of v-cells—adaptive cells—and a small container labeled *aminoglycoside antibiotic*: the amino-gly-something he was looking for. He set the items beside the crate and continued, stacking contents in small piles at the edge of the box after he was done with them.

During his search, Salem kept a look out for something that might harm the invading critter. Some kind of neurotoxin or something. He happened across a sulfur-based acid, a vial inside of its own cloudy container, marked clearly with the compound. Salem slid it along the bottom of the crate, having been instructed several times never to touch the solution. It would certainly kill the alien. Then, it would burn through the floor until it ate through the gravity lining, disperse into a mist, and erode a very large hole through the exterior hull.

Click.

Salem stopped.

He held his breath, wasting precious time as he listened for more clicks. But no more came.

It's the ship.

The whole situation reminded Salem quite a bit of *The Kikogen*, a classic tale whose titular monster roamed the unpowered decks of Venthralli during hibernation. Over the cycles, kikogens had become a common fiend of stories, like ghosts, though every depiction was similar to the original. They had many legs, long claws, and scoured the decks for venth, much like the *Myzer's* hostile visitor, except that kikogens were always portrayed as larger than venth. It made Salem wonder, though, if, ages ago, someone had encountered one of these creatures, but the information had been lost to time and separated into fiction.

Fingers wrapped around a vial similar in shape to the sulfuric acid, without its own protective container, Salem removed an icy container filled with an aqueous hydrochloric acid solution rated for 8.9 syros: the disinfectant. He continued moving the unchecked items at the bottom of the crate around, hoping the PGH wrap wasn't in the other one. There was a malleable package on its side. A bandage, but not the kind he needed, one made from protein, glucose, and hyaluronic acid—

A "PGH" wrap...

The intercom in the next room sparked with conversation between Hathem and Ank, but Salem couldn't pay attention to it. He picked up the small collection of objects and gave the room one last look around, as if he might suddenly notice a loaded hull riveter left by the colony's mechanics.

No such miracle appeared, so he turned to leave.

Click click click click...

Salem froze. His body tensed. The sound was faint, like a small, faulty gear, but it grew nearer.

He leaned to look through the doorway. Straight ahead, from the corner that led to the science and medical offices, he saw the kikogen skittering in his direction, and as soon as his head peeked into view, it launched into a sprint, cutting off the desolate intersection between them.

Salem hesitated. He needed to race to the doorway and turn left, past storage one, but his body wouldn't let him. It couldn't willingly move him towards the deadly alien invader.

After that moment, it was too late.

He set the supplies down roughly, hoping that none broke, and looked around again for something to protect himself. He saw the open crate containing the sulfuric acid. He wondered how much the acid cloud would disperse after destroying the gravity lining—past the edge of storage two? Deep enough to eat through the fuel tank?

It didn't matter. The kikogen hopped through the door with a short chitter. Salem only had a beat before its claws were digging into his carapace.

He grabbed the lid to the crate, holding it by its sides, and raised it as the kikogen it lunged.

The blades pierced through the makeshift shield, digging half a digit through the lid. The tip of one scratched the edge of Salem's stomach plate.

He screamed out—not from pain, but from fear. The world shook around him, sharpened, his blood urging him to stay alive.

The claws retracted, and the kikogen fell to the ground by Salem's feet. He instinctively moved his foot away, sparing it from the claw that immediately dug down at it. The blade hit the ground, puncturing a small divot in the metal. Without pause, the kikogen hopped closer, appearing from beneath the container lid to slice at Salem's legs. He leapt back quickly, evading the claw by a digit, and slammed the edge of the lid down.

The creature shrieked. Salem pressed as hard as he could, pushing the bladed arm into the ground. The other claw lanced through the lid, appearing repeatedly on the other side as it ravaged the thin alloy.

Salem held the lid down with all of his might. The kikogen continued its assault on the box cover, struggling to pull its arm free. It tried to jump away, yanked into the ground by its pinned arm. The lid shook violently. The kikogen swiped its arm up at Salem's face, springing on its legs to get as close as possible. Salem leaned on the square metal, fighting the urge to pull his head away from the razor-like claw. If he flinched and leaned away, the creature would get free, and then it would cut his face open.

After a roté, the lid had been shredded. The frame began to bend under Salem's weight, moving his neck closer to the kikogen's swipes.

The next time the bladed arm cut through the alloy, Salem pushed the container lid forward in a scooping motion, kicking the bottom of what remained to flick the kikogen up and away. The box covering landed on it, but Salem didn't think that would slow it for any amount of time. He grabbed the medical supplies in haste and bolted for the door, careful not to clutch them too tightly.

Behind him, the lid thudded against the floor as the kikogen ran out from underneath.

At the risk of dropping the supplies, Salem sprinted out of storage two as fast as he could. He turned left, crashing shoulder-first against the wall of the adjacent corridor, arm squeezing around the bundle of materials. The cap of the syringe pressed into the pit of his elbow; his fingers gripped the hydrochloric acid vial so tightly he feared the frosted exterior might crack.

Five feet tapped along the floor. The kikogen skittered out of the storage room, voice clicking from inside, and emerged at the corner of Salem's vision, barely an arm's length away.

Legs pumping, he ran. He didn't dare look back, even as the creature shrieked and lunged across the narrow hallway.

A hollow *clang*, and the kikogen's blades struck the wall behind Salem. By the time it landed a beat later, Salem was fifteen digits further along the corridor, halfway to the next corridor. His arms bounced with every stride, his body tense.

"Get ready!" he called out. "It's behind me!"

Salem turned the corner between storage one and the reactor, bumping into the wall with his other shoulder. His hand squeezed around the acid, and the icy container slipped from his fingers up into the air.

He gasped, watching the vial arc up and away from him. It hovered in front of his eyes, as if time had slowed again.

Salem lowered his cradling arms, a slight bend in his knees, and rotated his body to dip the pile of medical supplies underneath the bulb. The hydrochloric acid landed on the packaged PGH wrap, rolling to Salem's chest and coming to rest.

The brief pause took Salem's lead away. The kikogen cleared the corner, again within jumping distance, and turned toward him.

A new sound came from its body, a rumbling sort of squeal.

And it slipped.

The two-legged side of its body lost traction in the turn, splaying it out along the ground.

Salem bolted for the engine room, passing the corridor from which he'd brought Olyké earlier. The clicking of the kikogen's feet resumed, growing nearer as he reached the engine room. He darted over the threshold, and by the time he'd turned to look back through the door, it had already sealed shut.

Olyké slid back down to the floor, her breaths quick and shallow. Dull *thunks* pulsed through the bulkhead.

"I'm back," Salem said into the intercom, elated by the sense of accomplishment and the safety he felt upon returning to the engine room, but the feeling was short-lived. He set the supplies on the ground, staring nervously at them while Hathem gave him detailed instructions to save Olyké's life.

Carefully, tightly, Salem wrapped the PGH bandage around Olyké's torso. With no knowledge of the kikogen's biology, Hathem's treatment plan was an educated guess using the materials available, and Salem had followed her instructions as best he could.

The bandage was already damp in the warmth of the engine room, and Salem wondered if it would be best to get Olyké somewhere colder. His first thought was the farm cabinet, a small room where their renewable rations grew. Many of the plants had died during the *Myzer's* periods of reduced power, but not all, so the cabinet—

"It's in the vents," Cejero's voice came through the intercom. "We can hear it nearby."

"How did it get there?" asked Plexie.

"Probably back through storage three."

"But how did it get back up through the vertical vent?"

"Who cares?" said Cejero. "Salem, get Olyké to the medical office. Hathem is on her way."

In a half-shuffle, Salem moved the colony administrator along the corridor of bunks. They turned through the common area, careful not to slip on the bedding as Salem bared half of Olyké's weight.

Click click click click…

Salem's eyes angled up. He followed the sound along the ceiling, down through the bunks, and toward the large vent junction that ran over his room. Could the kikogen be looking for up-wheel paths into the rooms they'd barricaded? Did it even possess that level of intelligence? Salem had considered the kikogen to be an animal, a large pest, but he had no reason to believe that to be the case.

After all, he'd thought the same way about quarry beasts up until this cycle.

Leaving Olyké in the medical office with Hathem, Salem joined the other three in the sensory room. It felt strange knocking on the bulkhead to get in, like they were grubs with forts.

"I've blocked off storage three," Plexie said, "so it should be trapped in the vents."

"It might cut itself out somewhere else," Salem said. "It has big claws. Its arms are just blades—this long." He held his hands a digit apart.

"Let's work fast, then," Cejero said. "We're going to vent it into space. If we can lock it in the narrower, outside-sealing duct, Plexie should be able to build up enough pressure to push it outside."

"The one that goes over your room," Plexie added.

Salem stared at the closed door, eyes squinted. Something about the plan bothered him, but he didn't know what. "I just heard it down there," he said. "The kikogen, I mean. That's what I've been calling it."

"Is that what it looks like?"

"A small one, kind of," he shrugged, his vacant gaze still locked on the door. "It has lots of legs, claws..." His eyes widened. "Wait a turn, we can't open any of the ducts that lead outside. We're in the middle of a jump."

"Yeah, we'll have to exit subspace first," Ank said casually, as if they somehow wouldn't exit subspace into the arcane medium.

And not just at the edge of the medium, either. They would be firmly in the thick of it.

"Will we be able to jump after we've done that?" Salem asked tactfully.

"Ank can!" she said cheerily, and despite everything Salem had heard about the arcane medium, that was good enough for him.

Jumping within the medium was assumed to be impossible, a task likened to throwing a ball directly into a cup on the other side of Venthralli while wearing a blackout helmet and being knocked around by people. A blind jump was more likely to land you in a sinkhole than a zone, and the best you could hope for was to land near the edge of a zone so that the medium could potentially push you to safety before you ran out of food.

But really, it wasn't supposed to be *impossible*; it was supposed to be impossible to calculate, which Salem had learned didn't necessarily mean "impossible for *Ank* to calculate."

"How fast is the kikogen?" Cejero asked. "Can we outrun it?"

"In a sprint, yeah," Salem said. "Not if you're weighed down. You wouldn't be able to outrun it in a space suit."

"In that case, you and I are going to go through the ship and figure out where it is. Plexie and Ank will close off as many air ducts as possible while leaving an open path to the target vent. Then, they'll send us to new locations to listen again. Alright?"

"Can we do that pressure loop thing?" Salem asked. "To make it go where we want?"

"This will be quicker," Ank said. "It's basically Bozrass' solution to the 'fugitive capture problem,' only instead of halving the space, we're going to close off about seven-eighths of it."

Salem didn't know who Bozrass was, but if Ank liked the plan, then it was a good one. And with such a simple task for Salem, there wasn't anything he could do to mess it up.

"Come on, let's go," Cejero said. He opened the door and stepped through, waving Salem along.

While Cejero roamed the common area and offices, Salem was tasked with the back right quarter of the ship. He moved between storage three and the engine room, looping around through the bare intersection, then back to storage.

The kikogen was either still or over by the bunks. Salem figured that it would try to get to the opening in storage three at some point, but so far, he'd heard nothing but the hum of the *Myzer's* engines pushing it through subspace, farther into the arcane medium.

After more loops than he could count, though he hadn't actually tried, Salem heard a noise in storage one while walking towards the engine room.

"—got it," Cejero's thin words flowed from the intercom. Salem hopped back to the doorway to listen. "Sounds like the common area, moving up towards the helm."

"It's here," Ank said. "Right outside the sensory room."

Thunk. Thunk.

Metal panels flipped closed, echoing down the corridors as Plexie systematically shut the outermost ducts.

Salem waited for his next instruction, hearing only the hum of the *Myzer's* engines. No voices or footsteps, no additional vents slamming closed. Nothing to indicate his next step.

After a roté, he wondered if Ank had meant the kikogen was right outside the door, in the corridor.

"Salem, head to the hall outside of my bunk," Ank finally said. "Cejero, go to the common area."

In their new positions, Salem and Cejero could talk easily, meaning they had restricted quite a bit of the kikogen's available range. Salem wondered how long those ducts could stay closed before affecting their air or heat. If it would even affect them at all. He'd never learned much about the life support systems. He felt silly for not taking the time to do that at some point.

"On its way down!" Cejero yelled. His voice was accompanied by the swelling *clicks* of the creature as it moved through the narrow vents.

The kikogen had moved more in the last half-circayd than the entire trip leading up to it. There had to be a reason for the sudden agitation. Had it been hibernating or nesting? Had it only now become hungry?

Thunk. Another vent closed.

Then, as the creature's footsteps faded, something strange happened to the ship. Something Salem knew inherently, though he'd never experienced it before. The ship...

Whirled.

Ank had pulled the *Myzer* out of subspace and into the arcane medium. The sensation was as if the ship had spun around itself, but the shipboard gravity had still kept Salem's feet in place. He'd always imagined the medium tossing a ship around uncontrollably, like rolling along the floor in a barrel. That's how the Energy Department described it.

Then again, the Energy Department also said that the ship was a bubble, its inhabitants isolated from the deadly universe around, and that wasn't so.

The four venth gathered in the bunk corridor, and Plexie ran directly into his room, which held a basic interface for the ship. It was a poor substitute for the primary control systems, but if a problem arose while they slept that prevented him from leaving his room, he needed to be able to quickly seal doors, adjust power supplies, or, more importantly right now, close sections of the ventilation system.

Wrangling the kikogen into the final duct was a tedious process. The long, narrow vent had several offshoots—small, but large enough for the kikogen to move through. Closing them required precise timing to ensure the kikogen was trapped in the "cannon duct," but the creature's location was anything but precise.

With her neck retracted, Ank gazed up at the ceiling. She heard the creature move, far away from the last remaining offshoot. "Now!" she yelled, and the last vent *thunked* closed.

"Okay, get ready." She pointed to the ceiling in front of Salem's bunk. "When it's around here, most of the air in the tunnel will be behind it, which should be enough to—"

Click, click, click.

The kikogen's feet clicked along the ceiling towards Ank's finger, searching for a way out of its tunnel prison.

"Now, Plexie!"

Ctshh—phwoop.

The heavy, exterior vent opened, dense and distant, creating a tight vortex of air through the lone duct. A loud *whooshing* ran through the ceiling, like heated water flowing through a pipe for just two beats.

The kikogen's body thunked along the duct once, then twice. A small, yellow-green tip appeared from the ceiling inside Salem's bunk, ripping through the vent and partway into the room.

The whooshing ended.

The claw remained.

A narrow breeze cascaded over Salem, whistling up through the ceiling around the kikogen's claw.

"Close it!" Ank yelled.

Cejero took a step back. "I don't—" he started, shaking his head. His fingers tapped nervously at his shell plates. "What else can we do?"

The breeze stopped, and Plexie ran out of his room. His eyes followed theirs to the small, unassuming dagger protruding from Salem's ceiling.

The arm vanished briefly, spearing back through farther.

Retreating to the engine room, Plexie reopened all of the vents except for the damaged one near storage three, allowing the kikogen to roam freely through the ceiling, again. That had stopped it from digging through the roof of Salem's room for the time being.

The engine room was still a bit warm from its time being closed off. Ank stood a few steps away from the others, out in the hall, listening for signs of the critter returning.

"None of the related cellular tests have been completed," Cejero said. "But I'm almost positive that hydro-sulfuric acid will kill it."

"I was told never to use that," Salem said, "even in an emergency."

"Yes, it will eat through the floor, but we've gone through enough of our food reserves that we could combine them all into one ration store. Those rooms are effectively sealed from the rest of the ship to allow for preservation without energy waste, and should be big enough that the acid cloud won't spread past the edge. It's the same material as the pressure room, so it's…"

Cejero stared off, then turned his gaze to Salem.

"Right," Salem nodded. "Let's do it in the pressure room."

"You're gonna burn through the tank," Plexie said, "or the refiner." He tapped idly on one of the dead machines nearby. "But… you know…we might be able to blow it out of the pressure room. I can disconnect the gas pump from in here. The exterior hatch would open while pressurized, and the differential should pull the creature outside. I don't think it'll be able to dig into the floor of the pressure room. It's basically a hull."

"Do you think we can lure it with food?" Cejero asked.

"I don't know. Aren't you the expert?"

"Yeah, Plex," Cejero said flatly, "I'm the expert on the alien species nobody knew existed until just now."

"Well then how would I know?"

"I was really asking Salem. He's dealt with it more than anyone."

The floor fell away in an unusual manner, like they were floating in liquid. The *Myzer's* desire to remain still was at odds with the arcane medium in which they resided. It bobbed flat to the side, then went still.

Salem's gaze wandered to the wall's edge, towards the suit closet. "I can lure it in," he said.

Cejero raised his palms. "Wait a turn. Maybe we should at least *try* food before we resort to that?"

"How long will that take?" Salem asked rhetorically. "For all we know, *we're* its food." He turned the corner and came to a stop, staring at his old suit. It was worn and weathered, more flexible now than any other. "I've escaped it twice, now. I can tell when it's going to jump." He looked to Ank for support. She didn't object, which meant she was on board.

"Hook yourself in," she told him, "and when it comes into the pressure room, hit the switch. Try not to let it get its claws into you."

"Thanks. I hadn't thought of that."

"I mean because it will be able to hold onto you and stay inside."

"Oh," Salem grunted. "Right…"

"After Salem gets changed," Plexie said, "I'll head to my bunk and open access to storage three. Then we can close ourselves in the engine room."

"Are we sure about this?" Cejero said nervously. Right then, he didn't seem to Salem like a senior crewmember. He had no experience or training for this problem. He was terrified, just like the rest of them. Unsure, just like them. They were all equally unequipped to deal with the creature.

Except for Salem. In a way, he was the universe's foremost expert on kikogens. The alien, not the story monster.

For the next hundred rotés, he was the senior crewmember.

"I'm sure," Salem said. "Let's do it."

Plexie worked to disable the pressure room's cycling process while Salem hooked the tether to his old space suit—ratty, frayed, and burned within threads of uselessness.

The way he figured, if the kikogen grabbed the material of his old suit, it was more likely to give way, and since he'd already stopped using it for collections, they wouldn't be losing another suit if it was torn.

The isolated, sound-dampened environment of the space suit made it difficult to hear the pentapedal steps on which Salem had relied. The kikogen could turn the corner right in front of the pressure room, and he wouldn't hear it coming.

The floor shook a bit under Salem's feet; he held onto the lever for support. "You done, yet, Plexie?"

With no one in the sensory room to radio Salem directly or patch the engine room's intercom, Plexie used the radio in his helmet, which lay on the floor near him. "Almost," he said. The sound echoed around the bend from the walls of the engine room a fraction of a beat later.

The whole process was taking longer than Salem had hoped. They should have rigged the gas pump before opening the vent to storage three.

Sharp, chartreuse legs appeared down the corridor ahead of Salem, past the lavatory by their bunks. The kikogen lingered at the intersection, almost as if looking around to get its bearings. A few beats later, via whatever means it used to view its surroundings, perhaps heat, it spotted Salem in the pressure room, tied to the ship by a metal cable, and while Salem hadn't been able to hear the creature's approaching footsteps, the shriek of its attack penetrated the material of his helmet just fine.

"It's here," Salem said, unable to filter the tremor from his voice. "One roté…"

For its size, the kikogen was fast. It halved the distance to the pressure room in a few beats, now just a couple of allos away.

"I don't have a roté," Salem said. The alien critter would soon be able to lunge, which Salem realized would require him to dodge away from the lever. He sidestepped twice, lingering in the center of the pressure room as the kikogen closed in.

One allo.

As it approached the threshold of the pressure room, twelve digits away, Salem saw a subtle bounce in its legs as all five touched the floor simultaneously.

Claws forward, the kikogen pounced. It careened towards Salem's chest, passing through the space he had occupied when it first left the ground.

He lunged to the door control, yelling, "It's in!"

With his hand on the lever, Salem watched the alien land gracefully on the floor near the exterior door. With or without the pump, he would have to cycle the pressure room. If the mechanisms operated normally, Salem would be trapped in the pressure room with the kikogen, and there would be no air to pull it outside when the door opened. Maybe it would die of exposure. Right beside Salem's bloody corpse.

He couldn't wait for Plexie. He threw the switch to close the interior door, dropping a curtain of shadow across the pressure room.

The kikogen turned back towards him.

As the last beam of horizontal light squeezed around it, it jumped again.

Claws out, the bug soared through the dark at Salem, outlined only by the pilot light of the pressure room. The interior door closed, trapping the two of them together.

Salem was off balance from the lunge to the lever. He was blocked on one side by the cable spool. His footing was weak, unable to even shift his weight to dive back to the side.

He raised his arm up, hoping to intercept the damage long enough to get his feet planted. Maybe even bat the kikogen away.

The outer door opened.

"Got it!" Plexie said.

The gale first appeared through a crack near the floor. It pulled at Salem's feet before filling the room, vacating the cubby of air in less than a beat. The kikogen's bounding attack slowed in the wind. It swung its scythes through the fleeting gasses, which yanked Salem towards it, placing him just within reach of its sharpened limbs.

One of the blades cut swiftly through Salem's tattered suit, opening a geyser of atmosphere from his sleeve.

Pain seared along his forearm beneath the jet of white air.

White air—frosted by the outside.

Not a drop of blood mixed in.

The kikogen hadn't cut him. It was just the cold burning along the opening in his sleeve.

The jet from Salem's pressed into the creature, and when all of the forces inside the pressure room were combined together, the ornery, green-yellow alien was left drifting towards the exterior door. It moved so slowly, it would've appeared stationary if not for the fact that Salem, too, was drifting towards the door, and the creature wasn't getting closer.

The kikogen waved its arms wildly at Salem, each swing coming within a digit of his suit. The pressure room fell away behind them. The cable slowly tightened and pulled against Salem's belt.

He marveled at the scene. In the absence of all air and heat, the kikogen wasn't dead. Not yet, anyway. And this wasn't any ordinary outside, either; the kikogen attacked repeatedly through the thick, brutal forces of the arcane medium, though as Salem watched, he noticed that the expanse didn't appear any different than usual.

"Are you okay?" Ank said, staticky, as if Salem were hundreds of wheels away. "What happened?"

Salem gripped the rupture in his suit, hissing at the burn spreading along his arm. The atmosphere pressed out from beneath his glove, cooling into a translucent mist in front of the kikogen.

"Yeah, I'm alright," he answered. "My sleeve is torn. That's all."

"The kikogen is gone?"

The cable stopped Salem at the exterior door, and as the alien's distance grew, its fight faded. He couldn't tell if it was dead or just idle, helpless to change its own fate.

"Yeah," he answered.

Even as he clutched a tear in his suit, Salem lingered at the end of the tether in the exposed pressure room, watching the kikogen drift away through the arcane medium.

CHAPTER 17
INSIDE THE MEDIUM

The wind of the *Myzer* almost knocked Salem over when it raced into the vacuum of the pressure room. With a breach in his suit, he couldn't wait for Plexie to reactivate the gas pump.

Ank and Cejero appeared behind the interior door as it opened.

"Great job!" Ank cheered. "What happened to it?"

"It's floating away from the ship," Salem said, adding, "but barely."

Normally, when something moved outside, it continued forever until it was stopped. Item drift was a constant problem for Salem while he was working, and as a result, it was a concept he understood inherently. Even in gravity, he was mindful of how much pressure he placed on items when he set them down. That wasn't necessarily how objects floated in the arcane medium, though. As the name implied, it was unpredictable.

"Is it possible for the arcane medium to push it back?" he asked. He set his helmet underneath the empty suit hook.

"Um…probably not," Ank said unconvincingly.

"Maybe I should change into another suit and go outside for a bit? Just to make sure it keeps moving away."

"Hathem wants to treat your frostburn immediately," Cejero said.

"And the longer we wait, the more difficult it will be to jump," Ank said. "We need to start now." She headed up towards the sensory room with Cejero. Salem followed along, ignoring his injury.

"And you're sure you can plot the jump?" he clarified.

"Yup!" Ank said. "There's been a lot of really interesting work done over the last ten cycles by a few venth, mostly Alazend, on modeling the effective forces of the arcane medium using six-dimensional field theory. We can use a variant of his algorithms to approximate our movements after breaching and plot a jump from that."

"Couldn't you just pilot us out, then?"

"That requires real-time data, which we don't have. The vector fields are a large-scale application. They can't tell us anything about our fine movements."

"So how can you jump?"

"We have stored data, silly suit. We can extrapolate with *math*."

"You still need to initialize the jump," Cejero grunted.

"I have a plan."

"Without sensors? I'd love to hear it."

They walked through the common area as Ank began explaining the mathematics to Cejero, which sounded extremely complex. She paused at the beginning of the opposite corridor, which wound up to the sensory room, and turned to Salem.

"Why are you coming with *us*?" she asked. "Go see Hathem."

"I'll go later," he said.

"You'll go now," she said, slapping his frostburn.

Sitting at the edge of the examination table Olyké lay on, Salem waited patiently while Hathem picked fragments of dead carapace from his forearm, preparing to treat and seal the burn.

"Okay, we're going to try again," Ank's voice came through the intercom. Hathem sighed, pulling the tweezers away from Salem. He and Olyké gripped the examination table; Hathem, the edge of the counter.

The ship threw Salem downward into the table, pressing it painfully against his butt before launching him to the floor by the doorway. Hathem and Olyké both fared better.

Ank's second attempt to jump the ship out of the arcane medium had gone as poorly as the first, throwing the crew around much like when they'd been evicted from subspace. As Salem had recently learned, the medium didn't just make the calculation of jump coordinates impossible—it made the mere act of entering subspace problematic, too. In keeping with the analogy for subspace travel, jumping required a running start, which the arcane medium prevented.

And every attempt used fuel.

"She's going to run the tank dry," Olyké grumbled weakly. Her body was covered in bandage wraps, though she did seem a lot better now that she wasn't actively bleeding. "I can't believe I let her pull us out of subspace between zones…If we're lucky, we'll get pushed back to the one we just left before we run out of power."

Hathem helped Salem up from the floor and seated him back on the bench near Olyké's feet, resuming the treatment of his dead shell matter.

"If Ank says she can jump out of the medium," she said pleasantly, "I believe her."

Salem had also been confident that Ank could calculate the incalculable and plot their jump, but even she had once admitted that piloting through the medium was impossible. That was effectively what initializing a jump into subspace required. The "run-up" required an active awareness of the ship's position in relation to the universe. In the zones, aiming that run-up was a routine process. In the medium, it was like running along a strip of ground that twisted while they ran in ways they could neither see nor feel, and hoping to lunge off the end at a very specific angle and velocity.

When they failed, they got knocked backwards onto the ground.

They could always just plot a course and let the ship jump, allowing the metaphorical ground to alter their path however it saw fit while they ran. It would result in a smooth jump, but it would also guarantee that they landed back in the medium somewhere.

Hathem took the pause between initializations to grab a protein binder that Cejero had taken to use on the kikogen leg.

Salem sat in the medical office with Olyké, who was already in a sour state. The frayed chitin on his arm began to itch, requiring a conscious effort not to touch it, as instructed.

"Salem, do you remember Jenithem?" Olyké asked. Her voice was soft and low, like rough soil being dumped onto the ground. "She was a civil engineer."

After some pause, Salem said, "She sounds familiar."

"Do you remember the power outage?" she asked. "You would have been fairly young."

That, Salem did remember. All of the power systems in the colony had shut off for part of a circayd. The rōshis had huddled all of the hatchlings and grubs into the Burrow with everyone else and lit fires.

"Yeah," he said. "I think I was one or two."

"That was during my second contribution cycle," she said. "I was still working on Bendil 2, tasking engineers for the power systems. Basic stuff. What happened was the main reactor had ruptured—a bunch of fluke issues all occurring at once—and as soon as it was obvious that the core was going to explode, I went through the regulations: evacuate all personnel, seal the affected area past the maximum damage estimate..."

"That makes sense," Salem said, too tired to inflect his voice.

"Jenithem came up with a way to prevent it, saving the colony a lot of material, energy, and ships. She *insisted* she could do it. And..." Olyké stared off through the cabinets. "I let her convince me. I cleared her. For something I knew I shouldn't have, and she died. Best engineer Venthralli had seen in generations, and I'm the reason she's gone."

Salem nodded quietly. He didn't quite know how to respond to a story like that.

"When my instincts tell me something is wrong, I have to listen to them. Right now, I'm being forced to ignore them because we have no other option, but it feels similar to that rupture. With you, it wasn't that I had ignored my instincts and regretted it. It was somebody else ignoring them, which is why I said I couldn't trust you and removed you."

"Yeah, I know," he said. "I'm sorry."

"No, Salem—" She sat up a bit, wincing. "I'm saying that I was wrong about that. You've put yourself in a lot of danger over these last sets. More than anybody else. And that initiative is the reason we're not all frozen back in that awful zone. You *are* trustworthy."

He smiled at the ground. "Thanks."

"And so, I've been thinking that...*if* we get back...I would remove the ship's handler restriction."

Salem blinked. That would place him back on the *Myzer*. "Oh," he said. He was never completely sure how to act around Olyké.

"If you want to, that is," she added, then sighed. "I don't think any of us will be faulted for grounding ourselves voluntarily after this trip. I know you were looking at moving to civil..."

"Yeah, but that would be instead of the labor tasks I usually do between excursions," he said eagerly.

Salem hadn't actually spent a lot of time considering the true gravity of the various situations they'd encountered throughout this excursion. He knew they were extreme, of course, but not in the wondrous way that finding alien ruins was. In horrific ways. Ways that would probably affect them forever. Stranded outside the excursion limit, boarded by violent alien invaders, untethered and isolated. They were truly living through the tales of nightmares.

"But in turn," Olyké said. "You have to trust me, too. When I tell you to abandon a task, it's not because I don't think you can do it— the whole reason you're here is that I didn't think we could shard-hop otherwise—it's because something else is giving me that same, dreadful feeling, and I won't be the cause of another person's death."

"Okay," Ank said through the intercom. "We're going to try again in a roté."

"Like now," Olyké sighed and rested her head back down, staring up at the ceiling. Were she ever likely to convey emotions,

Salem would have suspected her to be on the brink of tears. "She even reminds me of Jenithem."

Hathem returned with a fairly large jar of syrupy liquid. "I see that often," she said with a melancholy smile. "Just smaller. And cleaner."

The ship jolted again. Hathem held onto Salem, so he managed to remain on the table throughout.

"Shit," wheezed Olyké.

With each failed jump, the ship was moved in unknown ways, and the likelihood of their success dwindled further. Ank claimed that their position relative to the rest of the universe was actually somewhat calculable to a degree, but that the longer they waited, "the more unreliable the bijections between the coordinate memory and approximated third-order vector fields would become."

Whatever that meant.

It must have meant something to the universe, because other than ghost ships that appeared cycles after their crews had died, the only ships ever to exit the arcane medium had been piloted out from the very edge—a couple of wheels. Nobody had actually jumped out of the medium and into a zone.

It took Ank four tries.

Ank's "impossible" jump didn't go without complications. In addition to using a lot of extra fuel, she had to jump the *Myzer* into the easiest zone to plot a course for, which was the one they had just left. With no more shards in the zone, they replotted the same course, giving them a substantial energy deficit for the circayd.

Amidst the rhythmic snoozing of his crewmates, Salem lay awake in the common area, wondering about the light shard they were about to land beside. Would its light go away as soon as he cut into it, or would it take a few chunks, first? Or would there be multiple lights in multiple places?

They were just idle thoughts, designed to distract Salem from his true worry: that a quarry beast would come after them while he tried to collect it.

After much pondering, Salem decided he would simply cut up the light shard in whatever way would get it into the *Myzer* quickest, and not worry about the light at all.

The ship landed and the crew awoke. Ank skittered to the helm to locate the light shard within the zone.

Preparing for a long circayd of cutting, Salem ate another rotten-flavored vegetable, wondering how something so nutritious could taste so awful; it seemed counterproductive. He ate quickly, to avoid tasting the disgusting nutrients.

"Does knowing that the spike came from the kikogen change anything about it?" he asked Cejero.

"Not really," the science officer said. "It changes some of the significance of the findings, since we know it's not specifically from a quarry beast, but it's more of just a parameter to keep in mind. We know the two are connected in some way."

"We do?"

"Sure, think about it: how did the kikogen get onto the ship in the first place?"

Salem shrugged. "I don't know..."

"Well, where did you find its leg?"

"In storage three."

"And what else happened there?"

Salem thought for a moment. It felt kind of like a trick question. "Oh," he said. "The hull was breached."

"Breached by a *quarry beast*," Cejero clarified. "We're the only ship ever to have one of these creatures on board. The only one to survive, at least. We're also the only ship to be grabbed by a quarry beast and escape. Combine that with the fact that the kikogen cut its way into the vents at the same location the quarry beast opened our hull...it's a very low probability that they're coincidental. The kikogens might be small quarry beasts, or a related species that diverged over eons. Even if they're not genetically related, like a symbiotic lifeform—that means they live cooperatively with the quarry beasts—it still means they live in the same environments, so learning about the kikogens provides insights about the zero beasts."

"How?" Salem asked, poking at his remaining vegetables. Having a larger ration because of the amount of work he had to do later should have felt like a reward. If they were eating food prepared on the colony, it would have. But he was eating ship-grown vegetables...and eating more of them was a punishment.

"Well, the tissue appears to metabolize very slowly, which means the kikogens can go without food for long periods of time, especially if they're not moving much. That suggests the quarry beasts also don't eat often, either from similar genes or behavioral parallels. Now, a predator that doesn't eat often is in danger of running out of energy and starving, so it raises the possibility that our two-jump evasion isn't effective because it escapes their vision, but because it drains them of too much energy to justify further pursuit. Perhaps Relentless Bastard isn't keener, but simply eats very well."

"Wouldn't that mean *all* quarry beasts can see through subspace?" asked Plexie.

"To some degree, yes."

"But that's worse!"

"I agree, but we don't get to pick the truth, Plexie. And if that *is* the truth, it's better for us to know. Otherwise, yes, it is the more dangerous scenario. It means that the people who didn't make it back weren't eaten because of some error they made, but because a quarry beast felt secure enough to continue the hunt."

Salem didn't like that thought: that all quarry beasts could be as tenacious as Arby, but simply hadn't learned yet that there was a reward for it.

"Or, maybe we were right the first time," Cejero said with a smile. He must have noticed Salem's concern. "Maybe 'Arby,' as you call it, is just physiologically superior to other zero beasts."

Salem nodded thoughtfully and finished his fresh-but-spoiled produce, trying to get the haunting thought out of his head while he waited for Olyké to finally come back and give him the order to get dressed.

But it never came.

After locking themselves away in the sensory room for a couple of hundred rotés, Ank and Olyké returned to the common area.

"We have an incredible update!" Ank raved.

Plexie bounced upright in his seat. "You didn't name the zone, yet, did you?"

"I—no…why?"

"Can we name it 'Lone Tone's Bone Zone?'"

"*Lone Tone's Bone Zone…*" Ank chuckled. "Yes."

"Focus, please." Olyké's cheeks pulsed around her jaw.

Ank slammed a piece of parchment down on the table. "*These* are the errant radiation readings from when we first turned on the sensors after being stranded in the PFZ—"

"PFZ?" asked Hathem.

"Pile of Feces Zone."

"You didn't actually name it that, did you?"

"I sure did—screw that place."

"Ank," Hathem said, pausing tactfully, "perhaps you should start to consider the sort of legacy you want to leave behind…"

"I already have!" Ank said. "Brilliance and whimsy!" She pointed to a column of numbers with unexplained units beside them. "*These* are the equivalent bands from here in…" she looked at Plexie. "Lone Tone's Bone Zone?"

"Correct."

She laughed again. "Brilliant and whimsical," she acknowledged. "Now, these increases between the PFZ and LTBZ are marginal, which means that the light shard in question is *not* in this zone."

Ank seemed excited, but it sounded like bad news to Salem. Plexie leered at her for a while before shaking his head, removing the news through his earholes.

"How is that incredible!?" he wailed. "We came here specifically for that shard!"

Cejero said quietly, "Because it must be in the next zone..." he grinned, "and *massive*."

"Wellll..." Ank grimaced. "It's actually not in the next zone, either. I'll have to find us different shards to hop us to the end."

Cejero's face scrunched. "Why? We can't take this thing back with us, and it might not be of any use once we've harvested the mega shard."

"Because it *is* the mega shard!" Ank said. Her fingers riled into a drumroll, giddy from her reveal.

"It *might* be the mega shard," Olyké clarified. "We don't have the time or tools to do one of those long-term scans—"

"Selective rescanning."

"—to compare against these basic ones, so it might still be some-where along the way, or something else entirely."

Cejero stared at the numbers on the table. "Something else entirely..." he echoed, eyes tracking down the paper. He opened his mouth to say something, then stopped, looking back over the scribblings. Eventually, he poked at one of the columns. "Ank, are you *sure* these are correct?"

Ank scuttled around the table beside him, "Yup!" she said, guiding him through each value set. "This is luminosity, which is *so fun* to use for this! These are both arcane medium scattering—this one with Tieffer-waves included. This is restricted by the sensor, as usual. And, of course, invisible mass here, normal distribution scalar."

"Then this can't be a shard."

Ank frowned. "Yes it is. *I'm* the one who finds them, remember?"

"No, I mean…this is well past the mass threshold for a shard's structure." Cejero pointed to something on the page. "See how slowly these values increased?"

"Yeah. Because it's far away."

"Right, but if you repeat that, say, eight more times…" his finger dragged across. "Look how much radiation this would show."

"Because it's big."

"Okay, fine, but that would be…what? Four million?"

"Four-point…" Ank bit her tongue, "two-nine-ish? Two-nine-ssseven…" Her right eye squeezed inward. "Ffffive—"

"That's too much pressure. Even for a light shard." Cejero fell back into his seat. "I think…" He paused, jaw open. "I think this might be a star."

"No way!" Plexie fell off the bench.

"There could be reasons we've never considered that would explain this. It could be a new phenomenon entirely, problems with the sensors…" he stared at the readings. "But, otherwise…our current understanding of fusion indicates that this should be a star."

Hathem rubbed her chin. "We certainly can't harvest a star," she said. "We probably can't get anywhere near it."

"No, we'd be cooked alive."

"Regardless of what it is, we need fuel to get there," Olyké said. "Not to mention home. Find us something within a jump, Ank."

"Consider it done!" Ank ran over the table and out towards the sensory room. Half a roté later, she poked her head back around the corner. "Well? Who's coming with me?" she said. "Come on, Salem!"

"Why me?"

"Because you're the one who needs the company, not Ank!" she said, running partway down the hall before doubling back again.

Salem grabbed an armful of his things and ran after her, ready to sit in the sensory room for circayds if that's how long it took for her to find a trail of shards that led them to a star.

A real star.

CHAPTER 18
Discovery

Lounging around the sensory room while Ank searched for fuel, Salem became aware of how much he had begun to take her talents for granted. Even little things, like how she always positioned their shards on the pressure-door-side of the ship.

With any other navigator, searching for fuel out here would have taken a quarter of a set, with Salem returning to the helm every circayd, hoping that they would find an adjacent shard before they all died in Lone Tone's Bone Zone. It was why most of a navigator's work was done before the excursion, over the course of sets.

With Ank, there was no surprise when she found a sizable shard within a jump.

As Salem reflected, though, he decided that it couldn't be considered pure luck to have her there. The only reason they knew about the mega shard—the star—in the first place was because of Ank, so there was a self-fulfilling aspect to it all. No other navigator could have paved their way through uncharted space as Ank had because no other navigator could have made a discovery of such consequence that an excursion like this would be warranted.

To Salem's surprise, the thrill of the star's existence diminished quickly. Several collections after LTBZ, the tiny white dot remained unchanged. Same size, same color—white with a tinge of ultraviolet if he stared at it for a while. Cejero insisted that the star was growing, but to such a small degree that they wouldn't notice until they were in the same zone. Ank insisted they were nearing that zone. It was so close that it had become a point of excitement for everyone.

Whenever Salem did a shard grab, though, he looked at it and saw nothing more than a hallucination.

The *Myzer* touched down on an average-sized deadworld in a zone called Prestigose. Its surface was grey. Darker than his space suit but lighter than the *Myzer*—like the space suit of an engineer after a long circayd of work. The area in front of the pressure room was a flat, featureless clearing. There was no dust or powder on the ground, just a few sporadic pieces of rubble, broken away from the surface by past impacts.

"Alright, I dub thee…" Salem began. He blew the rest of the air from his lungs, giving his duty a moment of consideration while he got his bearings in the deadworld's gravity. He didn't want to bestow an unfitting name out of carelessness. "Clandix."

"Sorry to disturb you, Clandix," said Cejero. "We won't be here for long."

Salem strode out from the ship, knocking a pebble away with the toe of his boot. "Clandix," he decreed, "was responsible for protecting all of the other deadworlds from being burned by their star."

"How noble of them," Cejero droned.

Homing radar in hand, Salem stopped four allos out from the pressure room. He spun around fully, shining his lantern across the flat, silver clearing, briefly catching the edge of the *Myzer's* hull behind him. The beam swung past Cejero, who stared off at the dot of light in the distance. His body twisted slightly to angle the visor of the suit he and Plexie now shared.

"See?" Salem said. "It's not at all bigger."

"I see, Salem. And I'm telling you, that's normal." Cejero turned away from the star with a laugh. "Well, not *normal*," he added. "But, you know…expected."

Salem did another full rotation with his lantern. "I don't see anything here."

"Me either."

"Keep looking," Ank said. "It's not very big. Maybe two chunks or so."

Cejero shined his own light at the ground, dragging it slowly outward and away. Eventually, the beam faded and disappeared, too far to send any of its photons back. The surface of Clandix was unusually bare and even. No trenches, not even the little, circular valleys that covered most deadworlds. It was just flat and grey.

The pair walked around the perimeter of the *Myzer*, searching every digit of the hard, pale ground. There was a slight bounce to the surface, like heavily compacted soil. They checked an entire quarter-wheel radius around the site and found nothing.

Salem finally asked, "Ank, how far away could it be from the location you gave me?"

"Maybe an allo," she said. "There shouldn't be any margin of error when we're this close and locked with its movement."

Salem groaned, long and loud, embellishing the emotion for everyone to hear. "Is it buried?"

"Either that," Cejero said, "or we're in the wrong location."

"Then it's buried," Ank said.

With another airy groan, Salem walked over to the cart storage cabinet to pull out digging equipment. Shards weren't usually too far underground, but digging them up was exhausting and time-consuming, which took up a lot of extra air. On the other hand, it meant the shard was bigger than Ank had calculated, because its mass was being hidden by the ground.

Salem placed the digging device at the expected location of the shard and extended its legs out. The "strut scooper" was preferable to a shovel, but it had limits. It was basically a bucket-shaped shovel that rotated down and up in a vertical loop through the use of a crank. Mechanisms in the machine angled the scoop throughout the motion, pulling dirt from the ground and dumping it to the side when it rotated around. Salem would then lower the scoop down after each rotation to dig farther into the deadworld. The strut scooper could make a grub-sized hole about a third of an allo down, which was usually far enough to spot a shard. By making a grid of holes an allo apart, Salem usually found buried shards before his air tank ran out.

If not, he'd have to dig with manual instruments.

He set his flashlight on the other side of the strut scooper, faced towards the hole so he could see its reflection on the shard, should he expose it. The crank usually stopped moving when the scoop hit a shard, but the machine was also designed to carve through compacted dirt, so if Salem put his weight into it, he might start shaving pieces of the shard off. He could also feel the difference through the handle and into his suit, but the light allowed him to pay less attention. Which was nice, because, as far as tasks went, this was the most tedious. More so than cutting up a twenty-chunk starshard.

Salem turned the crank, periodically pulling at a ratchet lever to lower the scoop another digit. He gazed over to the star. It hovered near the ground, just barely visible above the deadworld's mass. He still couldn't shake the feeling that it was a hallucination: one they all shared. After all, he and Plexie both heard Arby talk to them, which Cejero had said was because of their shared experience in hearing the un-venth's growl. Couldn't they all be seeing the same phantasmic light? They spent a lot more time in pairs, now. Maybe it was the subtler, earlier stage of outside sickness.

Having collected all of the dirt he needed from Clandix—and not being able to cycle back into the *Myzer* until the shard was collected—Cejero wandered out to the edge of Salem's flashlight, idly investigating the area while Salem turned the crank of the strut scooper.

"Is this one of those shallow grave deadworlds?" Salem asked. Cejero had once explained that there was a certain type of deadworld for which all shards would be either on the surface or buried very close to it, which he had referred to as "shallow graves." Salem really wanted Clandix to be that type.

"Non-volcanic," Cejero said. The faint reflection of his own lantern ebbed and flowed out in the darkness. "Or, non-volcanic prior to the nearest supernova." His light began to brighten, sweeping across the ground nearer to Salem. "I haven't seen a single crater, so probably not. Don't worry, though. The shard won't be too deep. We wouldn't have seen it, otherwise."

Cejero had said that before, as well, but Salem didn't know how true it was. He'd once had to dig nearly an allo down to reach a shard.

They switched places for a little bit, with Salem scooping the loosened soil away from the hole as it fell out of the strut scooper. Soon after, they reached the device's maximum depth and moved it an allo closer to the *Myzer*.

When the second hole was about twelve digits deep, a dark glint bounced up from the bottom.

The material looked dark, almost opaque in the ground.

"Whoa," Salem grunted.

It was a chemically-hardened starshard. Similar to a light shard, but without the light. Or the cavity. This one appeared to be especially dense. It looked almost like metal.

"Now *that's* intriguing," Cejero hummed. "Hold on for a turn, Salem. I want to get samples of the soil around it."

Salem started pushing the mound of loose dirt farther from the hole, making room to expand. The easiest method was to move the strut scooper directly to the side and carve another hole until the entire shard was exposed. Then, he could use that loose dirt to build a ramp and pull the chunks up it.

After dropping into the hole and collecting his sample, Cejero climbed awkwardly back out to the surface, sliding his leg up over the lip and scooting across the ground until he could stand.

"You think that dirt is different?" Salem asked.

Cejero brushed the residue from the front of his suit. "I think this deadworld was once much, much larger."

Salem turned the crank, lowering the scoop to begin the adjacent hole. "Because of this shard?"

Cejero picked up the shovel, casually dragging the dirt dumped by the scoop away from the hole. "Some of the planets were much larger than any deadworld, but comprised mostly of gas or liquid."

"Like Soupworld!" Salem said. He smiled to himself, excited by the notion that his fictional planet could have been real.

"Ah, sure," Cejero said. He dragged a small pile of dirt away from the hole. "The cores of those worlds were solid due to the pressure. So much pressure, in fact, that some people have calculated that it could have created chemically-hardened shards all on its own—heat gel that was thrown into a gas planet. Later on, that gas would have been burned up or pushed away by the nearest supernova, probably the outer layers of the core, too, leaving behind the rock we're standing on."

"Is that why it's so smooth?"

"Perhaps. It's worth looking into. All sorts of elements could be in these cores." Cejero dumped some more of the freshly scooped soil into another sample bag. "The softness of the surface might mean some of that gas or liquid solidified and settled down."

Salem wound up having to switch his tank before finishing the collection, but the shard was also twice the size Ank had predicted with her scans. And since it was ultra-dense, Cejero suspected it would then be twice as much fuel for its size once refined.

It was a good haul. One that would get them all the way to the star at their destination.

The *Myzer's* final jump to the star was possibly the longest jump of their journey. Shard-hopping through their adventure had forced them into dozens of not-so-ideal zone transitions, either to obtain fuel or conserve it. Longer jumps had been forgone as a luxury, so once the star was within their grasp, the crew wanted to get there without further delay. They had energy to spare, so Ank plotted a two-circayd jump to the Stellar Zone.

Excitement flooded the air supply. Plexie was so energized that he forgot to perform the jump's post-initialization checks until Ank asked about them. Hathem smiled about nothing all circayd long, Cejero hummed. Even Olyké was in a good mood, only once mentioning in two circayds that they were, technically, not even halfway done with their mission.

For Salem, it meant a sleepless eve in the common area. Plexie snored lightly beside him, the engines rumbled beneath them. Lying on his back, Salem stared through the darkness at the outline where the ceiling hit the wall, thinking about the mega shard. What would it look like when he went outside? Would it blind him? Burn him? All the stories about ancient stars claimed that they were required to create new forms of life—a prospect that both invigorated and petrified Salem. Would those lifeforms be like the quarry beasts? Would they refuse to share their heat with Venthralli?

He rolled to his side in search of a comfortable position, desperate for rest before whatever the following circayd would bring.

"Come to our light," came a rumbling voice.

Salem gulped, rocking back supine and covering his ears. He wanted to shout at the quarry beast, to tell it to go fry itself in the star, but he couldn't. Not without waking everyone else.

Everyone else…

Everyone else was there. They were all sleeping in the same room *specifically* to prevent outside sickness.

"Not sick," the voice said. *"Awake…returning."*

"What do you mean?" Salem whispered. So quietly that the hazy cloud above him was the only indication he'd spoken.

"Welcome to our home."

"Hey," another voice whispered. Ank rolled to her side, her purple frame outlined in the dark by the tiny emergency light in the corner. "Are you awake?"

"Yeah."

"What do you think it's gonna look like?"

"Arby?"

"What?" she squeaked. Her carapace scraped against the floor as she sat up. "No, the star."

"Oh, I don't know," Salem shrugged. "It's supposed to be a giant ball of fire, right?"

"Uh-huh—why did you think I meant that quarry beast?"

"I think it likes light," he said. "And everyone says life came from stars..." He didn't want to tell her about the voice. It wasn't exactly a lie. Just a fractional truth. Ank liked fractions. "Do you think there will be aliens on it?" he asked. "Ones that like the heat?"

"That would be so weird!" she whispered with undue joy. "Is this what you think about when you're not sleeping?"

"Not all the time."

"Go to sleep!" Cejero hissed, his body still.

"Sorry!" they both whispered, but Salem didn't sleep. Not from lack of trying, nor excitement, but because even though the voice had ceased, he wasn't supposed to have heard it at all.

Late in the circayd, the *Myzer* bucked beneath their feet, placing the crew at the edge of what Ank had named the Stellar Zone. It was nearly time for sleep, but since they were planning to spend a couple of circayds in the zone, they could get a start on their first tasks. It would probably take a while just to figure out what could be accomplished without cooking them alive.

Eagerly, Plexie guided everyone to the sensory room to watch Ank take her first look at the nearby cosmos. Hathem scurried like she was ten again—Salem wouldn't be surprised if she went outside at some point during the upcoming circayds just to look at the radioactive generator, death be damned.

Only, there was no generator.

"T—this..." Ank stuttered. Her eyes darted across the readout, returning to the top before dragging down again. A fissure rose in her throat. "This isn't as bright as it's supposed to be."

"It will be plenty bright," Cejero said.

"No, it's...only marginally brighter than before the jump," she said, handing a page to Cejero.

He scanned the parchment up and down. The sides of his eyes dropped. "Shit..."

"No!" wailed Plexie. "After all of that?"

"Calm down, Plex. We might've just landed across the zone."

"Don't you tell me to calm down! You just lost an entire *star!*"

"I'm looking for it!" Ank squealed.

Salem wanted to tell everyone to stop yelling so Ank could work, but he didn't actually know how bad this was. If one of them said they were all going to die because of this, he would have no knowledge to refute it.

Ank punched away at the keys. "One of these should contain an anomaly," she said. "A large one. I'll try...inverted gravity extrapolation, thermal outlining..."

For twenty-five rotés, they watched Ank pull information from the *Myzer's* various eyes. She copied down some of it, wrote a few calculations, then stared at the page blankly.

"Well?" asked Olyké.

Ank shook her head. "It isn't here."

"Could it be in the next zone?"

"At this point," Cejero droned, "with these changes...it could be thousands of jumps away."

Olyké's eyes squeezed together, her jaw clenched. "*What?*"

"We don't really know. This is all unprecedented..."

Olyké stared at the consoles. Salem could practically see the steam rising up from her plates. The room was silent aside from the light whir of the machines and the rumble of the idle engine.

The silence was finally broken by Olyké letting out a long, throaty scream. "*Fuuuck!*" she yelled, swinging her fist against the wall beside her. Her carapace struck the metal with a dull *thud*, probably hurting her hand.

The crew watched quietly.

She hit the wall again, screaming, "*Fuuuck!*" She winced and rubbed the side of her hand. Her shell heaved around her lungs. "Just do a regular fucking shard search," she spat towards Ank. "See if we can find something that way."

Absorbing stress from the air, as purple-shelled venth often did, and likely blaming herself for their predicament, Ank sobbed softly while she performed the measurements used to locate inner-zone starshards. Once upon a time, she had excitedly explained the process to Salem, which involved bouncing signals off small angles of space and then measuring the responses to rule out anomalies like invisible mass clusters. When Ank was training, a navigator Salem's age had lauded her ability to intuitively decipher between proper readouts and cosmic trickery.

Ank finally cheered, languidly, cutting a bit into the tension.

"I found something," she said. She scooted to the panel on her right, rotating a dial downward. "There's a really big shard here. It has to be at least an allo wide and tall."

"That's around twenty chunks," said Plexie. "Depending on the depth. With the fuel we have, using optimal jumps, that might even be enough to get us back to the excursion limit."

Olyké glared at the discarded readout, as if the paper itself had taken their star away.

"Alright, we'll grab this consolation shard," she said, turning to Ank. "That'll give you and Cejero time to figure out what to make of these readings."

The floor rocked gently underfoot as the *Myzer* rotated toward the shard. The ship retched once, beginning its path along the inappropriately named Stellar Zone.

Starshards were larger in volume than their refined gel would ultimately be, which made it somewhat difficult to gauge how much of the tank a shard would fill up. When it was the size of a domicile, like the one in the Stellar Zone, there was little ambiguity. It would certainly fill the rest of the *Myzer's* tank.

Processing a shard of that size took a while, usually requiring a pause after four or five chunks to allow the reactor to refine them before adding more. Starting so late in the circayd, Salem and Hathem were only able to chunk off about four pieces before bed, anyway. The mega shard glowed in the distance, tiny as ever, indistinguishable from itself in previous zones.

Salem hoped Ank and Cejero could make sense of it all. Even if it turned out to be a star they could never reach, that would be something. It would make the expedition worthwhile to the colony. And if they collected that first anchor shard on their way back, the *Myzer* would return with more fuel than it left with, also.

Salem and Hathem only received one update as they chunked off the quartet of 0.4-allo cubes and fed each to the reactor.

"Designation changes aren't permitted," Ank said, "but nothing we've done past the excursion limit will reach the colony until we return, anyway."

Salem looked at Hathem. "Okay…"

"So, I am renaming this zone the 'Mirage Zone.'"

"It's definitely not here?"

"Or any zone nearby," Ank groaned.

Oddly enough, when the star vanished, so did Salem's concerns regarding it. He collected the first chunks of the domicile-sized shard with no expectations of a scientific breakthrough, nor anticipation of a quarry beast hive, making the mundane chore of his contribution role almost relaxing. And affording him his most restful night of the journey.

Upon waking, Salem went right back to work. He immediately cut off a single chunk, allowing the *Myzer* to process it while he switched to a batching procedure. He cut up the entire shard—an impressive haul of twenty-seven chunks in total—and fed them one by one into the reactor until the fourth of the batch, at which point the refiner started rejecting them.

"That's it for now," Plexie told him. "It needs a couple hundred rotés to catch up. Olyké wants you inside, anyway."

"Why?"

"I don't know, she told us to come to the sensory room. I'll meet you at the pressure door."

Salem checked that none of the remaining chunks were drifting away, leaving them clustered together like eighteen fruit on a shrub.

He glided over to the pressure door, taking one last glance at what he believed to be a distant star as it fell behind the hull of the *Myzer*.

Salem shut his air tank off and set his helmet by the door. The effort required to shed the suit and put it back on wasn't worth a couple of hundred rotés of added comfort, so he followed Hathem and Plexie through the cold narrows of the *Myzer* in his hefty clothing.

They came across Olyké and Cejero waiting in the common area, the color in their carapace washed out.

"What's going on?" Hathem asked. "You two look flush."

"Let's wait for Ank," Olyké said. "She's compiling some long-distance scans the ship has been running."

"Is something wrong?"

"Yes."

Cejero gave no effort to explain, making the reticence of their colony administrator all the more disconcerting. Salem looked at Hathem, who merely gave him a shrug and waited.

When Ank finally made her way to the common area, there was no rapid pattering of her hands and feet against the floor, no haphazard flailing of limbs brainwashed by excitement. Her steps were heavy and lethargic, one at a time until she appeared.

Cejero's back straightened, wobbling as he turned in his chair.

"Well?"

"It traveled exactly one thousand light-rotés."

Olyké leaned her forehead against her fingers and closed her eyes. She let out a disparaged, defeated laugh. "Well…fuck."

"Yeah…" Ank sat at the table and pouted. "It's a bummer."

"Okay, please explain, now," Hathem said. Her gaze darted between the three morose venth. "*What* traveled a thousand light-rotés?"

Ank looked to Cejero. Neither were eager to explain.

"This light we're seeing," he said. "It's not a star. Not really."

"Do you know what it is?"

"Yes, it's…" He shook his head in disbelief. "It's all of them."

Hathem didn't seem to know what Cejero was saying, which made Salem feel a lot better for not knowing, either. She started to become annoyed. "What does that mean, Cejero? All of *what*?"

"All of the stars. Millions of them. Billions. Maybe more."

Hathem recoiled back, mouth agape. "Ech—" she started, her words replaced by a cough. Like her tongue had forgotten how to formulate speech. "W–what?" she finally said. "Didn't they all explode?"

"Supernovae, yes. Eons ago. And we've always believed that the matter from those stars dissipated through the outside indefinitely, until nothing was left aside from sinkholes and the occasional deadworld. Species like the precursor to the venth would have been forced to live in isolated structures to survive, or flee on ships like Venthralli, dying out slowly over the following millions or billions of cycles."

"But now…?"

"It appears that the stellar debris was drawn back to the gravitational center of the universe. Perhaps augmented by the arcane medium or…super particles of invisible mass or something. The deadworlds weren't the planets farthest from a nearby star. They were farthest from the center of the universe. *We* were farthest from the center. Our ancestors."

"Isn't this a big deal?" Plexie asked. "Why is everyone sad about it?"

Ank's breath spread across the table in a thin haze. "I thought the measurements were increasing because we were moving towards it," she said. "But it was moving towards us, too. That's why I kept under-calculating the mass."

"The stars are moving towards us?" Salem asked.

"That much mass creates unfathomable pressure," Cejero explained. "And heat. It's how the universe is believed to have originally begun: all matter existed at a single, infinitely dense point, which then expanded outward."

"I've been overlapping the results of a few different sensors," Ank said, "to see how fast the heat is moving—measuring the distance a particular thermal level expands over the course of a thousand rotés…and it moved a thousand light-rotés."

"What's a light-roté?" asked Salem.

"The distance light travels over a roté," Cejero said. "Around twenty-nine million wheels."

Ank stared sadly at the table. "Twenty-nine million, four hundred fifty-three thousand, one hundred—"

"That's how fast the *heat* is moving towards us?" Hathem's voice broke. "The speed of light? Wouldn't that mean the stars are all going supernova again? All at the same time?"

"Sort of. I guess you could call it a hypernova."

"Why isn't the light approaching, then?" Hathem asked. "Salem keeps saying it hasn't moved."

Cejero gave an exhausted laugh. "Because those are just photons. The light we're seeing is, technically, from the past. When we finally see that light growing in size, it absolutely *will* be moving at the speed of light. A cosmic explosion that will destroy everything in our current universe."

"My god…"

Cejero nodded. "Once we notice an increase in our surrounding heat, it'll be a fraction of a beat away."

"At least we'll be nice and crispy for the quarry beasts," Salem said dully.

"Oh, the quarry beasts are as good as gone. I don't see how they could know it's coming. Venthralli isn't even aware. The radiation heat will fry everyone long before the so-called 'starfire' reaches them. They might even get crushed by waves of invisible mass."

"Then it's up to us to warn them," Olyké said. "How long until this reaches the colony?"

"The initial wave of radiation shouldn't reach Talesk-Venthralli until the end of the cycle." He gave a shrug. "With a margin of error, of course, but there's still time."

A quiet whine left Plexie's throat. "Venthralli isn't ready to make repeated jumps like that..." he squeaked. "to keep in front of the explosion."

Olyké stood up from the table, stretching her back out. "We have to let the colony worry about that. Our only concern is getting the information back to them." She looked between Ank and Plexie. "If we collect everything outside, can we get back to the excursion limit without stopping for extra shards?"

They exchanged a glance. "Maybe..." Plexie said. "It'll be close."

"Salem, Hathem, and Plexie, grab those shard chunks as quickly as you can without flooding the refiner. Ank, find us the path with the longest average jump—we need to minimize our initialization costs. Cejero, gather any data you can on this hypernova while we're still in the zone. If this all goes smoothly, we'll be in subspace for the next half of a set."

Cejero rose with a nod. "I'll note what I can," he said. "A lot of fundamental truths were just upended, though. As far as we know, Venthralli is plummeting towards the center of the universe as we speak."

"Is that actually possible?"

He shrugged. "We've been using photon travel to determine neutral positioning for cycles—what we call our 'cosmic anchor'— but it's constrained by the arcane medium. If the medium, itself, is contracting—"

"You're the Science Officer. It's your call what to prioritize."

"We should start by documenting a slew of redshifts," he told Ank. "That'll be the most useful overall, and maybe we can determine if our baseline has been skewed—"

"Quiet!" Ank sat up stiffly. The room dropped dead, filled only by the idle hum of the engines and life support. When Salem strained, he could hear the distant beeps of the sensory room performing whatever searches Ank had left it to accomplish.

Her eyes widened. "Oh no!" she cried. She sprang up from her seat and scurried out of the common area on all fours. A dense pit formed in Salem's stomach. He and Plexie exchanged a glance and ran after Ank, the three older venth lagging in their wake.

"What is it?" Plexie called out as they ran down the corridor. They neared the sensory room door and slowed to a stop. A white light flashed inside, timed with a grating, siren-like sound. Plexie leaned against the bulkhead's frame, huffing at the crisp air. Salem squatted slightly, allowing his suit's rigidity to support his body.

Olyké and Cejero brushed past him. Hathem glanced over his head at the pulsing lights.

"Oh no..." she moaned, spinning to run back down the hall. "Plexie, Salem, let's go!"

Without question, they followed, retracing their path through the corridors of the *Myzer*. Salem grunted through his hindered step; the sounds of the sensory room quieted behind him.

"I'm sorry! I'm sorry!" Ank cried. "I've had all the sensors..."

Her voice evaporated as Salem ran across the bedding in the common area. He had a surprisingly difficult time keeping up with Hathem's long strides, hop-jogging behind her.

"What's going on?" Plexie screamed.

"We need to siphon fuel out of the reactor!"

"What's happening with the reactor?"

"Nothing," Hathem called back. "It's—"

Clunk-clunk-clunk-clunk-clunk-clunk-clunk!

The loud, rapid pounding of the quarry beast permeated across the side of the *Myzer*. Hathem stopped in her tracks, head retreating back into the top of her shell. Her eyes followed the sound along the corridor ceiling.

Her voice wisped out.

"It's here."

CHAPTER 19
THE SIEGE OF THE MYZER

Hathem burst through the doorway of the *Myzer's* engine room. The mysterious actions of the quarry beast outside sizzled through the hull; a scratching from beneath, a whine from above.

"It's right on the reactor," Ank's voice buzzed. The ship jolted an allo back and forth as she tried to pull it from the beast's clutches, throwing Plexie from his feet inside the doorway.

"We just need one jump," Hathem said. She careened left towards the cubby housing the shard boxes. Plexie's fingers scraped the floor as he reached the reactor, scrambling up to two feet and colliding with the panels in lieu of slowing down.

Salem followed Hathem to the shard boxes. "One jump for what?" he huffed. With the *Myzer* already in the claws of the quarry beast, he didn't see much point in shutting down the reactor. It wouldn't be fooled anymore.

Hathem dragged a shard box across the floor. "To get out of the zone!" She yelled over the squealing metal of the box against the floor. "If it drains all of our fuel, the colony will be consumed by the nova."

Salem removed one of the heavy containers from the shelf, its back end crashing to the ground. "What about the quarry beast?" he shouted back.

"We need to harm it enough to give us time to replace the gel and jump…" She grunted, pulling at the box, "or kill it."

Salem paused, hand resting on the box handle.

Never before had he heard someone suggest killing a quarry beast to be a possible solution, and with no trace of embellishment or exaggeration, Hathem's words to that point were inspiring, because what Salem *did* know was that they were the only crew to escape the clutches of an un-venth, on the only vessel to have accomplished that feat.

They had escaped before.

They could do it again.

Worrisome creaks filtered into the engine room, the lights above their heads shuttered. Salem pulled his shard box along behind Hathem. Ahead, Plexie connected a wide tube with a slanted edge to a once-covered port on the rearmost wall. With the first shard box opened beneath the spout, Plexie pulled a small lever recessed into the adjacent machine.

A viscous gurgle came from the angled tip of the makeshift drain, followed by a thick stream of glowing atoms spewing from the opening. Opaque, white steam rose into the air.

If Salem's memory was correct, which it often was not, the shard boxes couldn't hold the gel in this form indefinitely. They were designed to keep unrefined shards from evaporating, not to contain the liquid inferno of their refined sludge. Closing the lid would prolong that timeframe, but for how long, he did not know.

Plexie watched the heated sludge pool in front of him, his face bright in its glow. "Salem, can you start the preparations to ignite the fuel reserves?" he asked. "The same as the heat-strip prep."

"No, we'll be stranded," Hathem said.

"Not an actual heat-strip," he explained. "After we fill the boxes, we can seal off the engine room and ignite the remainder. That'll blow the quarry beast off of the reactor, and we can feed fuel directly into the distributor column for each jump back."

Hathem stared past the glowing stream for half a roté, her shell wavered in the hot air. "Okay, yes. That could work. Tell Olyké. I'll grab the last box."

Salem leapt over to the radio, relaying Plexie's idea through the sound of boiling propellant.

"That's too risky," Olyké replied. "We might destroy too much to get home. We have to look at other options first."

"There won't be time!" Plexie yelled. Hathem pulled the last crate from its shelf with another *thud* and began dragging it towards the boiling gel.

After a lengthy pause, Olyké said, "Tell us when you're done filling the boxes," she said. "If we don't have anything better, we'll blow the reserves."

"Got it," Salem said.

"And bring the other suits up here with you."

"Right."

The pool of yellow neared the top of the box. The light danced radiantly along the corner walls, up until Plexie slammed the lid shut, prolonging the life of the box against its corrosive contents.

Salem and Plexie dragged the full container out into the hall. The back corners carved tiny ruts into the engine room floor, shaving the metal beneath. Salem feared that the box would be damaged to the point of leaking across the corridor, but it didn't.

They pulled the box over the lip of the bulkhead, leaving it still in the hall.

But the sound of flaying metal continued.

Darkness swamped the halls, not unlike the outside. A few moments later, the *Myzer's* emergency lights kicked on, bathing the ship in a dim, orange hue to spare them from disorientation. A flat horn sounded throughout the ship, the significance of which was unknown to Salem—an alarm he'd never heard before.

They rushed to the second shard box and moved it under the spigot, reopening the flow of heat gel. Hathem dropped the end of the last one beside them.

"There's three," she exhaled.

Her next words were replaced by a gasp, sucking in the residual cloud of breath that had yet to vanish in the warm air.

The flow of heat gel dwindled, then stopped. The second crate was less than half full; the pool of fuel within settled calmly.

Plexie shut the valve off and on.

"What the heck?" he wailed, repeating the process a few more times with no effect.

"It drank the rest…" Hathem said quietly.

"Already?" he said. "There's no way!"

He lunged to the fuel hatch and cranked the handle, prying open the dense cover. There was no reflection from deep within, as there usually was, no blast of heat that could be felt across the room. It was just dark, tinted orange by the nearby emergency lights.

The tank had been emptied.

Emptied of fuel, but not empty. The reservoir's hull tore open, and a long, jagged spear burst into the engine room from the tank.

The scythe-like limb skewered Plexie through the lower neck, pushing easily through the back of his shell. Fragments of carapace flaked away from the appendage as each barb pushed through, soaking the floor behind him in thick chartreuse.

His body convulsed, but he gave no scream; just a single, gargling cough.

Salem darted towards Plexie, though to what action he wasn't sure. Hathem dug her fingers into his arm, anchoring him with her massive frame.

"*Next, you…*" The creature's voice rumbled into Salem's ears. He couldn't get swept up in hallucinations and ignored it, focusing instead on the drumming in his stomach. Dry bile worked its way up his abdomen. He forced it back down with a slow breath.

"We need to get out of here!" Hathem shouted over the droning alarm. Between each swell, the hiss of escaping gas emanated from within the tank, beyond the demon's spear.

Hathem kicked the lid of the partially filled box closed and heaved one side towards the door. Salem followed suit, wrapping his glove around the opposite handle and lifting.

He waddled the back end of the crate to the door. His legs grew softer with each step. The walls blurred as he shuffled into the hall.

The blade behind them retracted back into the reservoir, and with it, Plexie.

The roaring gale yanked Salem's feet out from under him, and the back of the shard box crashed to the floor. He clenched the handle tightly, legs swinging in the air as the exposure pulled him.

Hathem propped her back against the wall outside the door, rotating her torso to pull the box, and Salem, another twelve digits into the hall, growling through her teeth. She spun back into the gale, throwing her elbow against the door control, and sealed off the engine room.

The world around Salem continued to fizzle—the lines between the floor panels zigzagged in front of his eyes. A sob rose up his throat and out his mouth, causing him to finally void his stomach onto the grated floor.

Hathem dragged the shard box beside its heavier counterpart.

"Salem? Can you hear me?"

He grunted, "Uh huh…"

"Come on, get up," she said, but Salem couldn't. The butchering of Plexie remained in his mind. As faint as the sight had been in the dark engine room, it was still the most gruesome image Salem had ever seen, and it was too much. Salem wasn't squeamish—not like Ank or Cejero—but hearing Plexie's carapace shredding away from his body; seeing his insides pushed through his back, the vacancy in his face…it made Salem dizzy. He couldn't stand up.

Salem had known people who had died, but they were always older, and they always passed away elsewhere: a doctor's office or during hibernation. Not somebody his age. Not in front of him.

The powerful force of Hathem's arms pulled Salem from the ground, scraping the boots of his space suit along the floor. With his feet planted and stomach empty, the amber corridor around Salem came back into focus. Clear enough for him to realize that the scraping hadn't been from his boots at all. It was coming from the engine room. Like grubs scratching at the door.

"Suits…" Salem uttered.

"Good idea."

Hathem rounded the corner to the suit closet. Salem hobbled into the wall, clawing his way along as his equilibrium returned. As he got farther from the engine room door, the scraping quieted, falling behind the periodic ringing of the alarm.

From the orange haze of the nearby corridor, Ank appeared on all fours, running ahead of Olyké and Cejero.

She stood up beside Salem. "Did it work?"

"Did what work?"

"The fuel thing."

"We…never got a chance," he said. "It ate the rest."

"*Already?*" Cejero gasped. "How?" He looked around for a more knowledgeable explanation, spotting the sealed engine room. His eyes dropped. "Where's Plexie?"

Hathem thrust a suit into Cejero's hands—the one he and Plexie had been sharing for almost a set. He looked at the suit, its gloves stained with dark residue from the ship's machinery.

Ank whimpered. "What do we do now?"

"Get dressed," Olyké said, pulling the outerwear up around her shell. "The air is already thin, and we could depressurize at any beat."

Salem helped Hathem fit her shoulders through her oversized suit, her plates creaking from recent strain. More scratching came from above their heads. Salem's eyes grazed across the dark, orange ceiling plates. It sounded almost the same as—

Thud.

A conic dent formed in the engine room door, bending outward into the hall, then another. Salem stumbled back a step, blood surging through his arteries. He waited for a third hit against the door, watching through the thinning fog of his breath, but the commotion inside had paused.

The crash came from behind, farther down the hall by their bunks. A ceiling panel fell to the floor inside Salem's room, barely visible in the shadows created by the corridor's emergency lights.

And behind it fell a small creature, neither quarry beast nor venth, emitting an adorable, laughter-like chitter.

"A a kikogen!" Salem spat out. "In my room!"

The parasite screeched, charging towards them. Salem lunged for the suit cabinet, picking up the heat saw from the floor. He flicked it on in haste and spun around, back to the wall as the cutting edge warmed up.

Halfway into her suit, Ank hopped back, dropping the fabric down to her feet so she could step out of it.

The kikogen dug one of its claws into Ank's leg, then the other. The serrated arms dragged downward, spilling her blood over the creature's body while she bellowed through the air.

Taking a heavy step, Hathem planted her boot and kicked the small alien as hard as she could. It soared across the open area in front of the pressure room, smacking into the adjacent wall. It dropped to the ground belly-up, and as it tried to right itself, Hathem stomped the boot of her space suit onto its stomach, pressing all of her weight down. The creature's shell cracked under the force, but it seemed otherwise unharmed, squirming with vigor and swinging its limbs at her foot.

Salem ran beside her and pressed the blade of the heat saw against the front of the kikogen's body—what was probably its head. The blade wasn't sufficient for cutting carapace, but the creature screeched nonetheless, changing the focus of its attacks to Salem's hand. He pressed harder, fighting to keep the blade steady while the alien flailed. Its shell sizzled; the talons of its arms cycled rapidly. Every attack came within a digit of Salem's hand. It would only be a matter of beats before it finally connected and sliced through his glove.

But it never did. After an entire roté of burning the parasite's face, its cries finally subsided and its fight faded.

Hathem slammed her boot down on the limp creature one last time. The nauseating smell of charred skin assaulted Salem's nostrils. His shell heaved as his lungs struggled to oxygenate, gasping at the attenuated air. Every exhale formed a cloud as big as his head.

Thunk.

The icy mist of Salem's breath was pulled back around his face. The door to the engine room broke open into the hall. The five venth stumbled towards the depressurization a step. It was loud, but mild. The quarry beast must be covering the exposure in some way.

They had to preserve as much air as possible in the rest of the ship. Salem grabbed his helmet and made his way up towards the common area.

At least, he started to.

Motion caught his eye from beyond the broken door of the engine room. The movement grew closer, barely visible in the lightless opening until it finally emerged.

A pale, pink tendril wound its way slowly into the cabin from the reservoir. It slithered into the hall, whipping back and forth along the floor and walls like a recoiling cable. Filmy residue remained on every surface it grazed, freezing within beats.

The crew stared, stunned as they dressed—time they couldn't afford to lose.

"Everyone, get back!" Salem shouted over the turbulence. He turned and sprinted up the bunk corridor as fast as his suit would let him, helmet in his hand.

Turning down the offshoot towards the science office, he made his way up towards the medical office, leaping over the frame of the bulkhead before the junction and sealing it behind him. He ran up past the medical office and through the common area, legs chaffing against the rough material. He stepped back over the lip of the corridor leading to the bunks, closing the corridor seal.

Alone in the dark fog of the bunks, Salem paused, allowing his eyes to absorb the amber reflections of the scene. He placed his helmet on, twisting it back and forth as he walked along the bunks until the mechanisms lined up, then locked it down.

Through the haze, the slimy appendage materialized. It slid around the turn to the suit cabinet, probing for the crew nearby. Olyké and Cejero fumbled to get their suits the rest of the way on, but Ank still hadn't started. The gash in her leg was too large to clot even in the cold. Her shell rolled as she gasped at the weak air. The crew retreated farther into the nook, Ank half-carried by Hathem, her eyes fixated on the emerging tendril.

Salem sidled along the wall farthest from the prehensile digit—what was probably a tongue. After a couple of steps, he could see it in its entirety back through the engine room door. Through the narrow openings surrounding it, Salem could see more commotion.

It was three things. Squeezing their way through the available space in the broken door to the engine room.

Salem yelled over the fading wind, "More kikogens are coming!" but with his helmet on, only Hathem could hear him. One of the parasites spotted him immediately, breaking away from the others to cross the intersection towards him. Salem braced for the attack, heat saw held firmly in front of him.

Expecting the kikogen to lunge, he swiped downward through the dim light, striking the floor directly in front of the creature. Sparks leapt up from the impact of the hot blade, bathing the corridors in white light.

Over past the suit cabinet, the other two kikogens jumped up onto Cejero, digging their sharp, cutlass arms into his chest.

The four pointed limbs punctured rapidly into the suit hanging on his shoulder. Blood splattered across the fabric with each strike.

The flash lasted for only an instant before the sparks were snuffed by the cold, but the image remained burned into Salem's eyes while they readjusted to the dark.

The kikogen in front of Salem leapt up towards his stomach, appearing from the darkness caused by the flash. Salem recoiled in panic, flinch-swinging the heat saw up diagonally into the kikogen, smacking it with the cold side. A soft *thud* reverberated up his sleeve from the impact, sending the creature careening past him along the wall.

Salem couldn't hear any sound of pain from the animal, but judging by its frantic flailing, he hadn't caused too much damage to it. He stumbled away, heart pounding against his carapace. The heel of his boot caught the lip of the bulkhead, sending him into a backpedaling dance to remain upright farther down the bunk corridor.

Cejero's screams, carried through the air and into the unworn helmet radios, stopped. Olyké shouted something Salem couldn't hear, and in the distance, he could see the outline of Cejero's body fall to the floor. The kikogens started dragging him back to the encroaching tongue, fighting against Olyké while she held onto his bloodied space suit. They pulled harder, their claws tearing further through the ragged flesh.

After a few tugs, one of the kikogens abandoned the kill to charge Olyké. She let go, punting the creature with the toe of her boot, then retreated hastily. The quarry beast's tongue enveloped Cejero's body, swiftly pulling him back into the engine room and through the fractured fuel tank.

Ank limped along the wall, dragging her space suit behind her with glazed eyes, towards Salem in the bunk corridor. Between them, the third kikogen sprinted for Salem. He backed farther into the bunks, waiting for it to jump. Again, he panicked, swiping the blade down early and missing, showering the nearby area with white sparks.

This time, though, the embers landed mostly on the creature's shell, causing it to stop and flail.

In the brief illumination, Salem saw Ank and Olyké by the door to his room. He could hear Ank call to Olyké, "Get in!"

"No," Salem shouted, "Plexie's bunk!" But neither venth had their helmet on. He knocked the perturbed kikogen onto its back with his foot and ran to the others, his stride wide and cumbersome in the space suit.

Thankfully, Ank noticed the broken panel on the floor of Salem's bunk and pointed sleepily to Plexie's, veering Olyké. The colony administrator rushed them inside, followed shortly after by Salem and Hathem, each with a blood-soaked parasite on her heels.

With barely a hiss, the door closed shut. The creatures flung themselves against it, and their claws softly *clanged* through the alloy.

Crammed into the bunk of their late engineer, Ank fell against the bed, sliding to the floor to sit in her pooling blood. Hathem crouched awkwardly beside her, a difficult pose to take in a space suit, made worse by the tight confines. She removed her helmet, leaving the air valve to pump gasses into the bunk. Salem did the same, cold stabbing at his neck, and Olyké opened her valve.

"I need light," Hathem whispered. Salem and Olyké squinted through the dark room, unused for almost a set.

Rummaging through Plexie's stuff filled Salem with guilt, even though he knew Plexie would insist that they toss his bunk if it could save Ank. Hathem grabbed some of Plexie's bedding and crunched it around Ank's leg. The young venth clenched her teeth. Her breathing remained rapid and deep, even as the air density increased.

"Hurry," Hathem urged. "The wound is too big to frost-clot. I have to try to stop the bleeding, but I need light to do that."

On the back wall, Salem found the small interface that Plexie had used to adjust the *Myzer's* systems. It would run off of any available power source, so as long as they had emergency lights, it could turn on. It might produce more light than their helmets.

Clawing underneath Plexie's bed, Olyké removed a tube-like object. She held it up to her helmet light, flicking her finger at one side until a blue flame shot from the end, bathing the room in brown-grey.

"Cabin welder," she said. Cabin welders were used for fixing thin metals inside the ship, emitting smaller, cooler flames than similar tools used outside, which usually burned violet.

"That'll solve both," Hathem said, taking the welder from Olyké. She elongated the flame, lowering it near Ank's leg to examine the sopping wound. Two deep cuts formed on her thigh, one slightly above the other, and ran down to her knee, meeting halfway to form a Y-shape.

Thunder came in from the walls, pulsing the air as more of the *Myzer's* hull was shredded.

Hathem reduced the torch jet to its minimum. "Ank, this is going to hurt," she warned.

"I know."

"*A lot.*"

"Okay…"

"And you have to keep quiet."

Olyké handed some more of the bedside linen to Ank, who stuffed a wad into her mouth and bit.

With the steadiness of a surgeon, Hathem moved the torch towards Ank's leg. The blue glow on the shell plate narrowed and sharpened as the jet got closer. When it was half a digit away—still not even touching the plate—her carapace began to sizzle.

Memories of Plexie's shell melting against the engine ravaged Salem; it was just as nauseating the second time around. Ank screamed without pause, loudly, even through the icy cloth in her mouth. Salem put his helmet back on, anticipating a possible breach in response.

The smell was already inside.

Hathem jerked the torch away. "You have to hold still or this will take longer," she whispered.

"Mff tryffinff."

"Salem, hold her leg, please."

As instructed, Salem tried to keep Ank's hindlimb still while she instinctively pulled away from the flame. The torch flared through the lens of his visor, which smelled less potent as time went on, but he couldn't keep her leg stationary, even with Olyké's help. It wasn't until Ank became dizzy from pain and lightheaded from screaming that Hathem was able to cauterize the wound.

"Okay, all done!" she said cheerfully, as if she'd performed a minor procedure on a hatchling.

They helped Ank into her suit; she bore weight on her wounded leg surprisingly well.

"The heat saw hurts them," Salem said as he held the sleeve up for her to work her arm in. "I'll bet the torch does, too."

"Probably," Olyké grunted, fastening Ank's helmet down. "But I doubt it will do anything to the outside creature."

"Un-venth," Ank said woozily.

Olyké gave her an annoyed face. "We still need to figure out how to deal with it, and soon."

Ank took deep, deliberate breaths, filling her lungs with her new air supply. "We know the landing jets work," she said. "Which means either extreme heat or force."

"I don't think that will work on a regular quarry beast," Salem said. "The jet only worked on Relentless Bastard because it was smarter, but weaker, remember? We can't have been the first people to try burning one with a landing jet."

"Yeah...?" Ank gave Salem a confused look. "That's this one."

Salem blinked, stammering, "W–what? No...I'm talking about the one back at the excursion limit. The one from Hobblecob."

"Yeah," she said again. "That's this one."

Salem recoiled back a step into the wall. "But—that..."

He couldn't believe it. He didn't *want* to believe it. The voice he'd heard was supposed to be fake. It couldn't know anything that Salem didn't already know, because it was in his head. That's what Cejero had said. That's what Hathem had said.

But Salem had heard Arby's voice just rotés ago—his creeping outside sickness. Or, so he was told. If the beast attacking the *Myzer* was actually Relentless Bastard...

How could Salem have possibly known that?

"That can't be true," he said. "Are you sure?"

"Yup." Ank coughed. "It's pretty easy to tell, now."

"B–but we've jumped dozens of times. If it followed us, why wouldn't it have attacked us while we were stranded?"

Ank shrugged. "I dunno. But I was going to present the algorithm to the Exploratory Advisor when we got back. To try to build a more consistent system of identifying…"

Her voice fell out of Salem's head. Strangely, he felt no nausea. He heard no further taunts from the rumbling voice. He felt no terror, trauma, or panic.

He was angry. Spiteful.

Vengeful.

This single quarry beast had followed them across the entire damned universe…

It killed Plexie.

It killed Cejero.

And now, it was trying to kill every other venth. To make them extinct.

Fuck Arby.

"…but now, I guess there's no point," Ank finished.

"How do we kill it?" Salem asked with an energy he rarely possessed.

"I've been thinking," Hathem said as she fastened her helmet. Her voice rose through the radio. "Burning the fuel was probably our best chance at causing damage through its carapace, but we may be able to get it to ingest something hazardous."

Olyké thought to herself for a moment. "Like poison?"

"Poisons, chemicals…everything we can get our hands on from the offices and storage rooms."

"We don't have large amounts of those. Will they be enough?"

"Who knows?" Hathem said. "Some of them are potent enough to kill a venth from a few drops."

Olyké stared at the nearby wall, as if clear through to the outside. As much as Salem wanted to kill Relentless Bastard, it was an attempt at the impossible, and probably couldn't be done with small vials of chemicals. Causing it pain, though, or making it sick, was a feasible goal that they had already accomplished once. Without access to the engine room, chemicals were probably their best chance.

Salem looked at Ank to see if she had another idea, but she remained silent on the bed, wincing with every motion.

"Alright..." Olyké nodded, eyes still on the blank metal beside her. "We seal away the common area and helm, then reopen the back corridor to the medical office..."

She moved to the terminal at the back of the bunk and flicked it on. The light produced was weak and useless. "Ank, can you run?"

"I can three-leg."

"You and Hathem go to the medical office and lab," she instructed, selectively closing bulkheads throughout the ship and opening others. "Salem and I will do the storage rooms."

Gripping the heat saw, Salem prepared himself to face the kikogens presumably lying in wait. *Hopefully* lying in wait. It would be a lot worse to dig through the storage areas with three monsters roaming the halls like their namesake, unable to hear their approaching clicks through the helmet.

Salem looked at Ank again, half-expecting her to suddenly come up with a better way to kill the quarry beast. It was too fantastical. She had made a habit of coming up with quick, clever solutions, saving the crew multiple times, changing the way the colony saw the universe. Salem would be drifting through the Pile of Feces Zone right now, frozen, had Ank not meticulously calculated—

"Wait!" Salem blurted. "Do you have any more of those festival toys? The sparkling ones?"

Ank's face furrowed behind the curved plastic. "I doooo...?" she said quizzically, then her eyes bulged with electricity. "I do!"

Hathem ignited the torch. "We don't have time for this, grubs."

"No, we don't have time to go through the offices," Salem said. "But we have a shard box right in the hall that's half-filled with refined gel. If we're going to feed it something, why not that?"

"Using a sparkler fuse!" Ank said. "Like in the PFZ!"

Hathem nodded slowly. "Not knowing anything about its digestion—that might also ignite the gel in its stomach." She looked at Olyké. "How can we make sure it eats the box while the sparkler's still burning?"

The room went silent. No sounds came from the ship—nearly dead, itself. Olyké's face distorted. She answered quietly.

"Bait…"

Salem had arrived at the same conclusion, just as he knew that he would be the bait. It was his role on the ship; his role in the colony, really. To be expendable. To go outside and cut up shards with nothing more than worn fabric between him and instant demise. To end his lineage. He wanted nothing more than to go home and paint and never leave the colony again, but that couldn't happen if the *Myzer* was destroyed. Not if the universe consumed Venthralli.

Ank looked between Olyké and Salem, perplexed. Then, she realized that the bait wasn't just luring the quarry as Salem had with the kikogen, but sacrificing themselves to it.

"No!" Her eyes bulged. "We can't do that!"

The hull beside them boomed, heavy and hollow, then pressed inward. A *creak* spread across the bending metal. The quarry beast's arm-spike squeezed into the ship.

"I'll do it," Salem said, saving Olyké from ordering him. She shouldn't have to do that this circayd. Not after losing two people, already. Not after pulling on Cejero's mauled body to stop him from being taken away.

"No," Olyké said. "It's my ship—my responsibility. You and Ank take the heat saw and grab the sparkler. Hathem and I will move the full shard box into the corridor and seal it away. Everyone clear on that?"

They all nodded. Hathem hovered her palm over the door controls, giving them a beat to prepare for the skirmish that lay ahead.

Before they could take on Arby, they would have to deal with the kikogens.

CHAPTER 20
DOMESTIC XENOCIDE

A tear came from the wall of Plexie's bunk, dampened by the helmets of the *Myzer's* remaining crew as the sound grew into a muffled crescendo. The metal near the ceiling bent inward. A jagged, black spear pressed into the hull.

Hathem stood with her hand over the door control. "Opening!" she shouted, the radio crackling from the volume.

The door slid up, pulling some of the remaining air of Plexie's room out into the corridor. Two kikogens stood less than an allo away, fine even after prolonged exposure to the vacuum.

Salem rushed to the nearest one, not wanting to afford it time to lunge. The small aliens seemed surprised at the sudden appearance of the four venth, though they had no faces to indicate as much. Their reactions were sluggish, like they were waiting around for the quarry beast to finish its task.

The dull patter of Salem's footsteps floated up through the air of his suit, followed by an abdominal grunt as he swung the heat saw downward as hard as he could. The kikogen sprang to the side, and Salem's arm connected with the unoccupied floor on which it had stood, bouncing upward.

Ready for the kikogen's response, Salem mirrored its tactics by leaping to the side when it pounced. He rotated back, watching through the glare of his visor as the creature's sharp, purple-mottled scythes cut through empty space.

With two hands, he swung the heat saw through the air, using all of the might his space suit would allow.

And he whiffed.

The tiny creature landed beside Plexie's door, safely on its feet as Hathem and Ank exited the room. It could only enjoy its escape for a beat before Hathem angled the fully-powered torch flame against the back of its head area. The top of the kikogen's shell boiled; its claws swung up weakly. Within a couple of beats, the blue flame appeared underneath the creature, melting through its carapace. Its body collapsed to the ground in a small puddle of burnt entrails and molten flooring, the top half of its body no more than a smoldering hole.

The other kikogen stopped on its way to Hathem, dissuaded by the dancing jet of fire whose length exceeded its entire body. Salem took a long stride to the hesitant alien's flank, and rather than swinging and missing as he had so many times already, he pressed the saw into its side.

The violent critter swung its arms wildly at Salem, each swipe threatening to cut his suit. Gritting his teeth, he held the tool down firmly, pushing the heated blade harder into the critter's abdomen.

Then, one of the long, curved claws arced up, farther than its previous attacks, and connected with Salem's face.

Bonk.

He gasped at the impact. The back of the claw smacked into his visor, bouncing off without cracking the shatter-resistant material. Salem's hand shook, pulling the blade back a fraction of a digit.

His blood-colored foe didn't get another try. The imposing figure of the *Myzer's* doctor appeared beside him, adding the cabin torch to the onslaught. The animal's shell boiled beneath the extended flame, its screams preemptively silenced by the void as the flickering azure light cut into the floor beneath it, leaving a circular divot in the metal.

"Looks like the torch works," droned Hathem.

Olyké nudged one of the shard boxes with her foot. "Remember, there's at least one more," she said. She nudged the second box. "This one." She leaned over to grab a handle.

Skittering on three legs, Ank's fourth limb dangled freely as she followed Salem to the far end of the bunk corridor. Her room was only a couple of allos away, but that was far enough to lose sight of Hathem and Olyké in the amber darkness.

Wind pressed around Salem as the door to Ank's room opened, which at least indicated that the missing kikogen probably wasn't inside. Ank ran in to grab the sparkler while Salem waited near the door, arm cocked back with the heat saw.

Balancing on opposite limbs, Ank held the decoration up, its narrow outline barely visible in the glow of the emergency lights. "Got it!" she said triumphantly. Salem took the sparkler so Ank could walk, then cautiously led them out into the hall.

There was motion…a torn grate in the floor. Some kind of access point for wiring or piping. The last kikogen squeezed through the frayed metal and into the hall.

Having found much more success in the "press gently" tactic, Salem lowered the heat saw to the level of the kikogen and stepped forward, hoping to make contact before it could get completely into the corridor from the grate.

He was too slow. The kikogen cleared the opening and pronged at Salem, claws out.

Wise to their movements, he rotated his body and ducked away, allowing the creature to soar by. As it passed, its feet clicked against his visor. Salem swiped after it with the saw, catching only the vacuum.

Spinning from the graze against Salem's visor, the kikogen landed back-first against Ank's helmet, bouncing off to land on the ground, facing Salem. She pounced from her near-crawl and grabbed the creature's arms just below the start of its claws: what Salem considered its elbows.

Rolling onto her back, Ank suspended the creature above her, struggling to keep hold as it kicked frantically. She cried out, "Get it!"

The critter's legs tapped against Salem's glove as he pressed the hot blade to its stomach. A small trail of smoke trickled to the ground like billowing liquid.

"Come on!" he growled. After an entire roté of having its stomach burned with the saw, the kikogen continued to kick wildly, tough little bastard that it was.

Then, it kicked itself free.

The kikogen twisted one of its claws loose from Ank's grip and twirled around, dangling from the single arm she still held. Before it could cut her, she flung it backwards over her head.

The creature sailed end-over-end down the hall, past Salem. It careened off the wall, spinning like a top as it hit the ground.

Unsteadily, the creature rose to its feet, then dashed off to the pressure room.

"It's coming!" Salem said. "The other kikogen!"

The corridor ahead disappeared into nothingness, otherworldly in its orange haze. Salem ran after the fleeing monster, his steps sluggish in the rigid suit. After a few beats, the figures of Hathem and Olyké appeared through the dark, both clawing for the torch resting atop the stagnant shard box.

With all six limbs, the alien bug leapt at Hathem, tearing into her arm. A shrill scream pierced the radio's waves as she fell to the ground beside the kikogen. A jet of white air shot from her forearm. Blood trickled into the stream.

Olyké struck the cabin welder repeatedly, but the flame wouldn't start in the vacuum of the *Myzer*. The kikogen stabbed another claw into Hathem, digging deep into her shoulder.

The creature stabilized its footing beside Hathem and raised its other claw back, preparing for a barrage of punctures.

Continuing to charge forward, Salem arced the heat saw low and ran past Hathem, swatting the creature up and off. It hit the nearby wall, legs splayed out at odd angles when it landed on the ground. Salem pinned the closest leg down with the heated blade, pressing for what seemed like rotés, not daring to let up.

"Cold..." Hathem whispered, voice masked by the whistle of fleeting air. She pressed her glove against the opening in her side.

Eventually, the tension beneath the saw gave way, cutting through the kikogen's limb. Dark pink, almost red blood sprayed along the floor; a flash of white light flared as the blade pressed into metal.

No longer pinned, the kikogen flipped onto its stomach. Salem didn't let up on his assault, sawing into the creature's back. He practically fell on top of it, heat saw wedged between them, to stop it from turning around. To prevent the blades on its arms from facing him.

Eventually, it fell still.

Salem tossed the heat saw and sparkler on the floor, grabbing the handle opposite Olyké. They carried the full crate the last half-allo to the hatch.

"Ank, get in," Olyké ordered as she stepped backwards through the hatch, the sound coming from deep within her stomach as she lifted the shard box.

Without hesitation, Ank turned and hobbled back towards the bunks. She was the only one who could realistically get the *Myzer* back to the excursion limit. The colony depended on her survival, now.

Dropping the shard box in the hall, Salem ran back to help Hathem get through the bulkhead. The air escaping her suit was a gentle massage through his own. With a final step over the lip of the doorframe, Hathem fell against the brimming shard box. Small geysers of air sprayed between her gloved fingers.

Leaving her and Ank to find trapped atmosphere elsewhere in the ship, Salem vaulted backwards through the door, and it slid shut.

The quarry beast moved again, felt only as vibrations in the floor. Salem wagered it was returning to the bottom of the fuel tank somewhere. Perhaps it sensed its cronies were gone.

Or it was releasing more.

The only sounds Salem and Olyké heard were the other venth.

Hathem asked, "Can you help me up?" followed by grunts of agony and exhaustion as Ank took Hathem to the tangle of rooms still sealed with life support.

Salem followed Olyké back to the junction. His voice came out quiet and low, like it was someone else's. "I think it's under the fuel tank, again."

"I think so, too. Let's drag this in."

More rumbling beneath them. The absence of atmosphere created far more mystery than Salem would've hoped for in this situation. He couldn't accurately tell where the creature was, whether it was cutting through the hull or moving. He only knew it was close.

Laying the heat saw and sparkler atop, they carried the second crate back to the engine room. It was lighter than the other box, but still not an easy object to move swiftly, especially in full dress. Even empty shard boxes were clumsy.

Not wanting to spur an attack prematurely, they gently lowered the trunk down by the broken hatch. Plexie's frozen blood coated the ground beneath them, glinting in the light of the heat saw.

Olyké plucked the festival decoration off the box. "Grab the heat saw," she said, angling the top towards Salem. "Once this thing is lit," she said, "get back to the far corridor."

He tapped the heat saw to the sparkly end of their unwitting fuse, then touched it more firmly.

Nothing happened.

He scrunched his face at the saw, then held it down for half a roté, far longer than should be needed.

"It's not lighting!" he cried. He pulled the saw away and tapped it against the tip again, barely fomenting smoke to drip down. He tried again and again but couldn't foster any ignition from the tube.

Salem's eyes darted around the engine room. His suited body twisted frantically in search of something that could light the sparkler. Perhaps a hull welder? All of the room's contents had been removed in the breach.

The whoosh of Hathem's vacating air supply stopped, her helmet removed. Her voice was distant, speaking from nearby.

"Coat the tip of the sparkler in heat gel—"

Salem cursed himself, "Damn, that's right." He had needed to do the exact same thing for the untethered collection.

"—soak some of it up and allow it to ignite outside."

Olyké opened the shard box; its contents immediately softened into a near-frozen slushee. She plunged the tip of the thin cylinder into the gel, swirled it around, and held it towards Salem.

Tssssk.

He squinted against the sudden flare. A smile grew across Olyké's face, glowing in the sparkler's aura.

"Perfect," she said. She ogled at the toy: once a gimmicky object, now the catalyst for defeating a quarry beast. She stuck the dry end into the shard box and wedged it underneath the lid. The embossed patterns of the container rippled in the flickering light. "Now get back to the door, Salem. And don't argue."

Heat saw in hand, Salem waddled backwards through the engine room hatch.

Knowing what was about to happen to Olyké somehow made it harder. Plexie and Cejero had been taken suddenly. Faster than he could really process. This time, he knew what was coming. He wanted to say something meaningful or profound, but he couldn't think of any such words.

"Thanks, Olyké."

She gave him a curt nod, then started kicking her boot heel into the floor.

Repeatedly, she stomped, making as much ruckus as one could in a total vacuum.

"Ank, get ready with the other box," she said. "You might not have long to thaw the gel and pour it into the distributor column."

The ship rattled: the quarry beast shifting along the hull in response to Olyké's noise. This time, it wasn't difficult to tell where it was. The beast traveled quickly; the pulses from its legs swelled more than in previous movements.

"It's coming," Salem whispered, stepping further into the hall. Olyké clutched the handle, hands holding tightly in a reverse grip, and continued her barrage against the floor.

The slimy tendril darted in from the fuel reservoir, slithering out of the darkness. It swept agilely along the floor, colliding with Olyké and wrapping around her in one smooth motion, knocking the air from her lungs.

The powerful tongue pulled her off the floor with ease, crushing her torso. The shard box made a single hop across the ground, too heavy for Olyké to maintain a grip on amidst constriction, and her fingers slid off.

"No!" she cried with a hollow voice. Her hand reached out for the box as the tendril slammed her up into the ceiling. It retracted back through the hatch, vanishing with the *Myzer's* colony administrator.

No further screams; no commands.

Just silence.

Past the dancing shadows of the idle shard box, Salem stared at the opening through which Olyké had disappeared: a black wound torn in the fuel tank. His eyes bulged, jaw hung wide.

"What happened!?" Ank asked. She was answered by silence. "Salem, what's going on?"

"The box was too heavy..."

"Alright. I'm coming back. The two of us can carry it."

"No, stay there," Salem said. "You have to get the ship back to the excursion limit."

"There's not going to be anything to pilot in a turn, Salem, and Hathem can't leave the medical office until the reactor is back on." Her voice was uneven, rising and falling as she limped back to the engine room. "We don't have a lot of options."

She was right, too. Salem would need someone to help fasten him tightly to the shard box. He silently cursed the reliability of their ship; the misfortune of its gravity systems *not* failing. He knew there was a way to shut them off manually—specifically for when the power systems were destroyed—but like any essential system, it was a complex process that Salem didn't know. He was a shard handler. If he wanted to remove gravity, he just went—

Rushing to the shard box, Salem dragged the makeshift bomb away from the fuel hatch. The corners ground along the floor, sparkler glowing strong. His eyes remained locked on the opening from which the tendril had emerged, watching with frightened anticipation.

He growled with each burst of energy, throwing his weight against the dense crate, celebrating every step he took without the prehensile tongue's reemergence.

"What's wrong?!" Ank asked, short-winded.

"I'm taking it outside…errg—I can throw it."

"Okay. I'll help you get it there."

Salem yanked the box up over the rim of the doorway, far enough from the hole that Arby couldn't grab him without warning.

"It's not worth the risk," he said, "I'm almost there."

He rounded the corner by the suit closet. The entrance to the pressure room flickered in the light of the sparkler. In one roté, he'd be there, and with no air to cycle, he'd be outside instantly.

Salem neared the threshold of the pressure room, bomb in tow, when he saw motion through the orange haze.

The hatch to the bunks sprang open, and Ank's silhouette appeared in its place.

"The ship is about to be ripped in half, Salem!" she said, walking around the full shard in the bunk corridor. She stepped through the bulkhead, animated by the gel-soaked sparkler in front of Salem.

Click click click click.

Four rapid vibrations pattered beneath their feet: the un-venth shifting in response to the dragging shard box. Ank neared, fully illuminated by the fuse, and dread swept through Salem. It was as if, right in that moment, he could see the future—like he knew he was about to be forever separated from the figure before him.

"Ank, go back—" he started, but before he could finish, the floor punctured upward. The thick, outer hull of the *Myzer* tore open like a knife through warm foil. The rumble that would have been the deafening rip of the ship's exterior pulsed quietly through Salem's feet as the razored arm of Relentless Bastard plunged up into the hall.

Terror drained into Ank's eyes, the last time Salem saw them.

The ungodly spike punctured through Salem's lower back, covered in chartreuse entrails as it exited his stomach, effortlessly sliding through his shell. His entire field of vision was obscured instantly by the dark blade, partially masked by splashes of blood on his visor. The fleeting atmosphere of his suit carried the sounds of his cracking carapace. Air squeezed out around the serrated claw, spewing yellow-green blood from his abdomen, covering the shard box and craggy floor beyond. Salem's lungs wouldn't work; they couldn't work. The agony was so unbearable that it almost didn't exist.

Then, as fast as the pain had begun, it ended. A faint gargle left Salem's throat, barely louder than the gaseous hiss surrounding it, and numbness overtook him. The spear pulled him down through the floor, and the metal panels of Salem's nomadic home crunched him in two around Arby's arm as the predator collected its prey.

"Got you."

CHAPTER 21
ANK

The darkened, dying ship provided a sickening backdrop for the carnage that occurred before Ank. Salem's viscera glowed brilliantly behind the gel-fueled sparkler, its flame wavered as his liquid insides splashed over it.

And then the scythe retracted. The serrations of its blade gripped Salem's suit and carapace, pulling him along with it.

Then, they were gone.

"Salem…" Ank wept, not realizing she'd said it until long after. The festival light blurred through her moistening eyes as she crawled towards it. She groaned into the pain in her thigh, pulling herself along as light-footed as possible.

"Ank? What happened?" Hathem asked, though she knew damn well what had happened.

"It got him," Ank sniffled quietly.

"Where's the shard box?"

"Almost outside."

Ignoring her instincts, Ank peered into the hole ripped in the *Myzer's* floor. Some idiotic part of her brain thought maybe Salem was alive down there, hanging onto a piece of broken metal as if there was gravity outside, or another deck below—some scenario where she could save him.

Thankfully, she saw nothing but blackness.

The shard box rested atop the broken panels jutting up from the floor. With the lid cracked open, the slush inside had eaten partway through the sides. If Ank didn't get it to the un-venth soon, the heat gel would corrode the walls entirely, rendering the device useless.

Or blowing it up in her face.

With soft, quick steps, she pulled the box around the puncture, leaning lazily away from the container. She was exhausted from injury and exertion; each tug at the handle was weaker than the one before it, each step anticipated to be her last. She didn't know whether she would collapse to the floor, be impaled by Relentless Bastard, or get swarmed by kikogens, but they all seemed like even odds. And inevitable.

Clunk clunk clunk.

Ank paused.

The un-venth moved overhead. Or underneath. Certainly nearby. Away to the left somewhere.

"I'm in the pressure room," Ank exhaled. She shambled to the only remaining tether and slowly connected it to her suit.

With careful, determined motions, she unraveled half an allo of cable and locked the spool, then threw the switch for the pressure cycle. In the absence of air, there was already an equilibrium between the *Myzer*, the pressure room, and the outside, allowing the exterior door to open without pause. The mechanisms made a heavy *chunk*, and the door opened, revealing the solid black canvas of the universe.

Ank stared.

Never before had she seen the cosmic expanse with her own eyes. Where the walls of the pressure room ended, so did reality. It was disorienting; terrifying. The physical universe just sort of... ended. It gave her the unnerving sense, as illogical as it may be, that using her ocular lenses to absorb the infinite void would kill her. Like trying to pump fuel out of an empty tank and breaking the pump, only in this case, the pump was her brain.

Of course, as Ank had discovered during the last circayd, she wasn't staring at an infinite anything. Reality was not expanding indefinitely, as previously believed. In fact, reality was more finite now than at almost any other point in natural history.

Balancing on her good leg, Ank leaned her head out of the pressure room. She wasn't sure what she'd expected to see other than more nothingness, but that's exactly what she saw. Somewhere out there, the un-venth clung to the hull, but with no light, there wasn't even an outline of the creature to gauge its distance.

Ank didn't know what the quarry beast was supposed to look like; not really. Nobody did. Reliable imaging was a long-standing issue in the study of extra-Venthrallian life. A decent outline had been formed over the cycles using dead ones people had found, but only one of those was ever viewed up close. Seeing any large object outside was difficult. It required a lot of time, energy, and light, and even then, it was a puzzle being pieced together by fragments, much like images of Venthralli itself.

Gently, Ank tugged upward on the box handle. It floated above the floor, the gel inside frozen from exposure. With steady, deliberate motions, she swung the bomb outside. Its weight nearly pulled her off her foot when she stopped it from sailing away. The festival toy shone like a beacon through the darkness, which made Ank suddenly uneasy.

Alas, there were no *thumping* steps of the quarry beast repositioning itself, no tendril snaking around the door.

Leaving the safety of the pressure room, Ank took an uneven step outside, allowing the slack of the tether to run through her fingers until she was beside the corroding shard box. The light of the sparkler only illuminated the hull for half an allo before it grew dark, but Ank was relieved to see that Arby was not right beside her.

Not wanting to leave the doorway, Ank checked up and down the side of the ship, then along the direction she knew it had gone.

Beyond the brightened section of hull, a thin line glistened in the darkness—a shallow curve that ran perpendicular to the *Myzer*, ending at its hull. A second, fainter line extended downwards from the first, perhaps one of the barbed limbs that clutched venth ships and impaled their crews.

Ank's chest tightened, blood flowing tensely from her heart. She didn't know if the un-venth could see her. She didn't even know if it could see at all.

With as much maneuverability as the cumbersome suit allowed, Ank placed both hands and her good leg against the side of the shard box, as if she were skittering along its surface, and lunged, sending the frozen combustible towards its target. She careened in the opposite direction, soon stopped by the tether pulling tight and swinging her into the ship. Her injured leg collided with the metal, sending a bolt of pain up her side and a vibration through the hull.

Groaning, Ank reoriented herself towards the door.

The glimmering light shrank slowly as it floated away. Along the hull of the *Myzer*, a soft, yellow glow traced beside the container.

"The box is on its way," she said. "The sparkler's still working."

The pair of sprites grew smaller, and another formed on the un-venth's carapace, warped by either texture or curvature. It moved along the side of the alien towards the approaching sparkler.

Ank pulled herself back to the pressure room along the short tether. She couldn't say with certainty that the bomb would hurt the un-venth, so it may not earn her much time. She had to get the *Myzer* jumping as quickly as possible.

Ank lingered by the entrance to the cubby; she couldn't help herself. She needed to see what kind of damage the explosive did.

The box hit the creature's shell, met by the glow that had moved along the carapace. A small circle of the creature's body remained illuminated, glowing brightly where two of its legs connected to its body. Each one extended out past the circle, into darkness.

The box became almost still upon impact, spinning gently beside the quarry beast, and the sparkler jostled free of the lid. The two objects danced separately in space. The circle of brightened carapace grew and dimmed as the festival light twirled.

"Oh no..." Ank exhaled. There wasn't time to unspool enough cable to get down there. She would have to unhook herself, float over, and shove the sparkler back into the box.

"What's wrong?" Hathem asked. Her voice was soft, as if she was worried it might carry through space and alert the predator.

Using the thick fingers of her suit gloves, Ank pried at the tether's hook, which was frustratingly difficult to unlatch. She continued to fumble with the hook, wondering who had designed them so poorly. Obviously, someone who had never once—

The quarry beast shifted behind the tiny light.

Ank froze.

Her nerves worked overtime to pull in every detail available, eyes expanding across her face. The leg joints moved out of the light. The thick hide slid by slowly.

"Ank?"

"Hold on…"

A series of unidentifiable nooks and crevasses came into the light and left. Then, something decidedly different appeared. A pale, pink opening in the darkness, ending abruptly in the center at a circular wall similar to its carapace, maybe to protect its innards from the outside.

No tongue lashed at the warm object beside the orifice. There was only the maw. Large, horrifying, and vivid in the glow of the sparkler. Ank could just barely make out small crystals forming on the inside of the mouth as it chomped down on the box and sparkler, surrounding both of them in darkness.

The ship jolted beside Ank, quickly and repeatedly. She couldn't see the un-venth approaching. She could only see the ship moving in relation to her; hear the rumbling from Hathem's exposed helmet radio.

It was moving along the hull towards Ank.

Turning to pull herself into the pressure room, Ank re-tore the gash in her leg, howling as a fresh stream of blood cascaded down into her boot.

"What happened?" Hathem asked, but Ank didn't respond. She had moments to get inside and shut the door.

She pulled at the tether, guiding her toes down to the metal.

The creature's footsteps stopped.

Within the lightless expanse, the body of the quarry beast illuminated once again, clinging to the hull. A pair of rumbles swept through the *Myzer's* cabin, one overlapping the other. A jet of flame and smoke flashed out of the beast's mouth and scorched the side of the ship. As the light extinguished, a fountain of dark-pink blood sprayed across the hull.

Ank was thrown violently into the back of the pressure room, or more accurately, the pressure room slapped into Ank as it rotated around its center of mass. She hit the interior door and bounced back outside, stopping when the tether pulled taut.

"Oof!"

"Ank, can you hear me?" Hathem asked. "What's going on?"

Floating outside the pressure room, Ank looked into the darkness beside the *Myzer*. There was no movement, no rattling of the ship, no thumping through the helmet radio. She wanted to yell something triumphantly at the dying quarry beast, but as her blood had already formed a deep pool in her shoe, yelling wasn't an option for her.

Screw you, Arby.

"I think it's dead," Ank groaned.

"Are you sure?"

Straining her eyes to absorb every spare particle of light from her helmet that might reflect off of the un-venth, Ank scoured for signs of movement. After half a roté, she thought she saw the chance glint of a large object rotating away from the ship. Slowly. The way a dead thing would.

"Pretty sure."

"That's…incredible, grub!" Hathem said tiredly. "Are you hurt?"

"Mmhmm," Ank hummed.

She felt along the edge of the pressure room for the lever, lungs taking in deep, heavy breaths from the air tank. Using the cable spool as leverage, she flipped the switch, again requiring no time to equalize the vacuums. The ground pulled Ank back towards it, and her legs collapsed under her.

"I need to put gel in…in the distributor…column," she said. In the orange light, she disconnected the tether with comparative ease.

"We can do that later."

"Nope. The…air."

On her three undamaged limbs, Ank slowly skittered—more of a crawl, really—back to the shard box sitting like weighted scrap in the corridor. Blood splashed up her freely dangling leg, sloshing into the rest of her suit. The hall began to blur, but she kept clawing her way towards the shard box.

Had Ank been in the right state of mind, she would have gone straight to the medical offices. She and Hathem could reroute air and treat her injuries before returning to the rest of the ship. They would have time to make the *Myzer* spaceworthy and transfer what little fuel they had into the distributor column.

Instead, her body became heavy, her arms buckled, and she collapsed to the floor beside the box.

There was beeping.

Annoying beeping.

Ank awoke tired, like she hadn't slept for an entire hibernation. She was more tired than she had ever been in her entire life, and she was being prevented from sleeping by whatever was beeping.

"Hathem?" she meekly called. She couldn't remember much of what happened after she killed Relentless Bastard. The image of its innards vacating through its mouth remained clear in her memory, but everything else was just swirling blackness.

A line of synthetic carapace coated Ank's leg where the stomach bug had stabbed her—a noticeable contrast to the beautiful purple hue of her plates. She blinked a few times, trying to focus on the room around her through a pounding headache. She was in the *Myzer's* medical office, or the medical office of another energy collector. The door was closed. Ank's suit lay on a chair across the room, Hathem's in a pile on the floor nearby.

Definitely the *Myzer*.

"Hathem?" she called louder.

Presumably—*hopefully*—Hathem was somewhere else in the ship, alive, with ample life support.

Soon enough, the door to the medical office slid open, and in ducked Ank's sole remaining crewmate.

"You made it!" Hathem said with a tinge of relief that was rare for the seasoned doctor.

"I made it."

"You've got quite the genes, grubbo." Hathem reached for one of the nearby machines, a sizable frostburn scar on her arm, and checked its readout.

"How did I get here?"

"I found you by the rear junction, next to the heat gel, and carried you here. I clogged my suit's tears with synthetic carapace. It's no insulation, but it worked enough to get to you and bring you back."

Ank looked at the suit piled on the floor. "Thanks."

"You are quite welcome," she hummed. "Besides, I don't think either of us is likely to return alone."

Ank had been so focused on surviving the attack that she'd completely forgotten about the return trip. They had a long path ahead of them, and right now, lying on the medical table, Ank didn't feel up for another journey like that.

She lay back against the bed. "How far have we gotten?"

"Nowhere."

Ank immediately sat up again. She figured Hathem would have at least done one jump to get them out of the zone. Ank didn't want to be here anymore. "We're still in the Mirage Zone?"

"Yes," Hathem said. "We've got a lot of patching up to do before the ship can go anywhere."

"Is Arby...?"

"Still dead," Hathem smiled. "You might want to go collect yourself some proof for the folks back home. I don't think anyone will believe you killed a zero beast. Sorry, an *un-venth*." She pushed on Ank's stomach to lay her back down. "Rest for now. I need to make more sustainable alterations to my suit before we can try to seal up the damage. Should you choose to ignore me and wander around, do not open any doors in the rear corridors past the common area."

"I would never..." Ank lied. She always moved when told to stay put. But on this circayd, the attraction of sleep was simply too great.

Ank's body ached.

All circayd, every circayd.

For the first two, she searched the nearby zones for starshards while Hathem did her best to patch up the *Myzer's* damaged exterior. At one point, Ank took Hathem's advice and went outside to try to cut off a piece of the un-venth. Not for fame or celebrity, but for credence to a story that could easily be shrugged off as outside sickness. Venthralli would be faced with urgent, sweeping decisions upon the *Myzer's* return, so anything that could expedite those discussions was worth bringing back.

If the colony then chose to revere Ank for slaughtering a quarry beast...that was their prerogative.

And sure, she may mention it when it comes up naturally in conversation—and sometimes when it doesn't—but who could blame her? She was but a mere mortal.

A mortal *slayer of gods*.

Several times, Ank forced herself to approach the ghoulish mass beside their ship only to find that nothing aboard the *Myzer* could sever its carapace. She tried taking off a piece of the tongue, too, frozen into a spike as it hung stupidly out of the creature's mouth, but after extensive thawing and boiling of the soft tissue, Ank became squeamish and instead decided to collect some of the frozen blood scattered nearby. She was also plagued by the fear of coming across the partially masticated or digested bodies of one of her crewmates, which hastened her attempts to cut through the unventh.

So, in the Mirage Zone the corpse would remain. They had kikogen bodies, which should be enough, even though they were clearly not quarry beasts. Scientists would probably spend cycles upon cycles studying them.

With a new surge of paranoia, Ank skipped the *Myzer* between zones, scouring for sizable enough shards to jump to a few more. Luckily, the reactor still worked, so they didn't have to run the ship on crude gel. They dumped the refined gel directly into shard boxes through a spout in the engine room, storing it until they needed to pour it into the distributor column. If the boxes remained closed until they needed to be filled or dumped, they should last all the way home without corroding through.

To expedite their pace, most of the *Myzer's* systems were shut off throughout the trip. All of the bunks were frozen out completely, as were the storage areas, non-medical offices, and some of the engine's failsafes. The farm cabinet had frozen out during the attack, killing off all of their supplemental nutrient plants, but the last yield had, in turn, frozen over, preserving them. With only two people to feed, their combined rations should sustain them, even if their trip got prolonged by the unforeseen.

Every roté Hathem wasn't outside collecting a shard, she and Ank were in the same room to prevent outside sickness.

Unfortunately, other ailments turned out to be unpreventable in their situation.

A dozen jumps into their return trip, a rare ailment called Chitin Wither Disease fell upon Ank: when a venth's body began to shrivel up and pull on the inside of their carapace. Hathem suspected it was a combination of several factors: primarily stress, malnourishment, and exhaustion. Every motion Ank made was painful, and would likely remain so until long after they returned home.

If they returned home.

On only two occasions did Ank have to redirect their path after spotting an un-venth in the next zone, neither of which cost them much fuel. It was such a notable difference from their trip out that Ank wondered if the un-venth could somehow smell the blood of Relentless Bastard coating the hull and veered away because of it. Smelling outside did seem a bit far-fetched.

Ank got them more than halfway home before landing in a zone that harbored a quarry beast she hadn't seen prior. After everything they had been through, the positive sighting of an un-venth signature was overwhelming for Ank, but their two-venth husk crew managed to execute the standard evasion swiftly. Despite Ank's reticence towards the maneuver, two jumps later, they were safe.

The way things should have been.

The way they'd always been before Arby.

I should have cut his tongue off, she thought.

After what felt like an entire contribution period, but was more like a set, Ank was jostled awake from the common area floor.

"Ow…" she groaned halfheartedly. It was more of a dry joke than genuine anguish. She'd long ago become used to the discomfort.

"Sorry, grub," Hathem said softly. "If you spent some time outside, you could alleviate that pain a little."

Hathem had suggested the same thing before, but Ank didn't think it was worth wasting the energy to cycle the pressure room and refill the air tanks. She just wanted to get home as fast as possible, CWD be damned.

"I'm fine," she muttered. "What's up?"

"We're about to land," Hathem said. "I thought you'd want to send the information yourself."

The disorientation of being stirred awake fell away. Throughout the trip, Ank had prepared a full transmission of data to send to Venthralli the moment they landed in the excursion limit, and for the last eleven thousand rotés, the *Myzer* had been jumping to a zone within that radius.

The moment the engines began to fizzle, Ank sent the stream of data. Everything they'd learned about the hypernova, the quarry beasts, the arcane medium…all of it.

Whether or not Venthralli would take the appropriate steps was up to them. The *Myzer* had completed its task, preventing the losses accrued from being in vain.

EPILOGUE
Novum Aera

"Excavation Team Four says they're ready to leave."

A young venth stood in Ank's doorway, awaiting her blessing to ensure that the departing crew had the most accurate information available for their multi-cycle mission.

Ank looked up from her workstation, her plates creaking loudly.

"Wonderful!" she told the assistant cosmologist. "I have nothing new, so they're free to leave."

In the past, Ank would add that she'd see them in a few cycles, but at this stage in her life, that wasn't likely to be true. Most venth would have ended their contribution period six cycles ago, but Ank truly didn't know what else to do with her time.

The first cycles of the new era had been frightening and dangerous. Radiation sickness had been widespread throughout the colony. Administrative groups had struggled to figure out how far Venthralli needed to be from the hypernova to keep people safe, as well as how to obtain the energy required to maintain that pace, because the one way they *couldn't* acquire energy was through starshards. The small globs of heat gel were effectively extinct, evaporated into the hot universe. Shards certainly existed at the edge of space, far from the expanding heat, where it was still 0 Syrolacs, but by the time Venthralli could have reached those areas, the fuel would have sizzled up.

Fortunately, the source of their problem had also afforded its solution. The colony required less energy to maintain life support than it used to, and once they'd figured out how to shield Venthralli from the surge in radiation, they were able to harvest the excess to supplement their needs. The technology was still progressing, but for the time being—almost twenty cycles later—their energy problems had mostly stabilized.

As far as eras went, it was simultaneously exciting and mundane. Most experts, including Ank, believed the hypernova to be a recreation of the circumstances that borne the original universe. As incredible as that was, it would take hundreds of millions of cycles for the hot matter to cool off and form into planets and stars. For Venthralli, the new universe would only ever exist as it did now, and the only astral bodies they would ever see were the dying race of deadworlds, each waiting to be incinerated by the violent waves of stardust.

Venthralli would remain forever at the edge of the universe, locked in a carefully-metered contest with radiation.

Every cycle, a few excavation teams were sent into deep space, far ahead of the hypernova, to mine a deadworld before it was consumed expanding universe. The teams then spent half of a cycle setting up and two cycles mining before the colony caught up and retrieved them with the materials they'd collected.

Finding those worlds had become laughably simple. The cosmos was much brighter in the circayds after Venthralli began its race with the great expansion. If Ank were to go outside, it would look just as dark and empty as ever—sans a single dot of light—but when it came to instruments and sensors, the difference was astonishing.

It was also safer. A conversation had arisen early on, regarding whether the venth had a moral obligation to save the quarry beasts, but it was immediately forced into hibernation. There was no shortage of dangers, and being able to plot excavations without worrying about crews being eaten was a luxury Ank had never taken for granted. Eventually, Venthralli appeared to have left the natural range of the quarry beasts. It had only taken eight cycles of constant jumping towards the edge of the universe.

Perhaps even more beneficial than the absence of quarry beasts was the information gained by the new era's radiation. The brightened universe hadn't just made deadworlds easier to find; it also allowed the venth to reliably determine which ones contained valuable materials, such as soft metals or combustible liquids, guaranteeing that every mining operation yielded bounties that improved Venthralli's infrastructure.

And now, there was even a proposal to use the excess resources to begin construction of a second colony, allowing the venth to expand their population capacity for the first time in recorded history. It seemed like an inevitable advancement to Ank—one that would begin long after she had died.

She couldn't imagine living in a different colony, anyway.

The departure of the fifth and final excavation team of the cycle meant that Ank's work was nearly over. It would take them a set to out-jump Venthralli and exceed the comms range—what used to be called the excursion limit, and during that time, the crew might encounter a problem or question requiring Ank's input. Otherwise, she had completed her duties for the cycle.

And her contribution to the colony.

Leaving the exploration offices, Ank made her way up to the second deck of Venthia. It was a long hike; her old legs wavered with each step up the ramp from Bendil. She angled herself across the deck, shuffling to the same café she sat in once every five circayds.

"Happy circayd, Ank!" welcomed Velka, the venth who operated the service hut. "One immunode coming up!"

Velka was a sort of chef, but only dealt in water-based foods: shavings mixed with juices and resins such. Ank's body had come to require quite a few vitamins and nutrients at regular intervals, all of which were provided by the immunode.

Ank crossed the room to sit by the opposite wall. It was farther than the tables near the door, but the journey was always worth it. By the time she arrived and seated herself, Velka had already set the juice blend down on the table. Ank shaved down the ball with deliberate bites from her worn teeth, reflecting on the work she'd accomplished over the cycles. At almost twenty-seven cycles old, with an increasing collection of ailments, she was unlikely to survive the upcoming hibernation. It would be a shock to everyone if she awoke next cycle, herself included.

Ank was thankful to be facing a peaceful death in hibernation, lucky to have lived a long and wondrous life.

In her youth, Ank had calculated the hypernova's radiation rings, now measured by Ank Intervals, and at only eight cycles old, she had been entrusted to plot the colony's jump path. Then, after formalizing those theorems to be calculated easily by others, she'd turned her attention to the reformation of the universe, and subsequently remodeled the venth's entire understanding of it.

The arcane medium was expanding, as were the zones within. Someone else had made that observation before Ank's time, but where it had previously been seen as evidence of heat death—the theory that all energy was dispersing infinitely, and would eventually spread into nothingness—it now appeared that the expanding medium was a result of the hypernova, which indicated that, at one point, the zones had shrunk and gotten closer together. Theoretically, that meant the zones would become massive in the distant future, and the arcane medium would become so weak it was practically non-existent.

The model also supported Ank's other famous theorem: the variable rate of electromagnetic acceleration due to invisible mass, or "Ank Factor." For ten cycles, often while performing other duties, Ank had assisted others in calculating the radiation race, collating data in the process. The result of those efforts wound up being a mathematical description of the universe's formation—a formula that calculated the universe. It was her legacy. The thing that had solidified her name in the tomes of history even before her death.

The expansion of the universe, it turned out, was slowing. That wasn't a revelation in its own right—it was just gravity—but since most of the mass in the universe was of the invisible variety, it had created unexpected differences. The initial burst from the hypernova had been invisible mass, which pulled the starfire along with it for a couple of beats, accelerating it until it finally overtook the initial burst and continued past. Ever since, the invisible mass has been pulling back at the radiation surge, slowing the universe's expansion of matter. It was the only thing preventing that matter—which would eventually become stars and planets—from drifting away forever.

However, because the invisible mass didn't physically interact with regular matter, as the nova slowed down, billions of cycles in the future, the initial wave of invisible mass would eventually overtake it again, slinging the universe forward for a second acceleration. Then, as the invisible mass reached the apex of its own journey, forming into a spherical ring like the shockwave of an explosion, it would compress back on itself, reversing the entire process of the hypernova back to its origin. The dead stars and worlds would be pulled back to the center of the universe, again leaving behind errant deadworlds and sinkholes among the condensing arcane medium.

One of Ank's colleagues, with whom she'd argued continuously, believed that the universe's eventual collapse was caused by the arcane medium—that it was some sort of boundary that would be pushed into a thin band, and in its entirety, would be too dense to be penetrated by the hypernova, bouncing all matter backwards.

This was, of course, idiotic, because it implied that venth ships routinely accomplished something that the universe itself could not.

Ridiculous.

Moreover, Ank had tested her model against *literally* everything. You could even apply the Ank Factor to Alazend's Algorithms and see the vector fields approach zero without contradicting the radiation rings...

It was all very sound.

Ank hadn't spent the entirety of the last nineteen cycles submerged in a world of sensors, formulae, and theorems. Once the colony had built up a surplus of materials, she'd spent half of a cycle developing a stable, improved version of the gel box she had used on the *Myzer*: a delicious barrel of combustible, pressurized gasses and brittle metal fragments she called a "shatterglass bomb." Every crew carried one, though only two had ever been needed for an un-venth. Now, they all ended up being used for blast mining once they hit their instability dates and needed to be replaced.

After that, Ank moved to Materials Acquisitions, where she oversaw two excavation teams, spending the better part of five cycles living on deadworlds. She'd had the pleasure of personally mentoring her own genetic offspring, one of whom had inherited her chromatic gene—a rare occurrence between two generations—one who had worked on her ship while she was a lead, and another who had worked at her second mining outpost.

It was just about the best life Ank could have lived. Filled with brilliance and whimsy.

Halfway into her immunode, Ank gazed across the café, smiling at the faded paint adorning the opposite wall.

She didn't think about Salem nearly as much as she used to, but whenever she came to Velka's café, she did. She used to often tell people that she had known the venth on the teal mountain, reciting stories to anyone who would listen about her cycle aboard the *Myzer*.

This circayd, her mind wandered to death, and what would happen when it finally took her. Some venth swore that there was another life afterwards, an eternal one outside of the physical world. As a venth of science, Ank didn't believe such things, but it was still fun to think about, and if there was one thing Ank *did* know, it was that the universe was full of magic and mystery.

Gazing at the chipped, blue-green peak, she imagined being reunited with the little venth on its side. Telling Salem all about her life and offspring. She wondered whether he would be old like her, or she young like him. Would they have bodies at all, or be formless energies in a timeless expanse?

In all likelihood, Ank's neurons would simply stop firing. Her consciousness would end, and her molecules would be converted to fertilizer, returning her to the same energy that permeated throughout the universe.

Whether or not the colony continued to prosper was no longer up to Ank, nor did it really matter on the cosmic scale. If the venth continued to thrive after her demise, they would cease being venth some circayd, just as the venth had ceased being their planetary ancestors. That was just how life worked.

All that truly mattered was that, on this circayd, the venth were alive, and they would likely be that way tomorrow.

It was for that reason Ank had told stories in the café of the *Myzer's* crew. They were a reminder of what the venth used to do to survive. The lengths they went in order to find minuscule amounts of heat, so that the venth of tomorrow could be. For all of Ank's accolades, her greatest accomplishment belonged to those who died in the Mirage Zone. Salem, Olyké, Plexie, and Cejero were heroes from a lost era, memorialized for the gift they had given the venth. A gift more incredible, more unique, than any other gift throughout time.

Venthralli had survived the end of the universe.

THANKS FOR READING!

I hope you enjoyed reading this story as much as I did writing it.

If you have a moment to **leave a quick review** on your platform of purchase or preference, your feedback is greatly appreciated!

-Travis Stecher

Learn about upcoming books and exclusive deals in my infrequent newsletter:

www.TravisStecher.com/writing/newsletter

Also Available

DILATION
A 10,000-YEAR SCI-FI EPIC

"Ingenious..." ★★★★★
"Skillful, epic sci-fi."
- Independent Book Review

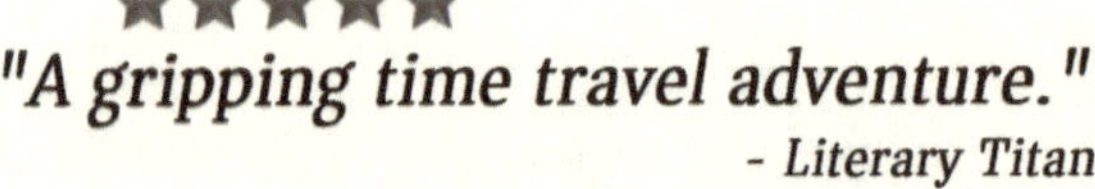

★★★★★
"A gripping time travel adventure."
- Literary Titan

Bibliography

Bolonkin, Alexander. (2009). Man in Outer Space Without a Special Space Suit. *American Journal of Engineering and Applied Sciences,* 2(4), 573-579. doi:10.3844/ajeassp.2009.573.579

Bothwell, Matthew. (2021). *The Invisible Universe.* Oneworld Publications.

Cain, Fraser. (2015, December 14). How does the sun produce energy? *Phys.org.* Retrieved July 14, 2022 from https://phys.org/news/2015-12-sun-energy.html

Emsley, John. (2001). *Nature's Building Blocks.* New Edition 2011 by Oxford University Press.

Hutchison, Grant. (2017, March 27). Coriolis effect in a rotating space habitat. *The Oikofuge.* Retrieved November 20, 2024 from https://oikofuge.com/coriolis-effect-rotating-space-habitat

Jones, Trevor. (2020, March 19). Types of stars. *AstroBackyard.* Retrieved July 14, 2022 from https://astrobackyard.com/types-of-stars

Livitski, Rich. (2014, 25 August). What would a bucketful of our Sun contain? *Astronomy Magazine.* October 2014 issue.

Mack, Katie. (2020). *The End of Everything (Astrophysically Speaking).* Scribner, imprint of Simon and Schuster.

Ohtake, Takeshi. (1993, April). Freezing points of H2SO4 aqueous solutions and formation of stratospheric ice clouds. *Tellus B: Chemical and Physical Meteorology,* 45(2), 138-144. doi:10.3402/tellusb.v45i2.15588

Patenall, Bethany, Kristyn Carter, and Matthew Ramsey. (2024, January). Kick-Starting Wound Healing: A Review of Pro-Healing Drugs. *International Journal of Molecular Sciences,* 25(2), 1304. doi:10.3390/ijms25021304

Pérez-Pereira, Noelia, et al. (2022, July 11). Prediction of the minimum effective size of a population viable in the long term. *Biodiversity and Conservation,* 2022(31), 2763–2780. doi: 10.1007/s10531-022-02456-z

Pont, Federico, et al. (2005). A planet-sized transiting star around
OGLE-TR-122 - Accurate mass and radius near the
Hydrogen-burning limit. *Astronomy and Astrophysics, 433*(2),
L21-L24. doi:10.1051/0004-6361:200500025

Silvera, Isaac, and John Cole. (2010). Metallic hydrogen: The most
powerful rocket fuel yet to exist. *Journal of Physics: Conference
Series, 215.* doi:10.1088/1742-6596/215/1/012194

Wenhao, Zhang. (2021). Influence of Temperature and
Concentration on Viscosity of Complex Fluids. *Journal of
Physics: Conference Series, 1965.*
doi:10.1088/1742-6596/1965/1/012064

About the Author

Travis Stecher is an award-winning author, musician, and screenwriter in Los Angeles, California. After earning his degree in mathematics from UCLA, he worked in multiple industries before finally leaving to pursue creative efforts. He's an operatic singer of six octaves, a multi-disciplined martial artist, and an award-winning mascot.